BIRDS OF WONDER

A Novel

Cynthia Robinson

BIRDS OF WONDER

A Novel

There are birds small enough to live forever…
Donald Revell

Standing Stone Books is an imprint of **Standing Stone Studios,** an organization dedicated to the promotion of the literary and visual arts.

Mailing address:
1897 State Route 91, Fabius, New York 13063

Web address:
standlngstonebooks.net

Email:
standingstonebooks@gmail.com

Distributor:
Small Press Distribution
1341 Seventh Avenue
Berkeley, California 94710-1409
Spdbooks.org

ISBN: 978-1-64136-526-0

Library of Congress Control Number: 2017964408

Book Design: Adam Rozum

Standing Stone Books is a member of the Community of Literary Magazines and Presses
Clmp.org

For every broken girl.
     And every good-as-new one too.

Saturday

I

Jes
Beatrice
Edward
Jes
Liam
Connor
Waldo

II

Beatrice
Edward
Jes
Liam
Connor
Waldo

Sunday

I

Beatrice
Edward
Jes
Liam
Connor
Waldo

II

Beatrice
Edward
Jes
Liam
Connor
Waldo

Monday

Beatrice
Edward
Jes
Liam
Connor
Waldo

A Friday in November

Jes

Saturday

I

Jes

Jes tossed the contents of the glove compartment onto the passenger seat—flashlight, two ossified sticks of gum, an old breathalyzer, the pre-digital model. Somewhere was dry shampoo, the most significant advance in personal hygiene since the invention of soap.

She'd planned to be at her desk by now, mowing through a stack of case reports before her boss rolled in with his 7-11 donuts and sports bar hangover.

Finally, buried between the folds of a crumpled map of New York State. Pssssst, and her hair was…better.

She wriggled out of last night's jeans and into the uniform pants she kept stashed under the seat. Earlier that morning, on her way out of the unfamiliar house, she'd glanced longingly into the master bath—parade of grooming products, plush towels on the racks.

But if she turned on the shower, she'd have woken him. And then she would have been late. Very late.

What was his name?

She had absolutely no idea.

Her mouth felt like sand. She extracted her toothbrush from the clutter on the seat, stuck it in her uniform pocket. One good thing you could say for police issue clothing, pockets.

Another must-do before she headed in: a new ring tone for her mother.

Braying ass?

‿

Beatrice

Shuffling down the hall of her house, her yipping beagle dancing at her feet, Beatrice hummed in time to the slap of her slippers against the carpet runner. After a few measures, the meandering notes marshaled themselves into a tune, the idyllic harmonies of the seduction aria, *"La ci darem la mano,"* from *Don Giovanni*. Ah, the genius of Mozart.

At the threshold to the kitchen, she bent down to scratch Geneva's ears. Blinking in the brightness—she loved the generous windows above the sink—Beatrice inhaled deeply, anticipating the rich aroma of the French roast that would be waiting in the pot of her coffee maker, courtesy of the infallible timer.

Instead, her nostrils filled with the sour tang of overripe tomatoes.

The coffee pot was cold to the touch—she'd forgotten to set the infallible timer. The source of the acrid smell was beside the dish drainer; tomatoes in meaty red chunks glistened beneath a busy cloud of fruit flies. Peeled, cored, and diced into cubes, intended for gazpacho. Extra ripe, soft in places; in her hands they'd felt like heavy red balloons of juice. She hadn't finished the soup because her daughter had called to cancel their dinner plans. Vague, weedy complications had sprung up in Jes's life—again—at the last minute. Beatrice frowned. The August morning unsettled itself, hazy and leisurely sliding into too-humid and wrong.

She mopped the tomatoes into the disposal, her mind replaying the argument—despite her best efforts—while she prepared the coffee. Jes telling Beatrice she was being ridiculous—no one made plans days in advance anymore. Jes finally disclosing, at Beatrice's increasingly heated insistence, the reason for the cancellation.

"I have a date."

In the background, Beatrice had heard glasses and bottles clinking, loud conversations, bursts of laughter. Jes was in a bar. "And you didn't know about this...*date* when we made our plans?"

"Okay, not a date. A Thing That Came Up."

"More like a *hook-up*," Beatrice had slammed her knife down on the tomatoes, cell phone crunched uncomfortably between ear and shoulder. "Don't think I don't know what those things are called. And don't think word doesn't get around in this town about who's...*hooking up*." The guidance counselor at the high school where she taught English literature delighted in informing Beatrice where her daughter had last been spotted, and with whom.

"Oh, please." Beatrice knew that voice from her daughter's adolescence—Jes had been a quietly difficult teenager, only her father had been able to manage her.

Beatrice sipped her coffee at the front window, holding the mug under her nose—the aroma drowned the smell of rotten tomatoes. She pushed away the memory of her own shrill voice, "You're throwing your life away, *that*'s what!" There'd been a short silence, followed by her daughter's icy enunciation: "God forbid I have a life like yours."

The bank president—the latest name dropped by the guidance counselor—was old enough to be Jes's father. Literally—he was the same age Charles would be (four years Beatrice's junior) if he were still alive. Beatrice had shouted that, too, just before Jes hung up.

On good days, Jes was like garlic, strangely beautiful to behold and, when treated with proper care, inimitably sweet and nutty. On bad days, she was more like horseradish—fragile white flowers and abundant green leaves attached to a root so pungent the faintest whiff would make your eyes water.

Jes *was* throwing her life away, squandering her youth and attractiveness—these things had a certain shelf-life. Heading straight toward a dead end, and she'd be there sooner than she thought. Beatrice sighed and tried to focus her attention on her well-tended flower beds.

Hollyhocks, hydrangeas—lovely ruffled globes of pale blue. Dragon's blood, nestled in the shade of the old oak, surrounded by rows of fussy cyclamen. Jes considered gardening a waste of time. But then Jes had no time for beautiful things that lacked a practical purpose.

Parking her empty mug on the sill, Beatrice began the daily search for Geneva's leash. She found it in the study draped around the neck of a dressmaker's mannequin, the ends lost in the folds of an elaborate gown. The costume she used for the Duchess of Malfi, title character of John Webster's seventeenth-century tragedy (Beatrice's favorite among her rotation of student productions—*A Midsummer Night's Dream* was so predictable as to be almost dreary). Beatrice had been mending the lace at the neckline, torn during the death scene in the previous performance—it was hard to die convincingly without doing damage to the costume.

She'd also had to let the bodice out; this year's Duchess, Amber Inglin, was a round, ripe peach of a girl. Previously Beatrice had tended toward the Japanese eggplant variety—understated curves, dark and brooding, appropriate for the somber Mr. Webster—and Amber was a bright, sunny change.

Except for the tattoo. An enormous peacock, its tail feathers fanned across the back of the girl's hand, enveloping her wrist like a colorful silk glove, glowing iridescent under the stage lights. Fortunately they'd worn sleeves long in the seventeenth century—a woman's bare hands were considered an erotic sight. It could have been worse, snakes, or fairies, or one like Jes's, which Jes herself, regrettably, described as a 'tramp stamp'. A peacock was in reasonably good taste. Charles, her late husband, had been partial to peacocks.

Rehearsals started in two weeks, with the production slated for the week before Thanksgiving—fall was, without question, Beatrice's favorite season. Her mood lightened with the thought of the auditorium full of slightly scandalized parents. No production of Webster's Jacobean masterpiece was a success to Beatrice unless at least one mother called the principal's office the next morning to complain.

Snapping the leash onto Geneva's collar, Beatrice ignored the portrait in the entry hall. It was a seventeenth-century original, and bore a distinct resemblance to her daughter.

Given the lack of signature or attribution, the bespectacled owner of the antiquarian shop had let her have it for a song. The young woman was dressed in a red satin gown and an over-garment of gold brocade lined with fur, her honey-colored hair pulled back smooth from the pale, sober oval of her face. Beatrice had fashioned the Duchess's costume after the gown in the portrait, imagining how the colors would bring out her daughter's peculiar beauty when she was old enough for the part.

Years (and several Duchesses) later, when Jes had finally tried the costume on, the likeness had been uncanny. And still was, or would be, if Jes ever wore anything besides jeans.

Following Geneva down the driveway, Beatrice passed under the bird house Jes and her father had hung years ago in the birch tree. They'd spent hours at the window in the study, whispering so as not to startle the birds, making notes, passing binoculars stealthily from hand to hand.

At the bus stop on the corner Beatrice turned left onto Willet Drive, a winding road bordered by two- and three-story lakefront homes. Geneva's tags jingling, they passed well-kept Victorian mansions, a modernistic Bauhaus-type structure that looked as though it would be more comfortable in Holland. A shadowy stretch of woods where daubs of gold were just beginning to appear among the deep green leaves. Then the angular, wood-trimmed stucco of the Walshes' Prairie Style mansion, curving into view around an elongated bend.

Liam Walsh, a handsome, burly man with a smile worthy of a toothpaste commercial, who'd made a name for himself in the courts and the school system as a tireless advocate for children unfortunate enough to land in the custody of Child Services. His altruism, in Beatrice's opinion, was rendered considerably less self-sacrificing by the fact that his wife was loaded.

Beatrice stepped over the shallow ditch into tall, tangled grass. Geneva was advancing at a trot now. Sweat soaked through the back of Beatrice's shirt in big, irregular patches; she could feel it making circles around her armpits. Her shins swished with difficulty through a dense patch of weeds ready to burst with seed; the Walshes should really mow all the way out to the street.

Jes was over thirty. Jes could make her own decisions. The guidance counselor was a bored, small-minded busybody. Jes had just been chatting with the bank president. In a bar, yes, so what of it?

And Jes did have a point: what daughter wanted her life to resemble her mother's? But a surge of indignation jostled aside the reasonable thought—there was nothing wrong with Beatrice's life. Beatrice realized she was muttering to herself. She stopped. These imaginary conversations were becoming a habit.

Then Geneva began to bark, lunging forward and straining at her leash. Beatrice's arm straightened with a painful jerk as she broke into an awkward run.

Near the fence at the back corner of the field, Geneva came to a sudden stop, tripping her mistress who nearly fell. The dog's nose was working furiously among the weeds and Beatrice bent over to catch her breath.

It was then that she saw the curl. A lovely, shiny curl of hair the color of coral tea roses that wrapped itself around twigs and weeds, and then disappeared beneath an overgrown forsythia. So very Pre-Raphaelite!

Beatrice reached to touch the curl, brushing the weeds aside.

Nothing could have prepared her for the image of the peacock. Suddenly, there it was: tail-feathers fully unfurled, luminous blues and greens shimmering between blades of grass.

And then red, marbled with pink, around two imperfect circles of bone-white with dark centers. A space where there shouldn't be one—ground visible, covered with grass, and some clover. Red again—an image of the tomatoes on the kitchen counter flashed across Beatrice's mind—surrounding two more bone-white circles.

The hand bearing the peacock was severed, that was why Beatrice could see a sliver of ground where basic biology dictated there should be skin. There was a clean cut five inches or so above the wrist, just missing the edge of the peacock's tail, the muscles and tendons—the bones—neatly sliced through like a Swiss round steak prepared by an expert butcher.

Beatrice's mind had been taken over by a calm, rational scientist voice, now explaining to her in a precisely measured way that the hand must have been severed by some terribly sharp instrument in order to produce such a clean cut. Beatrice thought again of the tomatoes, chopping them into cubes. She started backward, bile rising in her throat. Dimly, as though from very far away, she heard Geneva's frantic barks.

Having seen the tattoo, Beatrice would have required no further confirmation of the body's identity. But the beautiful face was there, too, pale skin dusted with freckles, blond brows, partially veiled by the forsythia branches. The eyes were open, the skin around them smudged with the remnants of a heavy makeup job. Amber Inglin's mouth formed a flattened "o", as though death had surprised her in the midst of a conversation.

She was naked. As is often the case with Titian-haired women, Amber's skin was startlingly white, nestled in the deep green of the grass. Before Beatrice could look away, the scientist in her brain—certainly male—registered that Amber's breasts were full, and that the triangle of hair covering her pubis was the same color as the curl. Peach.

Later, she would remember not having noticed any blood.

Beatrice staggered backward, away from the bushes, wrapping Geneva's leash around her wrist. Geneva tried to lunge forward again, toward the body, her anxious yip sputtering into a guttural whine when the leash brought her up short. Nausea churned through the two cups of coffee in Beatrice's stomach. She gave up control, vomiting a surprising quantity of bitter liquid into a gap between the branches of a creeping juniper. She straightened and wiped the back of her hand across her mouth.

She had to call Jes. She pulled her cell phone from her pocket. She hadn't wanted a cell phone—people looked so silly walking down the street talking into their hands, or swiping a little screen with their grubby forefingers—but Jes had made her get one. Beatrice's hand shook as she dialed her daughter's number. She mixed up the prefix twice, and then remembered speed dial.

When Jes answered, Beatrice opened her mouth but her vocal cords were unwilling to cooperate. Her throat felt full of stones.

"Mom?" Jes sounded distracted at first, maybe sleepy—it was early, wasn't today her day off?—and then Beatrice heard the icy voice from last night. "Mom? *Hello*? Are you there?"

Cell phones showed the caller's number. Beatrice always forgot that.

"I…," Beatrice began. "It's terrible…it's… you have to get here!" Beatrice choked on a sob. She raised a hand to her mouth and realized that her cheeks were wet. She hadn't been aware she was crying. She tried to swallow and choked again. Those were sobs, hundreds of them, not stones.

"Mom? Where are you? What's going on?" Impatience and concern in equal parts.

Beatrice took a breath. She'd intended for it to be deep, but it caught and her voice came out on a sob. "There's a body, under some bushes. It's… oh, I can't bear to say it. It's one of my students. My Duchess, for the fall production, Amber Inglin. She's *dead*!"

"Where, Mom? Where are you?"

Beatrice spoke but a riding lawnmower rounded the corner of the Walshes' grand house at the other end of the field, trailing some sort of contraption behind it and drowning out Beatrice's reply. She tried again. "At the edge of the Walshes' field. Beside some bushes. Forsythias."

She had no idea why she'd added the detail about the forsythias—Jes wouldn't recognize a tulip, let alone a spring-flowering bush in the middle of August. Her head seemed to float, far above her feet in their clogs. She was conscious, in a terrible way, of the presence of Amber Inglin's body, to her left, not far away at all, but she kept her eyes on her shoes. Clogs. Impractical for walking across fields. She didn't want to faint. Blades of cut grass stuck to the scuffed tips.

"Mom, what are you…"

The lawn mower was back and Beatrice missed her daughter's next words.

Once the mower disappeared behind the house again, Jes's voice returned, the syllables short and icy. "What are you doing in Liam Walsh's field?"

"Walking the dog."

A crackling silence and then, "You're walking the dog in Liam Walsh's field?"

"It's where I've always walked her. What does it *matter*? My *student*…" Beatrice swallowed with difficulty. "My *student* — my *Duchess* — has been *murdered*. Get here, please." Beatrice choked, had to stop to cough. She was glad to stop speaking.

"I'm on my way." Jes's voice was businesslike now, competent. Beatrice could hear clattering in the background.

Geneva was determined to dive back into the bushes. Beatrice had a task — keep the dog under control. She must not faint or the dog could slip away, return to that terrible…

"Wait for me there. Don't touch the body. And don't call the station. I'll call them once I get there. I'll be there as soon as I can."

"Hurry." Beatrice felt the need to lean against something. The air was heavy and humid, oppressive. She made her way to a shady patch, away from the forsythias but not too far — she felt she shouldn't leave the girl alone — and leaned against the fence.

A sluggish breeze blew across her cheeks, producing the momentary illusion of coolness — she had stopped crying but her face was still wet. With the coolness came a gust of fruity sweetness. At her feet blackberry bushes twined through the slats in the fence, weighted down with dark purple fruit. The berries glinted wetly in places, oozing juice. The sun had heated the fruit past the point of ripeness, releasing perfume that announced the descent to decay. Beatrice fought back a dry heave.

The nausea was followed by an unworthy thought. If Amber Inglin was lying dead — naked and dead; Beatrice shuddered — under the forsythias, who would play the Duchess? What a thing to be thinking about; Beatrice shook her head. Queen Anne's lace waved gracefully at her feet, bringing her mind back to the sleeve, to the lace cuff that almost hid the tattoo, to the costume and to Amber wearing it. She was so perfect for the part that Beatrice hadn't bothered with an understudy.

With the exception of her daughter, Amber Inglin was the most gifted student actress Beatrice had ever encountered. Jes, of course, had had the advantage of early exposure to culture, but a girl like Amber didn't have anybody serving it up on a silver platter. And she was a peach, delicately colored and curved, sweet but not cloying. Her face was period-perfect, as though God himself had breathed life into a Hans Holbein portrait. Exactly right for Webster's Duchess.

Beatrice wiped her hands across her eyes, over her cheeks. She shouldn't be thinking about acting, shouldn't even remember there was a production, except that, once the school year was upon her—with the exception of food and flowers—she rarely thought about anything else. Well, besides Jes. And the dog. She did think about the dog.

When Beatrice first called her to the front of the class, Amber had rolled her eyes and taken her time about getting there. But once the role of the Duchess took hold of her, she stood up straight and projected as though she'd been acting all her life. Her classmates were silent—you could've heard a pin drop. Her voice was melodious and commanding all at once, her gestures grave and graceful. She was a natural, made for Shakespeare and the Jacobeans. By the end of Amber Inglin's first reading, Beatrice's heart was pounding with the euphoria of discovery. A jewel in the rough, to be sure, but one that Beatrice could polish. There'd been that model, back in the 80s, from some podunk town in Alabama. Her mentor had taken her to New York and gotten her signed with an agency. These rags to riches tales happened all the time!

The girl's eyes had opened wide at Beatrice's descriptions of London—the Globe theater, the Royal Academy of Dramatic Art. *Me? I could go there?* Her own brisk, *Well, I don't see why not!* And the germ of a pleasant inspiration: someone would need to accompany the child, and why not herself—indeed, who else?

The image of those features, alive with excitement, metamorphosed in Beatrice's mind to the face she'd seen through the forsythia branches: still, pupils glazed, pewter-colored eyeshadow garish in the morning light. The faintness returned and Beatrice leaned hard against the fence. She remembered the girl's childlike scent of soap-and-nothing-else. She and the girl, bending over a complex scene from the script. The scent, so clean and uncomplicated, had been perfect for her character: throughout the play, the Duchess, though surrounded by depravity of the basest sort, maintains her purity of heart.

Beatrice forced herself to stare at her clogs: clunky shoes, ugly almost, but practical. She no longer needed to wear beautiful things. That was behind her. Jes was taking forever. Beatrice put a hand to her forehead and closed her eyes.

She opened them at the sound of a motor coming to a stop.

Jes, in the police car, alone. Beatrice had been expecting her daughter's partner, Drew, a broad-backed man, fifty pounds overweight, with a florid face and the vocabulary of a slow tenth-grader. As if reading her mind, Jes called out from across the field, her voice echoing strangely, as if from a much greater distance. "I'll call Drew in a second—I didn't want to wait for him."

Geneva began to bark as Jes approached at a trot.

Her daughter had been on the force for two years now, but Jes's delicate face and slight body still looked all wrong in the gray polyester uniform. It must be scratchy and uncomfortable, even with its short sleeves for summer. Jes's dark blond hair was wound into a no-nonsense coil at the nape of her neck. Beatrice understood Jes's efforts to conform to the conformist culture of a police station, but she preferred it down.

"Where's the body?" Jes didn't sound winded, despite the jog and the heat—the job kept her in excellent physical shape, one positive thing to be said for it.

"Under the bushes." Beatrice pointed without looking.

Jes regarded Beatrice with narrowed eyes from behind aviator-frame sunglasses that Beatrice couldn't help but notice were the wrong shape for her daughter's face. "You didn't touch her, right, Mom?"

"Only the hair, with one finger." Beatrice tried to keep the quaver out of her voice—displays of emotion made her daughter uncomfortable. "She was my best Duchess."

"You and Geneva need to come away…" Her daughter's hand on her arm was firm. Beatrice allowed Jes to lead her toward an old oak several yards from the fence. "Stay here." She spoke as if to the dog, but it was for both of them.

Beatrice seated herself stiffly and leaned against the tree trunk, placing Geneva inside the space created by her crossed legs.

"Drink some water. You look like hell." Jes held out a plastic bottle stamped with *Tompkins County Criminal Investigative Division*.

"Amber was only sixteen. She had such a wonderful career ahead of her—she might have done great, great things. She didn't even get to have her opening night."

Jes didn't respond.

She was extracting a roll of yellow police tape from her pack. She attached one end to the fence and walked to the tree beneath which Beatrice now sat, wrapping the tape around the trunk and securing it. "Keep the dog behind this line. There might be evidence under all this grass, but I'll never find it if you guys trample all over everything."

Beatrice nodded.

"And drink your water. You're going to get heat stroke."

The water bottle felt like a chunk of ice in Beatrice's hand. She opened it and took a small sip. Her stomach protested. When Jes turned and walked a few paces toward the center of the field, drawing her phone from her pocket, Beatrice closed the bottle again.

She could hear her daughter's authoritative voice, "Terence? We've got a possible homicide in the vacant field beside 469 Willet Drive. Call Drew and get here as soon as you can, okay?"

Beatrice rubbed the water bottle across her forehead. The coldness helped her focus her thoughts. She found police protocol impenetrable. If she remembered correctly, Terence was some sort of lackey, and Drew was Jes's partner. Shouldn't Jes be calling Drew? But she understood so little about Jes these days.

She'd given her daughter a Shakespearean name, Jesca. Some believe it was first used by the Bard in *The Merchant of Venice*, for Shylock's daughter. She'd insisted on the Shakespearean spelling over the more common contemporary form, "Jessica." Beatrice remembered the erudite pleasure of penning the name on her daughter's birth certificate. The baffled clerk had already misspelled it twice.

Throughout Jes's childhood and adolescence, despite her keen aptitude for the sciences, which were Charles's terrain, Beatrice had indulged herself with visions of her daughter on the stage, perhaps even— one day—that of the Globe itself. Jes's success as the Duchess during her senior year of high school, and her obvious enjoyment of her role— she hadn't even seemed to mind taking direction from her mother—had filled Beatrice with joy. After Jes's call from Berkeley to tell her she'd declared her major in Theater Studies, Beatrice had been giddy for days. Jes had actually declared a double major, it was true, in animal biology, but Beatrice had been sure the higher calling of Art would win her daughter over in the end.

Beatrice's own doctorate in English Lit was never completed— everyone, it seemed, wanted to supervise a dissertation on Shakespeare, but no one would touch Webster. She probably could've picked it up again once Charles landed the chair in ornithology, but…well, she hadn't.

Everything—Beatrice had always told herself—would be different for her daughter.

And it was. She just hadn't imagined this kind of different. Squandering her youth hanging around in bars and *hooking up*. A job that made little or no use of Jes's intellect and expensive education. An unattractive uniform that didn't show off her lovely figure. Colleagues who wouldn't know Webster from Webster's, and didn't care. Drug addicts, domestic violence, petty theft. And, now, a dead body. The dead body of the most talented student Beatrice had ever taught. Beatrice choked back a sob.

Another vehicle pulled up behind Jes's squad car. Drew and a tall, lanky man in need of a haircut rushed toward the center of the field, shouldering heavy looking black backpacks. A series of sharp metallic clicks came from the shutter of her daughter's camera.

The clicks stopped. Jes was returning the camera to its case. She knelt beside the girl's body, fitting rubber gloves onto her hands.

Beatrice leaned her head against the rough bark of the tree. Her raw throat ached. She closed her burning eyes.

A sound made her open them to see Jes holding the girl's detached hand between her two gloved ones, examining it with clinical interest. So deathly white. That hand, alive, gracefully balancing the tattered Penguin edition of Webster's masterpiece, as Amber Inglin had stood before the mesmerized class and become the Duchess of Malfi.

The nausea returned. Beatrice wiped a film of sweat from the back of her neck. "Honey," her voice was faint, "I need you to do that somewhere I can't see it."

"Sorry." Jes turned her back, blocking her mother's view.

But not before Beatrice had noticed that the nails were painted electric blue. Such an unnatural color amid so much nature. Beatrice wiped at tears and clamped her lips together, fighting back a sob.

⌒

Edward

Edward reproduced the gently sloping arcs of his sister's eyebrows with rapid, feathery strokes. He liked Sara's features when she was sleeping—placid and still, not talking, or yelling. Or laughing in hoarse shouts that became sobs that took hours to grind down to silence.

Women shouldn't yell.

The scratch of his pencil across good paper—the best paper, which he couldn't afford; his bills were late, his credit in tatters—was the only sound in the room. Edward shaded from dark to light and back to dark again, across the rounded orb beneath the lid, the fine indentation of temple thrown into shadow by the early light creeping across the walls of the boathouse. For the fringe of lashes, he held the pencil point at a glancing angle—Edward imagined a gray moth, wings folded, perched on his sister's peaceful cheek.

Peace was not a concept he associated with Sara. She'd started drinking at thirteen, had two abortions by the time she graduated high school. Lived briefly with each of five men. Been married to one. Tried to have a child, but the doctor had told her she was infertile, probably a good thing.

Sara's marriage had been bad from the beginning. Bad mostly because of Sara—her husband had gotten tired of finding liquor bottles every time he opened a drawer, sick of Sara breaking all their plates with monthly regularity.

The boyfriends since didn't stay around long enough to invest in Sara's well-being, and there hadn't been one for a while.

When she wasn't drinking, Sara made sculpture, using carving and intarsia on found wood to create tableaux. Depicting domestic scenes, the crafting and details were so exquisite they "took your breath away"–in the words of one besotted (and trite) critic.

Making sculpture made Sara thirsty, and when she'd finished a piece, she'd disappear. She'd show up days later at Edward's door, reeking and disheveled, filled with crazy stories of where she'd been.

Her gallerist in the trendy Chelsea space was tolerant of her drunken bouts, her disappearances. He encouraged her to drink at openings—she was good, animated and charming, until she turned bad (Sara could be an ugly drunk), by which time the opening was wrapping up and, with Edward's help, he could get her out the back door. Each Sara Friis tableau brought in at least $25,000—the limited, unreliable supply pushed the

29

prices up.

While they were growing up Sara's young face had delighted him. Angular and puckish, with a pointed chin and pearly teeth. More than missing that face, Edward mourned it.

His sister had been a perfect girl.

Asleep, he could almost see that face again.

Neither Sara, with her irregular substitute teacher's paychecks from the Brooklyn school system—"I'm really good with study hall"—nor Edward, an adjunct instructor of painting at a state college up the Hudson, could afford vacations. Instead, they came upstate to their older sister's lakefront house. Cate tolerated them, with the unspoken understanding that Edward—as usual—would keep Sara under control.

During their first summer at Cate and Bill-the-obscenely-rich-cardiologist's palatial summer 'cottage', they'd decided to sleep in the boathouse. Like the main house, it faced the lake, but stood some yards away, at the edge of a shallow strip of woods. The boathouse was untouched by Cate's omnivorous decorators—she used it for storage.

Among the jumble of boxes and crates they'd salvaged old bunk beds, from the room they'd shared in their parents' old house across town, until Edward had left for college. Sara in the top bunk, Edward in the bottom. From these exact beds they'd made plans to be artists together in New York or Paris or London or Hong Kong. Sweet times.

Edward had begun to draw before he could talk, and once Sara reached adolescence, he'd only drawn her. Sara reading, Sara vacuuming the living room on Saturday, before she was allowed to go to the mall with her friends. Sara putting on makeup, Sara smoking. Sara smiling crookedly, wasted and pretending not to be. Sara through the crack in the bathroom door—she'd never locked it; Edward had kept the hinges oiled—to the sight line from the mirror to his sister's body in the steamy bath.

When she started passing out, he began to draw her asleep.

On the nights she spent at his down-at-heel NoHo loft, she'd be passed out for hours on the old couch in his front room, surrounded by the paints and tools and glues and thinners that colonized all available space. The lamplight was soft, forgiving. What Sara's face needed.

Closing his sketchbook, Edward stood up from the old chair that had been their mother's, enjoying the coolness of the concrete floor beneath his bare feet. He paused a moment to admire their symmetry, the cleanly delineated beds of the nails; he had beautiful feet, nearly perfect.

On his way to the bathroom, he stopped at the window and opened it to the familiar smell of the lake: high humidity and algae. The boathouse stood on a slight rise, the window affording a clear view of the water, the back yards of other well-heeled home-owners. The Garrisons next door—he was some muckety-muck at the university, Edward had forgotten what the wife did. Beyond, an open field edged with woods and then the Walshes' Frank Lloyd Wright extravaganza. The husband was unimportant to Edward, but Basia Walsh, a close friend of Cate's, was a gallerist.

Basia owned the gallery in town where Cate's current favorite artist was showing his mediocre paintings. A "get," Cate called him, all the way from *Amsterdam* (Cate's eyebrows shot up, corrugating her forehead, when she said "Amsterdam")—he had ties to the area, a local boy made good. Tonight was the opening.

More importantly, tonight Edward would speak with Basia. He'd guilt Cate into helping him get her alone. He, too, was a local boy, and Basia could give him a leg up.

The truth was things were a little desperate as far as his career was concerned. The week before he'd driven up from the city, his third-rate NYC gallery had dropped him—the idiot owner disagreed with the bold new direction Edward's work was taking. And this quite possibly on the strength of the mean little frown with which the phone-answering bimbo at the front desk—some socialite's daughter—had greeted his last batch of slides.

But Basia would see what his erstwhile gallerist could not. Maybe she'd even get him reviewed. He'd get a new line on the bio, then get another urban gallery, maybe somewhere edgy, out in Red Hook.

The view through the window held him: the tops of the trees were turning. August was only beginning, but his students would already be buying their supplies. He wondered how many he'd have, whether any of them would be even slightly talented.

They'd be sure to give him the classroom next to the restrooms again. While Edward lectured concerning the relative virtues of linseed oil versus walnut as a medium, the flimsy walls would let through the sound of flushing toilets. He'd have to repeat himself after each flush, while the students tittered behind their easels.

The price he paid for his stubborn naturalism, his refusal to let go of skin and eyes and hair. He'd found the true soul of painting, though his colleagues dismissed his work as mere exercises.

They didn't get it, the supreme aptness of the human being—certain instantiations of the human being—not as a bleak mirror of the dreary ugliness and inanity of daily life, but for the expression of higher truths. They didn't grasp the transcendent potential of physical perfection, its tragically fleeting sublimity—this sublimity, indeed, rested in perfection's fleeting nature.

But some day they would. The real world was a horrible place full of terrorists and beeping devices: his calling as an artist was to distract discerning viewers from that fact, even for a few brief minutes.

Edward smiled at the trees, a secret certainty warming him as he envisioned the current canvas in his studio. Soon—he was sure—the critics with their intricate phrases of praise and witty criticism would review him, his work. Important. Relevant. Revelatory. Breathtaking.

He could almost taste the words. He'd read them aloud, first to himself and later to friends at a restaurant over dinner—by then he would have a set of beautiful friends. Friends of a like mind, who understood him. *Appreciated* him.

Or perhaps to a lover early on a Sunday morning, while the vinegary smell of ink on newsprint mixed with bodies and sheets still warm with sex. Or maybe even to his wife over breakfast—other people got married, why not him? His imaginings stopped there.

In the real world, it was Sara's reviews (when she was producing) that they read at brunch on Sundays—brunch was one meal he could get Sara to eat, no matter how hung over she was. And Sara's reviews were always good; the art world loved a self-destructive and brilliant drunk. One day she'd slice off a finger, maybe even on purpose, and the art world would love that too. But his turn would come. He'd earned it.

Edward removed his glasses and placed them carefully on the bathroom windowsill. A crisp slap of cold water across his face, and he bent toward the old pewter-framed mirror, to run a comb through his thinning hair. The blond hid the gray well, he told himself. And the chin-length cut was still trendy. His face surprised him, with its square jaw and precisely sculpted features, ice-blue eyes framed by the long, fanning lashes of a young girl.

A perfect face.

Sometimes, catching his reflection in a shop window or a mirror above the bar of a downtown restaurant—he charged an expensive meal once a month to his one remaining credit card—he wondered who the handsome man was, and thought it a pity that he walked or sat or ate alone.

Edward entered the corner of the boathouse that served as their joint studio. On Sara's worktable, a dusty chaos of shavings, burls, knives, and a grinding wheel, untouched for over a month.

His easel was beside the window, where he could work with his back to her. Beside it was his paint stand, where daubs of oil paint circled precisely around the edges of his palette, from dark to light. On the nearby table, patches of color blended into varied skin tones ranged across a rectangle of freezer paper—the best surface for mixing.

Edward painted girls. Girls, in fact, were his discovery.

He found them, mostly in magazines, the filthier the better. They had to be white, so the light could shine *through* the skin, not just on it. His chosen ones, he cleaned up. Heads and shoulders—never bodies. Faces framed by billows of hair you could sink your face into, necks like warm, slender columns of marble, clavicles bowed like a bird's wing, the hollows dark and secretive. With every passing week, his girls were inching closer and closer toward perfection—according to his particular definition of the term—frozen in that exquisite moment between the ages of fifteen and eighteen, when molecules and cells twine themselves into lustrous hair, clear pink nails, skin like butter and cream.

His girls, though *idealized*—his gallerist wielded the adjective like a bludgeon; Edward would have bet his nonexistent retirement savings the woman had never read Plato—were also heart-stoppingly close to real. Each eyelash a whip of three-dimensional beauty, skin textured to believability, inviting touch—he'd learned a thing or two from his days as a photorealist, his girls looked as though they might burst right off the canvas. But they were frozen there, in space and in time, in the moment *he* had captured, saving them from the inevitable slide—from perfection there was nowhere to go but down—into the prosaic, the everyday, decay and decrepitude.

And his girls represented a sacrifice. Up until two years ago, he'd had a good gallery in MidTown. But then he'd been doing something the art world recognized, derivative though it was. A well-known critic had even attended Edward's MFA show—he now wrote for the *The New Yorker*; Edward kept a notebook of his reviews, penning dissenting comments, precisely and in red, in the margins. The man had hailed his work as a new twist in Photorealism—meat-packing district diner scenes, transvestites after they'd been clubbing all night. The later the better—the baggier the under-eye circles, the redder the zits and the scars beneath the makeup. His work had been lauded because of the outré subject matter (it was a cheap shot and he'd known exactly what he was doing when he'd taken it). Following the critic's review, he'd begun to sell, at first only a trickle, it was true, but he'd been on his way, even a couple of musems had bought small pieces, and eventually he was living decently on the sale of his work, the leaner times supplemented with the steadiness of underpaid teaching.

But then had come the epiphany. One summer evening after an opening—not his, but an artist also represented by his gallery, they'd been a kind of fraternity back then, now they all avoided him—he'd followed a golden-haired girl through the park, the dying light on her skin wouldn't let him do otherwise. Even though he'd lost her—and he'd had no idea what he'd have said even if he'd caught up to her—by the time he'd reached his studio, he'd known he couldn't keep doing it. Serving up the drearily grotesque because it sold, his tranny diner denizens keeping risibly elite company with the middle-aged faces and bodies of Chuck Close; the bloated, cellulite-dimpled Florida Tourist sculptures of Duane Hansen— as real as a loudmouthed great aunt and just as horrifying; Richard Estes' over-shiny cars, motorcycles, and urban blight.

He could no longer claim, along with those charlatans of the realer-than-real, to render his subjects with dispassionate exactitude, offering no social comment whatsoever. Those images spoke for themselves, both his own and the masterpieces of his masters: beneath their dubious veneer of objectivity, they *celebrated* ugliness, cheapness, tackiness—all that was tawdry about mass-market culture. They mocked it, but they *were* it, and he couldn't be a participant anymore.

There, in his studio, the traffic hurtling beneath his open window toward the Holland tunnel, gas fumes making him slightly high—late lafternoon rush hour was the worst, the ugliest, the most toxic—there, staring at his canvases, he'd seen. The fatal error of the Photorealists was to attempt to unite art with life—the last one who'd managed to walk that tightrope had been Jan van Eyck, and he'd been dead for half a millennium. The goddamned Dutch—van Eyck's descendents had betrayed him, he must have been roiling in his tomb—had started down the road to perdition with their stripped-of-hidden-meaning genre scenes—Frans Hals among the most egregious—which, when combined with the poison of Industrialism a few centuries later, had combusted into something inoperable.

Then the plague had gone global, the tainted bloodline eventually manifesting itself in Sara, who, with her everyday objects—however ironically kitsch—made the same mistake. Art was not life. Art's purpose was to transcend: it had never been intended to do anything but. With Beethoven's ninth blaring from his speakers and making the floor quake, he'd destroyed every painting in his studio with an exacto knife. It had felt like carving up the body of an unfaithful beloved—grief and fury in equal measure. He was trashing his livelihood deliberately, tens of thousands of dollars, but it had to be done.

Then he'd started all over again.

Someday an *intelligent* critic would grasp the feat Edward had achieved, at once transcending the flagrant ugliness of Photorealism and stripping bare Abstract Expressionism's failed grasp at sublimity (which was like vomiting, or ejaculating, onto a canvas, there was no control involved—case in point: Jackson Pollock, who'd spent most of his life sloppily drunk, chasing bar sluts). Edward, on the other hand, had trapped the transcendent in the very hairs of his paintbrush, embodying it in woman, caught at the fleeting moment of her greatest physical perfection. He'd saved those girls, the ones he'd chosen. He might even have saved the world.

Sara called his work sexist, but then she would.

To the lake house he'd only brought the canvas of the brunette, his favorite.

She'd started out in one of the magazines, standing, straddled across a chair, breasts thrust forward, light from a window behind her throwing the small tangle of hair between her legs into relief, highlighting the slit of flesh at the center. Edward had felt a hardening in his groin at the sight of her, but stopped himself. He'd forced his eyes back to her face—her mouth was open, as though asking a question.

He'd answered by cutting the face out from the rest of her. She was one of the lucky ones, the ones he could fix.

When he'd first started buying them, he'd hidden the magazines in drawers. Then, emboldened—his was a higher purpose—he'd let them migrate into stacks under the bed, out of sight but within easy reach.

With Sara around, he'd shove them in the drawers, but he had long stretches of hours to himself, while she slept on the couch in the front room, to take the magazines out and study them.

The brunette was perfect now. He'd made her strawberry blonde, lightening her skin with cadmium yellow blended directly into lead white—hard to find, because of the lead, but worth the trouble. Graced now by an idealized beauty, she glowed, as though with a mystical, interior light, her eyes closed, abandoned to sleep.

Gazing at perfection was more pleasurable when no gaze was returned, when no interchange was possible. Conversation was so awkward.

Besides Sara as she used to be, Edward had only ever seen two perfect girls in the flesh. The first had come during the prior summer at Cate's, when he'd let Sara convince him to rent a stand at the annual crafts fair— she liked to say, usually around the third drink, that art was for the people too. And she was broke, having used her cut of her most recent sale to pay off her maxed-out credit card and three months of back-rent, and there'd be no more home-room subbing in Brooklyn till September.

Sara's sculptures, made quickly and cheaply especially for the event, and for the people, had all sold within the first hour (bought unironically by tourists, which proved how dangerously close to craft she in fact trod, though she'd brushed him off, as she usually did, when he'd pointed this out). Then they'd sat sweating in the shade for four more, while Edward produced portraits of squirming children. Till Edward had insisted that they leave.

While Sara broke down the card tables he'd been replacing his pencils in their flat metal box. A cool shadow had fallen over his lap and hands, and he'd looked up, expecting Sara. Instead, before him stood a breathtaking girl of fifteen or sixteen, accompanied by a nondescript teenaged boy—the boys all looked alike to Edward. The boy had stupidly refused to leave the girl's side while Edward worked, so he'd feigned dissatisfaction with his first efforts, ripping the initial sketch from his artist's pad and starting over. Later, once the boy had paid and they'd gone, Edward had retrieved the rejected sketch from the ground and taken it home with him, where he could take his time working on the girl.

He still had her. Blond and ethereal, kept under glass so she wouldn't smudge.

Last night he'd seen the second perfect girl—perfect if he could have scraped the slutty makeup away.

The babysitter, a luminous gift. When she'd arrived he'd been in the kitchen downing a shot of vodka, to ease himself toward the cocktail party

36

at Cate's country club (which he'd hated, as he'd known he would, but it was part of the win-Cate-to-reach-Basia campaign). He'd figured probably not worth a smarmy excuse for invading the TV room to get a look. But how wrong he'd been.

Cate had asked him to drive her home, after the cocktail party. Which had given him a perfectly legitimate reason, while his tight-assed sister rummaged through her purse and then kitchen drawers for a twenty, to sit down, without seeming weird, beside her on the porch steps. Her name was Amber, a name from a trailer park. But he could forgive her that, forgive her anything. He'd noted a stirring in the lower part of his abdomen—which he'd corralled, controlled—as he asked Amber what she studied.

She was going to major in drama, she told him. Her low, resonant voice did not disappoint.

She was just back that morning from a theater workshop. She was in a play, at the high school, *The Duchess of Malfi*. Actually, she was the star, she'd confessed, with a grin of pure pleasure and pride, as she tucked a curl of strawberry-blonde hair behind her ear. The hair was perfect, a rare color shared only by Botticelli's Venus-on-a-half-shell.

When Edward told her he'd played the malcontent Bosola as a senior, in Ms. Beatrice Ousterhout's class, in the fall production, Amber's laugh was incredulous. Ms. Ousterhout was her favorite teacher. She'd asked if they'd had the costumes yet, in his year. They hadn't – Ms. Ousterhout had wanted everyone in black jeans and T-shirts, even the Duchess and Cariola.

"I guess minimalism was hip around here in the eighties," he'd said. He'd been pleased with his unaccustomed quickness and offhand delivery, as though he had such conversations with girls every day, made them throw back their heads and laugh like she did then, baring her teeth between lips that didn't yet need lipstick.

Once Cate had found the twenty he and Amber had stood up from the steps and walked side by side toward his van and it hit him: maybe everything didn't always have to be out of his reach.

The sun was sinking, lazy and fat and golden, and inside the car was intimate, almost conspiratorial. Amber told him she lived on Stanton Road, but she didn't want to go there. She wanted to be dropped off near the municipal pool, in front of the city library. He'd acceded; Stanton Road was close, and the library was on the other side of town. The drive would give him fifteen more minutes with her. And now they had a secret.

The windows down, her hair blowing into her face. Absently, she'd knotted it in a ponytail holder at the nape of her neck. He'd seen the tattoo of a bird on her left wrist, large and showy, an imperfection. He could paint it away.

His glances had been short, surreptitious. Controlled.

She was perfection incarnate. Hair the hundred warm hues of a ripe peach. And her skin, translucent and pale, but with undertones of violet, rose, cerulean, changing as the van passed into shadow beneath thick trees and out into the open again. Perfectly smooth, not a single imperfection— freckles being so common an accompaniment to Titian hair, what were the chances?

He'd pictured her sleeping, imagined how he'd whip orange and warm gold into her hair, melt her skin into swirls of rose and coral, shoot it through with light. Build the darks into the paler tones, the opposite of what he'd been taught; the secret, never shared with students, behind his girls' inner light. The fingertips of his right hand had begun to tingle.

Leaving the car, she'd shouldered her backpack and extracted her phone. He'd watched in the rearview mirror as she'd disappeard into the trees, talking into her cell, cradled against her face.

Edward closed his eyes. He could see her still, almost smell her.

Perfect.

He slipped the notebook of Sara drawings inside a drawer in his table, pushing it to the back. Around his neck he strung a pair of binoculars and left the boathouse, easing the screen door shut so as not to disturb his sleeping sister.

Edward paused on the steps, squinting out past the slice of deep blue lake, over bulrushes and water weeds toward Walsh's field, then headed toward the house.

He preferred the side entrance because it took him through the laundry room, the only place not contaminated by Cate's regrettable taste for hack-job minimalism. If he hurried into the kitchen, keeping his back to the eastern wall throughout his breakfast preparations, he could avoid the beige-toned mess that occupied pride of place.

Edward would have chosen an entirely different color scheme for a kitchen. The bland, grey-green walls absorbed light, but gave none back. Like Cate—correct, and always in good taste, but never warm.

He'd never had the slightest inclination to draw Cate.

"Damn!" Edward's hand, holding the plastic coffee scoop, banged against the barista-quality coffee machine, sending a dusting of finely ground espresso across the countertop.

Thinking of his work—the possibility that he might *die* an undiscovered genius—and his sister Cate—who could help him so much if she only *would*—made his hands shake, the left one worse than the right.

He dumped the contents of the plastic scoop back into the coffee container and grabbed a sponge from the sink. The gray stone countertop— imported from somewhere, probably Italy—was textured into wrinkles and folds like the skin of an elephant. The powdery bits of coffee got trapped between the ridges.

Cate would find the telltale black flecks anyway. Knowing he'd been in her kitchen, making coffee, she'd look for them—suspicious, birdlike, her head bobbing out from her skinny neck as she talked about a German movie or French cheese while she ran her finger across the base of the Japanese knife stand.

Through the window, a bright flutter of color caught his eye. Edward left his clean-up and raised the binoculars. Closer than the Walshes' place, at the edge of the lawn next door, the neighbor was stretching—flirty pink sports bra, tiny, hip-hugging shorts. Late thirties, Marla or Marta, Mar-Something.

Her thighs were too muscular; there was a point beyond which you shouldn't push it. Her nothing-special face, with its weirdly juvenile upturned nose, was hidden by a visor, pink to match the bra, but he'd seen all he needed to at Cate's barbecues. When Mar-Something bent forward to stretch her hamstrings, pushing with her personally-trained arms against a tree trunk, Edward could see her panty line, though he didn't want to.

No woman over twenty should wear pink.

A little later her daughters would come out to the dock they shared with the Walshes, laden down with iThings and towels and suntan lotion. Both were short and stocky like their mother, though the younger one still had the wide-eyed, soft-faced look of a child. In year or two, she'd get a chin like her sister's. Like their mother's—weak chins were hereditary, and they ruined a face.

Edward watched as Mar-Something jogged off, skirting the edge of the field. He kept the binoculars trained on her until she disappeared around a bend in the road.

"No coffee yet?" Sara's voice rattled him. "I slept like shit."

Three martinis and wine with dinner last night, more wine at the country club. Cate wouldn't be taking her there again. When he'd come back from his chauffeuring errand Cate had been in bed, but Sara was still drinking with Bill. Edward had walked through the door into another argument about Palestine.

Bill-the-cardiologist was a dyed-in-the-wool liberal on every subject except Israel, for which he broke out the yarmulke and side curls. Edward stayed away from politics – politicians were all the same, and none of it mattered anyway—but the drunker Sara got, the harder she fought about Palestinian children and land mines and statehood for all.

Sara's face was puffy, the bags under her eyes papery in the dappled light of the kitchen. Then a brief mirage: the cool, serene perfection of sleep returned to her face as she stepped out of the light.

"Hurry it up, I need caffeine." Sara opened the refrigerator and the apparition vanished. She held the door with her hip, and took out two gallons of milk—Cate's 2% in her left hand, whole in her right, for the two of them.

"You can put hers back. She's at the country club—the Saab's already gone." Edward was working the coffee machine, still finding tiny, soft flecks of espresso. He flicked at them with his fingers, finally blew them under the Cuisinart. "And it's a massage day."

Edward and Sara would have the deck, the lake, the house, to themselves until lunch.

Sara filled a glass with water from the tap—an automatic filter was in place, to make sure Perfect Offspring Boy-and-Girl consumed no impurities. She reached into the cabinet, removed a small vial of Ibuprofen, spilling three out into her hand. As she swallowed, her eyes met Edward's. She smiled her half-smile at him and, for a frozen moment, the morning felt right.

Edward and Sara in Cate's big kitchen, drinking her expensive coffee, with the sun melting over the countertop in squares like pats of butter going soft around the edges.

They were getting away with something. Like when they were teenagers, sneaking into Cate's bedroom while she went out on dates with the captain of the field hockey team. They'd pull her Stevie Nicks albums out of their sleeves and place the shiny black discs on the record player they were never, ever supposed to touch.

Edward could tell Sara was thinking about the record player, too, in the silent, empty kitchen, without either of them needing to mention it. The two of them, always, against Cate. He liked that.

When Sara replaced Cate's carton of milk, the refrigerator light picked up the gray strands that twined through the blond skein of her ponytail. Their hair still matched. Now she wore loose, shapeless cutoffs and a loose, shapeless T-shirt, no bra.

Back when Sara was perfect, they'd laughed together at Cate because she wasn't. Now Sara didn't care.

"Not like that, Edward." Sara's breasts swayed beneath the T-shirt as she took charge of frothing the milk. Hangovers didn't mess up her competence with coffee makers. "It'll go flat again. You never know when to stop, do you?" It was true—he didn't. Edward had always pulled the loose thread just a little further, squeezed the pet hamster just a little harder. Pulled, squeezed, knowing all the while he couldn't undo.

Sara poured the over-frothed milk down the sink and reached across him for the carton. Despite himself, Edward felt a woozy shudder of distaste as his sister's nipple grazed his arm, through the flimsy fabric.

Sara's voice broke through the loud, sucking whoosh of the machine. "Jesus, Edward, you're such a perv."

"What?" Edward's hand shook; the cups of espresso clattered together.

"Ready for the lake, I see." With her free hand, Sara held the binoculars away from her, like an offending piece of leftover food or trash.

"I always… there are birds." *Put the goddamned binoculars down.*

"Yeah, birds. Right. With tits and ass. The Garrison girls come out to the dock at, what, nine? With their little towels and their little bikinis?"

"They don't wear bikinis." Edward wanted to swallow the words back down, but they were out. He bit his tongue. He'd never learn.

"Whatever." Sara returned the binoculars to the counter with a clatter. Edward resisted the impulse to reach for them—not now—and concentrated on balancing the cups.

Sara knew he watched. He knew how much she drank. It was a trade-off.

There were movements across the Garrisons' yard, at the edge of the Walshes' field. His hand wanted to grab the binoculars. He held his coffee mug, tight. Not yet.

Cereal in one hand, coffee in the other, Sara opened the sliding door onto the deck with her foot. "Bring your fucking binoculars," she called to him. "You can see better from out here."

"In a minute." He watched his sister settle into a deck chair. When she pulled her sunglasses over her eyes, he raised the binoculars.

A harsh streak of light struck Edward's eyes. He put the binoculars down. The Saab was back in the driveway—the light had bounced off the windshield.

In a flurried, bourgeois bustle, Cate and the Perfect Offspring gathered their paraphernalia from the trunk. The Perfect Offspring's hair was dry—swimming class must have been canceled, occasioning the early return home. Edward cursed under his breath.

There was movement over in the Walshes' field. Edward raised the binoculars again. A police car crawled along the road beside the field, gliding to a stop among the Queen Anne's lace at the edge.

The door on the driver's side opened and a uniformed woman got out. Dark-blonde, her hair wound into a twist. She crossed the ditch and advanced with long strides, then began to run.

Edward heard the click of the screen door to the laundry room, then the voices of Cate and the Perfect Offspring. He shoved the binoculars into the tea-towel drawer—once Cate had disappeared into the bathroom for her shower, he would retrieve them. To watch.

Jes

"*Pavo muticus imperator.*"

Jes pronounced the Latin words under her breath as she examined the elaborate tattoo extending from the back of the hand around to the delicate underside of the wrist. According to protocol, she shouldn't have picked up the hand until forensics had finished. But forensics, on Saturdays, was Jes (under, theoretically, the supervision of her supervisor, for whom she should probably wait). But there was something under the fingernails.

She wanted to know what. Now, not three hours from now.

It was dirt.

Jes ran her gloved finger down the bird's neck. A male peacock. The artist had gotten the intricate markings around the eyes right, the beaded appearance of the forehead, the proud crest. He, or she, must have had access to good photographs.

The spreading tailfeathers hid old scars.

The hand felt heavy, waterlogged. Dead. The synthetic azure of the manicure—the polish was chipped—clashed with the medicinal aqua of Jes's surgical gloves, with the brilliant blue eyes at the tips of the peacock's tail feathers.

In Thailand Jes's father had pointed out the drabber, dowdier female peacocks. Pea *hens*, he'd whispered, holding his best field binoculars, the Bushnell Legend Ultras, up to her eyes. His hands were fine and clean, with long, elgant fingers. Breathing in the sulfurous, loamy smell of the fertile marshes, Jes remembered the feel of the baby hairs at her hairline and temples frizzing. Her hair was curly like her mother's; her father's was straight and fine. The male bird had spread its tail feathers then. They made a sound like the opening of her grandmother's carved bone fan.

"A courting ritual," her father had murmured, his breath damp and warm on her neck.

She put the girl's hand with its peacock tattoo down carefully where she'd found it. Jes could feel the sweat now, gathering in her armpits and around her bra, trickling down the insides of her thighs. She could smell her own acidity mixing with newly cut grass and wet dirt. She shut the discomfort out. Sweat, heat, itchy trousers, none of it mattered.

This mattered. The girl, what had happened to her.

Getting the guy, making him pay.

The chances of a she-perp were pretty minimal; in cases like this one, women were exponentially more likely to be the victims. Which was not exactly news. But there were so many more ways now for the creeps to identify and pursue targets, just being a girl constituted a sigificant risk factor.

Jes flipped through the shots she'd taken of the hand with its intricate tattoo. Her first real case. She'd gladly put in an eternity of boring, nothing-happening, 8 a.m.-call Saturdays if she could undo what had been done to this girl.

She could at least nail the bastard and put him away for life. Do something that mattered, instead of rounding up a bunch of druggies and then letting them go—state rehab facilities were maxed out, with mile-long waiting lists—knowing she'd be rounding them up all over again before the week was out.

This job hadn't been what Jes had expected, or what she'd prepared for. She'd sat through two years of seminars—profiling; crime scene forensics; deviance and normative social behavior; obsessive-compulsive tendencies in sexual predators—before writing her too-good thesis about too-awful trophy collecting among serial killers. "The prose is excellent, but why do you even want to think about things like that?" her mother had asked, pushing the sheaf of papers back across the coffee table toward Jes.

Then had come fitness tests, police entrance exams, interviews, and finally graduation. All of it a long, gray institutional tunnel at the end of which the only decent job at her pay grade had brought her back here, home, to a college town barely big enough to have an airport, where some clothing stores didn't bother to carry anything smaller than Extra Large. Where her mother could invite her to dinner via voice mail whenever she felt like it and expect her to show up. Like last night.

Jes took final shots of the ground surrounding the body—the grass was trampled, flattened, likely by her own boots and her mother's Flintstone clogs—before returning her camera to its case and kneeling beside the girl. She checked the undersides of arms, the insides of thighs, running her fingers from armpit to wrist, groin to ankle. Dozens of square inches of healthy skin, no needle marks anywhere. The girl wasn't a junky. That already made her exceptional.

For the two years she'd been on the squad, Jes had seen nothing but junkies, skinny rat-assed humans in torn jeans, arms like twigs, hair like straw, missing teeth. At first, she'd felt sorry for them. Now they just pissed her off.

As did the woefully inadequate system for dealing with them.

Most people who live here think Ithaca is too nice for junkies. And most people think the pedestrian streets downtown go dead after the restaurants shut at midnight. Jes could enlighten most people about a thing or two. Yesterday one of the girls had a bunch of stolen debit card numbers on her, along with thirty-two $100 gift cards from The Gap. Drew had called the state Identity Theft unit and they'd sent a guy over from Albany.

While Jes did damage control on the debit cards, Drew and the Albany guy took their coffee into Drew's office and talked for half an hour with the door closed. Then they sent the girl to Albion for a couple of nights, to see if she'd roll on somebody bigger.

Jes had thought about telling them they should put her right back where they found her, because that was where she was headed, and sooner rather than later (unless of course they planned on setting up a rehab program that actually worked, like in Sweden, where the kids worked outside and ate organic and had ridiculously low recidivism–good luck getting *that* through the state legislature).

But Double-Wide Drew did everything by the book. So arrestee-du-jour girl went to Albion Correctional, to waste some taxpayer money while she learned from high-risk inmates about new and ingenious places on her body to stick a needle. Insteps were good, lots of veins there.

This girl's insteps were pearly and smooth, the soles of her feet soft as though she'd never stepped on anything rougher than a cloud. Toenails neatly clipped, painted the same bright blue as the fingernails. Not a runaway — their feet were destroyed after a week or two on the street. This girl hadn't been outside long. If at all.

The creep had probably kept her somewhere carefully hidden, until he got ready to kill and dump her.

Jes sat back on her heels, surveying the position of the body, still half-hidden by a screen of leafy branches. Whoever had done this was definitely a royal scumbag, but not a typical serial killer: shoving the girl up under the bushes like that instead of leaving her out in the open, for all to see; cutting off her hand — they usually took fingers or toes. No scratch marks or defensive wounds. And why had he left it?

Maybe she knew him. "Shithead," Jes muttered.

Pretty much everyone thought this job was wrong for Jes. Her mother was ridiculous on the subject. Her name around the station was College.

Werner, her immediate superior, Deputy Chief of Police and D.W.'s uncle, didn't care for the class of individuals he termed "intellectual snobs," which included anyone who had gone to school out of state. "Over-qualified," Werner had pronounced, skeptical behind his messy desk, as he'd first handed Jes her badge and gun.

And Jes agreed. But babysitting junkies wasn't what she'd been hired to do. She'd been hired to do *this*. Terrible and hard to see as it was. Jes gently opened the girl's mouth, lifted her tongue and looked underneath, then reached her fingers down the throat—with some difficulty; it was getting stiff—to check for obstructions. She was working quickly. By the time Werner and his nephew got here, she'd have the initial exam wrapped up.

They could call her "College" all they wanted. Jes's performance review was on Monday: she'd get a commendation for her work on this case whether Drew liked it or not. She already had three, all for junky crap, but still three more than him. Couple more and she could request a transfer. To anywhere, she wasn't particular, as long as it put distance between her and her mother.

Jes stared at the hand on the ground beside her. The fingers fanned open with a curious grace. Why cut it off if you weren't planning to take it with you? For effect, she supposed. Or maybe he'd dropped it. Something could've spooked him, maybe a passing car or an animal – there were a lot of deer in the area.

What was it with sicko creeps and teenaged girls? You could call it paraphilia, as did one camp of the neuropsychologists whose papers she'd consulted for her thesis, or you could try to reconstruct the etiology of the deviant's sexual orientation—Jes's personal shorthand for this school of thought was *"Blame It on His Mother"*—but it always came down to the same thing. You didn't need abstruse scientific terminology to explain the simple fact that most men were hardwired to want to screw young women.

But the freaks wanted to kill them.

"She was sixteen." Her mother's words startled her; Jes had forgotten she was there. "Barely old enough to drive."

Jes didn't answer.

"I can tell you what I know about her?" She sounded tentative, fragile.

"Absolutely, Mom." Jes opened a sterilized plastic vial and began scraping with a forensic blade beneath the blue fingernails of the intact

46

right hand. Dirt. The nails on the severed hand were clean. The dirt bothered her—why the right hand and nowhere else? "It needs to be a formal statement, though. I shouldn't be the one to do it. Drew can talk to you when he gets here."

If it hadn't been for Beatrice, someone else would be processing the scene, maybe even D.W. himself.

Jes secured the scrapings, then began to photograph the body. As her finger clicked the shutter—sternum, gentle slope of hips, soft layer of fat across the belly—the crunching of tires over gravel reached her in the too-loud way of sounds traveling over open spaces. She looked up. A second squad car was pulling up behind hers. Terence got out of the passenger's side, shaggy bangs flopping over his eyes. Werner had given up on the regulation haircut—Terence was too good in the lab. Her partner's big, square head emerged from the driver's side, with its military-issue crew cut.

Drew talked about the first Gulf War as though he personally had driven a tank up and down the Highway of Death until it was safe for babies in strollers, but Jes's quick snoop through his file—left carelessly open on a desk—had told her he was never shipped further than the Wiesbaden Training Area.

And the physical fitness exam had been waived in Drew's case—the guy must weigh at least 240. Terence had let that one slip one night after the third round of beers Jes had bought.

Drew jogged across the field, accentuating the heaviness of his body. When he reached Jes, he wiped sweat from his forehead. His pale eyes took in the tape, the array of tools on the ground at her feet. "Aren't you off today, College?"

Jes began to prepare a label for the vial of fingernail scrapings. "Nope." He knew perfectly well she wasn't.

Drew had written a formal memo against the department's decision to hire her. The drafts were still on his computer (he should know better than to choose his dog's name as a password): lack of experience; female detectives were handicapped in violent situations. Even this: too much higher education made for too little common sense. None of it had stuck.

Jes stood, sealing the vial inside a manila evidence bag. "There's nothing here – no footprints, no blood, no fibers. We're going to have to cast the net wide. Let's start the cordon over by the end of the fence and run it down to those trees, then about half-way into the field."

"Right, Jes." Terence's voice, usually lazy and good-natured, sounded strained. Jes noticed that he kept his face turned away from the body.

"Cause of death?" Drew's eyes, even behind his sunglasses, were easy to follow: straight to the breasts. Yesterday, Jes had seen him sizing up junkie girl's ass, what little there was of it, as she climbed into the back of the van.

"Dunno yet." Jes bent to retrieve the camera. "No bruises on the neck or ligature marks. No blood in the throat. No sign of petechial hemorrhage. When we get her back to the lab, we can check to see if the hyoid's broken, but I'd bet against it."

"Holy shit, is that her hand?" Drew craned his neck, trying to get a better view.

She ignored that, watching his eyes scan down from the girl's breasts over her belly to her mound. Then he hunched violently forward, broad back straining the seams of his uniform shirt. A wet, choking sound filled the air. Drops of vomit splashed too close to the girl's belly.

Once the heaves had stopped, Drew spat several times into the bushes and wiped his hands on the grass, then turned to face Jes. "This doesn't bother you?"

"What do you think?"

Drew was fixated on the droplets of vomit that speckled the cuffs of his trousers, scrubbing at them with a Kleenex he'd produced from his shirt pocket. "You called Werner yet?"

Jes wrinkled her nose at the sour smell. There was no hard and fast rule, but it was generally acknowledged that Werner should get a call when an unusual case presented itself. Procedure was Drew's thing—and he was well aware that it wasn't hers.

Jes's phone was out first.

"What's up?" Werner sounded like he'd been on a Red Bull drip.

"We have a body. Female." She pushed her sunglasses over her eyes, shutting Drew out. "A pedestrian found her in an empty field out on Willet. Cause of death unknown, possible sexual assault. Her left hand and partial forearm have been amputated, but were found on the scene."

"Is the pedestrian still at the scene?"

"Yes." Jes adjusted her sunglasses. "Actually, it was my mother, out walking her dog." The statement, she knew, shrank her down to size, but it was unavoidable. She didn't mention having driven to the scene before informing her colleagues. She could almost hear Drew ticking off procedural violations and breaches of protocol on his mental whiteboard.

"Werner," Jes plunged in, "looks like a sex crime. Am I primary?"

Werner's voice came back, studied and thoughtful. "Yep. But work closely with Drew. He's got a lot of years under his belt on narcotics and I'd bet my retirement account there's drugs mixed up in this." She heard a motor start up on Werner's end.

"Sure – I'm on it." Jes pocketed her phone, glancing down at the girl's track-free arms, smooth insteps. *Drugs, my ass.* Let them chase red herrings down rabbit holes while she cracked the case on her own. "Werner says I'm P.I."

Drew's face registered a pasty mixture of resentment and residual queasiness.

Werner joined them, head smooth from one edge of his neat gray goatee to the other. Werner didn't like stubble. He stared down at the body for a few seconds, running a palm back and forth across his bald head, as though he could polish the problem away.

Jes suspected Werner was thinking about the budget cuts, the subject of yesterday's demoralizing staff meeting. There hadn't been a sensational murder case in Ithaca since the two cheerleaders, back in the 80s. A quiet neighbor living in a trailer on the back of one of their father's properties had sawed the bodies into pieces so small some of them had never been found. If you got the perp, a case like that could make a department and a career. If you didn't, it could ruin you. But catching criminals took money.

"Okay, let's see what we've got here." Jes's criminology professors had all had Manhattan accents, or Brooklyn ones, but Werner's was a local voice. Werner knelt beside the girl, removing a surgical thermometer from his pocket—the budget cuts had reduced the medical examiner's office to strictly Monday-Friday. "Jesus, did you puke on her, Ashton?"

"Drew doesn't do so well with dead bodies."

"I'm hung over." *Right.*

"You drink a whole keg? Stinks like hell." Werner's meaty fingers curled around the girl's ankle, lifting her nearly rigid leg. "Did you get a reading on the liver temp?"

"Time of death sometime between ten and midnight last night."

"Sounds about right," Werner said. "She's stiff as a board."

Jes made a note in a small spiral notebook she carried in her shirt pocket. Drew was typing with his big thumbs into his knock-off smart phone. He tried to edge his way between Jes and his uncle. "We need to get drug tests run ASAP—that'll tell me a lot. Six to one she was doping."

"Everything gets channeled through me." Jes kept her voice cool, neutral. "I'm the primary. There are no needle marks on her anywhere, I checked. A rape kit might be more to the point."

"Rape kit first," Werner said. "Best chance of turning up a suspect. Then we start on the toxic substance workup." Not looking at Drew or at her. Saving his nephew's face. "We know anything about her?"

Now Jes had the advantage. "Sixteen years old, local high-school girl." Jes called out to her mother, "What did you say her name was?"

"Amber Inglin. She had the starring role in a play I'm directing." Her mother's voice sounded reedy, close to breaking. "She was in the foster system. She lived out on Stanton Road, with a couple named Wilbur and two other kids."

"Why's she all the way over there?" Werner jerked his head in the direction of Jes's mother.

"The dog wouldn't stay away from the body. Drew, maybe you could take my mother's deposition." Jes pulled rank before Drew could deliver any smirking comment. "I can't do it—violation of protocol."

"I'll talk to her." Werner said. "Drew, you knock on that door over there, see if they heard anything. Lawyer's place. Nice guy, Liam Walsh."

Liam Walsh, one of the more memorable of Jes's late-spring drive-bys. A thrill sought, caught, and experienced. Then released back to his wife, his big house, and his magazine-shot lawn. No harm, no foul.

Drive-bys were the key to a low-maintenance emotional life. Much less complicated than boyfriends. She hadn't had one of those since her sophomore year at Berkeley.

While Werner spoke to her mother, Jes studied the grasses and weeds flattened by the body, unwilling to confront the girl's glassy, unfocused gaze. What a way to go. And before you were even old enough to vote. All the Teflon on the planet wouldn't make notification any easier. And the words would be coming from her mouth; no way she'd trust D.W. to deliver such a message. A glint between the leaves caught her eye. A cell phone, probably the girl's. She slipped the phone into an evidence bag, stowed it in her backpack—fuck protocol, forensics wouldn't be open for business again till Monday. As if pervs operated nine to five. Thank you, budget cuts. She'd check it for prints herself. She brought her face close to the ground, making sure she hadn't missed anything else.

Two long, curved feathers, one crossed over the other, stripes of creamy beige and brown blending into the grass flattened by the girl's head. From an owl—no mistaking the comb-like flutings along the outer edge. *"Fimbriae"*—Jes could almost hear her father—"so its flight will be silent." Fuck forensics. She'd do it herself. Jes placed the feathers into a plastic evidence bag, and into her backpack with the phone. Massive violation of protocol, but Werner and D.W. would take the lazy way out, anything to get themselves out of uniform and into their stupid fishing boat. This was not drugs, it was something else, and she was going to work through the weekend to figure out what.

After a few moments, Drew called, "Nobody here!"

Jes looked toward the house. Nice back porch. Perfect for Saturday morning brunch and the New York Times in matching spa robes. No thanks. Just the sex, please.

Drew returned, joined by Terence, who'd finished canvassing the ditch for footprints. Werner assigned tasks. "Terence, load the body up—I guess we'll have to transport her in my car. Use some plastic sheeting or something. We can't leave her out here in this heat. How come you guys didn't bring the van?"

"Terence didn't–" Drew started. Nothing was ever his fault.

"Never mind. Get her down to the deposit." Werner waved a fly away from his face with an irritated motion of his hand. Werner didn't dissimulate well. "I'll do the preliminary autopsy so we can get the samples to the lab. Maybe they can put a rush on it. Unlikely." He studied their faces as though their joint presence bothered him. "Walsh bought a vineyard near Homer not long ago; he may be out there. And his wife's got a gallery on the Commons. Pillar-of-the-community types, so handle with care."

Liam Walsh had definitely been a pillar when she'd climbed astride him and gripped his scrotum, handling him with anything but care. All her drive-bys liked fierceness, a change from their blasé lives.

"Let's talk to them before informing the family. I'll be in the lab—call me as soon as you have anything." Werner vaulted back across the fence with unexpected athletic grace and started toward his car, head glinting in the sun.

With Werner gone, Jes grabbed the reins. "Let's hit the gallery first—meet you there." Drew stood for a moment, scrolling through the notes on his phone before starting toward his car at a lumbering jog, without acknowledging Jes's directive.

Jes stuck her keys into the ignition. She'd let Drew barrel over to the gallery first, then have to cool his heels while he waited for her—no questioning could begin without the P.I.

A cardinal perched on the wrought-iron scroll above the mailbox at the end of the drive. *"The Walshes."*

She'd met Liam Walsh at Corks and More, a doctor-and-lawyer hangout on the upscale end of her rotation of bars. Not a sure bet, like the Velvet Dog, but she'd had reasonably good luck there. And it was good to mix it up, instead of staking out the same place night after night. That could get a girl a reputation.

Actually, she had a reputation.

The drive-by rules included never having seconds (twice with the same guy on the same night didn't count); never handing out her phone number (though sometimes she took theirs if they were insistent, discarding them later); and never, ever bringing them to her place. Their houses were nicer anyway.

Most were professional men in their forties and fifties. All were married—less prone to attachment than the single ones. And Jes liked testing that stability, giving a rocking jolt to the conjugal equilibrium and then disappearing. She wasn't endangering anything that wasn't already dangling over the abyss. How happy could they be, if they hooked up with her?

Some of the lawyers—surprise, surprise—were already infamous for dipping into the pool of law students who interned at their firms—the county clerk was a gossip, and she liked free lattes. The law students were handy— they graduated and moved to L.A. or Chicago or Manhattan. Case closed.

Sometimes she imagined the drive-by going on a family vacation, putting up the Christmas tree, entertaining dinner guests alongside his wife. And maybe his daughter. The images filled her with a wistful sadness, but also with an absurd feeling of safety, of security: somewhere a family, a mother, father, and daughter, were happy. Like before her father's expeditions to places farther and farther away, before his residencies at labs in Brazil and Thailand and Mauritania, before his constant absence.

A pair of grackles took flight from the weeds that lined the ditch, sun glinting off their inky wings. *Quiscalus quiscula.* The first Latin bird name Jes had learned. Her father had smiled his crooked smile as she giggled over the silly-sounding syllables.

Jes eased the car off the shoulder and onto the road. She was about to meet a drive-by's wife, a violation of a rule so obvious that it didn't need to be made.

The road into town rolled past fields of hay that belonged to a horse farm, where Jes had hidden one night late with her father, tracking owls. An adult female's wingspan had darkened the moon for a brief second, turning the stalks from silver to black. Jes thought of the feathers in the plastic bag. Sometimes serial killers left souvenirs. Less frequent than trophy-taking, but it happened. What was the intention behind owl feathers?

Basia Walsh's gallery was downtown, at the southwest corner of the square known as The Commons, surrounded by trendy restaurants and shops. *B. Walsh Fine Arts*, a smallish space with disproportionately high ceilings and windows almost as tall, paintings still in brown paper wrapping, stacked in corners, waiting to be hung. Wide swathes of focused light lit up the sand-colored walls, the chrome frame of the glass-topped desk, the expensive highlights and lowlights of B. Walsh's shoulder-length, drive-by-wife bob.

Across the table Drew's bulk pushed against the minimalist edges of a yellow armchair, phone balanced on his knee, thick fingers poised over the keyboard. Looking foolish.

Basia Walsh's face was an elegant oval with a finely drawn jawline, dramatic hazel eyes placed at a slight slant, the nose strong, a bit broad at the nostrils—a face that, in youth, might have been unremarkable but, in middle age, was stunning. The lines beside her full mouth were the only ones visible in the well-maintained skin. Jes thought of the expensive creams and cosmetics arrayed across marble vanities in master bathrooms. Sometimes the medicine cabinets held prescription sleep-aids—she always checked—guaranteed to knock you senseless in fifteen minutes flat. In case marriage hadn't numbed you enough already.

"Please excuse the mess, we're getting ready for an opening tonight." Basia Walsh's voice was finely modulated, echoing her sleek, coiffed appearance. A rich voice. There'd been voices like hers at Berkeley.

Jes rounded the couch and pulled forward a low-slung chair made of polished blond wood, nudging aside a pile of Styrofoam packing peanuts with her boot. "Detective Jesca Ashton, Tompkins County Investigative Division."

Jes felt the woman's eyes catalogue her features, her body, then dismiss her. Score one for the uniform. She felt a strong urge to look straight into those eyes and announce, "I fucked your husband. And he liked it. What do you think of that?"

Drew began a pompous line of questioning, cocking an eyebrow upward in his best imitation of the lead detective on C.S.I. Miami. He had hundreds of episodes downloaded onto his precious phone, watched them over lunch every day. "Mrs. Walsh, can you verify your whereabouts yesterday evening between the hours of nine and midnight?"

Mrs. Walsh answered Drew's questions slowly, enunciating carefully, as though she were conceding a gracious favor. She'd been at a cocktail at the country club—Jes swallowed a smirk—then out to dinner with friends, leaving the restaurant a little after ten and arriving home around half past. She listed several persons with whom she'd conversed at the cocktail party and gave the names of the friends with whom she'd had dinner, producing a receipt from the restaurant with a time stamp of 10:12.

When Jes showed her the feathers in their bag (Drew shot her a look, which Jes ignored), Basia Walsh shook her shiny head, reaching forward to straighten a stack of pamphlets with an artist's photo on the front. With the movements of her hand—tanned, moisturized, coral-colored nails—came a waft of crisp, lemony perfume.

Jes replaced the feathers into her pack. "Was Mr. Walsh with you last night?"

"Only at the cocktail—he had some work to do. He was there when I got home."

Drew edged forward on the yellow plywood chair which tilted up off the back two of its delicate legs. Basia Walsh blinked, worried about the chair. "Mrs. Walsh," the D.W. gotcha voice, "I have it on good authority that Miss Inglin was known to your husband." A text from Werner, no doubt, on which she hadn't been copied. Not on purpose, necessarily—Werner was still figuring out his new phone. Jes resisted the temptation to roll her eyes. "He worked on her placement case...or perhaps you don't recall that instance."

Drew should stick to two-dollar words.

"Of course." Basia Walsh's voice was edged with just the right amount of concern. "He works for the city, Child Services. He's out at the vineyard, I can give you directions."

Home, husband—these people sleepwalked through their lives. "I know the place." Let her wonder. Jes thanked Basia Walsh for her time, left her card. Said she'd be in touch if they required further information.

Basia Walsh studied Jes's card, then placed it carefully on the table. Her polite smile didn't reach her eyes. "You can see yourselves out, I presume."

Outside, the glare hit hard.

"You enter the feathers into the log?" Drew squinted, more gotcha.

"Yup."

"Once they're in the log they're supposed to go to the station."

"Fucking lab's closed til Monday, might as well make use of them. They're safe in their baggie."

"Violation of protocol."

"We have a dead sixteen-year-old girl. You think she'd give a shit about protocol?"

Drew shook his head and jangled his keys. The sound was loud, aggressive. Jes was used to him. "So where's the vineyard?"

"We'll go to the Wilburs first."

"But Werner said—"

"I'm running this. Notification first—let's get it done, before they hear it on the news. And I'll do the talking."

In the car Jes put gloves on and pulled out the girl's phone.

Off-brand, cheap, no password.

She scrolled through the recent texts. One call late last evening—9:03—to a number linked to "Connor and Megan." Probably the two other foster kids; Jes made a note of the names. Before that, two weeks without calls or texts, which was strange for anyone, but especially so for a sixteen-year-old. Then, starting mid-afternoon yesterday, a short volley of texts to and from "Connor and Megan"—"r u back?," "yeah," "sweet".

Someone named Darla. "Lasagna in fridge, pre-heat oven 350 45 min don't 4get salad." Probably the foster mother.

She checked the phone numbers. Not that many. Among them was "Liam." Which would be none other than Mr. Liam Walsh, esq. Child Services, made sense. But still—that plus the field, maybe one coincidence too many.

Would Liam Walsh fuck a sixteen-year-old girl?

Maybe. A disturbing number of men would, if given the chance. Especially if they thought there wouldn't be consequences—foster kids were low-risk targets, right up there with prostitutes and junkies.

But would he kill her?

Walsh didn't look the type. But then they never did.

Liam

The second squad car disappeared down the steep gravel drive, leaving behind a tight-stretched silence.

Frank broke it. "Want me to send the men back in? Those canopies need pruning pretty bad." Heavy lopping shears balanced in one hand, a saw in the other. "Vines are going crazy."

This year they'd gone cold-turkey—no more chemical growth inhibitors. Now eager new shoots and leaves appeared practically overnight.

The crew still clustered around the picnic table, holding mugs of coffee long gone cold, murmuring. *Muchacha. Muerta. Terrible.* And *migra.* The men were worried about deportation.

"*No migra.*" Frank spoke over his shoulder. "No INS, *sólo policía normal. No hay problema.*"

But there was a problem. The soft Spanish words didn't drown out the ones Detective Jesca Ashton had spoken, now playing on endless loop in his head.

"Don't leave town"—she'd said that right before she left, preceded by "person of interest." And the girl's face was there too. Amber Inglin's pretty, scared face, dropped into his mind like a quarter into the coke machine Frank insisted they have for the crew.

The girl, lying in his field, decay already starting—it was hot. Imagining flies attracted by the sweetish smell of recent death, he fought off nausea. The line of trees at the back of the eastern vineyard wavered into a strange, watery mirage. Or maybe she wasn't there anymore—they'd have removed her by now, to the coroner's, or a morgue.

He wiped at the trickle of sweat tickling down the back of his neck. He'd caught the word "reveal," pronounced by Detective Jesca Ashton in answer to a question from Frank that the buzzing in his brain hadn't let him hear. The word had sounded strange, foreign.

"What?" His own voice had been loud, too loud, surprising him, making Detective Jesca Ashton, cool in her gray uniform—did the woman not sweat?—repeat her answer—"I *said* I can't reveal the details of the investigation at the present time"—and turn and look at him. Notice the drops on his forehead, around his hairline. He'd seen her eyes take them in, register them, begin to interpret them. Which had made him sweat harder, trying to blink the girl's face away, or at least back into the fog that had gathered inside his head.

That was still there. He felt as though nothing around him were real, not the vines, not the men. The only real thing was what had happened to the girl.

When the first squad car appeared he'd been thinking about fog, about how there hadn't been any, like sometimes happened in late summer, in the early morning. Fog was hard on grapes—devastating even—this far into the season, and the weather had been nuts. Crazy warm days in February— thank God the buds hadn't burst—hard frost in March. Torrential rains in April, and it hadn't gotten cold enough all winter to kill the insects off. But his vines were hearty. He'd been congratulating himself, as though he were somehow responsible, in control of fog or no fog.

In control of shit nothing, more like it.

"Start again?" Frank's gravelly prompt pulled him back, centered him. Work: vines, pruning, keep the men calm.

"Yeah, go ahead." Liam wiped more sweat from his neck. "I have to make some phone calls. Be out in a while."

Not that they needed his help, Frank ran a top-notch crew, but Liam liked the weight of the shears and the saw, the vines bending in his hands, calluses, the perfect hard-working days of high summer rolling toward harvest. The feeling of accomplishment, of all having done something together, something *good*, as he himself—*el patrón*, the men called him— snipped the first bunches of round, purple grapes from the vine.

He knew this: he wouldn't be feeling good about much of anything for a good long while.

The day had started off about as perfect as they got, with a sleepy kiss from his gorgeous wife before she burrowed back beneath the crazy-expensive sheets. At 54, Basia still turned heads, including his. He'd married up, in every sense of the word.

From his office window he'd looked out at the hills covered with vines, *his* vines, rows of healthy green canopies twining toward the horizon, sheltering fruit. Just yesterday he'd noticed the change in color, green mellowing into gold on the Riesling, tinges of purple around the edges of the Pinot, a softening of the fruit under the skin— *Veraison*—the most vulnerable moment in the growing cycle.

Happening earlier than it used to—though the broader implications were troubling, more days of sun were not necessarily a bad thing, in the short term, for upstate wineries. A bumper crop, especially the Riesling, it would have notes from the native bell flower and marsh marigold he'd planted along the edge of the field, another step toward the holy grail of organic certification. Last year's Riesling had been stellar—award-winning, in fact—but there hadn't been enough of it. This vintage would put Vestri on the map—reviews, restaurants, shows, tastings. The orders were already piling up on his desk.

Booting up the computer, he'd enjoyed eavesdropping through the open window on Frank, speaking to one of the men in the bad Spanish that everyone seemed to understand. Basia called Frank "one of the more successful" of her husband's rehabilitation projects; Liam had found him among the work-release gardening crew that kept the courthouse grounds. Not every vineyard could boast a reformed alcoholic as a foreman. Frank could even taste the product, though he spat afterwards.

The morning had followed his usual pattern, working steadily for three hours, accompanied by the faint metallic singing of pruning shears, then breaking for the communal coffee. The men brought their own lunches but Liam served the ten-o'clock *merienda* himself: *café de olla*—he'd bought the clay pot, the *olla de barro*, on vacation in Mexico, and had found a specialty store to supply the raw cane sugar, spices, and dark roasted coffee beans.

Carrying the tray to the picnic table beneath the old oak, inhaling the aromas of nutmeg, coffee, and ripening grapes, he'd felt the rightness of the world. The rightness of these men, good workers, grateful to him for the work, grateful for the coffee that tasted like home.

When the first squad car had sped up the driveby, he'd been explaining—through Frank and between sips of coffee—why fog, *niebla*, was bad.

Then the car had stopped and Detective Jesca Ashton had stepped out of it.

She was his only slip-up. Not like he hadn't had other opportunities. Dozens, in fact, but he'd always resisted.

And then he hadn't. Something about her wouldn't let him.

Afterward he'd felt like a jerk. Not to mention an idiot, for risking his marriage, and his sweet, easy life. The vineyard. Everything. For a lay.

He'd spent the last two months avoiding Corks and More.

Today he'd watched her—he couldn't help it—as she bent back into the squad car, searching for something, gray uniform trousers hugging her ass. A beautifully sculpted, perfectly rounded ass. A spectacular ass. As she'd straightened and turned to face the group, he'd looked away sharply, her silhouette still imprinted on his retina. An afterimage he wished he could erase: two months ago, he'd sunk his fingers, then his teeth, into that spectacular ass. The vividness of the memory shook him.

In the shade of the oak she'd pushed up her sunglasses, and he'd remembered her eyes were green. They'd lit on his for a sliver of a second then slid out toward the vines. To the spot where they'd had frenzied, panting, hard-biting sex.

Explosive, earth-moving, soul-rumbling sex. Twice. He'd forgotten it could be like that.

Basia had asked about the spreading purple bruise on his shoulder. Fortunately Detective Jesca Ashton's teeth hadn't left marks, and there were a hundred ways to get bruises on a vineyard.

The first lie he'd ever told his wife.

He'd been so sure he'd never cheat, contemptuous of friends and colleagues who risked perfectly good marriages because they couldn't keep their pants zipped. Until that night at the new pub across from the courthouse, when Detective Jesca Ashton had grinned at him from down the bar, hair waving to her waist, China-doll teeth glinting in the dim light. When he was young he'd had a thing for long hair.

He'd watched her eating a huge plate of home fries—double order, she'd told him—mixing hot sauce into her ketchup, licking her fingers. A soccer match had been on the television above the bar, a rerun. She was rooting for Lithuania, though they had already lost. She said she liked an underdog.

He'd liked that.

A commercial had come on with a cartoon stork, and she'd asked if he'd ever seen storks having sex. He'd had no idea what she'd say or do next, and he'd liked that too. He'd found himself telling her about the vineyard and she'd wanted to see it. Right then.

The whole thing had blind-sided him, or the sex part had. Even with her beat-up Jetta following him out to Vestri, he hadn't let himself see what was happening, what he was about to do. A new friend, maybe, this

31-year-old, dirty blonde cop with a wicked laugh and a tattoo on her lower back.

He'd shown her around. She'd asked all kinds of questions about the plants—they'd been just beginning to bud then—and listened attentively to the answers, like she really wanted to know. When the sun was fully down he'd brought a bottle of Riesling out to the porch, and at some point he'd gone in for another.

When he'd come back out she was walking barefoot in the grass. She'd smiled up at him standing there on the porch and said how good everything smelled at night. Then she'd wandered into the vines, so small she almost disappeared between the rows of plants. Not even looking back, as though she'd known what he'd do, each step a natural consequence of the last. Each leading to a next, and then a next. The ease of the whole thing sent a shiver through him now. Shocking, when you thought about it. What *had* he been thinking?

"Mr. Walsh." Having found whatever she was looking for, she'd straightened, closed the car door. Faced him with a professional nod, pulling a small spiral notepad from her uniform shirt pocket. "I'm Detective Jesca Ashton, Tompkins County Investigative Division." As if he didn't know.

He'd watched her take in the mid-morning spread, the men standing round the shaded table. Frank's tanned, muscular arms crossed over his chest. Frank didn't have a good record with cops.

"I'll need everyone over here, please."

The men had formed a half-circle around her, Waldo's head and broad shoulders standing out above the others. Another misfit, rescued from the ragged halfway house across from Liam's law office. Graying hair, fine and wispy like a young child's, Waldo was the only American among the workers. Records listed a sudden onset of schizophrenia in late adolescence, just after his mother's death. Committed by his half-brother— they didn't want him on the Onondaga reservation anymore, stirring up trouble; he wasn't even real Indian, the mother had been a hanger-on, a wanna-be. They hadn't wanted her around either. Why a schizophrenic was housed with low-level criminals on the road to reintegration was a mystery Liam had never been able to solve. What he had been able to do was bring Waldo to a better place.

As Detective Jesca Ashton was stating the few facts of the case she was "at liberty to disclose," with Frank translating, a blur of white had shot from between the vines. Waldo's dog, baptized with the strange name of Galizur, had wrapped himself around his master's shins. Some of the men took a step back. Jesca Ashton hadn't blinked.

She'd held up a plastic bag containing two long feathers. "These were found beneath Ms. Inglin's head." Her tone was flat, precise. "They'd been placed in the form of a cross. Docs this sound familiar to anyone?"

Frank's prompt *nope* had sounded churlish.

Her eyes had circled the group, lighting briefly on each face. The men shook their heads. "Mr. Walsh?"

"Not at all." Wrong answer, too wordy, a simple *no* would have done the trick.

She'd put the bag away. "I need to establish everyone's whereabouts last night between the hours of nine and midnight."

Each day one of the men with papers drove the others in a van, out and back from a strip of track apartments in a cheaper town twenty miles away. There'd been murmuring in Spanish and then Frank's explanation. "Went home around eight, no stops, then back this morning."

"What about you?"

"Date. Girl named Andie." Frank's latest aging blonde "fuck-buddy" in Frank parlance.

"Does Andie have a last name?"

"She does but I don't know it. Only met her last week." Frank's eyes had swept the detective's body, lingering over her hips. Frank was a good foreman. And an equal-opportunity fornicator, the radar was never off. "You can find her easy—massage therapist, got a website. We were at her place, take-out Thai and a movie. She keeps receipts. That would be an alibi, right?"

"If it checks out."

Frank had uncrossed his arms. "We were out again, around eleven, place where she knows the bartender, down on Clinton. I got the receipt. Coke for me, rum and Coke for her. She likes to drink, so I let her." A Frank grin. He pulled a wad of detritus from his pocket—chewing gum wrappers, a ponytail holder, miscellaneous scraps of paper, all balled together by lint.

Detective Jesca Ashton had examined the crumpled receipt and handed it back, eyes flicking across Frank's solid shoulders. Maybe she was equal-opportunity, too.

Then she'd turned to him. "Mr. Walsh, you said you did not

accompany your wife to dinner after the...ah..."—she consulted notes—"country-club cocktail?"

"No." Fine, he belonged to the country club. So did every other lawyer in town. She hadn't had any objections to lawyers when she was on all fours in the dirt, doing her bit to reestablish the organic balance of the *terroir*. He'd blinked (which he probably should not have done), the image in his mind far too clear for comfort.

"What did you do?"

"Went home, worked on payroll. I was there when my wife got back. Ask her." Had he sounded defensive? Undoubtedly.

"I have." Of course she'd already have been to the gallery—she'd go there first, it was the closest to the field. Where they'd found the girl. The idea of Basia answering Detective Jesca Ashton's questions had made him suddenly queasy. "Now, about Ms. Inglin's...*apprenticeship* here at the vineyard. At the time of her death it was ongoing?"

"Yep. She was due to start again next week."

"She'd been away?" The scribbling had stopped. Detective Jessica Ashton's hand raised, pen poised.

"To a theater camp, last two weeks of July."

"I see. You were close to her then?"

"She worked here, so I knew her schedule. Makes sense, no?" Smart-ass, one more of those and she'd likely have cuffed him.

The sound of her pen scratching across paper had been the only response. "The...*apprenticeship* program...continued...even after you were no longer affiliated with Child and Family Services?"

"Yes." Halfway through the second bottle his Riesling, right before she'd headed into the vines, he'd told her he was planning to quit. Spill your guts to a one-night-stand and then repent at leisure. "It wasn't a program—there were no state funds involved. It was something I set up on my own." A mosquito bite on his elbow had begun to itch and he'd scratched it. Shouldn't have; fidgeting would read as nervous.

"So it was a personal arrangement, between you and the girl."

She'd really been gunning for him. Did they give these people seminars in word-twisting? He was a lawyer, he knew the answer to that: of course they did. Cop 101. It was what they were paid for, he shouldn't have let it rattle him. "There were five kids who worked here. *Are* five. Or four, now." He'd uncrossed his arms, tried to relax his shoulders.

Detective Jesca Ashton had looked up then, held his eyes with hers.

"Didn't you resign your position at Child Services?"

She *knew* that. "Yes." He'd waited for her to look away first. Bad plan, letting a cop think she was getting to you.

When he'd told Basia he wanted to focus on Vestri, she'd nodded her understanding, it wasn't like they needed the money. He hadn't said more; CS case details—the raw ugliness, the triaging of misery—made his wife uncomfortable.

But Detective Jesca Ashton had listened, that night on the porch, her face thoughtful, feet propped on the porch railing, drinking and watching the night settle. Deadbeat dads, crack babies, pregnant teenagers, toddlers with dislocated shoulders and cigarette burns, taking them out of one circle of hell and sticking them into another, only slightly better. That wasn't helping them, he'd told her, and she'd agreed. Helping them was what he did when he brought them out to Vestri. She'd agreed with that, too.

That night Detective Jesca Ashton had said he shouldn't think twice.

Today she'd recognized a chink when she saw one.

At the word from Frank, the men filed back into the vines, tramping over the exact spot where he'd first been unfaithful to his wife, with a detective who now had him in her sights as a possible criminal.

After they'd finished, she'd looked out toward the lake, not at him. They probably shouldn't see one another again. Their jobs, it could get messy. He was married, she wasn't looking for a relationship.

This after he'd shown his full hand, aces and all, suggesting she drive out again the next night or the next. In the adrenaline rush of powerful, unexpected sex he'd babbled. He'd make her dinner, he'd told her, he wasn't a bad cook, and the dirty bare feet, the racer-striped panties, suggested she likely couldn't fry an egg. He'd actually said all that, so sure he'd been.

And she'd said no.

Once the Jetta's tail lights had disappeared down the driveway he'd seen how right she was, what a good thing it was she'd gone. His own sheer idiocy had left him shaking.

He'd taken a shower, driven home. Slept next to Basia.

He'd closed the chapter, buried the file, started feeling okay about himself again.

Until today.

She'd kept after him like a terrier with a rat. "So you kept Ms. Inglin in your employ after you were no longer affiliated with Child Services?"

He'd felt a hot jolt of irritation, she was playing with him. A second squad car had sped up the driveway then, saved him from a rash answer.

A heavy-set blond guy with a ruddy face, tight uniform, had lumbered over. She'd looked up at him, then back down to her scribble pad, dismissive. "What happened to you? Traffic?"

"Yeah, I..."

"Never mind, I'm finishing up."

"Did you—"

"I did. I've got this." The stocky cop had receded, balls busted. "Mr. Walsh, you were saying? The vineyard...*program*?"

"They liked it here—they *like* it. I kept them *all* on, not just the...not just Ms. Inglin. It's good for them—they work outside, have responsibility, learn marketable skills. Get paid." She *knew* that, all of it. What had she been trying to get him to say?

"When was the last time you saw Ms. Inglin?"

"End of June, not long before she left for theater camp. She helped serve cheese at a tasting." She'd worn a short skirt, bright lipstick. All the men had noticed her.

More pen scratches. "No communication with her since then?"

"No."

Detective Jesca Ashton had reached into her hip pocket, Frank's eyes following her hand. Checking her out—Frank really should develop a filter or two. "Call if you think of additional information."

Now she gave him her card.

"Thanks for your time, Mr. Walsh." She'd stepped out of the shade, lowering her sunglasses, coolly, professionally, as though they'd never set eyes on one another until today. "I have to ask you not to leave town for a while."

And the girl's face—white and startled, eyes wide open, gray and clear—had dropped into his brain.

Where it was now, where it might always stay.

Liam collected the empty coffee cups and carried the tray toward the house, his pulse heavy. The beautiful day had soured, rotted.

In the mudroom a row of boots—his own and the girl's, toes and soles covered with a light coating of mud. Above her boots, work clothes, hanging on pegs: a flannel shirt, jeans.

She'd been easy, friendly, with the pot-dealer kid, sharing jokes no one else got. Said hi to Waldo, stopped to pet the dog.

Early signs of wear and tear etched into her milky, freckled skin. A smile that knew things she shouldn't know, not at her age. Once, when he was young, he'd kissed a girl like that. Her mouth had tasted of beer and smoke. Only once; he'd been a smart kid and smart kids, even poor ones, didn't kiss girls like that.

The girl's DNA would be all over the mudroom, all over the kitchen. He could call Detective Jesca Ashton and tell her that. Be helpful. What they called 'getting out in front of it.' Which he should do. Any lawyer knew that.

But that would bring her back out here. And he'd had all he could take of Detective Jesca Ashton for one day.

He loaded the cups into the dishwasher. The girl had worked hard and never complained. She'd lifted, carried, tied, trimmed. Swept, scrubbed, poured, wiped. Not like the other two she'd brought with her the first time, twins dressed all in black. By mid-morning they'd been high, the boy snapping pictures with his camera, the girl stopping every few feet between the vines to stare at the sky. He'd had them back once more, but Frank had caught them smoking a joint in the woods when they were supposed to be applying copper spray to newly flowered vines. That night he'd discovered $200 missing from the till in the tasting room where they'd been stocking glasses.

Amber Inglin brought trouble of a different kind, making the air around her seem to hum. Making Frank stand up straight and smooth his prematurely gray ponytail. "Too young for me," he'd said, lighting a Marlboro. "Too bad. I should be more of a jerk."

The Mexicans had gotten reprimanded after one of them cornered her in the tool shed. Never clear what he'd done, exactly—the girl had just shrugged, said she could take care of herself.

Liam had told Frank to get rid of the guy. Deportation was no joke, he'd heard Frank tell the men later, which was what jail bait would get you. Then the Spanish got thick and fast and Liam had lost the thread. The man didn't come back which, Frank said, was too bad because he was a good worker. "But we don't want problems, not that kind."

After that, back in the spring, during the late frost, the girl had been here all the way through, sleeping on a cot in the kitchen (with signed permission from the foster parents, he should have told Detective Jesca

Ashton that) and rousing everyone when the alarm went off every two hours. By then he'd been taking the grand front stairs instead of the steep, narrow back ones, so as not to see her pale shoulder peeping out from the forest-green sleeping bag.

In the office Liam decided he'd make the calls later. Right now he felt scattered, off his game.

His eyes raked over the papers and invoice forms cluttered across the desk. From a silver frame his daughter smiled, proudly holding a diploma from Yale. Cassie. Dark hair, glossy to her shoulders. The straight white teeth of good nutrition and top-notch orthodontists. Young and fearless and ready to conquer the world.

Another, this time wearing the blue, black and gold regalia of Columbia Law. With shorter hair—a sophisticated cut, just grazing her jawline—and the more defined features of early adulthood, the spitting image of her mother.

But she was like him, or like he used to be. Hotshot property lawyer specializing in the complicated lease laws of lower Manhattan, she was even at his old firm. And she'd make partner, like he'd done. Until, nine years ago, he'd made a screeching U-turn, taken the job with CS, and moved his bemused but uncomplaining wife, along with his less-pleased fifteen-year-old daughter, upstate.

Cassie had been overjoyed at the acceptance to Columbia, the opportunity to live in the city again. But Cassie was sweet and down to earth, when she wasn't sharking around a courtroom in $400 pumps and a sharp-as-tacks pencil skirt. She had a shelter dog.

Next to the desk was the scarred gray filing cabinet, sole artifact of his now-defunct law career. Noisy when it opened and closed, old style— the cases on his docket.

He hadn't opened the cabinet since he'd brought it out. Didn't need to, he knew what was in there.

All too well.

The vineyard was for them, for the kids flung out of their flimsy-walled houses into the roiling system, scrambling, hanging on for dear life in better-than-nothing foster homes. He'd weeded out the ones where the girls were touched or worse, assuming they told. A lot of them didn't, but he'd learned to see it in their faces, their slouching shoulders. He'd taken the girl out of a place like that, put her in with the Wilburs. Not ideal, the guy was nuts, but probably not a toucher.

Some of them hardened up, started using what they had as leverage. Like this girl.

He could only bring so many out to Vestri, it was a small operation, but the ones he employed he helped. Of that he was certain.

He looked around the room. The place was a mess, and he didn't want to be inside anymore. He took his pruning tools from the shelf in the mudroom. He'd join the men in the field.

Waldo was standing under the tree, waiting. The faint, ripe odor of benzene he brought with him was stronger than usual, probably the heat. The dog was close at his feet, never seeming to mind the smell.

"You can come inside anytime you want."

Waldo nodded but didn't move. He was strange about doors, thresholds, didn't appear to like to cross them. He held out a feather, gray with a black tip. "From a pigeon, for your spirit."

The first feather had been red.

Waldo had been part of the same grounds crew that had given him Frank. At recess one morning in the middle of a bad case, Liam had stepped outside the courthouse, needing air. A tall man with graying hair and an angelic face had put down his pinking shears and stepped from behind a boxwood hedge to offer Liam a cardinal feather. "For sadness."

And then he'd bent again to his task, pruning a bed of impatiens gone leggy. Slow, methodical, his big hands gentle, soon leaving the pinking shears in the grass to work with his forefinger and thumb. He seemed to be murmuring to the plants. After a few minutes, Liam had realized that he felt better. Infinitessimally—what awaited him in the courtroom would curdle most people's stomachs—but better. He kept the feather.

A few weeks later, he'd seen the man tending a sick rose bush, still whispering. When it flowered once more, at the end of a hard, hot summer, Liam hadn't hesitated: he wanted that man's magic touch for his vines. His contacts in the system greased the wheels, and Waldo had joined the crew three years ago, just in time for harvest.

Waldo's hands hung at his sides, fingers opening and closing around fistfuls of air. He was never still. "Let's get to work."

Liam let Waldo lead the way into the vines. As usual, they'd be pruning partners—the Mexicans found him too strange. *Brujo*, was the word.

Connor

Cradling the camera—a Nikon D7 100, a hand-me-down from his art teacher when she bought a new one—Connor crawled on his knees and elbows, making the sun and shadows work for him until all five of the pads on the cat's paw exploded into moonscape worlds, pocked by meteor-crater pores. He pushed the hair out of his eyes and adjusted the focus. In black-and-white mode, with the ISO lowered as far as it would go, the lens magnified the claws into sickles, each pitch-black hair defined by sharp, clear edges, the tips like points of spears. The cat's tear-shaped nostrils expanded and contracted, thin slits of green pupil visible under half-closed lids.

A macro lens would come in handy, but Connor was used to making the most of the 50 mm, even if he lost some depth of field in exchange for the surreal quality he was after. He'd buy a macro when he got to L.A., when he'd made some decent cash.

He snapped ten shots, angling the camera. His teacher said he had an instinct for composition. The hundreds of images on his camera and on memory cards—of the cat, but mostly other things, more artistic shots—were supposed to be for his senior show next spring. By then he'd be gone.

In L.A., he'd be a real photographer. His sister Megan would help, somehow. He'd figure out how when they got there. Makeup, maybe. Or something.

He'd model his work on the sleek, futuristic compositions of Frank Horvat and Stephane Sednaoui. Like in his favorite shot by Sednaoui—cut from a magazine and taped to the wall above his bed—where the model wore a black dress and gestured with her hands in a mannered, angular way against a wrinkled backdrop of gray fabric that might be a sheet. You couldn't tell if she was lying down or standing up.

L.A. would be hard. He'd need to find an insider to show him the ropes. He was open to anything: film, publicity, landscape, portraits of rich people or famous people or both. If he had trouble getting gigs, he'd get a bike—steal one if he had to—and become a paparazzi.

Connor's mouth was cottony, like the morning after a rave. He looked around for his water bottle, made of recycled aluminum and stamped with "One Less Plastic Bottle." He took a drink. They had money to buy stuff now—mirror aviator-frame sunglasses, Converse high-tops and jeans.

Designer water bottles. A new phone, all the glow sticks they wanted, and still plenty left over for the California Fund.

Tom and Darla, the current foster parents, didn't seem to notice the new stuff. When he wasn't at the church, Tom was in the basement, mixing music for Sunday services, 'CWM': "Christian Worship Music." Tom sold CDs which apparently some loser people still actually bought—and MP3 downloads from the church's webpage. Synthesizers, electric piano, and Tom's breathy voice singing about reaching for Jesus's hand through the clouds. Tom said he'd gotten orders from as far away as Alaska and even one from China.

He could hear Darla in the kitchen now—pots and pans clattering, a tinny thread of Christian easy-listening spiraling out from her radio. She was making lunch.

Connor wasn't hungry.

Darla hadn't asked about Amber. It was like she hadn't even figured out Amber was gone. She was weird like that—so high on Jesus she didn't care what the foster kids did, or what happened to them.

Connor could feel his sister watching him—feigning sleep. Head dark against the peeling paint, legs stretched out along the rickety porch railing. White plastic ear-buds draped around her neck, phone in her hand. She'd painted her fingernails blue, the same color as Amber. The underside of her wrist was turned in toward her stomach, protectively. The guy at the tattoo place had said not to get sunburned, to be especially careful the first summer.

His sister and Amber had gotten matching peacock tattoos a few weeks after Christmas, two for the price of one, Amber's first purchase with the new money. Amber had wanted butterflies, but Connor had informed her that butterflies were lame.

It was when Amber first showed up that things begin to change with his sister. With the tattoos—Amber's idea, so of course Megan had wanted them too—he'd understood: Megan was closer to Amber than to him. Now there was someone else who counted in their secret world of two. Maybe more than he did.

Connor had found the peacocks. The peacocks were bad-ass, a kind they only had in Thailand, taking up a whole fold-out page of one of the the *National Geographics* stacked along the stairs down to Tom's studio. If it weren't for Darla—she made him keep his clutter confined to the basement studio, and the shed where he stored supplies for the End

Times—Tom would definitely be a hoarder, like on TV.

The afternoon they'd brought the magazine to the tattoo shop, it was already dark. There was no one but Enzo, the owner, forearms covered with coiling sea serpents and fire-breathing dragons.

Enzo had kept the magazine so he could work up the drawing. The wrist part would be especially tricky, he'd said, but Megan was whispering about something with Amber. While Enzo noted Megan's and Amber's appointments into his book, Connor had waited for Megan to say there should be three names instead of two—he and his sister did everything together—but she didn't. Only Megan and Amber would be getting tattoos.

When they'd gone back on Saturday there was a second artist there. The girls got inked at the same time. When the tip of the tattoo gun sliced through the surface of their skins to outline the peacocks, neither made a sound. For three hours while the lines were completed and the colors inked in, Connor had waited, sleeves rolled up to expose his own bare hands and forearms. Still Megan said nothing. Connor had pretended not to care.

The peacocks covered up the girls' scars: Amber's white, neat, carefully spaced, as though she'd mapped out a grid, Megan's angry pink ridges ripping across the underside of her left wrist.

Amber had come to Tom and Darla's the day she turned sixteen. That night they'd smoked some of Connor's weed. High and silly, Amber and Megan had held their wrists up to the lamp on Amber's bedside table. He'd watched in silence—already an outsider.

They'd cut in exactly the same place. Some days they'd probably even been cutting at the same time. They compared the tools they liked, and ways to sterilize them so you wouldn't get an infection. Razors were the best—it was easy to pull the blade out. Until her mother left, Amber had had all the razorblades she wanted—her mother was obsessed with shaving her legs.

Carpet staples were a decent substitute, Megan said, because no one missed them and they were easy to pull up, all you needed was a pen or a pencil.

They'd agreed bathtubs were the best place, but if you were in a house with a lot of other kids, it was hard to be alone in the bathroom for very long. You could do it outside somewhere, as long as you took rubbing alcohol and toilet paper. And a plastic bag, Megan had added, to pick up the trash. Megan was tidy.

Megan hadn't started cutting until they'd moved her to Groton, the year before Tom and Darla's, the year they'd spent apart. Megan had never told him where she'd gotten the scars. She'd told Amber the first night they met.

When the tattoos were done, waiting for the bus back to Tom and Darla's, Amber said there wouldn't be any more cutting, now that they had each other, now that they had the peacocks. He'd seen Amber smile at Megan, seen Megan's happy face lit by the streetlight. Since that afternoon Connor had never been entirely sure his sister knew he was there. A lot of the time, it felt as though he wasn't, at least as far as the two girls were concerned—they were in their own world.

The cat twitched and began to lick her paw. Megan's eyes were still closed. If she was awake, she didn't want him to know.

Looking at Megan was like staring into a mirror. Her hair was longer than his, and when she wore a dress and makeup it was easy to tell the difference between them, but Megan barely had any boobs, and her hips were as straight as his. In their black jeans and T-shirts—she was back to those today—it could be hard to guess which was which.

Except now, with the tattoo.

Megan never talked about the year she'd spent in Groton, after they'd been separated, after the night Mrs. Fitch shook them awake and dragged them into the police station because she thought they were doing stuff in Connor's bed.

The night cop at the front desk had looked startled, then embarrassed.

Even at twelve, Connor had had an idea of the sort of things Mrs. Fitch thought he'd done with Megan. Gareth at school had told him, while they smoked a cigarette he'd gotten Gareth to steal from the gym teacher's jacket, about girls with really huge tits in the magazines his dad kept underneath his workbench in the garage, girls with their legs open. Connor had seen photos like that, the pink between-place slick like your tonsils when you look down your own throat.

But he couldn't imagine being with a girl in a picture like that, or any girl. He wouldn't have minded seeing the tits if they were as big as Gareth said, but he could do without the between-the-legs part.

He could imagine kissing Gareth—and maybe more than that—but Gareth wouldn't like it, he'd been pretty sure about that.

That night they'd waited at the station for more than an hour before two detectives materialized out of the blackness beyond the door. The woman's eyes were small behind her thick-lensed glasses.

Connor had followed the muscular back of the male detective into a stale-smelling, windowless room. The man flipped a switch and fluorescent light flickered over the stained linoleum floor, illuminating a Formica table and scooped-out plastic chairs, one orange, one blue. Connor's memories of the night were like snapshots from a cheap camera.

The cop offered Connor a Coke from a vending machine in the corner. His voice sounded like he'd just woken up. His brown eyes slanted down at the corners, making him look sad and nice, younger than Connor had first thought. He acted friendly, like a soccer coach or a school counselor.

The can with the familiar red-and-white logo thudded out of the machine. Connor popped the top on his at the same time the detective did. The first fizzy mouthful was icy cold all the way down.

When Connor had drained the can he told the friendly cop how it was all a misunderstanding—he and Megan hadn't been doing anything, they were just hot. Their bedrooms were on the third floor, the attic really, and you could hardly breathe up there.

Before he'd gone to sleep he'd turned the fan on, and then Megan was next to the bed, shaking him and telling him to move over. She'd been about to cry. Megan never cried.

He'd made room for her, irritated, keeping the best pillow for himself.

Her face was sweaty and she'd swapped her pajama bottoms for cotton panties. The foster mother had taken away her fan after she'd been caught stealing a Mars bar from the 7-11. Connor had asked her to steal the candy, but for the friendly cop he'd left that part out.

The cop's phone had rung and he'd stood up from the table. He'd turned away from Connor, hunching over the phone, murmuring uh-huhs while the person at the other end talked. Finally, "Where should I bring him? Back here?"

In the waiting room neither his sister nor the lady detective with the thick glasses was anywhere to be seen. The night cop was watching a movie on his laptop. Connor had heard sirens, cars blowing up—a cop watching a cop movie.

"You can stay with me tonight and meet my dog." The detective had rested his hand on Connor's shoulder as he shepherded him through the door and across the empty parking lot toward his car, a red Toyota. Connor had been expecting a cop car. Inside, the air smelled like wet socks. "We'll go for pancakes tomorrow and then get you some clothes. Your stuff will be sent to your new placement in a couple of days."

Connor had liked the idea of a dog. Animals had been strictly forbidden at the last place. The prospect of pancakes drenched in syrup, maybe even blueberry, made his mouth water. It had been oatmeal every morning, cold and rubbery before the Fitch Bitch ever served it.

"It'll take them a few days to get a new placement for Megan."

Connor's hand had snuck toward the door handle, ready to bolt. "Megan has to come with me."

The silence had lasted forever. Connor's heart thudding, his stomach sinking toward his feet.

"I'll try." The friendly cop had ruffled Connor's hair. No one had ever done that before. It felt fake.

That night was the first one he'd ever spent without his sister. For the entire year Megan was in Groton, Connor had felt as though part of him—the best part, the smartest part—was missing. Megan understood the way things worked, and when they didn't, she fixed them. When their dad worked late at his bar or stayed out all night, when their mother left them, he'd always had Megan.

Megan got cookies or candy out of the neighbors, money out of their mother, promises out of their father. They knew he'd never keep the promises, but thinking about the guitar or the bike or the fishing trip was almost as good as having it. For days they'd spin out their fantasies, and Megan's were always better than his, as good as movies sometimes.

When Megan did his math homework for him he got A's.

And Megan told stories about California, about the wide streets lined with palm trees where everyone drove convertibles—that was the only kind of car they had in California. She talked about beaches crowded with movie stars and smelling of suntan oil like she'd already been there. In California no one had to go to school and everyone was in the movies.

Megan had started the California Fund even before they got dumped into the system. Whenever either of them earned money—for raking leaves or digging up a garden plot or washing cars—half of it went into the California Fund.

At first the fund had been mostly change, but there'd been two bills, a pair of twenties. Megan had stolen one out of the cash drawer at the bar while their parents were having a fight. The other she'd pulled out of Mr. Fitch's wallet when he was shoveling snow. Mr. Fitch deserved it, he was the worst one of all.

Megan stuffed the money into socks and hid them in her snow

boots. The socks had filled up faster since Amber came. The last time they'd counted the California Fund, there was $3,954.68. It had been close to $5,000.00· but they'd been spending a lot lately. Amber had started contributing later so she should get less, but when he reminded Megan she told him not to be a jerk.

The sticky sound of tires on hot asphalt made Connor look up from the cat shots he was reviewing. A cop car had turned onto their street. It passed all the other houses, then slowed and pulled into their driveway.

"Meg." He watched her open her eyes, not bothering to fake waking up, watched her eyes land on the squad car. The cops, he and Megan had been here before. But not like this.

Waldo

The men needed him. Working. He must hurry, not trip on roots. Newspapers crackling in his boots. Touching pine trunks—Waldo knew each one. Moss and resin on his fingertips.

The Amber girl had made him late. Stumbling on her under the tree, nearly falling on her beauty. Eye-tipped blue feathers twining her wrist, Waldo had bowed, kissed the ground—the all-knowing peacock. Friend of the angels, his mother had said, their messenger; amber was their seeing stone.

Light from the moon on her honey hair, her pearly skin. Eyes open but not looking. On her way now, changing over.

His mother had lain quiet and still like that, eyes not seeing. And then men had come, to take her away. One, in a black robe, had told him not to cry because the most important part of her was in heaven.

But she didn't stay there. Just like she'd promised.

When his mother first came back to earth she'd been a sparrow; Waldo had fed her—stale bits of scavenged cereal, through the wire and bars on his window.

Now she was an owl.

In the clearing, the sun hot was on his neck. His bones were tired, from the all-night Charity journey.

Charity journeys meant long walks. Hours and hours, miles and miles. Late at night, so the journeys would stay a secret. Do-gooding, his mother had said, was for God's eyes, not man's. When he was a child they'd gone all around the reservation, leaving loaves of bread on stoops, handmade dolls for the children. Five-dollar bills stuffed into mailboxes— his mother hadn't wanted money in the house. The lord gave you things so you could give them away.

With his mother at his side, he'd never tired. Not even his feet, in the old, worn-out moccasins she'd traded their shoes for.

But he'd been a boy then, not like now. His shoulders ached from the heavy pack, and his hands, a ring of dull fire circling each joint. Feet sore, head ringing like a bell—the scourges of old age.

His mother led him still, though in a different way. Flying ahead so he'd have to run to catch her, the pack banging against his back. Flapping up from behind, urging him on. Telling him who was in need. So many, so many, no rest for the weary. Trailer parks and motels, sad falling-down houses. Loaves of the bread he made himself, left on doorsteps. And spare sweaters—Liam gave them to him, out of kindness, why was Waldo always losing his sweater, but you only needed one.

Dollars into mailboxes—his mother didn't like it when he kept his pay.

In dirty alleys, sometimes boys and girls were sleeping, propped against dumpsters among crumpled beer cans and cigarette butts. His owl mother would swoop down and perch near the Charities, telling him, *This one.* Beside each he left a dollar. And a sandwich and a small jar of his boss's wine, for when they woke.

Beneath the head of each Charity, a feather, from the collection in his pocket. Bright color to help them heal, his mother told him which.

Waldo had given the Amber girl feathers, too; she'd threaded them with beads and wire—earrings. And the Amber girl had given him things. The dry raisins in little boxes; her trilling laugh, *I stole them, don't tell.* Raisins brought the brightest birds.

Birds were souls, his mother said. You never knew who you might be feeding.

The dog Galizur ran ahead, flashing white through the trees. His mother had found the dog, sung his name into Waldo's ear—she'd been a nuthatch then. Galizur, Hebrew for the archangel who kept the Secrets of the Lord.

Waldo too could keep secrets. Keep the voices always secret, or he'd be sent back. To them, and their pills that made the awful silence. Liam had found him there.

Liam was good. Good was green.

The Amber girl was special. He must keep her secret, hiding her beneath the bushes. Not even Liam could know. A special feather beneath her head. Another crossing it. His mother would see.

And he would see, too. Go back to her, to see the changing over. With his mother, the men hadn't let him see. This time, he'd witness the wonder.

Ahead, the vineyard house, high on a hill, winking white between the thinning trees. On the dirt road, the van. As he drew nearer, deep voices, the men; Waldo knew the set of each neck and shoulders, knew the names that matched.

Time now for working, without the Amber girl. Hidden inside the sad, a song of joy.

Waldo cradled his secret, held it next to his heart. Only the trees knew. And the bushes that hid her. Which bird would the Amber girl be?

Above his head, branches whispered, leaves shivering with delight.

II

Beatrice

The short walk home from Liam Walsh's field seemed interminable. The bright green lawns hurt Beatrice's eyes, colorful flowerbeds garish under a relentless sun.

At her front door a wrestling match with the key and the lock, teeth chattering, grateful no one could see her.

Inside a thick silence stunned her ears—if only she'd left the radio on, or remembered to wind the dining room clock. She stood immobilized at the threshold to the kitchen until she felt a sharp tug on her wrist from Geneva's leash; the dog wanted water.

Stinging tears flooded Beatrice's eyes—she could barely see to unhook the dog's leash. She felt unmoored, floating, the kitchen floor rolling beneath her feet.

She grasped the door jamb with both hands. Deep breaths: one, two. Fixate on something—a mound of tomatoes on the counter. The ones she'd missed with the sponge, a cloud of fruit flies swarming round. They'd have been sitting there since last night. Since Jes had hung up on her. And they looked...

With a shudder, Beatrice turned her back on the tomatoes and turned on the taps. Bending her head, she gulped, rinsed and spat, washing the sour taste of bile from her mouth.

The Chief of Police's questions had made her sweat. She rubbed cold water over her neck, her wrists.

That man, Jes's boss, was of mediocre intellect. He'd likely never read beyond *Great Expectations*—and that only because some teacher had forced him. How could Jes stand him?

Those questions of his.

What time had she gotten to the field?

She'd talked too fast, 7:45, maybe ten to eight, she hadn't been wearing a watch.

He'd reminded her that she'd called Jes from her cell phone—Jes had made her get the damned thing—the time would have been *indicated* on the screen. *Indicated*, what a pompous-word.

The Chief of Police made notes.

Had she said damned aloud?

Had she seen anyone else between the moment she left home and the moment she found the remains?

Remains, another television cop show word. She'd almost retched. The man on the mower…

The Chief of Police had jotted that down. Had she touched the body or moved it?

Did the curl of peach-colored hair count? No.

What had she been doing prior to setting out on her walk?

Sleeping, waking up, having coffee.

The Chief made more notes. Where had she been last night?

At home, cooking for Jes. At home, ceasing to cook for Jes. Ordering Chinese food. Eating Chinese food. Drinking wine, finishing the half bottle, "Oh, and a glass of wine," she'd told the chief.

Could her whereabouts between the hours of nine and eleven p.m. be verified?

Verify her whereabouts. Another stale phrase. No. She could have if Jes hadn't cancelled, but she'd been alone.

Then he'd handed her his card, telling her to call him if she thought of anything else. Or inform Jes—she was the P.I.

Her face must have betrayed her confusion; the chief had clarified: "Principal Investigator." At least the bald man knew enough to recognize potential where he saw it.

Beatrice looked around the kitchen, avoiding the terrible memory of the body. That belonged to her Duchess. Her breath was coming too quicky. Was she about to hyperventilate? Focus, she told herself, re-establish normalcy.

What *was* normal?

When someone—*any*one—died, the normal thing to do was to bring the family food. She would bake.

Beatrice waved the flies away from the fruit bowl, corralling her mind before it could begin to list other things that attracted flies. A seasonal tart would be tasteful but there were only two plums, their skin subtly corrugated by the beginnings of wrinkles. Lasagna was out of the question—her stomach roiled at the thought of the tomatoes.

Prunes. A plastic container of prunes, for the days she couldn't face bran flakes.

She'd bake a prune-and-rum cake, Jes's holiday favorite. And her husband's. Well, it had been.

Now she had a sense of purpose, which shoved the flies and the oozing blackberries and the tomatoes, along with other unnameables, firmly into the darkest closet her brain had to offer and slammed the door. She simply could *not*... she'd come apart at the seams. Focus. Baking. Her hand shook as she reached for her recipe box. She steadied it.

It had been years since she'd made a prune-and-rum cake. Charles was gone, Jes had lost her appetite for it. In fact, Jes seemed to have lost her appetite for the holidays altogether, or for spending them with Beatrice — surely her daughter shouldn't have had to work two Christmases in a row.

It was noon by the time the cake came out of the oven. Her stomach emitted a low, querulous rumble.

She'd not eaten breakfast. She shouldn't set off for the Wilburs on an empty stomach. Best to eat something.

A chunk of day-old baguette spread with Camembert, a prudent portion, not excessive, a *normal* amount of Camembert. Hands steady — she was regaining control, she'd managed to concentrate on the cake for the entire morning — she carried her tray into the study, the dog following the scent of cheese.

In the study, the air was stifling — she'd forgotten to close the drapes on the south window. Moving a stack of files aside, she reached for the fan. It needed to face her, while she sat on the couch to eat. She looked around for an uncluttered surface.

A stack of boxes by the window, just the right height. Beatrice hadn't moved the boxes since the day they'd arrived from Charles's lab in Thailand. She'd given herself permission to ignore them for the first year of widowhood, and then the second. On the third anniversary of her husband's death, she'd thought about asking Jes to unpack them, then decided against it — Jes had been particularly distant then. Midway through the fourth year, she'd draped the boxes in a colorful Paisley shawl and they'd become a plant stand. The ferns could live on the carpet until the heat broke.

Charles had loved that carpet, covered with his favorite of all birds, the nightingale. Nightingales eating berries, beaks open in song, or in pairs. He'd bought the carpet at an antique dealer's in London, and no matter how worn or frayed it got — and it hadn't been in mint condition to start with — he wouldn't hear of replacing it.

Nor would Jes. As soon as it was unrolled, she'd refused to take her naps anywhere else: she wanted to sleep among the birds. Later, she'd done her homework there when her father was away. Which had been often.

When Charles wasn't directing students or working until all hours at the ornithology lab, he was documenting rare and near-extinct species in the Congo or the Amazon or the wilds of deepest Tanzania.

Charles's absences had lasted for weeks, sometimes months: wide stretches of time that all but erased his flickering existence from Beatrice's consciousness. Even now, ten years after his death, Beatrice sometimes forgot and imagined him tramping through an emerald forest in khaki walking gear, not missing her. She'd never pictured him missing her. Beatrice turned on the fan and settled down to her lunch. She offered the dog a crust of bread, without cheese. Cheese was terrible for dogs.

Glancing up from the dog Beatrice's eyes fell upon the dummy. The last crust of cheesy baguette stuck in her throat—the tomato-red of the severed end of Amber Inglin's wrist seemed to peep from beneath the lace cuff of the Duchess's gown. The girl's pale throat and chest, her clavicles, appeared to surface from within the linen-covered tailor's form, making the embroidered bodice rise, as though with the intake of air. Beatrice stood hastily, the rattling tray startling Geneva. Heart thudding, she rummaged in her sewing basket until she found a piece of black satin, which she draped, shawl-like, around the dummy's truncated shoulders. She stepped back and looked, then unfolded the fabric and covered the entire torso of the dummy—only the hem of the Duchess's over-garment showed beneath the black. At the mannequin's base, on the floor, Beatrice arranged the jet-bead rosary and prayer book props, things the Duchess carried when she fled her murderous brothers under the pretext of a pilgrimage to the shrine at Loreto. She backed up a few paces to view her somber tribute, her pulse returning to normal. It was right. *She* was right to do something, to honor her Duchess.

Only two weeks remained until the first day of school, the start of rehearsals for a play that now lacked an actress in the starring role. The production must carry on, her brain announced, in Amber Inglin's honor.

Though no Duchess could ever *replace* Amber, she'd have to cast another. Focus, she told herself. She needed to make a list of the runners-up from the spring tryouts. After some minutes of digging through a mountain of manila folders, Beatrice found the ones with the fuchsia-colored post-its. She shouldn't have the files at home—removing sensitive student information from the principal's office was a violation of numerous rules and probably the law as well. But the principal's secretary, unlike Jes, appreciated Beatrice's baking at holiday time. And she, like Beatrice, considered the principal an idiot and welcomed an opportunity to flout protocol.

On her way back to the couch Beatrice's toe caught the edge of the carpet, and she staggered, the folders sliding from her arms. Heavens, she was so unsteady today!

She knelt to gather up the files. On top was Amber Inglin's. She gave a gasp. Still on her knees, hands shaking slightly, she opened the folder. She hadn't read it prior to casting because Amber Inglin had been so perfect that Beatrice hadn't wanted the slightest doubt to mar her joy in finding such a Duchess. With children in the foster system, one never knew; sometimes ignorance was indeed bliss.

Inglin, said the file, was the father's name. Doug Inglin, deceased. The mother's whereabouts were unknown.

Two foster homes before Amber's present one, unspecified problems in each.

Jes would want to know about the two previous foster homes. Beatrice returned to the couch. She'd call with the background information on the girl, and she'd ask about rescheduling their dinner, as an afterthought.

Her call was sent to voice mail, where her daughter's voice instructed her to dial 9-1-1 if there was an emergency. It was 1:30. Jes might be on lunch break. Beatrice felt a twinge of irritation. She should have left her phone on. "Honey, I've made a prune-and-rum cake for the Wilburs, but wanted to be sure you've been there before I take it. Could you call me, please? And I happen to have Amber's file at home—some information that might interest you."

She'd wait to mention the dinner plans when Jes called back.

Beatrice made notes for Jes—erratic mother, possibly alcoholic father, the names of Amber's current foster siblings, Connor and Megan Sorensen, in the classroom across the hall from Beatrice's. The boy, especially, was trouble; it was all in the file.

Beatrice put her pen down. Why did Jes avoid her? She leaned back into the pile of throw pillows. She felt drained, exhausted. She closed her eyes. Behind her lids the dead girl's face hovered by the dressmaker's dummy.

Beatrice sat up slowly. Of course. Amber Inglin should be buried in state, attired as the Duchess of Malfi. A meaningful life, everyone should see that. A meaningful, *talented* life.

She could give the dress to the foster parents when she delivered the cake. Or that would be too soon. She'd *offer* them the dress.

The dog was licking her glasses. Groggy, Beatrice sat up and removed them from her nose and Geneva's reach, wiping the lenses against her sweatpants. The clock read 5:25—how had the entire afternoon had slipped away, with the cake sitting on the counter, undelivered? Bearice rose abruptly from the couch, her head swimming dizzily for a moment, and hurried to the kitchen.

The icing had dripped a tiny bit, and Beatrice removed the excess with her finger, which she licked.

She exchanged her sweatpants for a pair of rumpled summer slacks and a teacherly eyelet blouse, and located her car keys. At the hallway mirror, the portrait of the unknown young woman looking somberly on, Beatrice secured her Thespian Society pin to her collar (passion for the theater required dedicated missionaries, even under the saddest of circumstances).

The 1993 Volvo had belonged to Charles. It lacked functioning air-conditioning, so Beatrice opened the windows, doing her best to shield the cake from dust. She'd need to drive fast to keep the icing from melting.

Stanton Road was a long road, winding past the university where the houses were brick or clapboard, surrounded by old trees, with dramatic views of the river. Further out, houses were smaller, dingier, set in ragged yards with rusting swing sets.

Tom and Darla Wilbur's house was a rundown saltbox—paint peeling, front porch sagging. Cars spilled out of the driveway and onto the street. A sign on a piece of cardboard warned, in angry all-caps, MEDIA STAY AWAY. Around it, a makeshift shrine—teddy bears, bouquets of flowers drooping in cellophane wrapping.

Beatrice parked behind a white van bearing a complicated logo—a hand issuing forth from a bank of clouds, cupping an anchor that radiated Heavenly Light. Beneath, the words "Anchor New Life Church. Tom Wilbur, Pastor." Beatrice knew the 'church,' a big metal shed behind the airport. On Sunday mornings you could hear the shouting all the way to the terminal.

Balancing the cake, Beatrice approached the shoddy house. A black-and-white cat hissed from under the steps.

The front door opened and a ponderous arm ushered Beatrice inside.

The arm belonged to an obese blond woman in magenta polyester pedal-pushers and a flowing kimono. She took the cake from Beatrice's hands and placed it on a crowded table amid a dozen or so similar offerings—lasagna, of course. Beatrice looked quickly away, fixating on a framed photograph of Amber at the center of the table, next to a bouquet of roses, red.

The obese woman was introducing herself—Deaconess Arlene Jackson. She handed Beatrice a ribbon and a safety pin. "Pink is breast cancer, so we decided to go with pale green. The promise of young life, cut tragically short." The Deaconess's own prow-like chest was already adorned with a green ribbon, pinned between a diminutive American flag and a Support Our Troops button. "We haven't given a statement yet. How did you hear?" The Deaconess raised an eyebrow, suddenly inquisitorial.

"My daughter," Beatrice explained, glad for the first time of Jes's chosen profession, "She's the lead investigator in the case. I'm Beatrice Ousterhout, Amber's English teacher. I'm directing the show she was to star in." Beatrice adjusted the pin on her collar. "It opens in November, and of course we'll be dedicating it to her." She found herself enfolded by the ponderous arms, inhaling L'Air du Temps.

"Lord bless you!" The Deaconess's voice was deep with emotion. "I don't know what we'd do without our dedicated, self-sacrificing educators! And your daughter, too, at the service of this great, God-loving land!" The Deaconess wiped tears with one hand, retaining Beatrice at her side with the other. "Tom!" The shout, from the depths of the Deaconess's lungs, startled Beatrice. "Tom! You *must* come and meet Amber's English teacher!"

A red-bearded man separated himself from a huddle of men and women balancing paper plates. He approached, hand outstretched.

"Her daughter's leading the investigation!" The Deaconess's chest heaved. "And Miss Beatrice!"—the Deaconess placed her hand over her heart, as though pledging allegiance to the flag—"*Miss Beatrice* is the director of Amber's *play*! They're going to *dedicate* the production to her! What a *lovely* way for her legacy to live on."

With a final squeeze to Beatrice's arm, the Deaconess sailed across the room, docking in front of the sofa. A woman sat slumped, face in hands, flanked by two other women, also plump and pale. One offered a can of Coke, the other rubbed the woman's hunched back. Just as Beatrice was preparing to introduce the topic of the Duchess's gown, the woman raised her face and let out a terrible wail. Beatrice's heart thrashed in her chest like a frightened rabbit.

"I need to see about my wife," Tom Wilbur was extracting a card. "But let's be in touch—maybe you'd like to be involved with the memorial service."

The visit to the Wilburs had been shorter and tardier than she'd intended, but Beatrice drove home filled with purpose. The foster mother clearly wasn't ready to discuss such things, but Tom Wilbur would likely be open to the donation of the costume. This of course raised the question of its replacement, and Beatrice was up to the task. Normalcy. Focus. Projects. The more the better.

She was three quarters of the way home before it dawned on her that she hadn't seen the twins. Maybe they'd been in another room, with friends of their own. Teenagers reacted in unpredictable ways to the death of a loved one. Beatrice remembered Jes after Charles's death, stonily silent. What her daughter was feeling was so often a puzzle. Beatrice glanced down at her silent phone.

Pulling in, she noticed that the front flowerbeds looked parched. The hydrangeas looked especially accusatory, blooms hanging limp, leaves starting to curl around the edges. She'd forgotten to water last night—the phone call with Jes had discombobulated her.

Relieved at the excuse to remain outside, Beatrice opened the front door and called for Geneva, who came bounding out. Beatrice set the garden hose nozzle to maximum strength, spraying the bushes. The hiss was soothing, and the dog ran through the drops with excited leaps. The water brought a merciful coolness, a freshening. Everything was peaceful, green. Alive.

A sharp tap on her shoulder, and Beatrice jumped.

"Mom! Are you going deaf? I asked how you're doing."

Jes was still in uniform, and her squad car was in the driveway, but Beatrice hadn't heard a thing. Police cars should make more noise.

"I'm...okay." Beatrice gave her daughter the answer she clearly wanted. "Didn't you get my message?" Her voice sounded more peevish than she'd intended. Beatrice dragged the hose toward the front flower beds.

Jes followed, performing some sort of operation on her phone. "Sorry—must've missed it."

Beatrice sprayed the flowers. "Since you're here, maybe you'd like a quick dinner?" Better this way—casual, impromptu, no need to even mention last night. "I was about to throw something together."

"I'm on my way to do some work stuff."

"Perhaps tomorrow, then." Beatrice kept her voice light. "I could make us something special."

"Maybe."

She couldn't stop herself, "If I were you, I'd take a good hard look at Liam Walsh."

"*Mom*—"

"She was found in *his* field, after all. I'm not accusing him of anything, but still. Maybe you should look into the foster father, although he doesn't seem the type…"

"This isn't some who-dun-it parlor game." The edge in Jes's voice was close to frigid.

Beatrice's throat felt tight, "You think I don't know that?"

"And what the hell are you wearing?" Jes's eyes were aimed at Beatrice's chest. The green ribbon—she'd forgotten it.

"They were handing them out at the Wilburs'."

"I can't believe you went over there."

"I took a cake. It seemed the least I could do." Her words sounded trite. "If you'd checked your messages, you could've returned my call and asked me not to go, if that was your preference."

"Like anyone could ever stop you." Her daughter was glaring at her. "Whatever, it's done now." Jes looked away. "Actually, I needed to ask you something. Do you know a guy named Edward Friis? Born here, lives down in the city. Painter. Comes back every summer with his sisters. One has a place by the lake, the other side of Walsh's field. I thought you might have taught him."

A face materialized from some long closed compartment of Beatrice's memory. Tall, thin, good bones. Handsome in a diluted sort of way.

Edward Friis. He'd played "Bosola," the malcontent, the first year of *Malfi*. Painfully shy, she'd had to urge him constantly to project. He'd reminded her vaguely of Charles. "Now that you mention him, yes, I do remember. Had a bit of an unnatural attachment to his sister, if you ask me. The younger one. Sara, I think it was. Why?"

"He drove Amber Inglin home last night from a baby-sitting gig, or he says he did."

"What? You think he could've—" She remembered Edward Friis's hands. Epecially long, with elegant fingers.

"I am looking at all the possibilities." Jes pocketed her phone. "I'd better get going."

Beatrice watched her daughter's car back out of the driveway. A breeze picked up, blowing droplets of water into her face, dampening her blouse. She turned off the spray, shivering under the sudden chill, and wound the hose into its unweildy coil. Enough gardening for the evening.

Bending down to shove the coil under a bush, Amber Inglin's white face surfaced from among the leaves. Beatrice drew a sharp breath, stumbling backward. She blinked rapidly and the hydrangea blooms swam back into focus, their soft blue deepened by the gathering dusk.

~

Edward

Cate was back too early. The kitchen got loud and disorderly: grocery bags rattling, the cappuccino machine whirring and gurgling as though it might choke. Cate debating for ten minutes—in her saccharine mommy voice—how the Perfect Offspring should spend their morning, since swimming class—he'd guessed right—had been cancelled.

The sun was too strong for their skins, they'd burn. No swimming and no dock until afternoon. They could just this once watch TV before lunch, the history channel, what did Uncle Edward think? *She had controls on the TV, and what twelve-year-old hadn't figured out a way around those? His niece and nephew were hideously indulged, but they weren't stupid.* That's what Uncle Edward thought. With difficulty he steadied the tremor in his left hand; he needed Cate today. Tonight.

The Perfect Offspring thundered up the stairs, and Edward snuck a look out the window. Another squad car now, parked behind the woman's, two cops. He couldn't see what they were doing without binoculars.

When it seemed that Cate was headed out to the deck, Edward's hand moved in the direction of the drawer handle. She stopped, though, in front of the toaster, eyes trained on the stray flecks of espresso; Edward had forgotten them. She put her mug down and scrubbed with a sponge while she talked about the art opening. Edward followed her with a paper towel, making appropriate comments and wiping where there was nothing to wipe: the-way-to-Basia-through-Cate was paved with obeisance to the muddy, infelicitous abstractions of the unfortunate body of work that Edward had privately baptized *Disasters in Beige*.

Mr. Amsterdam was showing exciting new work tonight, Cate said, his best yet. Such a shame—Cate's head shook as she attacked the countertop, the tiny flaccid pouch of skin beneath her chin wobbling with the movements of her arm—she had no wall space left.

Try the toolshed, or the attic. Edward swallowed the words, hating that he needed his sister Cate, who had never given him even a molecule of artistic credit, to get to Basia.

Finally Cate disappeared onto the deck. Edward pulled the binoculars greedily from the drawer. This must be how meth addicts felt when a fix was in sight. But almost immediately he heard the discreet swoosh of the sliding door; she'd forgotten suntan oil. He'd only had time to glimpse yellow police tape, a stocky bald guy in uniform, talking to a woman holding a dog's leash. At last Cate took her cappuccino, probably stone cold by now, out to her lounge chair. He picked up the binoculars and looked again, but the woman and the dog were gone. The squad cars had disappeared.

The Garrison girls were out on the dock, but Edward wasn't in the mood for Garrison Girls.

He sat in the sun with greased-up Cate and sleeping Sara until noon, then made sandwiches for lunch—more good will into the bank for tonight: Brie and cranberry marmelade with mesclun greens from the gourmet section at the supermarket. He took the Perfect Offsprings' plates up to the TV room—they'd found a way around the history channel to something dumb and animated—then his sisters' plates out to the deck. Sara woke with an appetite, a good sign.

From the deck he could see that the field was empty. A piece of police tape had come unmoored; it floated lazily, a kite's tail on a still day. All was quiet. He cleared the table, leaving his sisters with fresh glasses of iced tea and whatever they found to talk about. Neither had noticed the activity in the Walshes' field.

Alone in the kitchen, he tucked the binoculars against his chest and hurried back to the boathouse, back to the new girl.

He'd begin with the dark tones and leave the pale ones for when the sun shifted; the light was too harsh now, washing thick and yellow through the open window.

Computer screens were tricky—pixelation, bothersome reflections—and Sara's laptop was ancient; its humming disturbed his concentration, made him feel as though there were someone watching.

He preferred magazines: it was easy to imagine the silky paper as skin. But he'd only brought two from the city, and magazines were hard to find around here, all the adolescents must be wanking to Japanese animé. His only option was the convenience store, the same one he'd gone to with Sara as teenagers, to buy cigarettes. The same guy still behind the counter, a train wreck of his former self, but he recognized Edward.

He angled the computer away from the glare. Head, strawberry blonde, and bust—vanilla scoops of cleavage spilling over electric green bra. Shoulders rounded with a sweet layer of baby fat beneath buttery skin; lips pouting, shiny under cheap pink gloss. Flavored, no doubt, like the tubes he fingered in his dusty corner drugstore in Manhattan. Teenage-sounding colors—Bubble-Gum Pink, Raspberry Float, Cherries Jubilee.

Someone in an office was making up names that sounded just porny enough.

He'd found her on a website that made you pay (there was an ocean of filth out there for free, but the quality was often poor and pixelated, the facial features hard to see), which he could ill afford, but once his credit card had opened the gates, he'd realized he'd stumbled his way into paradise. He'd clicked quickly past the silly ones—pillow fights, homework, ice-cream cones, two friends caught in the act of whispering, the dark-haired one glancing slyly into the camera—and gotten to where he needed to be.

The girl's innocence was marred by too much eye make-up, dark and smeared beyond the contours of her lids. Slutty. Like Sara on the morning after a bad episode.

But he could clean her up.

Outline first—cheeks, brows, hollow of the neck. He flexed his hands. They felt fluid, strong. He glanced down at their pleasing proportions, clean oval nails, the skin kept smooth with Nivea cream. He moved the brush softly over the girl's lids, closed them. Better. Not perfect. Not yet.

A sharp knock on the door twanged his nerves, causing his hand to skitter across the canvas, the brush cutting a slash of muddy brown from the girl's left eye down to the corner of her mouth.

"Edward Friis?" A slight figure, still in shadow, was visible through the screen door. "Detective Jesca Ashton, Tompkins County Investigative Division. I'd like to ask you some questions." She held something up for his inspection: her badge. "May I come in?"

The detective was already opening the door. It squeaked. Edward's chest tightened. *Yes* was the only acceptable answer. "Ah…of course."

She stepped in and he recognized the police woman he'd seen through the binoculars, running toward the center of Liam Walsh's field. His palms began to sweat.

He'd have to scrub the new girl's face, because of the brown gash. Or maybe start her over—she was ruined. Not something he should be thinking about, but he felt the urgency. He must fix it quickly. Now.

But the detective was already at his side. Too late.

She was scanning Sara's worktable—the carving knives and burl on top; the piece of wood beneath, a heavy cleaver beside it. Edward quietly closed the computer.

"Your sister tells me you drove her sitter home last night, a girl named Amber Inglin?" The detective had a low voice, lower than his own.

"Yes, I did." Would the policewoman look at his canvas? Of course she would look at his canvas. She'd see the gash in the girl's face, think he'd made it on purpose. Could he clean it while he talked to her? If he crossed the room, to the rags and turpentine, he'd leave the space in front of the easel open, for her to move into. Better to stay where he was. He shifted his weight, partially blocking the detective's view.

"What time was that, would you say?"

There was scarcely room for words in his throat. "Around eight thirty. Quarter to nine maybe."

"And you left her at her residence?"

"Yes." He sounded too breathy. Inhale slowly, exhale. Steady the hand and the twitching foot.

"And what time was that?"

"Nine, couple minutes after. Why?" He wanted the 'why' back—too late, it was out. Most people would ask why, though, wouldn't they? 'Why' was a logical, legitimate question.

"She's deceased."

His foot was making the stool legs rattle. He moved it to the floor.

His perfect girl.

"I…that's…unfortunate." He swallowed. Wrong word. "Terrible. How?" No, not *how*. "I mean, where?" Wrong, but less wrong. Anyone would ask that.

"I'm afraid I can't discuss the details of the investigation."

Should he tell the detective he'd seen her in the field, with the other officers? An innocent person would say he'd seen her. "Was it in the Walshes' field? That would explain the activity I saw earlier, over there." He swallowed, but the knot remained.

The field was too far away for him to have seen *activity* without binoculars. Now the detective was looking at the binoculars; why hadn't he put them away?

Birding was big in the area, everyone knew that.

He'd been birdwatching, he'd say, and happened to see the *activity* while spotting…spotted somethings. Think of a bird name, a rare one. Think of any bird name.

Think.

He couldn't.

Edward noticed the quiet. How long had there been silence in the boathouse? Several seconds, too many. He cleared his throat—another mistake, the knot turned it into a cough. A loud cough, a nervous cough.

The detective was examining his worktable now—not touching anything, but it felt as though she were. It felt as though she were touching *everything*.

Her eyes were on the paper, with its smears of fleshtones, his palette knife laid across it. Edward leaned forward, his shoulder casting a merciful shadow across the canvas, softening the gash in the girl's cheek.

"Did anyone see Ms. Inglin leave your vehicle last night?"

The perfect girl had *tried* to talk to him, she'd *wanted* to, but he'd botched it.

What do you do?

Teach painting, at a college up the Hudson.

Cool.

His turn, it should have been simple, but he couldn't get any more words out. She'd starting rummaging in some bag she had, and texting on her phone.

He'd taken them through the slow traffic of downtown, more time with her: save this. Eyes on her phone—her grin wry; he didn't like what the grin did to her face—she hadn't noticed the detour. The outdoor cafes all full, the sunset still happening on jittery slow-mo.

Looking up, like she'd just remembered he was there, she'd pulled out a cigarette. *You don't mind, right?*

And he'd let her, of course he'd let her, even though his van would stink for days.

He'd cleared his throat. The words were there, lined up and precise and ready—*I'd really like to draw you, no, to paint you, would you sit for me?*—all he had to do was pronounce them.

He was just getting the first one out, past his very slight stutter, when she cackled, her laugh was a *cackle*, it hurt his ears. Of course it wasn't at him or what he was asking because she hadn't heard, she was laughing at something on her phone.

But it had been as though she'd laughed at him. He'd felt the heat and the shame of it and so she might as well have. Making a face, still looking at her phone, she'd pulled something else out of her bag, cellophane crackling.

Stop doing that.

It's cool, dude, it's gum—I'm done smoking, and you said it was okay.

No, I mean with your face.

The car getting darker, her eyes big and round. A loud, decisive thump, she'd startled, the doors had locked, his hand had slipped. *What the fuck—* Her mouth open, inside was masticated gum, pale pink and rubbery. The perfect girl, jerking the door handle. *Let me out. I'll take you. I said I want out. I'll take you, just stop, be quiet.* His hands micro-shaking, wrapped around the steering wheel, from where they should not come free.

I'm calling 9-1-1, you crazy psycho fuck, her hand pulling at the lock, hard.

Be assertive, say what you want for once. According to Sara, that was his biggest problem in life, he didn't ask. *I want to paint you, won't you let me paint you?* The words finally out, but by then her whole body was scrambling. *Don't you dare touch me.* Her hand, yanking, the lock popping up, not broken, and that had changed the look on her face, she could get out.

Somehow he'd gotten them out of the downtown bar area and into a tangle of vaguely ramshackle residential streets. She'd pushed the door open with her foot—flimsy pink flip flops, chipped sparkly polish on her toenails, she couldn't possibly run in those shoes, his brain had thought that—*You're a fucking freak.* His hands were shaking so hard they rattled the steering wheel in its loose screws.

Standing on the unnaturally green grass of a deserted front yard, at a safe distance from him, she'd shouldered her backpack slowly, with... *disdain.* Disdain was the word. Hurried away, talking into her cell, the phone held in her perfect hand like a beloved thing. She'd glanced once back at him, but only once. Left him to the dead street, to the evening, darkening fast as a new bruise, houses blank-eyed with the quiet despair of a Hopper painting.

"Mr. Friis, I asked whether anyone saw Ms. Inglin leave your vehicle last night. Please answer my question."

"No." He started to swallow, then stopped. He might choke on the knot.

"Where did you go after you left her?"

His heart fluttered . "The Green Frogge, out on the edge of town." Fingers into his back pocket, pulling out his wallet. All receipts were fair game for the under-employed, his accountant had said, save everything. There it was, paid with cash.

"I had two martinis." He'd considered ordering a third. Good thing he hadn't. Two was sociable, normal; three was nervous, suspect even. "I cashed out at 12:14." He thrust the neatly creased piece of paper at the detective.

"Any way to corroborate the time you arrived?" She had tiny hands, too delicate for her voice.

"I think it was around ten, quarter to. I go there a lot, the bartender knows me." Did she? He'd never talked to her, except to order his drinks. Fortyish, years poorly worn. Bleached hair, no chest to speak of, flat ass.

The detective made a note on a pad, then handed the receipt back. "Please hang on to this."

The detective's phone rang and she excused herself.

Edward listened. "Oil." the detective sounded like she was repeating what the caller had said. "Eight...inches...above the knee." She scribbled on the pad, then hung up.

The detective was staring at his palette, not the flesh tones, but the scumbled yellows at the top. Edward used them for hair.

"What's the name of this color?" She pointed at a delicate, washed-out lemon. The color of pale blond hair in full sun.

His mouth was parched. Breathe—steady, in, out. "'Icterine yellow.' Very difficult to find." The words came out raspy. He'd never used the color before this week.

The art supply store in town, sadly undersupplied, was out of every other specialized yellow; the clerk had no idea when new stock would arrive. But then Edward had found the dusty carton. Classic white tubes, each marked with a swatch of pure, shimmering blond.

Back in his van, he'd perforated the seal of one smooth tube—slowly, so he could feel it give—and breathed the faint odor of petroleum, with intimate undertones of sweat or some other secretion. The paint smelled alive.

A globule of paint had dropped onto the seat, pigment siding easily away from the oleaginous medium. He'd checked for a cloth in the glove compartment, found none, made a mental note to clean the spot with paint thinner. But he'd forgotten.

"There was a spot of oil paint on the girl's thigh." As though she'd read his mind. "Made by a small, high-end manufacturer located in Maine. Icterine yellow. Our lab guy's good." The detective's eyes met his and held them until he looked away. He dipped his brush into the glistening mud-brown mound on his mixing paper, feigning concentration—he had other, more important business to attend to. She should see that.

And she would. This woman noticed everything.

"I spilled a drop the other day in my van, just after I'd been to the paint store." Was that the right tone? "She must have sat on it."

"We'll need to examine your vehicle." The floor seemed to buckle; the stool on which he sat, to wobble. "But first I need a sample of the paint." The detective extracted a small manila envelope from a pouch attached to her belt, followed by a cotton swab sealed in plastic.

His "Of course, no trouble at all" issued from the highest, tightest register of his voice, above the knot, which now threatened to cut off his air supply. Once she had the paint would she pull another swab out of her pouch, ask to place it in his mouth? Wasn't that what happened next?

His hand shook as he smeared a bead of Icterine yellow on the swab. He babbled that the color bore the name of a rare bird, found only in Europe. It had a yellow breast. The word 'breast' sounded hideous, pornographic.

"*Hippolais icterina*," Detective Jesca Ashton sliced the Latin syllables with scientific precision as she sealed the swab inside the envelope. "It winters in Africa, so I wouldn't say its territory was limited to Europe. And that color is found only on the breasts of the very young birds."

The detective's gaze was locked on his easel. The afternoon light fell full onto the canvas, onto the girl's half-drawn face, the brutal, muddy gash beneath her eye.

Silence. The detective was the sharpest woman he'd ever met. Everything about her cut straight to the bone.

"Thank you for your time, Mr. Friis. I'll be in touch." Edward followed, managing to overtake her at the door, hold it open for her.

"You're welcome." He sounded smarmy. Fake. He sounded guilty.

Outside, in the beating sun, Cate and Sara were standing by the grill. Cate fiddled with the gas dial—uselessly; no one was grilling anything. Sara wasn't bothering to pretend. They were waiting for him.

Edward walked the detective to her car, matching his stride to hers. An innocent informant, ambling at a comfortable gait. Nothing to hide.

Detective Jesca Ashton gave him her card. "I have to ask you not to leave town for the next several days." She opened the squad car, reached into a metal box sitting on the passenger's seat. When she faced Edward again, she held a roll of yellow tape—*crime scene* tape—which she began to wrap around his van. "I'll send my colleagues to examine your vehicle."

Cate had stopped doing whatever she was doing with the dial. She leaned forward a little, listening openly. Sara's posture mimicked Cate's. As the detective backed her car down the driveway, Cate spoke. "Awful about the girl."

"Terrible." Sara shook her head.

"I'm thinking maybe you shouldn't come to the opening tonight, Edward," Cate said. "How's it going to look?"

"How's *what* going to look?" Edward met Cate's gaze and held it, always best to take the offensive where Cate was concerned. "I'm apparently a 'person of interest,' and she asked me—not *told* me, *asked* me—not to leave town, which I had no plans of doing anyway. 'Person of interest' is equivalent neither to 'suspect' nor to 'criminal'."

Cate raised a professionally-plucked eyebrow. Sara's eyebrow arced upward too, her chin lifting. A bad sign. Like a canny stray dog, Sara chose to ally with strength. She could switch sides five times over the course of a single argument between her siblings, depending on who was winning.

"It would be a bit strange if I *weren't* a 'person of interest'"—Edward heard his voice thin and high—"given that I drove her home last night." His throat constricted around the lie. He hadn't corrected Detective Jesca Ashton's assumption and specified that, at the girl's own request, he'd left her…elsewhere. On the green grass. Hurrying away from him. 'Drive her home' was a pat, cliché sort of phrase: he'd repeated it at least twice without thinking through the implications. Now he couldn't change it. That was what liars did. And criminals.

Behind his sisters, the manicured lawn stretched lazily to the water's edge, lounge chairs inviting, each with its own brightly striped umbrella. The Perfect Offspring lay on facing beach towels, heads together like an ad for local tourism. The Garrison girls were performing handstands and back-flips in the water beyond.

"No one has to know the police were here, unless you tell them." *And mar the perfection of this lovely bourgeois idyll*. The words were so acid he almost spat, if only to get the taste out of his mouth.

Cate's eyebrow was up again; she was looking at his taped-up van.

He tried for light, ironic. "Okay, the police have clearly been here. So maybe you *should* tell people, a patron with a psycopathic brother might put an edge on all that beige."

But Cate wasn't laughing (neither, therefore, was Sara). "Not funny, Edward." Cate was looking at him, too long and too hard. Not characteristic: her eyes were always flitting from children to yard to house to car—did a window need Windexing, a Perfect Offspring's hair brushing? Her gaze remained steady, traveling slowly downward from his eyes to his hands, his arms. He wished she'd stop.

And then she did, distracted. "Shit! I don't have a sitter. I can't take the kids tonight. I have to focus on Renn, make sure he meets the right people." Renn. Was that even a name? Did Mr. Amsterdam even know his sister's first name? "I'll need Sara there." Sara, who was famous even if she was a sodden drunken mess. Who was gregarious—or would be, for that crucial hour before she got obnoxious.

Cate's eyes narrowed. "Edward, maybe you..." A beat of silence, followed by a tight little shake of her head. "No." She waved a hand in the direction of the water. "Gaby!"

Back inside, Cate suggested pisco sours. Sara began chopping limes—her loyalties for the evening were clear.

The tart bite of the lime surprised Edward with its rightness, the pisco cushioning into a billowy numbness that put the detective and her yellow tape far out of his mind. Back in the boathouse he selected slides, the best of his perfect girls to show to Basia Walsh, certain to blow away anything Renn the Hack from Amsterdam had on offer. The brunette? Definitely the brunette, with the dimple in her chin. And the lifeguard, from the poster he'd taken from the munipical pool, where he swam laps. Skinny little townie. Brief memory of tight, lean body in standard-issue swimsuit, the smell of chlorine. He'd worked particularly hard to clean her up.

The slides chosen, Edward stood before the mirror in his briefs. His abdomen was taut, the musculature chiseled—150 sit-ups every morning, no transfats or processed foods. Sculpted pecs, a swimmer's shoulders; he turned, admiring the bulge of his genitals, generous even when he was soft.

Clothes. Overdressing would be presumptuous. But too casual would be unprofessional. His dress shirts were frayed at the collar. When forced to choose between clothes and paints, Edward chose paints. But Basia had money, lots of money, and he must look *successful*.

He finally settled on a black T-shirt and olive khaki shorts with a tone-y belt. His legs were tanned, glutes, quads and calves defined from his daily swim in the lake. His moccasins were scuffed, but the Burberry tag was visible on the side. Basia would know status labels.

The pisco sours had staying power—driving toward the gallery along tree-lined streets, his window open to the lingering summer twilight, Edward felt almost happy. The slides were on his lap. Not all art consisted of amorphous beige blobs, and Basia Walsh certainly knew that, even if his pretentious, provincial sister did not.

He'd tell Basia he'd shown in Manhattan, which was not a lie. True, his last real show was five years ago, all work from the pre-epiphany period, but he could skate right over that and by the time she saw his CV she'd be so taken with his perfect girls that nothing else would matter.

On the Commons, a sizeable crowd was gathering. Two men were setting up speakers. A concert of some sort, free and bad. He hoped the gallery would be quiet enough for serious conversation.

The milling people slowed Edward down. By the time he reached the gallery Cate had swept Sara over to the bar, leaving Edward to negotiate his entrance alone.

He snagged a list of Renn from Amsterdam's work from the stack beside the door and crossed the room hurriedly, placing a brotherly hand on Cate's shoulder. Act the part. Inside a gallery now, for the first time in months, he'd do anything for a show. "Good crowd, for August."

Cate turned, eyes surprised, uneasy, as though she'd forgotten his very existence, and now was sorry she'd let him come. Maybe even that he was alive. In her hands, two plastic cups of wine, red for herself and a double dose of white for Sara. She nodded stiffly, as if she'd never met him. Bearing the brimming cups, she glided into the crowd. Sara's eyes met his, briefly. "She wants me to..."—a tiny, apologetic shrug—"you know. Catch you later."

The choices—red wasn't an option in this heat—were a greenish Pinot Grigio or a French Semillon. The Semillon was bathwater. Not chilled for long enough, heightening the sour notes. But he pulled it to the back of his mouth, forced it down. He needed to get a buzz going to talk to her. To Basia.

Fifty or sixty people were clustered about the dimly-lit space. He consulted the paper. The cheapest painting was $5,000. He performed some quick calculations in his head, taking mental inventory of his studio. One show here and he could breathe easy for months.

The crowd had pooled into small groups, backs to the paintings, some fanning themselves with the pricelists. Judging from attire, locals and summer people in roughly equal parts. The country club contingent hovered near the bar, sexagenarians in plaid golf pants and flourescent Polo shirts, their wives stuffed into too-young sundresses. The vegetarian collective wore up-market jeans and gently-used T-shirts, their female consorts in loose, baggy neutrals confected of fair-trade hemp.

A pugnosed man sporting rimless spectacles and a meager brown ponytail approached Cate and Sara. He wore a white linen Sherwani paired with harem trousers and huaraches. From across the room, Edward had dismissed him as a local, yet another victim to the town's indiscriminate fascination with ethnic chic. At the man's touch on her shoulder, Cate turned, features stretched into a mawkish smile of alcohol-fueled delight. She gestured first toward the ersatz Swami, then toward Sara. Introductions. They dressed like that in Amsterdam?

Sara was still in the good place, the Zone of Magnanimity, the easy stride she hit about an hour before the crash (which would be abrupt and brutal—Cate might not be familiar with Sara's trajectory). She waved a hand toward the pale-toned canvases—were people's livingroom walls truly in need of more beige squares and circles?—saying something complimentary. The man brought his hands together as though in prayer and bowed his head. Where did he think he was? An ashram? He'd actually *believe* the minimalist bullshit about the eternal mysticism of pure geometric forms, transmitted from enlightened mind to enlightened mind down through the ages. He probably did yoga and meditated, taking bargain Euro-jet flights to retreats in SomeWhereAbad, to draw mandalas in the sand.

Renn from Amsterdam. Edward had pictured him differently, pretentious linen shirt and black jeans—more like himself.

Cate shepherded her charges toward an elegant woman holding court with regal self-assurance. Basia. Next to her was Cate's husband Bill, who shouldn't wear plaid pants, not even on the golf course. Cate leaned against him, sliding an arm around his waist. Bill's white-toothed grin didn't betray the fact that he'd rather be anywhere else that involved beer and a flat-screen TV. Next to him stood a tall, sandy-haired man who might be Basia's husband.

Edward took a hefty swallow of the bathwater Semillon. Irritation rustled through his chest. Cate could make a minimal effort to include him — she'd seen him standing in the corner, alone.

But wait. On the other side of Basia — Edward's heart plunged into his intestines — this couldn't be so, but it was — stood The Critic, come all the way from Manhattan. Twenty-five years older than when he'd glowingly reviewed Edward's first shameful forays into Photorealism. But there was no mistaking the leonine head of iron-grey hair. The wry goatee and mustache, the shiny little lenses of the round little glasses. The breezy summer suit. No ascot today, it must be too hot. Though you'd never know it from looking at the man.

The circle broadened to include Sara and Mr. Amsterdam, each of whose hands The Critic shook warmly, effusively. Edward shook his head. Was was he the only one who perceived the glaring pusilanimity of the beige squares and circles?

Perfection was plethora, Edward wanted to shout, not pared-down simplicity! Sublimity lived in flesh, not in triangles and squares, and it was fleeting, not eternal, hence its preciousness!

He thought of approaching the laughing, archly bantering group, to impart his truths, envisioning their stunned faces, mouths still open but finally silent.

But he couldn't, not now. His hands were shaking, violently.

The Critic soon took his leave — a kiss to Basia on each cheek, this was wonderful, thanks so much, oh, no trouble at all to stop by, his partner had a place on the next lake over, handing his card round the elite inner circle. His gaze slid across Edward on his way toward the door, with no sign of recognition.

Half an hour went by, and still no inviting gesture from Cate, not even an acknowledgement. Sara had abandoned Renn from Amsterdam to his prayers and latched onto one of the sexagenarians, a shock of white hair offering startling contrast to his deeply tanned — and pleased — face: Sara might be the wrong side of forty, but she was still a generation younger than him. One of the straps of Sara's green dress had slipped from her shoulder, revealing her white bra, dotted — as Edward knew — with chaste rosettes. He'd undressed his sister plenty of times, when she was too drunk to know she'd pissed herself. Or worse.

Basia Walsh approached the bar alone, waiting to refill her glass.

Now or never. Edward reached her in two long strides.

"Basia?"

She turned. The air around her was fresh and citrusy. Her face registered a pleasant interest.

"Edward Friis." He held out a hand, stiffening his elbow to control the tremor.

But her hands were full—he hadn't seen the second glass from where he'd been standing. She had to put one back down on the bar, twist awkwardly. He was standing too close. Her eyes questioned. Who was he, exactly?

"Cate's brother." Of course, Cate went by "Howell" now. The only Friis Basia would recognize would be Sara. He glanced down for an instant, at his graceful ankles sliding into the Burberry moccasins—unfortunately, the room was too crowded for Basia to appreciate them—while he made his smile into what he knew a woman like Basia would want to see. "She's told me so much about you…" True, if you counted conversations with Sara at which he'd been present too. "She's meant to introduce us for a while now…show you some of my work…" Not exactly true, but not exactly untrue either. As in, Cate had never said definitively she didn't want him approaching Basia.

He laughed—why was he laughing?—then de-escalated the laugh into a discreet cough and cleared his throat. "Great opening, by the way. Love the new work." The order was wrong, the compliments, however insincere, should have come first. Too late now.

But Basia's bright smile was encouraging. "He's just wonderful, and we're so lucky to have snagged him while he's this side of the Atlantic." She gazed around the gallery, as if bewitched. "The *profound simplicity…*" Basia Walsh definitely did yoga.

"I…ah…" Edward glanced around the gallery, nodding. "I'm more… representational… idealized, the Platonic potential of the human form…" What shit was he spouting? Get it together, or at least take a stab. "Actually, *he* reviewed me." Which sounded unhinged: Edward corrected course; he'd almost said The Critic. "Barstow, that is." Dangerously close to an outright lie; the yellowed clipping was so old its edges were beginning to crumble. And concerned with work that he himself now eschewed. Edward knew, in his heart of hearts, that The Critic would laugh outright at his perfect girls. His back teeth ground together. His facial muscles began to contract. He smiled harder and held the sleeve of slides up. In Manhattan he'd never *dream* of taking slides to another artist's opening.

Basia let out a surprised little "oh," but took the slides anyway and stepped toward the track light trained on one of Renn from Amsterdam's smaller, more intimate canvases: a sand-colored field—textured, possibly *with* sand; was there no end to the triteness?—from which the ghost of a square attempted to emerge. Take a sip of wine, appear interested in her reaction, but relaxed, confident. Maybe Basia was a trailblazer, not afraid to champion non-obvious causes. Able to spot genius. Not fearful of being first.

Basia briefly held the slides up to the light and Edward held his breath, watching her face. Slowly, what had been a pleasant, professional smile, which he'd thought was headed toward serious appraisal and then appreciation, became a puzzled frown. Which she quickly rescued and tucked back behind that smile, which he now saw was completely false.

Basia hurriedly placed the sleeve of slides on her desk. "I'll take a better look at these later. Lots of distractions around now..." She was saving his face, because he was Cate's brother. But she hadn't gotten it, she was blind to his unique achievement. The knot in Edward's throat was tight and hard. The slides would stay on her desk for a few days, maybe a week, and then likely wend their way back to him, horror of horrors, via *Cate*. Perhaps with a polite little note—thanks for the opportunity, not right for my gallery, best of luck elsewhere. Another, for his collection. "Thanks for coming. Enjoy this wonderful work!" A whiff of clean, lemony dismissal as she left.

Edward felt dark, infantile, as though his first-grade teacher hadn't properly appreciated his art project. He felt his bowels loosen. But he faced the wall nearest him, feigning interest, absorption—Basia might be watching. Perhaps she would look again, later, alone again in her gallery. Perhaps he'd see.

Beige, beige, an endless sea of hopeless, stifling beige, it threatened to plunge him into despair. Were these people *afraid* of color? But something beautiful stood in front of the painting—a shimmering flicker of loveliness, maybe even of perfection.

A girl. Dark blonde, petite hands jammed into the pockets of her jeans. A warm tremor rippled through his lower belly, close to his groin. Delicate nose, small mouth, hair falling in disorderly waves over tanned shoulders. From his height, looking down, her eyelids appeared closed, ash-blond lashes fanning out toward her cheekbones.

The girl moved away, stopping before a large canvas: gradations in beige. He thought he saw a smirk flicker across her lovely mouth: a kindred spirit?

What a profile she had. Early twenties, possibly a young twenty-five—older than the ones that usually stirred him. Small breasts discreetly outlined by a white tanktop, an elaborately fringed scarf loosely wrapped her neck. Ahh, what a neck, a sweetly curved, perfect neck.

He needed to see all of her, but first he needed a pick-up. More buzz equalled more bathwater, but he could look at the girl while he forced it down.

"Semillon, please." The bartender was a smooth-faced young man with the kind of androgynous appeal he himself had once cultivated, could still pull off a decade ago. But not now. An actor, or a musician. Maybe even a painter. Edward felt a mean pang of envy, almost hatred. The handsome young man had yet to fail. Maybe he wouldn't.

The girl stood now before a series of washed-out circles. Not beige, but pale yellow—the "new" work, perhaps? Now she was definitely smirking.

Edward imagined asking the girl if she'd like a glass of wine, fetching it for her. Smoothly handing it to her while firing off, without a single stutter, the perfect one-liner about the Emperor of Minimalism wearing not even minimal clothes.

She fanned herself absently with the program held in her left hand. A beautiful, graceful hand, a *perfect* hand. She stopped and extracted a ponytail holder from her pocket. Her gaze on the pointless field of yellow, she swept up the thick mass of her hair, raised arms framing her face.

Disappointment squelched Edward's pleasant thrum; she was at least ten years older than he'd thought, a woman, not a girl.

She turned, winding her hair into a knot, and the tepid wine in his mouth went bitter. Edward spat. Not just any woman, but Detective Jesca Ashton. Maybe Detective Ashton was staring at that particular canvas because it was *yellow*. And because *he'd* been standing near it. Detective Jesca Ashton had come to Basia's opening with the specific intention of observing *him*.

His heart slammed against his ribcage. His hands shook. If he tried to speak, his voice would shoot up into its highest register, even tremble. And what could he say? He'd already said plenty, more would just make things worse.

Instead, he carefully placed his glass on a tray and walked—slowly, casual was the look he wanted—toward the group clustered around Sara. She was telling an anecdote, swaying a little on her feet. The tanned sexagenarian still hovered, hand near her elbow. Sara's laughter was shrill, careening dangerously toward the bad place.

Suddenly Cate was gripping his upper arm, nails cutting into the flesh. "You were *supposed* to keep her under control." Mossy fuzz of too-warm red on her breath. "You need to get her home. *Now*." Cate shoved car keys into his hand. "Do *not* take her into the house—the kids don't need to see her like that."

"Got it." Edward edged his way into the group surrounding Sara. "Come on, we need to get you out of here." She ignored him. He gripped her wrist and pulled. Still she prattled on, as though he weren't there. He pulled again, harder than he'd intended. Sara stumbled. Her weight threw him off balance; through the soft sole of his Burberry moccasin, he felt his heel grind someone else's foot against the floor.

He turned to apologize. To Detective Jesca Ashton. The woman was tailing him. His larynx swelled. He managed a croaky, "Sorry."

"No problem." She took a cool step back.

Sara was trying to pull free from his grasp. "*Edward*, I am having *fun*." She was in the petulant phase. Not ready to detonate, but it wouldn't be long. Edward wrapped his arm around Sara's shoulders, a concerned, brotherly hug—the detective was watching—and propelled her, stumbling, through the door.

Outside the number of people milling around the Commons had doubled, maybe tripled. A police barricade had been set up at one end. He'd been expecting loud, bad music but there was none. There were pale green ribbons everywhere, tied around columns, festooning the stage, pinned to chests. Lit candles were passing from hand to hand near them. The whole Commons shimmered and wavered, liquified by the hundreds of tiny flames, pointillist light spilling into the street and down the sidewalk in both directions.

What was going on? Edward took anxious shallow breaths of humid air, keeping Sara close in case she tried to duck him again. He probably hadn't filled his lungs fully for the past hour, no wonder he felt light-headed. A shrill electronic squeal cut through the soupy air. Onstage a woman in a loose smock and bright pink pedal pushers was tapping her nail on a microphone, making amplified electronic pops that hurt Edward's ears.

She grasped the microphone with her hand and began to speak. "My fellow Ithacans, we are gathered here on this sad night because of *evil*." She droned on, sing-song, hitting the word 'evil' again, several times, hard.

And then he saw the images of her face, Amber's. She was everywhere, she'd surrounded him.

Sara tight against his side, they were hemmed in by waving placards, held by people in shorts and boxy T-shirts, *Justice for Amber. Death Penalty For Pedophiles. Fry the Bastard*. On each placard was the face of his perfect girl, fifty times, a hundred times, more.

And then his sister was weeping loudly, lurching into someone's arms. Halo of frizzed hair around a big head, glasses. Lumpy hips in badly cut trousers. "Mrs. O.!" Sara wailed. "Oh, Mrs. O.! This is so terrible! That poor girl!" His head ached. How had Beatrice Ousterhout snuck into his nightmare?

"Sara, talented Sara! My favorite scene painter! How wonderful to see you, even under these sad circumstances. You would have adored her—she was a wonderful Duchess." Beatrice Ousterhout was rocking his sister in her arms, the flame on her candle too close to the green sundress. Edward bent forward and blew it out. Beatrice Ousterhout's eyes pulled to the sudden spot of darkness, landed on his face. The eyes widened, her mouth opening as though to speak.

She was pre-empted by another deafening squeal from the sound system. Two uniformed police officers stood at the foot of the stage, eyes scanning the crowd. Not far away stood Detective Jesca Ashton, from this distance a girl again, features delicate above the brilliant purple scarf.

Beatrice Ousterhout's flabby arm wrapped around Sara's shoulders, "That's my *daughter*! She's the P.I.!"

Edward found that hard to believe, the lovely young woman and the frowsy Mrs. O. "Excuse me, Mrs. Ousterhout. I need to get my sister home—she's not well." Understatement of the century.

He pushed Sara onto the sidewalk and across the blockaded street, but she stumbled at the edge of the parking lot, grazing her knee on the curb. "God *damn* it, Edward, let me *go*!" From the back of the crowd, a large man, bearing Amber Inglin's face on his menacing placard—*Bring Back the Chair!*—turned and looked accusingly at Edward.

Sara tried to pull away while he struggled with the car door— Cate's goddamned Volvo, the lock always stuck. His own van was still trussed in yellow tape. His grip tightened around Sara's arm, too tight; he'd likely bruised her. But she wouldn't bend down, wouldn't go inside. Instead, she landed a sharp kick on his shin. Sucking in his breath at the vicious slash of pain, Edward shoved her into the front seat. He heard a crack—she must have hit her head on the dashboard—and a squeal. Sara made things far worse than they needed to be, her specialty.

"You're a fucking asshole, Edward." Sara slumped against the door, arm resting across her lap at an odd angle. "This is abuse. I'm calling the police."

Praying Sara would pass out—she had to be close—he ignored her, manoeuvering Cate's car between the illegally parked vehicles crowding the lot.

Detective Jesca Ashton's voice echoed in his head, her questions from this afternoon, accusing him. And the fat woman's croon, bouncing and sputtering through the lousy mic, he'd not caught her words. He'd been busy getting Sara away, but even without the words, the voices condemned him. *He hadn't done anything.*

Edward's nerves crackled. He gripped the steering wheel tightly, trying to quiet the feeling that everything was trembling, shaking, coming apart.

~

Jes

Jes didn't get the beige-on-beige thing. To her, the smudgy outline of a circle at the center of a square exactly resembled a calcified condom in its fraying wrapper, excavated from some sad guy's wallet.

Which was, without a doubt, not what the artist had intended. Maybe she should have taken an Art History course in college.

Her back to the artlovers, Jes felt her senses in overdrive. She overheard snatches of three conversations at once, knowing instantly the voice and face match; from among a cacophony of smells, she distinguished individual notes of perfume, aftershave, sweat.

On her left a man was standing too close, she could feel him watching her, creep. She moved away, down the row of paintings. Glancing back she recognized Edward Friis. Strange, lonely-looking, he seemed ill at ease. His alibi, like Liam Walsh's, was partially credible, with a few significant holes. But he was so nervous and jittery, the image of him coldly severing the girl's hand with...something crazy sharp; she still had to figure out what...was bizarre, implausible.

But Walsh. She stole a look at him across the gallery. She could see him going for the girl, could see things spiraling out of control—teenagers were hormonal scatter bombs, their brains not fully formed yet. Walsh would be really fucking smart about cleaning up after himself.

Pretending to study the beige squares and circles, Jes tracked the two men's movements around the gallery, and the wife's too. Basia Walsh was in high heels—even killer legs couldn't keep a husband on his leash—and an expensive-looking dress accented with chunky jewelry, each piece had probably cost as much as her car. Walsh checked in every tèn minutes or so, his hand briefly encircling his wife's waist. What a good boy. He moved from group to group, chatting and smiling his lawyer smile.

And wearing his lawyer pants—what was it with these people and beige? Maybe even the ones with the zipper Jes had broken when she'd yanked it down too hard. Basia must have dropped them off at the drycleaner's for him—that's what wives did. Or maybe he had a dozen identical pairs of khakis. Who knew, and who cared?

When she'd arrived, Basia was still greeting guests at the door. She'd offered a price list to Jes with a look of puzzled almost-recognition. "Detective Jesca Ashton, we met this morning. No one recognizes me out of uniform."

"Ah, yes." Despite the professional smile of welcome, Basia Walsh's eyes were wary, lingering for a fraction of a second too long on Jes's tank top, the bright silk scarf, the tight, faded jeans. "Enjoy the opening."

It was hot, she put her hair up. Edward Friis had moved to the bar. He was looking in her direction again. More like staring, mouth half-open. Freak, and not a criminal type, he'd botch shoplifting gum from Walmart. Walsh, however, gave every sign of being unconcerned by her presence. Lawyers were expert dissimulators, went with the careful cultivation of courtroom personality. Her phone vibrated, diverting her eyes from Liam Walsh's relaxed—*too* relaxed?—shoulders. "WHERE R U? VIGIL, COMMONS, 8 PM. PREP STATEMENT." Werner always typed in all-caps.

Jes glanced out the window. The Commons was teeming with bodies, all ages and sizes and all, without a doubt, sweaty—instead of relaxing its grip, the humidity had thickened like a slow-simmering soup as the afternoon slid into evening. People spilled from the square into the street and down the sidewalk in both directions. Where had they all come from?

She typed a few words on her phone. Of course. A webpage, with Amber Inglin's picture front and center, brimming over with indignant commentary in all-caps about police ineptness not even twelve hours into the investigation. The case had officially gone viral. Werner wouldn't be pleased. She texted back to her boss: "@B. Walsh's gallery, observing p-o-is. Should obsv vigil but 2 early 4 statement—bad idea."

Beyond the window, placards were passing from hand to hand. People pinned green ribbons to T-shirts and tube tops. Well-organized event, and fast—journalists hadn't started pestering her until early afternoon. Someone close to the foster family, most likely. Another vibration. Werner again. "U HAVE TO GIVE THEM STHING OR PRESS WILL START SPECULATING." The public clearly already had.

What to say? "The most viable suspect at present is the married man I fucked two months ago?" Jes shot another glance at Liam Walsh. She could compartmentalize as well as any wayward husband.

"u made me p.i. & p.i. sez no statemt. 2 soon."

A bright, sharp pain in her foot made her look up from her phone. She'd just been stepped on by a wild-eyed Edward Friis. He apologized over his shoulder. Did he not recognize her?

Maybe not; he had his hands full—his sister was acting up. Not the tightly-wound one who'd answered all her questions. The other, the flighty one was soused. They made an odd pair, poster children for co-dependency issues. Perfect subjects for therapy. If therapy worked, which she doubted.

Outside, Jes sidled her way to the front of the crowd while the foster father, Tom Wilbur, made his statement from the stage. The wife stood hunched, hands hanging by her sides, her face blank in a classic mask of shock. They wore matching oversized T-shirts, neon green with black letters outlined in scarlet. "JusticeForAmber.com, #FundTheFight." Beneath, in smaller but still-legible cursive, "Anchor New Life Church, Tom Wilbur, Pastor." Jes glanced back at the website, at the wierdly glowing anchor logo in the top right-hand corner. The fundies definitely knew how to jump onto a rolling bandwagon.

Tom Wilbur's voice gathered strength as he spoke, preacher style. They wanted the animal caught and caged, trusted the law to bring down the hammer of justice. Everything about him was big, ham-hock arms, close-set eyes that darted around the crowd.

Fundamentalists were like pressure cookers, Jes reflected, you had to keep the valve on the right setting, let the steam out. Which a lot of them didn't know how to do, as a couple of minutes watching the latest megachurch sex scandal explode all over cable news could tell you. But Tom Wilbur had an alibi. He'd been returning from a church retreat, his wife and another couple with him in the car. There were truck stop receipts: half a tank of gas, 10:03. Too bad. She could picture Tom Wilbur doing it. She made a mental note to get hold of the church's membership rolls. Maybe someone else had skipped the retreat.

A woman in Pepto-Bismol pink pedal pushers, breasts torpedoing before her in what had to be one heavy-duty brassiere, took the microphone and in almost a croon, picked up where Pastor Tom had left off, whipping the crowd into an angry froth. Her lipstick exactly matched the pants. You had to admire the attention to detail.

D.W. and Werner surfaced suddenly out of the crowd, bulky and obtrusive in their uniforms. Werner spotted her and they advanced—so much for discreet observation—parting the sea of placards. The girl, in the grainy, happy looking yearbook picture they'd used for the posters. Smiling photographs of murder victims were so much worse.

The woman on the stage saw them coming too, and asked the crowd for prayers for the brave officers of the law. D.W. gave a nod in response which, if intended to appear self-effacing, missed the mark wildly.

When a reporter stepped forward and snagged Werner, Jes ducked into the sea of hot, sweaty bodies before anyone had the chance to make *her* as a cop. When she looked back, Werner was speaking into a microphone bearing the logo of a local television station. Jes could tell from his serious frown that he was giving his "let's not get carried away" spiel, doubtless in answer to the "do-we-have-a-serial-killer" question. An exercise in futility, the horse was well out of the barn—at least four television crews had carved circles of bare pavement out of the crowd, lending added gravity to their serious-faced anchor-persons, sweating beneath focus lights.

D.W. stood a few feet from Werner, aping his uncle's authoritative posture, leaning too close to a blonde girl in denim miniskirt and pink halter top. Same age as Amber Inglin, same physical type. Jes ducked between two men holding placards, aimed her phone and snapped—you never knew.

As she pushed her way to the edge of the crowd, she studied the shot. D.W.'s hands resting on his hips, just above his holster. The blonde was a little blurry but obviously way too young to be on the receiving end of that leering smile.

Would he...? No, not likely—Drew was an oaf and a sleaze, but he'd barely been able to look at the body in Walsh's field this morning. She'd ask him for an alibi anyway. That would piss him off.

She needed someplace to think. A bar would be good, maybe the one where Edward Friis had drunk his martinis. She'd check out his alibi, though the time-stamp on the receipt looked real. As did his nervous condition—his hands had been shaking when he'd accepted his refill from the bartender. She could see him wanting the girl, bad. Maybe even wanting to do whatever had been done to her before she died—she didn't let herself dwell on that—but not having the stomach to carry it out.

She didn't want to think about Liam Walsh, what he might or might not have done. But she had to.

Jes cursed. Her Jetta was boxed into the far corner of the overflowing parking lot. Forget the car. She'd patronize a local bar and then walk the two miles home. Edward Friis's alibi could wait.

A flickering streetlight buzzed and sputtered. The sound system at the vigil was overloading the circuits. "Need a ride?" In his hybrid, Liam Walsh's profile stood out clearly against the fitful bluish glow: sloping nose; curious combination of soft mouth and jutting chin. He looked so... *nice*. Which of course meant nothing. "That mess in the parking lot won't unsnarl for hours." She shouldn't, she knew she shouldn't. Getting in the car with a suspect was a bad idea, for all sorts of reasons. Not to mention a violation of protocol. But as of right now Liam Walsh was her best bet for a serious suspect and she needed to get a better handle on him. Screw protocol. If cracking the case meant bending the rules, fine by her. The street was empty, no evening walkers, not even a bicycle. Who would see her?

"Sure, thanks." Sliding into the passenger seat, the sensory alertness she'd felt in the gallery was back, tingling in her nose, pulsing through her arms to the tips of her fingers. Dust on the upholstery, dried mud maybe— messy for a lawyer, probably not so much for a vintner. Still, it was *dirt*. The girl had had dirt under the fingernails of her intact right hand. The tingling sharpened, intensified. "Did you go out to the vigil?"

Walsh shook his big head, maybe a little too hard. "I hate those things. Bunch of people looking for a reason to get angry. The media gets hold of it and fans the flames. Whoever killed her is probably loving it."

The tingling rollercoastered now, down into her lower belly. "Why?"

"These people want notoricty."

Her libido began to purr. Fuck, she was kinky. Deeply fucking kinky. "Is that why you left the gallery through the back door, to avoid notoriety?"

Liam Walsh slammed his foot on the brake. "You think I had something to do with this?"

The incredulity was either genuine or a consummate lawyerly counterfeit. "You can't account for your whereabouts between ten and twelve last night."

"I told you, I was at home, working. My wife must have corroborated that."

"The chronology has holes big enough to drive a truck through." Which, as a lawyer, he must surely know. Ergo, he didn't have anything better. Jes pushed him. "You knew this girl well, and she was found in your field. That makes you a person of interest. Maybe a suspect."

The raised eyebrows of indignation—possibly manufactured, possibly not. "I wouldn't hurt... *anyone*, let alone a girl... a girl I went to a lot of trouble to *help*."

"She was beautiful and she was young." Jes locked eyes with Walsh. "You had access." He looked away. "She had your number in her phone." A vibration against Jes's hip, D.W. texting. What the hell did *he* want?

"I was her Child Services lawyer," Liam Walsh's lawyer voice sounded tense. "Later, she worked for me. Like I told you." And distinctly defensive.

She looked at her phone. "*New York State Police Code, Section 4.29. Improper fraternization with suspects and informants will result in termination.*' *C U Monday, College.*"

A photo: her opening Liam Walsh's car door. Blurry, pixelated, but identifiable.

Bastard would rat her out—probably already had. But to fire her there'd have to be an inquiry. In the meantime, the most Werner could do was suspend her, and he wouldn't do that if she was making headway on the case.

D.W. was treating this like some kind of game, and he was playing out of his league. Jes opened the pic of Drew leering at the pretty blonde teen. Send? Along with a smart-ass question about his whereabouts last night between 9 and midnight?

Nope, keep it for a rainy day (you never knew) and don't sink to his level.

Jes typed rapidly—*I'm fact-finding*. If they fired her, then so be it, but she'd nail this case first.

A rocking jolt as they crossed the railroad tracks. They passed a McDonald's, a strip-mall, a tire-repair shop, suburban clutter unrolling along the secondary road that led out of town. And toward Vestri. "What the fuck are you doing?"

The car picked up speed, merging with Route 93. "I want to finish our conversation."

"So you're kidnapping me?"

"You never told me where to turn."

Jes's nerve-endings crackled and she opened her window to the warm, humid air. The risk sensors in her brain vibrated. She should insist on being driven home. Or just get out of the car and run. But she didn't feel scared exactly. What she felt was turned on. Something in her had *let* him drive right past her street. She'd seen the stop sign out of the corner of her eye, the pale pink house on the corner, Victorian lattice-work painted purple (there was truly no accounting for taste). And she hadn't said a word.

Low hills rolled past, dotted with stands of trees. Barns, a silo, thick woods in the distance edging the darkening sky. Remote. Her phone had only two bars of reception. And who would she call? The tuning fork in her gut hummed. "Alright. Why don't you tell me about Amber Inglin's...

job at your vineyard."

"Be glad to." Walsh's eyes were fixed on the road. His skin looked freshly shaved—must've cleaned himself up for his wife's opening. She remembered reddish stubble, going grey. Rashy splotches of beard burn on the insides of her thighs. "It's hard work. Everything from pruning and tying up plants to keeping the books. She was great, she could do all of it."

"Lots of opportunity to be alone with her?"

"I *cared* about her. Why in hell would I *kill* her?"

"Things can spin out of control. Especially when there's sex involved." He knew this firsthand. From her.

"I never *touched* her, okay? *Never*." Walsh pounded his palm against the steering wheel. Some innocent people got angry when you pushed them past whatever point they considered reasonable (a relative and highly individualized concept). And some guilty people feigned anger. Really well. "I was looking *out* for her, okay!? I *wanted* to get her *out* of the Wilburs'." He stopped, was silent for a second or two. Sighed in a controlled sort of way, seemed to take himself in hand. "The twins are pretty wild, especially the boy... I was considering asking your mother if she'd take her in."

Jes snorted in disbelief.

"I didn't know she was your mother then. I thought it might work— it was only for a year."

"My mother can't keep up with her own *dog*."

"She does good work with those kids."

"Whatever. Her house is a disaster. She lets her milk go bad."

His eyes still on the road, she studied him. Maybe he was okay—not a creep. Not a perv. Throw him a bone. "Is there anyone besides your wife who can corroborate that you went straight home after the country club shin-dig? Or that you stayed there until she got home? A neighbor, maybe, who saw you get out of your car and walk up the driveway? And not come back out?"

Walsh sighed again. "No."

They were starting the ascent up the long, winding drive toward Vestri. The air was cooler than in town—higher elevation. And lighter, not as humid. The smell of the vines rolled in, tangy, a hint of spice. She'd recognize the scent anywhere.

Gravel crackled as Walsh pulled the car to a stop. "Okay, for the sake of argument"—he spoke slowly—"let's assume I'm a psycho." The pitch on the tuning fork went higher. This was so wrong, so *bent*. "I raped her—I'm assuming she was raped?"

"Can't talk about it."

"Default assumption when girls are found in fields. What a sick world. So I raped her, and then I killed her. You can't believe I'd be stupid enough to dump her *in my own field*. I'm a *lawyer*, remember?" The edge was back.

"I remember."

A night-bird called, from the edge of the woods. It sounded like a nightingale, but nightingales weren't found in the U.S. Probably a Northern Mockingbird, *mimus polyglottos*. Avian shape-shifters, they could impersonate anything.

Liam Walsh pushed open the door on the driver's side. She got out and faced him over the hood of the car. "Ingenious way to throw us off?" He was easily a foot taller than she was. His hands were twice the size of hers.

"I know you want to collar someone for this. But I'm not your guy. I needed her help around here—running a vineyard is insane. And *I* was helping *her*. From a purely logical point of view it makes no sense." His eyes found hers this time, his gaze steady. "Are we good now?"

His arguments were logical, and five seconds was a record for a stare-down—the guilty ones rarely made it past the count of two. And if he was innocent... Jes pushed away the tingling—cardinal drive-by rule, no repeats—and took a new tack. You never knew, especially with the smart ones. "Your wife could be covering for you."

"*What?*"

"Spouses are legally protected from incriminating one another. You're a lawyer, you know that."

"I didn't do it." The words dropped one at a time.

"So you said."

"What do you want, a DNA sample?" Walsh slammed the door. The car rocked. He was *pissed*. Just follow it, she told herself, see where this goes. "We can settle this right now. All we need is a Q-Tip. Let's go." Either he was innocent—the tuning fork hummed—or he wanted to get her inside, where she'd be easier to corner and control. He must have seen she wasn't packing, he'd know where to look for telltale bulges. Jes squared her shoulders. Risk was part of the gig. The tuning fork hummed louder.

Walsh headed for the converted farmhouse, steps crunching hard into the gravel. Jes walked behind, measuring his shoulders with her eyes. She'd stay out of his reach, and she knew some moves she was pretty sure he wouldn't be expecting.

The screen door whined open, slapped shut behind them. They crossed a big dark kitchen. Walsh left the lights off and started up the stairs, angry footsteps loud in the old house. Jes followed. He stopped at the door to a bathroom and slammed on the light. He jerked open a medicine cabinet. "Inside of the cheek, right?"

The bathroom was a mess. Towels on the floor, or thrown haphazardly over the shower rod. On the vanity, a tube of toothpaste missing its cap, a soap-caked shaving stand. And soap, no dish. A man bathroom.

In the corner, atop a pile of socks and briefs that hadn't made it into the overflowing hamper, a baby-blue thong. "Whose is *that*?" Jes pointed.

Liam Walsh paused, Q-Tip in hand. "How the hell do I know? Frank brings girls out here all the time. It's not Amber Inglin's, I can tell you that. But you won't believe *me*, so why don't you find out for yourself?" He reached down with his free hand and thrust the panties at Jes. "Take 'em to the lab and knock yourself out." Jes took a step backward.

"Now you're afraid of me? Should've thought of that before you got in the car." He swabbed furiously with the Q-Tip, talking around it. In the harsh light she saw the tiny space between his two front teeth. Her tongue remembered licking over it.

"Not afraid." Jes ignored the underwear. "Just prudent." Only she wasn't. And they both knew it.

Two angry steps and they were back on the landing. Liam Walsh stomped down the stairs, letting her follow, back to where she'd have several get-away options. He wasn't planning to deck her. Or chloroform her. Or kill her.

In the tasting room he rifled through a stack of mail on the bar. "I know you people prefer manila, but this will have to do." With sharp, precise motions he opened an envelope, threw the sheet of paper it contained to the floor, and dropped the cotton swab inside. He held it out to her. "Have at it."

If they actually gave up their DNA, they stood a 99.32384% chance of being innocent—she had a ridiculous capacity for the retention of statistics.

"Okay. I will." The sensory vibrations roller-coastered through her belly and then down. Her problem with rules was that she bent them all, even the ones she made herself. Maybe especially those. Jes leaned forward and covered Liam Walsh's mouth with her own.

He jerked away, breathing hard. "What are you, crazy?"

Jes rubbed her lips together. "Yeah, maybe."

Walsh studied her, hands on his hips, his expression unreadable. "You got anything to drink around here?"

"It's a *vineyard*."

"And I'm *thirsty*."

He gave his head a shake. "What the hell." He bent down, pulled a bottle from under the bar. It looked like whiskey. "I'm way past wine. Let's go outside, I need some air."

It was cool on the porch. The moon was high, close to full. Across the road, at the bottom of the hill, the lake shone silver.

"She had some problems, but she was a great kid." He hadn't brought glasses so he took a long pull, then handed her the bottle. "She deserved to live long enough to see her life get better. I really hope you catch the piece of shit."

Jes took a swig and handed it back. "I will."

She ran a finger down his arm. He didn't pull away. Instead he stood and pulled her toward the vines. The sex was rough. She made sure of that.

Upstairs, the second time was slow and sweet and gentle. She hadn't been expecting that.

When they'd finished, he rolled into the hollow in the middle of the fold-out sofa, his arms around her like a nest, pulling her to him. Soon she felt breath along her neck, shallow and even, and soon after that, she felt drowsy. She closed her eyes, just for a minute.

She felt a warm arm, wrapped around her waist. The gentle pressure against her back: a body spooned perfectly around hers. She nestled against it. The bedroom—not hers; whose was it?—was cool, a window must be open. Country air, good for sleeping. If she matched her breathing to that of the body behind her, she'd float like a feather, back down into unconsciousness.

Which she absolutely should *not* do. She jerked herself awake. Shit. She'd fallen asleep with a drive-by. And worse, she'd liked it.

A thin stripe of light shone between ill-fitting curtains, sewn for another window. Clothes draped over chairs, his arms around her in the bed. Everything was domestic. The drive-by rules had been shot to hell.

All but one. She didn't have to spend the night. She didn't have her car but she'd seen where he'd left his keys.

Jes sat up, gingerly disentangling her limbs from Liam Walsh's. He stirred, following her movements even as he slept.

She dressed in a hurry, making sure the envelope with the Q-Tip was still in her back pocket. She'd told D.W. she was fact-finding, and she'd have some facts to show. Fuck his stupid picture. Which he had, by now, without question, sent to his uncle. In a desk drawer she found more envelopes, then into the bathroom to retrieve the thong, she'd run it too. Everything would come up negative but it all represented due diligence.

A glimmer at the bottom of the trash can, white and pearly. The used condom, full of DNA, expertly tied off. And unadulterated (the Q-Tip, in its unsterilized environment, was likely corrupted eighteen ways to Sunday).

No evidence bags, her spare uniform pants were in her car. She folded the condom in a tissue and pocketed it. Just in case—the guilty 0.67616% had to come from somewhere. And unless they soaked the body in bleach, which you could smell from a mile off, the creeps always left something behind.

Jes descended the curving staircase at a quiet half-run. She'd leave Walsh's car in the convenience store parking lot across from the station, next door to a yuppy restaurant that had sprung up. Walsh's kind of place, he could have a locally-sourced spinach frittata and a hair of the dog. He wouldn't be needing his wheels for a while, he had a lot of whiskey to sleep off. That sleaze Frank could drive him in tomorrow.

He'd be pissed, but he'd get over it.

In the mudroom she grabbed tools, gloves. She'd run them at the lab—more due diligence, more insurance against D.W.'s stupid photo. Or, worst-case scenario, if she was wrong about Walsh there could still be something on them.

The sharp, pungent smell of the vine leaves was stronger now. Probably the dew.

At the foot of the drive, she looked back toward the house and frowned. If it wasn't Walsh, then who was it? *Think*. What did she have? Frank the sleaze? Her gut said no. Statutory rape, sure, but not against the girl's will, he'd want her to like it.

123

One of the vineyard guys, the Mexicans? Not likely, they'd need access to a vehicle, and more detailed knowledge of the area than papersless migrant laborers were likely to possess.

The fundie church was a possibility. Okay, she had a thing against bible beaters, but still; she'd make sure her prejudices stayed on the sidelines. She'd pay the Wilburs another visit first thing tomorrow. And press the twins for more info—they'd said there were no boyfriends in the picture, but another try at them was in order.

As was another look at Edward Friis.

Shit. Tomorrow was Sunday. Werner and D.W. would take their boat out fishing and stay all day.

Never mind them, she could get the under-utilized Terence to help her: Jes knew smart when she saw it. By Monday morning, before Werner even opened his mouth about the pic, he'd have to be thinking about writing up her commendation. She'd make sure Terence got one too.

Jes opened the armrest console and rummaged through Walsh's CDs. Led Zeppelin. She got Kashmir pumping out of the speakers. One thing you could say for over-forties, they had great music.

And the car had a nice pick-up. Hybrids, who knew?

She gunned the gas. The faster she got home—she needed at least *some* sleep—the faster she could make it happen. The poor kid deserved justice.

Jes could give her that at least.

Liam

Half-asleep, he tilted down the stairs to tell her they had to drive back to town. His shoulder was sore—a new bruise, courtesy of the China-doll teeth. Head full of cottony fog, eyes dry and scratchy. Tongue stuck to the roof of his mouth, an ugly hangover brewing.

His foot missed a step and he stumbled onto the landing, grabbing at the handrail. Righting himself, he smelled her on his clothes, remembered the sweet, electric surprise of unfamiliar mouth, hair, skin. The wave receded, left him feeling sick.

He'd done it again.

It wasn't just a one-off anymore, an aberration. Something he didn't do, not him. Now it was something he did do, had done. Twice.

He took a tentative step, running his fingers along the wall—where was the light switch? His hand lurched into empty darkness. He stood still for a moment, breathing. Get a grip.

But he didn't trust his feet to creep down a flight of stairs he'd taken two at a time without looking for three years. Didn't trust his hands— one still clenched around the handrail—to do what his brain told them to.

He no longer trusted *himself.*

In the kitchen he flicked the lights on, the sudden brightness hurting his eyes. No Detective Jesca Ashton in the kitchen.

Basia loved him, she said, because he was dependable. Solid.

Right now he felt anything but solid.

The tasting room was empty, made strange by shadows. His footfalls echoed.`

Sometimes, when she'd finished her work for the day, the girl had studied in the tasting room, saying it was quiet, she liked to be there. He'd stocked glasses, cleaned, inventoried, with her at one of the tables. She'd look up from her books to ask him about words whose meanings he suspected she already knew.

The last time he'd been awake at this hour the girl had been here. The sudden spring frost, Frank and the pot-dealing intern had staked cots in the tasting room, the girl's in the kitchen. From the sofa bed in the office he'd heard shuffles, giggles—children at a sleepover after lights-out. He'd thought of going downstairs to join in the punchy camaraderie, but knew he couldn't. He was the boss.

"Go to sleep you assholes," then the girl's laugh, later the men's snores.

His own exhausted sleep shattered by a spoon banging on a pot, and the girl again, "Rise and shine, people! It's cold as a motherfucker." Her bare feet skittering, stopping at the foot of the stairs. "Liam! Yo, Leeeeeeeeeeeeeeeam! Get your lazy butt out of bed!"

Thinking of her was a mistake, and he'd already made plenty for one night.

Perhaps the first mistake had been walking into the gallery full of well-dressed, well-connected people, parents and grandparents of Most-Likely-to-Succeeds. Tonight their insularity had filled him with disgust.

Before that, crossing the Commons, working his way through the gathering crowd, no warning that it had been about the girl. He'd been hurrying so he wouldn't be late.

He'd driven home to change into the khaki pants Basia had left hanging on the closet door. Buttoning the white linen shirt—she said it set off his tan—he'd looked out the window, seen yellow tape fluttering at the far edge of the field. He'd gazed absently out the same window this morning, lacing his belt through his jeans and thinking about Vestri. He likely could have seen the girl—her hand, maybe, or her bright hair. If he'd looked.

He should have been the one to find her. He could have covered her. That much, at least.

Starting the car, he'd picked up his phone. To call Basia: he wasn't up for socializing, not tonight.

But he couldn't let his wife down. *Right.*

Hurrying across the commons, looking up to see the girl's face on the many placards, he'd been blindsided.

And after that, everything had been wrong: Basia's cool hand circling his arm, her perfume—that he usually liked—too heavy, too close. Her voice, murmuring in his ear. She wasn't serving his wine tonight; she'd wanted to tell him before he went over to the bar. Because of a collector come all the way from Manhattan to buy paintings, an expert in Italian wines. He shouldn't be mad, please? Next time, Vestri wines front and center, promise. She'd given his arm a little *you-know-I-count-on-you* squeeze.

She was right, on a normal evening he would have been hurt, upset. Tonight he couldn't focus on anything but the poor girl. How did his wife not know that? It made it all worse, made Basia part of the rich insular world, a world where lives like Amber's didn't matter.

Outside the window, the crowd had thickened and spread, dense waves crested by ten, twenty, thirty repetitions of the girl's face. Pale, blown up, eyes pixelated and unfocused. Dead. He couldn't look away.

His fault, the girl.

"This whole thing is so awful. How on earth did she end up in our field?" Basia had said, almost as if the worst was that it happened on their property. She surely hadn't meant it the way it had sounded to him. Sober, with a nasty, throbbing headache, he saw that now.

"She wasn't some piece of trash." The words had come out harsher than he'd intended. He'd softened his tone. He wasn't talking to the room full of moneyed, potential purchasers of Art. He was talking to his *wife*, with whom he had a daughter, not many years older than Amber Inglin. "She was smart, funny, pretty. She had dreams, plans. She mattered."

Basia's eyes searching his face, shadow of a frown between her brows. "Of *course* she did. I'm just—" She straightened her already-perfect posture in the determined way she had when she'd made the decision to speak her mind. A quality of hers he admired. "It's probably not the best idea for you to get so involved in those kids' lives. It's wonderful that you take up their causes in court, you've helped so many of them. But there's no need to—"

Liam had felt a knot gather and harden in his chest. "No need to *what*?"

Basia sighed. "To get...so *close* to them. And bring this so close to *us*." She gestured discreetly with her head. "They're here now, the police. Or that detective is, the woman who came here this morning."

Detective Jesca Ashton was facing a row of paintings, dressed in tight jeans and a tank top, arms up, winding her hair into a messy knot. His stomach took a dip.

"Did you *say*...I don't know..."—Basia gave a tiny, tight shake to her head, her earrings tinkled—"*something*...to make her think she needed to be *here, tonight*?"

His wife seemed not to know what to do with her hands. Finally she crossed her arms, as though she were suddenly cold, fingers gripping tight, making indentations into her flesh.

Basia had lived her entire life without a single worry. She was the only child of wealthy, educated, supportive, and perfectly charming parents. She'd never even had to have a tooth filled, and her own child had never given her a moment's trouble.

127

And yet she was compassionate, he'd reminded himself. Giving. Basia was always attending benefits, writing checks for one cause and then another. Victims of hurricanes and tsunamis, domestic abuse and homelessness, all had benefited from her generosity.

Giving at a distance—something inside him had emitted the judgment, a sententious, querulous voice. Giving in the abstract. She didn't want the misery of others up close and in her face. Or on her property. Unwelcome clarity, fog suddenly lifting to offer a hard-edged view of something he'd prefer never to have seen.

"Liam, I'm very, very sorry about the girl—"

"Her name was Amber. Amber Inglin."

"I'm very sorry about Amber. I know you know that." Basia was fidgeting with the clasp on her bracelet. An antique.

Gold, studded with tourmaline and rare, cloudy-pink quartz.

A gift from him, for their twentieth anniversary. When had he decided such extravagant purchases weren't okay anymore?

Basia shook her head slowly. "She wasn't left just anywhere. She was left on our property. Or more to the point, perhaps, on *yours*. That worries me, and it *scares* me. Whoever hurt her maybe wanted to hurt you too." She sighed again, made a gesture toward the clusters of people gathered in front of the paintings. "I'm sorry, I really must get back."

He nodded, wishing it had occurred to her to cancel the opening. To drive out to Vestri instead, unasked, to see if he was okay.

He wasn't. Not even close.

From across the room he'd watched her turn up the sound system. Jazz, filling the gaps between conversations and clinking glassware. But the voices from the Commons still leaked through.

He'd headed for the bar, hating himself, needing to dull the edge.

In a corner, Detective Jesca Ashton. Eyes on the paintings, but he could feel her watching him, weighing, considering. He had to leave.

"Are you okay?" His wife again.

"Sure," he'd lied. "I'll be home later." The vineyard was always an excuse. He'd left through the back door avoiding the images of the girl, of Amber.

Another mistake was two shots of whiskey at an Irish bar, dark and grimy, a few blocks away.

And then the worst one: offering Detective Jesca Ashton a ride home when he'd stumbled over her, her beat-up Jetta hemmed in by

SUVs and news crew vans.

He had no idea where the impulse had come from. Suddenly his finger was pressing the button, the window was lowering. He was speaking. Words he'd never planned to say. And she was opening the door, sliding in. Her jean-clad legs beside him, inside his car.

Before he'd come upon her, he'd been telling himself how, when all this was over, he'd make a point of including Basia at Vestri. Once school started again and the interns were back, he'd ask her to come out (which he hadn't done in a while), so she could get to know the kids, get comfortable around them. See what he saw in them.

A harvest party, or something—Basia liked events. Maybe Thanksgiving.

Everything was fixable, if you tried hard enough.

Then the dead girl's face had flashed across his mind. Almost everything.

And then he'd seen Jesca Ashton.

In the car she'd asked questions and he'd answered, or tried to; she'd gone after him hard. Somewhere along the line, his judgment possibly skewed by the whiskey shots, it had seemed like a good idea to take her out to Vestri. Where she would be... reasonable? More likely to listen to him?

But she'd kept pelting him with questions until he'd shut her down with the goddamned Q-Tip.

Finally she'd said she believed him. But—the headache throbbed— she'd had no reason to be straight with him. He saw that now.

Then they were drinking on the porch. That had been a mistake too.

And then they were in the vines.

He'd taken grim comfort in the realness, the aliveness, of every piece of it. The taste of whiskey his tongue had wrested from her mouth. The pain of his knees hitting the ground as he took her down. A scrape mark red across her back, maybe from his nails, he'd seen it as he shoved her around to face him. Hot, searing pain as her teeth dug into his shoulder.

He'd dug into her too, deep and hard—she'd pushed him—leaving bruises behind, marking her thighs. He wasn't rough like that, never had been. Who *was* she?

Who was he?

He'd woken thinking he'd heard his name called from the foot of the stairs.

But the house was empty. There, on the bar in front of him, was his phone. His keys were not beside the phone, where he always left them.

Nor in his pocket. He retraced his steps. Not in the kitchen.

Through the fog outside the window he couldn't see his car. He could barely see the oak tree or the picnic table beneath it. Fog inside his head too.

He flung the door open, stepped out onto the stoop, moisture condensing onto his bare forearms. His parking space was empty—she'd taken his car, that's where his keys were. Why hadn't she woken him? Who took someone's car without asking? Who *was* she?

It was three AM, his phone said. When had the fog come up? It snaked through the grass at the edge of the driveway, creeping between the rows of vines to sit on his canopies, wicked white tongues curling around his grapes.

Liam grabbed his boots from the mudroom, shoved his feet in, no socks. A flashlight in hand, he waded into the rows of Riesling.

Exuberant canopies poked through the bird-nets. He shone the flashlight on the lighter undersides of leaves, crouching low, his thighs protesting, his stomach rolling into a knot. Maybe just shadows. He checked other leaves. Not shadows. Spots, dozens of them, and a deflated grape withering under a coating of fine fuzz.

Gray rot, "noble" rot. It had bloomed in the Reisling in a matter of hours. As it could, as it sometimes did. In the exact spot—he saw now—where he'd first had sex with Detective Jesca Ashton.

Furry blemishes on the next plant, and the next. Shrunken grapes. Liam began to run, overtaxed thigh muscles grabbing as the downgrade steepened.

Fruit flies would come and feed, worsen the damage, spreading the rot to his other fields on their microscopic wings and feet. He couldn't spray any more, he'd reached the limit allowed by organic practice. Spraying might not help anyway—once the gray fuzz bloomed, you cut your losses. Literally.

He pushed away images of his vines pruned back to stubs, wasted fruit piled at the edge of the field. Not real, not yet, but it would be, in as little as seventy-two hours, if he didn't stop it.

He'd call Frank. Get the men out here. A Sunday; he'd pay them double.

They'd have to remove the nets that protected from the birds. The gray rot would send the sugaring process into overdrive. Probably already had, noble rot could lie dormant for months, waiting for just the right conditions to bring it to ghastly, ghostly life. Not enough scarecrow balloons in all of New York State to keep a flock of determined birds away from a field of naked, vulnerable, over-sugared grapes.

For this he'd hovered over frost indexes throughout the spring. For this he'd sprayed with copper to beat back an incipient infestation of black rot in May.

Unbidden came an image from then: Frank and the pot-dealer aiming the applicator at the girl. She'd squealed then grabbed the irrigation hose, nozzle at full blast, spraying her attackers.

She'd been a good worker, keeping track of the application of the organic compounds, marking the calendar in the office. Every ten days in the sunniest parts, every seven in the shade, checking every plant once a week for signs of mold.

All so they could lose an entire field of Riesling, maybe more, to a plague of gray rot and a gaggle of grackles out for an easy sugar high.

Who had they called to identify her, in the morgue? The foster parents, they'd have called the Wilburs.

He was sprinting now, crazily, up and down between the rows of vines, punishing himself, ignoring the searing in his lungs, the sharp pains shooting up his shins. Seconds wouldn't matter, but he ran as though they did. Triage, the word pronounced itself in his head. Triage, triage, triage, in time with his pumping legs, feeling his gut bounce a little against the waistband of his jeans.

Now he had to spend the night at Vestri. And the next night. And the next, and every night until harvest. Which wouldn't please Basia, not one bit.

He stopped, gasping for breath. Take action. Start pruning. When the men got here they could help him burn the damaged trimmings, prevent the spread of more rot.

Liam jogged back to the mudroom. He turned on the light. The tool shelf was empty, except for a piece of paper. From a legal pad, it bore the logo of his old firm.

Unfamiliar handwriting, messy, hard to read. Initials scrawled across the bottom.

She was taking the tools and the gloves—*his* gloves—to the *lab*. To look for what? *Blood*?

His car would be in the parking lot across from the police station. Maybe he could call Frank. "Frank," by name, she didn't miss a trick. She reminded him of a set of car keys in the drawer upstairs, "Could be yours? J. A."

She'd been in his desk. After fucking him—after *listening* to him, after telling him she *believed* him—she'd cased the place.

He couldn't remember what he'd said to her, exactly. What she'd gotten him to say. And then made him think they were okay by screwing his brains out.

The woman was chaos personified.

He dialed Frank's number again. Still no answer. No surprise. Frank picked up for sex or money, little else.

No message from Basia. Way worse than ten messages from Basia.

He'd call her later. At a reasonable hour.

And give a reasonable (partial, he'd have to lie again) explanation.

And pray she wouldn't ask questions.

He found old shears in the tool shed, dull. Not sharpened since he'd bought the place. No gloves. He'd prune without them.

Within minutes he felt blisters blooming across his palms.

At the edge of the field, a tree seemed to clone itself, replicating its own sober trunk and branches, moving toward him. Blinking, he recognized Waldo emerging from the woods, and the dog of course, same color as the wretched fog.

"Goddam gray rot blooming all over the Riesling. Whole eastern vineyard." Liam rubbed the raw skin between his thumb and forefinger. "Get in here and help me!"

"I found the gray feather," Waldo balanced on the balls of his feet, one hand on the dog's head, the other taking a pinch of moist air, as if testing its consistency.

Something swayed on Waldo's chest. Liam squinted. Waldo was wearing some sort of elaborate necklace, or shield. He stepped closer to see it. Flat stones strung together with crazy macramé, twining down into beaded tips from which hung long dark-tipped feathers. "Owl," Detective Jesca Ashton had said, standing before the group of men, holding up her two feathers in their plastic bag. Waldo had been silent.

132

Once Liam had found Waldo at the edge of the Pinot field, hunched behind a thicket, the dog crouched beside him. "Owl," he'd whispered, gaze fixed on the trees, "Hunting." Then he'd said this: "My mother is an owl."

And Liam had decided not to think about it. Waldo was a good worker, had a kind of sixth sense with the plants. What went on in that crazy brain was Waldo's business.

Maybe Liam should have made it his.

"I will get my tools. We can work." Waldo loped off. He ran easily, fast—even for a younger man—disappearing into the woods with the dog close behind, a smear of white melting into the fog.

Waldo lived alone, in the caretaker's cabin, which Liam had provided. And never visited.

He had been shy around the girl, Liam had noticed that, seemed almost to fear her. Eyes cast toward the ground whenever she spoke to him, turning bright red when she handed him gifts from her pockets— treats for his bird feeders, a stick of gum.

Except for his mother, Waldo had never mentioned a woman.

Liam had bought Waldo his own set of tools, which Waldo kept in his cabin. He'd enjoyed the sight of Waldo emerging every morning, independent, dignified by work and purpose.

Would Waldo have…?

Unimaginable—Waldo was the gentlest man he'd ever known.

And calling Detective Jesca Ashton was the last thing in the world he wanted to do.

Connor

The flames shot upward, hissing and flaring as the pink bra melted. The cabin door was open, and all the windows, but the room was filling with smoke, making Connor's eyes burn. He clicked a picture of the flames. Megan threw in the matching pink thong. It disentegrated instantly, sparks snapping.

The fire had been his idea—burn the evidence, just like TV. In a pile beside the fireplace were two bed sheets, a pair of denim cut-offs, a lime-green bra and panties, and two pairs of platform stilettos. Amber had found them on sale at Target. Forty dollars from the California Fund, the shoes were an investment, she said.

The cabin was in the middle of a wooded stretch halfway between school and home. There was no path to it, just a gap in the split rail fence by the bus stop and knowing to keep the sounds of the cars and trucks behind you as you picked your way through the woods.

Connor had found the cabin. He found everything.

He'd thought about keeping the cabin to himself, to use for something only he would know about. Do photography, get high. Maybe bring a guy there, the one with the shaved head from the raves—he looked like he knew things. But in the end he'd told the girls about the cabin; in the system you had to band together, be loyal. Share what was good so you could share the bad stuff too.

It felt empty today, except for the smoke. Amber had always been with them. And quiet too. Amber was the loud one, always laughing.

The first day had been fun. Connor had pushed the door open slowly, making the most of the creaky hinges. "Creepy," Amber had giggled. When she'd stepped on the hearth, the loose bricks shifted. Megan had pulled a rickety chair up to the table and rolled a joint. Hers were neat and prim, like pencils. Connor's were fat—getting everyone too stoned, too quick.

Amber had popped open a beer, handing the can around. "This is awesome."

Amber could always get them beer. The wrecked old guy at the convenience store knew she was only sixteen but he sold to her anyway. Connor had seen him stare at her ass as she bent over to get the Budweiser from the cooler. Sometimes she'd stay that way a second or two longer than was strictly necessary. Once, outside, their six-pack safely double-bagged, "He can look all he wants. He ever tries to touch me, I'll knee him in the balls." Megan had snickered, shaking her hair back from her forehead and tucking it slowly behind one ear, another thing she'd copied from Amber.

She hadn't done that for a couple of days. Maybe with Amber gone it wasn't legit anymore.

Connor poked the fire with a stick. "We should leave while they're gone to the vigil." Connor nudged his sister's shoulder, but she didn't turn around. "Reef doesn't have to work tonight, he'll be home."

Reef, short for Reefer Man, was Connor's weed connection. Reef could get you anything else you wanted too.

"I don't want to stay with him." Megan threw a sheet in. The flames licked, like a hungry wicked mouth.

"He's got rad music, Meg. There's even A.C." In foster squats you were lucky if you could scare up a working fan. "And all the dope you can smoke." Reef worked the night shift at the Super 8 on the edge of town; minimum wage and an apartment at the back, with the curtains always closed. Inside, rows and rows of tender green marijuana plants in little pots, crowding every available surface, grow lights on 24/7. "Unless you have a better plan?" He knew she didn't.

The sheet smoldered. Megan took the stick from him and poked the fire, saying nothing.

"We should lay low for awhile. Reef says we can stay as long as we want." Connor kicked at the pile of stuff. The shoes would never burn, did she know that? Without Amber around, Megan was different. Now he was the one who had to make sure things worked. Would it be like this in California too? "Once Tom and Darla figure out we're gone, the first place they'll look is the bus station."

"I want to go to the vigil." Megan picked up the cut-offs, ready to throw them in. Still not looking at him.

"It's the perfect time to leave." Connor looked through his camera lens out the open door to where the sun beat down on the decrepit steps. That could be a cool picture, the bleached wood, cracked and dry from the sun, like in the desert. It would be cool to see a real desert. "We have to leave tonight, everyone will be somewhere else."

Megan was silent. Over the past two days, the codes between them had shifted. Now silence from Megan didn't mean she liked something, it just meant "okay."

"Hey, where's the phone?" Connor made his voice casual. He was transferring pictures onto a flash drive, deleting them from the camera's memory. "I'll take him the last ones."

Instead of handing the phone to him, Megan held it close to her chest. "She was our friend, Conn. It's not right."

"Meg, there's not even four thou in the fund after what you guys spent on all this stuff. That'll maybe buy the bus tickets and get us a place to stay for the first couple of weeks. *Maybe*. L.A.'s expensive." It was like when they were little, Connor trying to convince his sister to take a few dollars out of their mother's purse, for candy or video games at the mini-mart. His sister always put up one layer of resistance, maybe two, and then she'd do what he wanted.

"You can't sell pictures of a dead person." She sounded like she was going to cry.

"If she was here, she'd tell us to sell them. You know she would. She wouldn't want us in juvie, she'd want us in California." The fire snapped and hissed, strange sounds for summer. Megan was silent, but not "okay"-silent. "We're almost seventeen," Connor said. "They might even send us to real jail. You know what they do to fags in jail. Give me the phone." The sheets were now a pile of ashes but the shoes weren't catching. He held out his hand.

Finally Megan thrust hers out, fist still tight around the phone. Connor had to pry her fingers open. While Connor dialed, she poked at the shoes. Now she was crying for real.

The guy picked up on the third ring. "Yup."

Connor knew his voice, but he didn't know his name. And he didn't want to.

Connor had been careful. He took the long route back from their meetings, changed buses twice, choosing stops that were out in the open, without enclosed shelters or too many trees.

"Got a bunch for you." Connor deepened his voice when he talked to the guy. "I can get there by five."

"See you then." They each hung up.

The smoke smelled terrible. "I'll meet you back at the house. Don't go to the vigil, okay?"

Megan answered him this time, in a small voice. "Okay." She sniffled.

"We'll leave as soon as it gets dark."

Silence. "Okay"-silence. Megan nodded and swiped the back of one hand over her face. With the other, she poked at the shoes.

"Those shoes will never burn, Meg. You should bury them."

Connor walked through the woods to the bus stop and sat down in the shade. Across the field he could see the rich people's house. In L.A., once he'd sold lots of photographs, he'd buy a house like that, on the beach, with palm trees all around it, and a swimming pool for when they didn't feel like the ocean. A Jeep and matching motorbikes. He'd let Megan pick them out, whatever kind she wanted. They'd be a team again, just the two of them. Everything would be like before.

The bus was almost empty, only an old lady he'd seen before who always got off at the mall. Connor sat in the back, watching the succession of gas stations, fast-food restaurants, and strip malls crowding the edge of the road. One tired-looking house wedged onto a slice of brown lawn. He didn't know how much money he'd get today. He had some stuff, but it wasn't what the guy was expecting. The bus jolted over a pot hole. Three more stops. Connor took the camera out of its leather case.

He didn't feel like it, but he needed to look through the shots, to pick out the ones the guy would like. He'd look at the old ones first, he liked them. One of Megan and Amber, showing off their tattoos, wrists side by side. Then his favorite, a pillow fight in the TV room, Amber jumping on the sofa in a cut-off T-shirt and bright green underwear, Megan curled into a fetal position, laughing, feathers everywhere.

He'd met the guy at a moment just like this one, looking at pictures of the girls on his camera, playing magazine editor in his head. Nice composition, over-exposed, good light, too vertical.

A shadow had fallen over the screen. "They're pretty hot."

He'd looked up into a tanned face, solid-jawed like a fashion model's. Five o'clock shadow, sunglasses that looked expensive. Very white teeth, a front one missing a small chip.

"Did you take those?"

Connor had nodded.

"You're good."

He'd made sure his "Thanks" came out chill and nonchalant.

When the guy leaned in closer, Connor had caught a whiff of Dolce and Gabbana—he'd tried it on himself at the mall. Thinking maybe the guy was an agent or something he'd flipped slowly through pics, enjoying approval from someone who might matter. The guy had stopped him at a shot of Megan stepping out of the shower, a towel clutched around her. Her hair was wet and you could see the tops of her small breasts.

"You could get yourself some money for those." The guy's breath was minty but he wasn't chewing gum.

"Yeah?" Connor had acted more skeptical than he'd felt. "Who'd want to look at them?"

"Men." The guy sat down on the bench beside Connor. He was wearing faded jeans, a white T-shirt and a suit jacket that looked Italian. Little wrinkles fanning out, in a nice way, from his eyes. Connor had no idea how old he was, everyone he knew over thirty looked like hell.

"I have a website." The guy had pulled a sleek leather briefcase onto his lap and extracted a computer that looked too old and crappy for someone like him. Later on he would tell Connor that the old ones were the hardest to trace. "I'll give you a hundred bucks for the skinny black-haired chick in the towel and the pillow fight." The guy fingered some twenties so crisp Connor had wondered if they were fake.

"For...a porn site?"

"Not exactly. Those shots *aren't* porn and that's why they're good. All kinds of nasty shit out there for free—not a single pubic hair left to the imagination, just click, you can even zoom allllllll the way in—but it's random and impersonal and usually pretty bad. Lot of men out there willing to pay a lot of money for the *illusion*—long as it's believable—that they're interacting with a real live teenage girl. They don't want to go down for rape, statutory or otherwise, but they want to live the fantasy. And they'll wait to get what they want. They like to wait, even. Waiting's part of it. She can't be some skanky slut, she's gotta give it up little by ever-so-fucking little. They like the exclusivity. The scarcity, the just-for-them-ity...You've heard of the slow-food movement?"

Connor hadn't, but he'd nodded.

The guy didn't seem fooled, or particularly bothered. "Started in Italy?" Made sense, the jacket. "Like, the opposite of McDonald's... Now you got people driving all over Italy, and everywhere else for that matter, looking for just the right kind of tomato, otherwise no sauce. And they will wait to make that sauce, from scratch, until they get their perfect goddamned tomatoes, even if it takes all freaking month. And then they'll wait till those precious fucking tomatoes ripen on their goddamn

139

windowsills. Long as it takes, the red has to be just right, they want their perfect sauce.

"So, translate that into the world of porn and you make a killing." The guy had grinned, and Connor had grinned back, though he wasn't completely following.

Which maybe the guy had sensed, because he slowed down, looking Connor full in the face, from behind his cool sunglasses. "See, it's like this. You create enough desire for a specific girl, a girl who makes a guy the pics he asks for, but not right away, he has to ask two or three times... a girl who chats just with him, enough to keep him stringing along but never as much as he wants, and before you know it he's *begging* to pay three hundred bucks for a shot of her in her underwear, looking into the bathroom mirror and brushing her teeth."

"You mean they have to, like, chat with a bunch of gross old guys?"

"Hey! Not necessarily old, and not necessarily gross. A lot of them look like me." The guy had fake-punched Connor in the shoulder. Which Connor had sort of liked, the guy was definitely cool. The kind of guy Connor had imagined might be his friend, show him around, when he got to L.A. "And no, no direct contact, we create the personas, all I need from you is the visual material. And then you sit back and wait for the tide to roll in."

Connor's mouth had flooded with what he figured was the taste of money, a lot of it, metallic and a little bitter; he'd salivated so hard he'd had to swallow. But he was also a realist. The girls had limits. "They'd never go for it."

The guy shrugged, too bad, and snapped the laptop shut, folding the bills again. Connor had felt a stab of pain in his chest as the twenties disappeared into a pocket inside the guy's silk-lined jacket, he actually had a *money clip*. "I can give you a number to call if you change your mind."

At home, Connor had found Amber and Megan hunched over Tom's computer, beside stacks of church pamphlets that Tom and Darla left on people's doorsteps or in mailboxes. Tom allowed them an hour a day on the computer, but he kept track of the websites they visited.

They were looking at the page for the Yale School of Drama. Amber had decided she wanted to be an actress. Not the kind that makes millions of dollars in Hollywood, which she could totally have done, but some other stupid kind of actress, wearing old-fashioned clothes and talking weird. She never stopped talking about Mrs. Ousterhout, who had told her she could go to Yale, which was a load of shit, people like them didn't go to Yale. She'd gotten Megan to rehearse her lines with her and they'd started making dumb, nerdy jokes all the time, thee and thou and wouldst fain. Their new favorite things to call each other were slattern, wanton bawd, and strumpet, which Amber had said he couldn't be because he was a guy.

Way worse, Megan had started saying the East Coast was better than the West Coast. Which was making things tricky with the California fund.

Connor didn't have a lot of faith—maybe he should have sold the pics while he had the chance—but he'd told them about the hundred dollars. "He said you guys are *hot*," He'd mustered a grin. "Even you, Meg! A lot of gross old bums would want to look at you, I guess." Connor still hadn't been able to picture the guy's customers as anything other than nasty and ancient and limp-dicked and pathetic.

"Eeuuw." Megan had wrinkled her nose. But she hadn't said flat-out no.

"It's not like you have to meet them or anything. And a lot of it's just stupid shit like doing your homework in your underwear." Connor had pressed his case. "I'll be the one with the camera, you know it won't do anything for *me*. We take the pics, we give them to him, he does whatever, and we make some serious cash."

"How much?" Amber turned around in her chair.

"Tons," Connor had answered, watching Amber's face. Her eyes narrowed, like she was adding up numbers.

"Meg," Amber leaned toward to his sister, "We'll make so much money." He'd seen it then, how dumb he'd been. Megan's head was in the clouds all day long, but Amber was like him, she knew it took cash to make shit happen. He should have been a lot nicer to her a lot sooner. Amber put an arm around Megan's shoulder, pulling her closer. "We *have* to."

Connor had tensed, waiting for what his sister was going to say. After a second or two she'd nodded, "Okay."

That was how it had started. Fifty bucks a shot for the pics the guy kept, an extra ten or twenty for really hot ones. Once he'd given them a hundred for one of Amber by herself, in her plain, white everyday underwear. She was lying back in a pile of pillows, legs apart, looking up at the camera, one finger in her mouth and the other hand inside her panties.

Megan had thought of that pose. Once she got going, Megan always thought of the best ones.

Once the guy had shown Connor his website, RealGirl.com, made to look like the girls themselves had posted the pics—"self-submits," the guy called them—fantasy material for lonely, bored men out there, somewhere.

"They're willing to pay," he'd said. "So we serve it up."

Amber had wanted to see their pictures, so Meg did too.

They knew they'd get caught if they used Tom's computer, so they'd gone on the internet at the public library. For cover, Connor and Amber had asked questions at the front desk, then made their way to the row of old computers in the back, where Megan sat. There were other webpages that Megan had found with stupid names like "Barely Legal" and "Saucy Schoolgirls," or gross ones like "Hot Teen Pussy." Page after page of teasers that looked like they'd been snapped with a polaroid. Like the guy had said, you had to pay if you wanted to see better stuff.

A title in flashing green letters urged viewers to visit "Underage Underground."

Then suddenly Amber's face was staring out at them, pouty lips slathered with cherry lipgloss. Bare shoulders, you could see green bra straps and some boob—Amber's were a lot bigger than Megan's. Okay, so the guy had kind of lied. Or he was multi-purposing the pics, which wasn't part of what they had talked about, but Connor hadn't told him not to either. Maybe this was how it was, making serious money. You also had to make some compromises. Connor thought of the rapidly expanding California Fund and decided compromise was fine with him.

The guy had named green-bra girl "Hayley." Underneath her name, in hot pink, girly letters, it said, "I had to stay after school." In a sidebar, site members with screen names like Reddy2ParT, MotherLoad57 and HotRodRambo had written comments. "Hot little blond." "She needs a spanking." "Gimme summa that sweet cherry pie."

Amber hadn't been mad about the multi-purposed pics, she'd just laughed, a loud cackle in the library.

Another click and Megan was there too—black lipstick, hair slicked into two tight braids, named "Aimee," one of six "Little Goth Sluts." "The back door's open," said a conversation bubble beside her head. Users asked "Aimee" to "show it to them," or whether she was "tight." "Aimee" had written back, in bright orange letters, that she sure would and she sure was.

Connor had rolled his eyes about the black lipstick but they'd gotten a bonus for the made-to-orders.

"Check it out," Megan whispered. "We're famous." He'd thought then that maybe his sister was okay with compromise too.

He was at his stop.

He got off and waited on the bench, staring at his camera, making sure not to act like he was looking for someone. The guy had warned him about that.

It was always the same. The guy showed up a minute or two after Connor, carrying his briefcase. Usually they stayed at the bus stop. If it was raining, they walked across the road to a Denny's. It took a long time, making the drop-offs. Once Connor suggested he could just email the pics. The guy had looked at him with a hard edge in his colorless eyes—that was the only wrong thing about him, the dead eyes. "Do you want to go to jail?"

After the guy flipped through the pics, he would name a price. Connor always acted like he was considering the offer, but there was nothing to think over. The money in the California Fund was more than the three of them together had had in their entire lives.

Once Connor accepted, the guy would take the money clip, with its fat fold of bills, from the inside pocket of his Italian suit jacket—same one every time, no matter how hot or cold it was. He'd count out the money, in pristine tens and twenties, and read out a new cell number. Connor would type it into his phone and the guy would leave. Connor would cross the road to catch the bus back home, never once letting his eyes follow the guy.

This time, he told himself, with Amber gone, would be no different.

When Connor got home, the money in his sock, it was almost seven. Darla, her face red and blotchy, was sitting on the couch, where she'd been most of the time since the police had come. Tom was stapling big smiling pictures of Amber onto long wooden sticks. "Megan isn't feeling well," Tom said. Darla didn't say anything. "Go up and see her."

"Sure thing."

Sure thing, sure thing, the words drummed in Connor's head as he climbed the stairs. It *was* a sure thing, they'd be out of here and toking on a joint at Reef's before Tom and Darla were back from the vigil.

But nothing was ever a sure thing, he should know that. A little after 8:30

by now, after watching Megan try to decide which of three pairs of identical looking jeans to stuff into her backpack, a blue-white glow sliced across the room. Headlights in the driveway.

"God, Meg! We should've been out of here twenty minutes ago."

The screen door whined open, a key rattled in the lock. Voices murmured and then a woman called their names. One of the fundies—they all talked in the same fakey sweet way, like they thought Jesus was listening. "Darla was feeling faint, she's going to lie down for a while," the voice cooed. "Let me make you children some supper." She'd probably watch them eat and try to talk to them about heaven or being saved or some other crap.

Now they couldn't leave till tomorrow, maybe even tomorrow night. By which time all sorts of shit could happen, none of it good.

Waldo

In the place where the Amber girl should be, empty grass lying flat, a cool dark nest under the bush. He was too late, the changing had begun without him.

The feathers too were gone.

He must replace them, to help her find her way back.

Sunday

I

Beatrice

Beatrice hoisted her groceries to the kitchen counter, and stood for a moment to catch her breath. A lovely walk to the farmer's market; she hadn't made that trek in ages!

True, the humidity had been stifling, the stretch closest to the highway lined with jiffy-lubes and chain drugstores, and the rushing traffic had made Geneva skittish. But she'd spied wild salvia growing along the roadside, pushing bravely through the gravel. The bright blue blossoms were a bit bedraggled now, but a drink of water would fix that. They'd be a charming centerpiece for tonight's dinner table.

Humming — a pleasant tune she couldn't for the life of her recognize — Beatrice unloaded her purchases, stacking the plastic shopping bags beside the sink. As she put away dish soap, the words came. "*Though Philomela lost her love, Fresh note she warbleth, yes, again. Fa la la...*" Where were those words from? A madrigal, yes, definitely a madrigal, possibly Thomas Morley — the Elizabethans had been positively fascinated by the Filomela legend. And she had Filomela on the brain because... Beatrice stopped, a roll of paper towels in hand. Maybe Jes was right, she was going dotty. No, she had it. Because of the *paper*. Right there, on the kitchen table, she'd read it last night as she ate her dinner.

How could she possibly have forgotten? Yesterday evening, among the files of her actors, Beatrice had found an old paper of Jes's wedged between two contraband student folders. A lovely surprise to end a terrible day. She paused now, savoring the title: "Avian Symbolism in the Legend of *Filomela*."

The Filomela tale was one of Beatrice's favorites. Thereus, King of Thrace, having won the hand of Filomela's older sister Procne after routing the Barbarians at the gates of Athens, saw that his bride was lonely in her new home. Thinking to cheer her, Thereus brought Filomela to his court, but the young Filomela's beauty clouded the king's judgment. That's always how it was told, the girl's fault for being young. Possessed by uncontrollable lust, Thereus forced himself upon his sister-in-law. He then cut out her tongue, locked her in a dungeon, and told his wife her sister was dead.

And at the end, after a lot of frenzied chasing about, they were all turned into birds. Beatrice emptied the plums she'd bought into the fruit bowl, on top of others that were going soft. Wrinkly all over now. Perhaps she should discard them. But then again, she might get around to making jam.

She put away cereal and dogfood, making a mental note not to mix them up. Procne became a swallow, if she remembered it right, and Filomela a nightingale, and the lustful king a nasty hoopoe. Now, where was the garlic? Beatrice kicked at the plastic bags that had drifted to the floor. Geneva wouldn't have eaten garlic, would she?

Beatrice surveyed the kitchen. If she were a head of garlic, where would she hide? She peeped behind the crumb-spackled toaster, ran her fingers beneath the slippery edge of the dish drainer. When the heat broke she'd give the kitchen a good scrubbing. The refrigerator? Finally! A head of garlic, only semi-dry—she could trim away the brown bits—at the bottom of the cheese-and-charcuterie drawer. How had it gotten in there? She tasted it. Absolutely serviceable, still sharp even.

"Fresh note she warbleth, yes, again..."

Moreley wasn't alone, there'd been scads of Renaissance variants on the Filomela legend. Of course Shakespeare, with his frightful *Titus Andronica*, had taken things a bit far. Poor Lavinia, raped by *two* men who, once they'd done with her, cut out her tongue and amputated both her hands...

Beatrice shook her head, stopped the train of thought, but not in time. A vision of Amber Inglin's severed hand, the wrist to which it had formerly been attached, rolled across her mind. She gripped the refrigerator door for support. She'd been doing so well today, getting on with things.

She'd think of Jes's paper, of how delighted she'd been upon finding it. It had felt like having her daughter back.

Peering into the refrigerator, a wilted stalk of celery returning her gaze, Beatrice stopped. Where on earth had that ridiculous thought come from? She *had* her daughter, right here, just across town. How many mothers could say that? She was being foolish, and she should stop. Yes, throughout her childhood and teen years, Jes had been obsessed with birds birding and thus—logically—spent more time with her father, but she and Jes had always been close. They *were* close.

Jes had written the paper here, Beatrice remembered it well, she and her daughter had spent ten whole days together. Charles had died three months earlier. Jes, home between quarters, sitting on the nightingale carpet amid piles of books and notes, trying to finish an assignment she'd been unable to complete during exam period. Charles' death had been so hard on her.

What had she gone to the refrigerator for? The Cornish game hens. Beatrice scooped them up. Turning, her foot slid on a plastic bag. On her way down, she grasped at a chair as the pinkish hen bodies spilled from their paper wrapping, landing with a wet thud. The chair crashed to the floor and Beatrice was on all fours, her right knee throbbing dully.

The hens lay a few inches away, legs splayed, revealing emptied-out cavities. Why on earth hadn't the butcher trussed them with twine? Beatrice struggled to her feet and hurried the birds to the sink for a thorough rinse.

She wiped her wet hands on her slacks, and pulled a grease-specked card from the recipe box to refresh her memory concerning the preparation of apple and cornbread stuffing. Jes's favorite.

Jes hadn't answered either of her messages. Beatrice sighed. Sunday mornings were okay for not calling back, people slept late. But now it was *late* morning, Jes must have been awake for hours. And she was always fiddling with her phone; of course she'd seen the messages.

She was being silly, Jes had said so yesterday, when she'd stopped by. But had her daughter said definitively to reschedule dinner for tonight, or had she said *maybe*?

Well, even if she had, among the young, "maybe" meant "definitely." In her second message Beatrice had told Jes to come at seven. Jes was punctual, she would be here.

Her father had been punctual, maybe Jes had gotten that from him.

Beatrice reached for her cell. She could tell Jes she'd forgotten… what? Whipping cream, for the dessert. And to *please let Beatrice know* she was bringing it.

No. Beatrice drew her hand back. Let her call you for once.

The kitchen was too quiet. Beatrice turned on the radio, Schubert, or Schuman—something German. The morning host played far too many selections from the Romantic period. But indistinguishable German Romantics were better than silence. When Jes called, she'd hear the music, hear Beatrice busy and occupied and *not* waiting for the phone to ring.

The coffee pot began to gurgle. When had she put it on? Pure habit.

When it finally did ring, the high-pitched trill of the telephone made Beatrice jump. Her heart thumped out a glad, jaunty Schottish. Give it one more ring, she told herself, and answer with the relaxed-but-busy, morning-coffee voice.

Beatice picked up her cell, yet the ringing continued, twice more before she remembered the landline.

No one called her landline anymore.

"Beatrice." A man's voice spoke her name as though it were a statement of fact concerning some unfortunate event. "Principal Norton here."

She'd hoped not to have to deal with Norton for at least another week. Why on earth would he call her?

"Beatrice, are you there?" Norton's voice quavered with a hint of irritation.

She turned the radio off. "Mr. Norton." 'Mr.' was all he was getting out of her. "I'm here."

"The curriculum committee had an emergency meeting this morning."

"On a *Sunday*?"

"As I said, an emergency. I'm afraid I've got bad news. We've had to cancel your seminar. We need you to teach the American Literature survey this year."

It felt as though someone had punched her in the chest.

"Jenna won't be teaching it this term." Beatrice could hear papers rustling. "As you perhaps know, she's taking a sabbatical to work on her masters'."

Jenna Black. Twenty-seven, earnest, enthusiastic. And helpful, especially to Norton. A degree in Education instead of English literature. She invented learning games and made her students "journal." Which wasn't even a verb.

Norton cleared his throat. "As you undoubtedly do know, there is a state mandate that we offer AmLit every year—"

"What about Holly?," Beatrice interrupted, in the bright, can-do voice she knew he liked.

"On maternity leave." More papers rustling. "We can't entrust a core course to a substitute." The sequence of s's whistled through Norton's teeth. "I'm afraid your seminar must be suspended."

He was punishing her. Because she wasn't *youthful*. "But everything's already…"

"The seminar certainly"—Norton sounded prim—"cannot be held this semester, given recent, and most unfortunate, events." More sibillant consonants. "Miss Inglin was to play the female lead this year, was she not?"

"Yes, she…" Beatrice shifted. Sound *positive*, she told herself.

"Recasting will…"

"Beatrice, it is simply out of the question."

She took a deep breath. Show no panic: a calm, measured voice. "*Principal* Norton"—give him what he wants—"there are are more than two weeks until rehearsals are slated to start. Of course I'll never find another Duchess of her caliber"—good, use the future tense; it sounded inevitable—"but I believe it would be her preference, Amber's wish, for the show to go on." Beatrice winced as the platitude escaped her lips. "I'm dedicating the production to her memory."

"The school board will never—"

"I can do AmLit, too," she added quickly. "It'll mean an extra class for me, but I'll make it work."

Move the rehearsals to Saturdays, evenings. Everyone could come to her house, she'd cook. Spaghetti for thirty, maybe even home-made ice cream, the hand-crank freezer must still be in the attic somewhere.

"Webster, as you certainly must know, would be wildly inappropriate under the present circumstances."

"The…*circumstances* will no longer be present in November! The opening's almost three months away! And it will be in her honor!"

"I'm sorry, Beatrice." Of course he wasn't. "The committee's decision is final."

Beatrice held the receiver in her hand, only replacing it when her eardrums were assaulted by the frenetic beeping signal. She felt bereft. Empty afternoons, days, weeks—how to even begin to fill all those hours?

She started down the hall toward the study, Geneva trailing her, a tattered plastic bag floating behind like a lacey kite. At the front door a muggy billow of air, as she retrieved the newspaper from the doormat. On the front page Amber Inglin's face, smiling for the school photographer. In color. The same picture they'd used for the posters. "Mutilated Body of Local Teen Found in Field."

Tears began to gather. The print wavered. A preliminary autopsy was being performed, with results available later today. On her Duchess. The idea made her queasy. Where would they cut first, for an autopsy? Terrible.

In the study, she gazed around. On the floor, piles of books and folders, materials for her seminar, covered by a thin film of dust. The costumed dummies stood, betrayed and forlorn. She should wrap up the Duchess's gown for the Wilburs—no need for a replacement now. The tears spilled over.

Beatrice wiped at her eyes. The desk top was a cluttered mess. The picture window, where Charles and Jes had spent so many hours with their birding glasses, filthy. How had she allowed the study to slide into such slovenly disorder?

A thunderous racket shattered the silence and Geneva scuttled under the sofa with a yelp. Bewildered, Beatrice looked around the room. Behind her, the dog had knocked over a pile of empty packing boxes.

Another project she needed to finish. The university had been enthusiastic about her idea for the Charles Ashton Reading Room. The former colleague, whose name she could never remember, had said he'd be honored to edit a special issue of *Acta Ornithologica*, to celebrate the reading room's opening, perhaps Beatrice might like to contribute a short remembrance. Beatrice had taken some half-hearted notes that first afternoon, and then forgotten.

But the university hadn't—they'd sent the boxes over, for Charles's books, and hinted at the loan of some of Charles's watercolors—the rare species from Thailand. For which she had yet to make a serious search. In truth, she'd forgotten all about them, too.

She'd best stack the boxes again. Beatrice sighed, depositing the newspaper onto the coffee table. And something else along with it, whatever was that? Beatrice stared. When had she picked up Jes's paper?

And then she stared some more, the idea dawning slowly, complete and perfect in every way. There, on the table before her, lay the perfect basis upon which to craft a contribution to Charles's colleague's memorial volume. *Together*, with her daughter. The paper was almost publishable as it was, and with a bit of work—which would require Beatrice's collaboration (that was the best part)—it would be a lovely piece. She herself could write an introduction, setting the stage—the rainy afternoon, mother and daughter together before the fireplace in the study, surrounded by Charles's beloved books. Then help Jes work up the bibliographical references a bit, and *voilà*!

Why had this not occurred to her before? Tonight's dinner would not be just any dinner, it would be a celebration, to mark the beginning of a mother-daughter collaboration. An intellectual reawakening for Jes—finally, something worthy to occupy Jes's mind—and a plum of an article for Beatrice: Jenna Black wasn't the only one doing interesting things. Not that the public school system rewarded such efforts, but scholarship was its own reward!

A second flash of inspiration followed the first: they could illustrate the essay with Charles's watercolors! If she remembered correctly, Charles had studied hoopoes in Thailand, that nasty bird again. Well if he'd studied them, he'd drawn them. She'd find the perfect illustration for Jes's paper. It all came together! She could worry about Norton later.

The files were organized according to country and region. T for Thailand, but the drawer was empty, except for a thin folder marked "Timbuktu." Where could he have put them? A coolish puff of air across her cheek. The fan. Of course.

Battered and worn, Charles's boxes looked as though they'd made the journey from Chiang Mai to Ithaca on the open deck of an ocean liner. The first contained only clothing: cotton shirts, khaki pants with lots of pockets, Charles's uniform practically. They smelled musty and unfamiliar. Beatrice wrinkled her nose.

The second box contained field notes. The handwriting, at least, was familiar: small, uniform and slanted toward the left.

The drawings had to be in the final box. On top were sketch pads filled with quick skillful renderings of birds, the date, time and location noted in the lower right-hand corner. She lifted them out carefully. Beneath the sketchpads were the watercolors, nested between layers of yellowing onionskin paper.

Lifting off the onionskin, Beatrice caught her breath at the sheer abundance of detail, of color. The long-tailed Broadbill, resplendent in blue-green plumage. The next a Hooded Pitta—lime green breast, wings striped cerulean. She was careful to keep the tissue covering intact. Next the curvaceous silhouette of a Spoon-billed Pelican, angular wings and neck of the Oriental Darter, both marked in Charles's slanting letters as rare and endangered.

Last of all—good things come to she who waits!—three magnificent hoopoes, any one of which would beautifully illustrate Jes's essay.

She lined the hoopoes up along the wall. She'd let Jes choose.

Edward

Goggles on, Edward swam in the lake. Between the bulrushes flanking the pier a fish glinted silver. Pushing off the piling, he executed a varsity-level turn, drew a breath with the taint of rotting plants and petroleum.

Out to the middle then back in, fleeting snapshots of his sisters on the beach. Cate stretched out on a chaise-longue, still more than willing—at forty-nine—to don a bikini. Her husband Bill wasn't with them.

Did they still have sex? Arms slicing through the soft water, Edward wondered who visited whom in their designer his-and-hers bedrooms; if they knocked or just walked in.

Sara flitted helpfully about the shore, retrieving stray beach balls with her free arm. She was easy to spot because of the sling. Bill had called his nurse in even though it was Sunday, to help him set her broken wrist. Sara hadn't accused him openly of anything—she said she'd fallen, which was partly true. "No wood-carving for awhile," Bill had said, to everyone and no one, when they'd returned. Cate had offered her the couch in the airconditioned living room. Tonight, Edward would sleep in the boathouse alone.

He slowed to a crawl. This was the part of his swim where, on normal days, he savored the endorphin glow. But not today—the Sara situation bothered him. He was now without an ally. And Sara wasn't drinking, or so she said. She might actually mean it.

He preferred her drunk and dependent. On him.

He stood in the shallows, the sandy lake bottom molding itself to his heels. Edward removed his goggles and looked to where Sara stood with her good arm around Perfect Offspring Girl's shoulder—when had she ever done *that*? Cate had joined them at the water's edge, as had Bill, dressed for golf. Beyond them stood Detective Jesca Ashton, in her gray uniform.

They were all waiting for him.

Edward looked around for his towel. It was folded, where he'd left it, on top of the picnic basket under Cate's umbrella. Too far away, he'd have to break through the line formed by his sisters, his brother-in-law and the detective. That would be a mistake.

He shook the water from his hair. "Detective Ashton. Good afternoon.

More questions for us?"

But she was looking only at him.

"Actually, Mr. Friis, it's with you I need to speak. Would you like to go somewhere more private?"

"It's just my family here." Edward let cockiness creep into his voice. "Are you sure?"

Edward shrugged, "I've nothing to hide."

"Right." Detective Jesca Ashton pulled a pad from her shirt pocket, consulted notes. "Are you certain you left Ms. Inglin at the Wilbur residence on Friday night?"

Edward crossed his arms. Jesca Ashton's voice seemed suddenly much too close, like a ventriloquist's trick. Steady, look directly at her. "Ah, how stupid of me." Shake your head, rueful half-smile—absent-minded artist. "Of course not. She asked me to let her off in front of the public library. It's a turn of phrase, isn't it, 'driving someone home?'" He tried for light, relaxed. Missed. He wished the detective would remove her sunglasses.

"Did she say what she intended to do once you left her?" The detective's words were careful, leading him down a particular path, toward some predetermined conclusion.

"No she didn't." He licked his lips, swallowed, then wished he hadn't. He'd always been bothered by the protruberance of his adam's apple. There it was, his imperfection, bobbing up and down for all to see.

"Was anyone waiting for her?"

"No." Say more, anything, so she'd stop *looking* at him that way. Sudden, fleeting vision of the perfect girl, her back to him, hand cradling her *phone*. "She made a call."

"Yes, we have that." He could feel her closing in on him. "I must ask you again, Mr. Friis, and it is very important that you answer truthfully and completely. To your knowledge, did anyone witness Ms. Inglin leaving your van?"

The deserted street. No restaurants or bars with outside tables. Just the green yard, the blank-eyed house behind. "No. I already *told* you." His voice was high and small. Plaintive.

"It appears, then, that you were the last person to see Ms. Inglin alive." The detective was scribbling something into her awful little notebook. Awfuler still, she looked up, her gaze boring into him like a drill. He felt as though he might faint. "Mr. Friis, your failure to answer questions truthfully during our first interview gives me cause to seek a search warrant."

Edward avoided his sisters' eyes. What was the detective waiting for him to say?

"Under the terms of a search warrant, you do not retain the right to be present during inspection. Alternately, you may of your own free will allow me to inspect your quarters while you are present. Your choice."

Edward clenched his fists against his ribcage to quiet the tremors. "You'd have to get permission to inspect the boathouse from the owners—we are, after all, not on my property."

Edward was not surprised to hear Cate's voice almost breathless, "Of course, detective. Whatever you need." She was throwing him to the wolves.

Edward felt an urgent need to cover himself. He stepped forward—Detective Jesca Ashton straightened; could she possibly think he would try to run?—and retrieved his beach towel. At the boathouse door, he turned to the detective. "I'll just get dressed."

"If you're going inside, I'll need to go with you. I should inspect the premises exactly as you last left them."

Edward opened the door and allowed the detective to enter first. He wished his family would remain outside, but there was no way to frame the request without making things infinitely worse. The moment passed. His sisters, Bill, the Perfect Offspring, assembled in a half-circle around the adjacent twin beds.

Finally, in the dim interior, Detective Jesca Ashton removed her sunglasses. Her face and eyes were without expression. "Which of these beds is yours?"

Sara's voice now, "The one closest to the window. We share the closet, my stuff's to the right. And the chest of drawers. I have the bottom two." Edward stole a look at his sister's face. Gaunt and serious, she'd started to resemble Cate, *mean*. The drunken bitch *wanted* him arrested.

"Whose computer?"

Sara again, "It's mine but we both use it, to check email and stuff."

"I'll need to take it." Detective Jesca Ashton removed a pair of disposable gloves from her pocket. Plastic rustled as she placed the computer inside an evidence bag. She wrote a number on the bag with a sharpie. "And the tools." Loud clanking as the detective gathered Sara's saw and knives.

Sara opened her mouth, then clamped her lips together. Edward reached for the pair of khakis flung across his bed. He was so goddamned *cold*.

Detective Jesca Ashton—apparently possessed of freakishly overdevelopped peripheral vision—stepped between him and the bed. "Please don't touch anything until I've registered it." She picked up the khakis and deftly checked waistband, hems, seams, pockets, then held them out to him.

There was silence—why were they all watching?—while Edward fought to get his feet into the legs and pull the pants up his damp thighs. He felt something cold and wet around his buttocks, against his groin. The swimming trunks. He'd pulled the trousers on over wet swimming trunks.

The detective had her back to him now, opening drawers, leveling stacks of T-shirts and shorts, pulling pairs of socks apart. The easel was next and she stood looking at the new girl, immobile. He'd cleaned the painting up yesterday, the gash was gone. But she was staring too hard, too long. He should have left it alone.

Then, as if she'd planned it, Detective Jesca Ashton turned to his worktable, opened the drawer, and removed his binoculars and the Sara sketchbook.

She stared for a long moment at the binoculars, turning them over in her hands. She checked something, maybe the manufacturer's label, and made a note.

Then she rifled through the sketchpad. Looked up at Sara, rifled some more. "All these are your sister?"

"Yes." Edward swallowed. The lump in his throat almost choked him.

"Edward"—Sara spoke now, her voice rising—"*Edward*! What the…" She reached for the sketchbook. "What have you been *doing*?"

"Sorry," Detective Jesca Ashton was sealing the sketchpad into an evidence bag.

There was an awful silence in the room, and the detective opened the closet. With her plastic gloves, she rummaged through pockets, pulling out movie-ticket stubs, loose change, toll booth receipts. A long-forgotten condom, the wrapping frayed. He peeked at Sara whose lips were curling with disgust.

The detective slipped her hand under the faded bedspread, then inside the pillowcase. She knelt and raised a corner of the mattress. Edward felt a bilious undertow of nausea.

When the detective stood, she held the magazines. *Barely Legal* and *Next-Door Lolita*, the May issue. On the cover, a blonde girl in a short cheerleader skirt straddled a bleacher beside an out-of-focus football field. She hid her bare breasts with pompoms.

Sara reacted first, hurrying the Perfect Offspring toward the door.

Cate followed, "We'll be outside."

Bill's eyes met Edward's briefly—Edward thought he read a note of sympathy.

Alone with the detective now, the nausea was a tsunami, the sandwich and iced tea he'd had for lunch surging toward his throat.

"Are there more?" Detetective Jesca Ashton gestured with the magazines.

"No."

"What about on the computer?"

"Yes."

"I'll need you to come down to the station to answer a few more questions."

Edward nodded, an icy trail of sweat creeping down his bare back.

"Do you have the clothing you were wearing the night Ms. Inglin was killed?"

He reached inside the closet for the duffel bag that served as a hamper. It was heavy, he needed both hands, the towel fell to the floor. Shivering, he pulled out stale-smelling clothes until he found the jeans he'd worn to the cocktail. He handed them to the detective.

"No underwear?"

"I...ah...don't know which ones."

"Give me all of them." A thread of triumph ran through Jesca Ashton's voice.

Edward retrieved the towel, wrapping it around his shoulders like a blanket. "I have to get dressed, and I should probably take a shower. Shall I meet you at the station in an hour?" He tried for casual, as though he were arranging a coffee date with a coworker. He never had coffee dates with coworkers. Maybe that was his problem.

"The procedure is that you accompany me in the squad car," stated the detective. "When we're done, assuming things check out, you may phone one of your family members to pick you up, or I can have someone drive you. I'll wait outside while you dress."

He grabbed a T-Shirt from the heap on the floor—dirty, clean, he didn't bother to check.

When the screen door banged shut behind Detective Jesca Ashton, Edward knelt beside the toilet. The violent heaves brought tears. When the onslaught was over, he stood, looking for his toothbrush. No, he'd taken it into the house when he went to shave in the guest bath; the water pressure was better there. He turned on the creaky faucet, splashed his face and rinsed his mouth.

The bitter taste of bile remained while he dressed, while he exited the boathouse. Cate and Sara stood by the grill. The Perfect Offspring had disappeared inside. Bill was nowhere to be seen.

When he opened the passenger door, Detective Jesca Ashton informed him that it was customary for suspects to sit in the back seat. He could feel his sisters watching as the squad car started down the driveway.

The water from his swimming trunks was soaking through the khakis. Edward glanced at his lap. A dark, spreading stain, it looked as though he'd soiled himself.

Jes

In the back seat, Edward Friis was silent. And guilty as shit.

That final call from Amber Inglin's phone, to the foster-brother, had bothered her from the very beginning. This morning at the diner with Terence and gallons of coffee, she'd put it together: the twins had been home all evening. If Edward Friis had left Amber Inglin at the Wilburs' around nine, why would she have needed to call Connor Sorensen at 9:03? Friis had lied.

Terence had found semen in Friis's van.

Quick drive out to the Green Frogge to see if they could poke a hole in his alibi, they'd gotten there just before the lunch crowd.

The bartender remembered Edward Friis, "Wierdo. Sits by himself, stares at people." The first martini hadn't left the shaker til 11:30, she was absolutely sure—same time she'd served the first round to a bachelor party, priming the groom for the strip joint down the way.

Two and a half hours unaccounted for. Add that to the lie and he got a private party down at the precinct.

Jes glanced into the rearview mirror.

Maybe some of them *did* look the part: Edward Friis was a textbook perv. She'd even found birding glasses inside his worktable, along with the sleeping sister sketchbook. Swarowski binoculars; her father had had the same kind, worth nearly three thousand dollars.

Friis's little investment, so he could look long and hard before he bought. And, once it was all over, paint his pictures of young girls. Dead young girls—that girl on his easel hadn't been asleep. She'd been dead.

It was still hard to imagine him keeping his shakes under control long enough to swing an axe, but adrenaline could work wonders.

Or horrors.

Maybe Amber Inglin hadn't been his first, maybe there were others. The quiet ones were always the worst.

Taking him in without a warrant was a skate along the knife-edge of the Fourth Amendment, but once she had a confession protocol wouldn't matter. Consent searches weren't illegal: he'd consented, she'd searched. He could've stopped her at any time—say, when she'd pulled out the sketchbook, or the binoculars—had he but informed himself of his rights. Concerning which, by law, she was under no obligation to edify him unless he asked. Wrap this thing up and deliver it to Werner, D.W. standing by, looking dumb.

Jes glanced again at Friis. Handsome, tall, good teeth. But he repulsed her. Made her skin crawl. And that creepy space where he slept, with his *sister*. Like a cabin at a summer camp. Wierdly juvenile—bunk beds, a child's desk, flip-flops flung on the floor, beach towels on pegs.

Just having him in the car made her want a hot shower and strong soap. The weird thing was, he reminded her of her father. Not the early childhood father, the later one.

At the precinct Jes parked in the rear. Friis cowered in the back seat, looking like he'd just been slapped. "In there." She gestured toward a side entrance. "Walk in front of me, hands where I can see them."

His hair was dry now, corn-colored and streaked with gray. He must have combed it while he was in the bathroom doing whatever, puking. Edward Friis parted his hair in the middle, as had her father. Though in Thailand he'd begun parting it on the side. Eerily similar, Jes pushed the thought away.

The old interrogation room was windowless with a one-way mirror. More what she needed than the newly outfitted space at the opposite end of the hall. And more what Edward Friis deserved.

Jes watched Friis take in the metal table, the uncomfortable chair. "Sit down." He did. "I'll be back." Jes walked around to the one-way mirror. Where she could watch him.

He'd removed his glasses—silver wire, round lenses—and seemed to be looking for somewhere to place them, other than the stained surface of the table. Without the glasses, the resemblance to her father diminished.

Friis pushed his chair back—a hollow, scraping sound. Walked over to the glass, examining his face, now only inches from hers. Jes drew back in revulsion. A fleck of green, probably paint, on his right cheek. He licked a finger, scrubbed, then scratched with his fingernail, thin lips partially open. A net of fine lines fanned out from the corners of his cold blue eyes.

She'd take the evidence bags to the lab. And take her time about it, let Edward Friis stew a while.

Terence was alone in the lab. "Any sign of Werner?"

"In the deposit. He's with the M.E.—called her in on a *Sunday*. They're pretty worked up about this case."

"D.W. too?"

"Left a few minutes ago, some bee in his bonnet about the twins and drugs." Terence rolled his eyes. "One-track brain, that one."

Jes cast a sidelong glance at the stairway that led down to the deposit. She should probably brief Warner before she went back in to Friis. More to the point, she should've called him, and D.W., to tell them she was bringing Friis in. But she needed Friis on record, which could be stalled for hours if D.W. was allowed to muddy the water with his harebrained fixation on pills and needles. Fuck 'em, she told herself. Let's just get this done. Then they could thank her. "What else you got?"

"Tools are squeaky clean."

Not a surprise. She still had the condom in her pocket. She'd run it if the semen from Friis's van didn't stack up to anything found on the body. Which seemed about as likely as an August snowstorm coming up over Cayuga Lake. She wondered if Walsh had his car back yet, if he was pissed.

She'd apologize, in person. Soon as she had Friis in a prison-issue jumpsuit. Maybe a little celebratory drive-by repeat. She'd already busted her own protocol with Twice, so why not Thrice? But that was for later. "What about the fingernail scrapings?"

"Dirt. Bastard probably dragged her by her feet."

"Here's some more treasures for you." Jes deposited the plastic bags on the counter. "Process fast if you can, especially the briefs. I had Friis figured for a boxer man."

Terence snorted. "You're heartless."

"Yeah, but I'm good. By the way, I saw him in his Speedos earlier— he's *huge*."

"There's no justice in this world."

Jes removed the computer from its plastic envelope. "Full of nasty. Maybe set up a feed to my screen?"

"Right on." Terence opened the top, already tapping keys.

"I stuck him in Room A. If D.W. shows up do what you can to keep him away, okay?"

Terence dangled an aluminum evidence bag, pinkie curled. "Shiny-shiny, pretty-pretty. He's not hard to distract."

Laptop under her arm, Jes stopped at the drink machine. Anxiety produced drymouth—getting Edward Friis's DNA should be no problem at all. Check it against the semen from the van, the gobs of jizz that would undoubtedly be in Amber Inglin's rape kit. Lock it up, lock him down.

Her phone rang, Drew's number flashing on the screen. Jes turned it off. Next time she talked to *him* would be to announce she'd cracked the case.

She opened the door. Edward Friis looked up, eyes worried.

Jes placed the bottle on the table, unscrewed the top. "You must be thirsty."

"Oh, yes." He looked surprised, then ridiculously grateful. *Fool.* The tremor in his hand was worse now. While he drank, water ran down his chin onto his shirt.

As Jes opened her laptop, her mind produced an image of Edward Friis's hand, with its tremor, touching Amber Inglin's naked body. She fought back a grimace of disgust. "What puzzles me, Mr. Friis, is why you went to the trouble of amputating Miss Inglin's hand and then left it at the scene. Perhaps you could clarify that."

Friis choked, water splattered. "I never *touched* her." A fit of violent coughs, the bottle bounced to the floor.

Give him a few more minutes of marination. Jes retrieved the bottle. "I'll get you some more water." *And get this bottle to the lab.*

When she returned, Friis was polishing his glasses on the hem of his shirt. He appeared more composed. Time to rattle him, hard. "Too bad we don't live in Texas—I'd like to get you the chair. Or maybe you'd prefer lethal injection."

Edward Friis's face blanched. The left hand vibrating. "I did *not* kill her." His whiney voice grated her nerves. "I don't know what else to *say*." He wiped sweat from his forehead, even as he shivered with cold—on her way to the lab, Jes had set the air conditioning on high.

"We found semen in your van, *freak*." She banged the table with her open palm. Friis flinched. "I spared your family that one, but they'll hear *all* about it at trial." Edward Friis's mouth opened, spasming, a fish gasping for air. "Which did you do first, fuck her or kill her?" Jes pushed her face close to his, locked eyes. "Maybe you like them cold and compliant."

Edward Friis's whole body was shaking. "I…never…touched…her."

"Then how did the jizz get onto your van seat? What were you doing for *two fucking hours* before you went out for martinis?"

"After I left her I…drove to the lake and…masturbated. Then I fell asleep."

A brief, all-too-clear memory of Edward Friis in wet Speedos. "You know, you'd feel a lot better if you'd just admit what you did." She ran the bottle cap back and forth across the table, watching him flinch at the sound. "And if you're smart, you'll tell me *why*—any mitigating circumstances, better get them out in the open right now."

Edward Friis hunched forward, grasping the table with both hands. "I didn't hurt her." His voice broke. A deep breath that rattled into a sob.

"Just tell me."

He shook his head, eyes squeezed shut, tears sliding from the corners.

In the silence, Jes's computer beeped. The image feed began. Dozens, maybe hundreds, none older than fifteen or sixteen. Girls in pigtails, panties around their knees, squatting on toilets. Girls made up like whores, girls with no make-up. Air-brushed girls, girls with freckles and moles in tight focus.

Girls lying back, legs open, breasts in their own hands or in those of another girl. Frilly pink bedspreads. Fingers, hands, between legs.

"Mr. Friis, are you aware of the hundreds of pornographic images of underage girls on your sister's computer? I asume she didn't download them."

"I…" Edward Friis started, then clamped his lips together.

Jes let the silence go leaden, cold. The feed was still pushing images onto the screen. "Go on."

"I… perfect them."

"*Perfect* them?"

"Paint them, take away the filth, clean them up." He looked like he was trying to swallow.

"Have you ever attempted to contact any of the other young women you…*perfect*? In a chatroom, maybe? Or in the flesh?"

His voice rasped to a whisper. "It's just a fantasy…I would never actually do…anything." He leaned forward, as though begging her to understand. "You can't make adult women perfect."

Jes's gaze locked onto the computer screen. Amber Inglin's heavily made-up face stared out at her. Skimpy green bra, lots of cleavage. Straddled across a chair. Micro-short cut-offs, lacy edge of green panties.

Dozens more images of Amber, and others of a thin, dark-haired girl—where had she seen her before? "Mr. Friis." Jes imagined Edward Friis's face divided into squares and rectangles by the bars of a prison cell. "Perhaps you'd care to tell me what images of Amber Inglin are doing on here?"

"That's impossible." Edward Friis straightened his shoulders.

Jes turned the computer screen toward Friis. His skin went sallow beneath his summer tan. "Was cutting off Amber Inglin's hand part of her process of *perfection*?" No answer. Jes leaned back in her chair.

"I had no idea…"

"Sure you didn't." Jes shoved the confession form across the table with one hand, pulling handcuffs from her pocket with the other. "Edward Friis, you are under arrest for the rape and murder of Amber Inglin. You have the right to remain—" A knock. Terence, with the DNA results. Perfect timing.

The hall was dark after the flourescent glare. The figure at the door was too broad for Terence. "I need to talk to you," Werner said. "Now." His boneheaded nephew was behind him.

"I'm in the middle of making an arrest."

"Where the hell have you *been*, Jes?" She'd never seen Werner angry before. "Drew's been trying to reach you for hours. *Hours*." In the dark hallway she could see a smirk twisting the corners of D.W.'s mouth. "How long've you had that guy in there?"

"He's about to sign a confession."

"*What?* There is *no* convincing evidence linking him to this case." Hands on hips, Werner took up most of the hallway. He was hissing at her. "Connor and Megan Sorensen have *disappeared*. They could be guilty, have vital information, be in danger, or all three. But we have no way of knowing because *you*"—Werner was whisper-shouting now, his face inches from hers—"have lost your fucking *mind*!"

"He's got pictures of her on his computer, dozens of them! He lied about where he left her, and she's got his paint on her thigh. Not to mention the semen Terence found in his van—go back down there and run it against the DNA on the body. He should fry for this, but at least we can put him away for the rest of his wretched life." She waited for Werner's face to register comprehension, gratitude. Instead he shook his head.

"There is no semen—no DNA on her anywhere. And no vaginal trauma." Werner jerked his head in the direction of the closed door. "You can't hold him. *He didn't do it*."

"Tons of drugs in her system. MDA-laced ecstasy, MAOIs. Should've done the drug test first." Drew looked like he'd just won the state lottery. "She OD'd."

They were making no sense. "What about her hand? That didn't just *happen*."

"If you'd answer your goddamn phone, you'd know we think it was a lawnmower. Industrial one. Yard guy was at the Walsh place early yesterday." Werner exhaled hard.

"That's crazy. A lawnmower couldn't make that cut. And there'd be track marks."

"It's an attachment, for cutting fields. Pulls along behind the mower, no wheels. Drew drove to the guy's shop to check it out, while *you* were AWOL." Werner turned to his nephew. "You take a pic?"

Drew fiddled with his phone, stuck it back in his pocket. "Sent it to her, like three hours ago."

"Don't you check your email?" Werner's voice was a growl. "Go on, look. Better late than never."

A grin threatened to crack D.W.'s fat face wide open.

Jes pulled her phone from her pocket, scrolled through her inbox. "Yup. S'there." She flashed the image in Werner's direction; no way was she including D.W. "But that doesn't exculpate Friis from super-perv status. What are you planning to do about *him*?"

Jes could smell the stale coffee on Werner's breath as he got right in her face, "We have to let him go."

Disbelief made her head light, a strange balloon, hovering above her shoulders. "He's a scumbag, lower than low. He's got enough adolescent porn on that computer to paper a house. We can put him away for years on that!"

Drew shifted on his feet, eyes on his shiny shoes. Wonder what Terence could find on *his* computer?

"No, Jes," Werner was measuring his words, as though speaking to an idiot. "We can't. You got them without a warrant."

"It was a consent search!"

"Wouldn't stand up in court. And they're downloads. He's not distributing, just consuming. Legal gray area. First-year law student'd get those pics thrown out, you'd never even get him to trial." Jes could feel it coming—D.W. had wanted her gone since her first day on the job. Werner had resisted, but now the door was wide open. She pretended to fiddle with her email, slipping her phone into "record" mode. She wasn't going down easy.

"You fucked this up royally." Werner crossed his arms over his chest, gestured with his big head toward Edward Friss, shivering behind the closed door. "We'll be lucky if he doesn't slap a lawsuit on us. I've looked the other way on a whole lot of shit with you because you're good. Hot-headed but good. But this time you crossed the line. You're done. You're fired."

"You can't just do that." Jes thrust her chin out.

"Fight it if you want to." Werner shrugged. "I can definitely suspend you—indefinitely." Not true. Two-week limit barring exceptions from internal affairs. But the recording was the rope: let him hang himself, garnish with gender bias. She'd have him in a legal straitjacket in no time. "Leave your gun and badge on my desk."

"Yup." Jes watched Werner open the door to the interrogation room. Drew followed, muttering as he brushed past her, "See you around, College." The door clicked shut behind them.

She could also get him investigated for negligence: a computer full of underage porn and the fucking creep was going to walk?

Of course investigating Werner wouldn't solve the problem of Edward Friis: maybe he hadn't done it this time, but who was to say he wouldn't do something next week? Or next month? Porn was where they all got their start—Criminal Psych 101, first day of class. And when they consumed it in quantity, and escalated to embellishing (or, in Edward Friis's terms, 'cleaning it up'—Jes felt like spitting), look out. No one was even going to monitor the freak?

On her way to the lobby she dropped the badge onto Werner's messy desk, shoving it under a spilling stack of papers. Let him look for it. And he wasn't getting her gun. She jammed the revolver into her holster. Let him come after it. He'd never dare.

Outside the haze had gone. The LED on the bank clock registered 92 degrees.

"Just consuming," Werner had said. They could have prosecuted, or at least tried. Was it money? Every day was *Sophie's Choice* around the precinct—paperclips or tape, you couldn't have both.

Or maybe Werner thought 'just consuming' was okay.

Jes stared down at her phone, ripping through the missed calls. Three from her mother, last night. She rolled her eyes. Then came the boys. Drew. Werner, twice.

Liam Walsh. The *about-last-night-that-can't-happen-again-I'm-married* call, no doubt. Delete.

Werner again, then Drew. Then Werner, twenty minutes ago.

She stumbled, nearly fell. Managed to keep the phone in her hand, taking a cudgel-blow to the shin. It happened—walk around around staring at your phone, you ran into benches.

Doubled over, she cursed as she massaged her leg. No money to go after likely sex offenders, but plenty for benches no one ever sat on. And hardware to bolt them to the ground so no one would steal them. Her tax dollars at work.

By this time tomorow, Edward Friis would be wanking away (or worse) somewhere, Drew would have a commendation for taking a picture of a lawn-mower, and she'd have an internal affairs investigator up her ass.

Far worse, more girls like Amber Inglin would slip through the cracks, and it would be no one's fault.

Liam

Cicadas hummed over the clipping shears. The men piled the ruined canopies at the bottom of the hill. Even if a breeze came up, the spores wouldn't make it far—small comfort.

Puffing back up the steep incline with an empty wheelbarrow, Frank called to him, "How do you want us to burn them?"

"Use a couple of the metal drums from the garage. The men can take turns. Shady down there, it'll be a break from the heat."

Hotter than yesterday, but not enough to guarantee the death of the gray rot—for that, you needed upwards of 93 degrees, several hours straight, several days on end. And the humidity was making things worse.

Liam closed and opened the fingers of his right hand. The bloody blisters across his palm were hardening into scabs.

Frank was beside him, "Nasty."

"That's what pruning for four hours with no gloves'll get you."

A pair of grackles circled overhead, sounding rusty-hinge caws. Waldo straightened from the bales of netting and stood still, face upturned.

Frank shook his head. "Jesus, there he goes with the damn birds again."

Sweat made dark circles on Waldo's T-shirt, under his powerful arms, across his wide shoulders. Big hands, callouses so thick he didn't need gloves.

Liam froze. Those hands could have killed the girl, without much effort at all, maybe even without meaning to. Or in answer to instructions transmitted by some troubled part of his brain—Waldo had protested once about the way his meds made him feel, and Liam had allowed the prescription to lapse. Nature would be Waldo's medication, he'd decided—like he was qualified.

What had Waldo done?

Worse, what had *he* done with his good intentions?

Waldo had eyes only for the birds. Two more perched on the fence bordering the Riesling, beady-eyed, chests puffed out, wings glistening purple in the climbing sun.

The feathers.

He should call Jesca Ashton. What had happened last night didn't matter, what she'd done with his tools and his gloves and his car didn't matter. The tools she should have taken were lying in the grass at the edge of the field. And she wouldn't know that unless he told her.

"Lining up for lunch." Frank was talking about the birds. "They can smell the sugar from a mile away."

Glints flashed from the streamers of silver tape, ends limp in the still air, ineffective bird repellent. Like the yellow balloons, black and white triangles arranged at the center to represent a hawk's open maw, useless.

"We could shoot 'em."

Waldo stood erect, staring toward the trees, mouth open. Liam gestured with his head. "Not with him around. He'd lose it."

"Crazy motherfucker," Frank murmured.

He had to call Jesca Ashton, fast. "Let's not make him any crazier. I'll call around and check on propane cannons, only thing the birds respect." *Act normal.* Liam ran a hand across the canopy nearest him. Still wet with dew. "Once you get the fires going, get a couple of the guys and bring the frost-fans out. We have to lower the moisture level."

"On it."

In the office it was hot, close. Clothes piled on the floor, the sofa bed unmade. He called and got Detective Jesca Ashton's voice mail—a little jab in his stomach at the sound of her voice. He didn't want to but he thought about sex. With her.

Even *now*? What was wrong with him? He turned his back on the rumpled bed. "It's Liam Walsh. I think one of my men was involved in what happened to the girl. I can help you with him, he trusts me. Call me."

It was too awful to think about. Move forward, he told himself. One disaster at a time.

Five calls and no one in the area had cannons. Internet to the rescue. The auto-type in the search engine helpfully offered 'poplar.' Poplar Lane. Where Detective Jesca Ashton had told him she lived. He put the "r" back into 'propane'—he was a terrible typist.

Detective Jesca Ashton had no online presence, none at all. He knew this from the thousand other times he'd Googled her, but he'd checked again anyway, night before last. The night the girl died. While Basia was at a dinner that probably should have included him too.

He'd have had to show Jesca Ashton his searches if she'd pushed him for a better alibi (his was crap and they both knew it).

What would he have said? He couldn't even explain it to himself.

And it could look like stalking, to her. Maybe it was, or at least the internet kind. Was he a stalker?

Then a sudden image of Basia—his stomach took a dive, not the good kind—innocently sitting down at his computer, as she'd done sometimes, before he'd started keeping it mostly at Vestri—when, exactly, had he started doing that?—to search. Anything beginning with the letters J or A—he'd never learned to clear a search history and make it stick—and his goose was cooked. Burned, more like.

Focus on the goddamned cannons, he told himself. Plenty of problems right here in front of you.

Bye-Bye Birdie, based in Sarasota, carried the big propane guns. Liam bought three, paid extra for overnight shipping. In less than ten minutes he'd hemorrhaged two thousand dollars, spending money he didn't have, wouldn't recoup, not this year.

Basia would have given him money, had he asked. She'd paid for the house with a single check. But not asking Basia for money was a personal, private rule. Instead he'd taken out a loan, now long spent.

"Where were you last night?" Basia leaned against the door frame, cool in ivory silk. Like he'd conjured her. Impeccably dressed, but casual, like she'd just happened to grab the perfect thing off the back of a chair. He'd always loved that about her. His heart thudded dully. "I... here. Sorry. I should have called." How had he *forgotten*? "We've got gray rot. Bad—I was up all night, cutting my vines to bits. Not to mention my goddamn hands." He held them up. "Could lose the whole field of Riesling."

"Oh. That's not good. But if you were here, then why was your car in the parking lot across from the police station this morning?" What had Basia been doing near the police station?

"Couldn't be." The lie came easier than he'd have thought. The hangover helped, the tinny, tight alertness. "Ton of hybrids around now."

"That's what I thought, until I looked inside. Phone mount, thermos. Jacket. All yours."

"Oh...*right*!" Liam moved the mouse, making random clicks: attentive, but not worried enough about this conversation to stop working. "What with all hell breaking loose around here..." Not entirely a lie. "I loaned it to a friend." Entirely a lie, any way you cut it. "Frank took me in to get it, couple of hours ago."

Basia cocked her head, chin jutting forward, her "this-makes-no-sense" face. The puzzlement might be genuine or it might be for dramatic effect—he'd seen both—but either way, this wasn't headed anywhere good. Redirect, said his tired brain, distract. "Had to get everyone back out

177

here on a Sunday, it's been crazy..." He heard the lameness in his voice.

"Let's see..." Basia's eyes narrowed. Definitely dramatic effect, and she was annoyed. Liam felt himself shrink in his chair. His wife tapped her nose with one perfectly manicured finger. Pensive. Or—much worse—mock-pensive. "You were here, the car was in town, ergo you... loaned it to someone who'd come out here with you, yes?"

Liam's shoulders tensed. His wife's devastating logic, delivered in velvet tones—he'd enjoyed watching lawyer colleagues engage her in conversation across annual-benefit dinner tables, waiting for the moment when the colleague's posture would straighten, his expression sharpen.

"You know, Liam, in twenty-six years of marriage, I don't think there's been a single night when I didn't know where you were. When you didn't call. So something truly out of the ordinary must have happened last night." Maybe she should have been the lawyer. "Who came here with you?"

"No one." Bad move, the tired brain said. But it was out, so go with it. "Neighbor had an emergency. Guy that owns the next vineyard over, Ralph..." Was his name even Ralph?

"Liam—" Basia sighed. She looked as though she'd slept as badly as he had. And about as much. She inclined her head and massaged her temples for a moment. Thumb, middle finger, ring-finger. Her wedding ring gleamed. Then she stopped. "What's that?"

Liam forced his eyes to follow his wife's pointing finger to a spot of color in the sofa bed. Deep purple of a ripe plum. Shiny fabric, crumpled among the sheets.

"It looks like a scarf." Basia's tone was conversational, as though she were telling him what she'd had for brunch. Brunch. Her favorite Sunday brunch restaurant was on the same street as the police station, right next door to the convenience store parking lot. Fucking *Sunday brunch*. What a stupid word, what a stupid concept.

He remembered untwining the scarf from Detective Jesca Ashton's neck—the jab pricked at him, below the belt—and sinking his teeth in deep. The taste of salt, of dried sweat. He'd never tasted his wife's sweat: a strange thought, but something he knew, suddenly, to be true. If he didn't pick the scarf up, Basia would. He reached down.

"I think it belonged to the girl." Maybe he could save this. "She worked up here sometimes, on the computer. This place is a wreck."

"May I see it?"

Liam surrendered the scarf.

"It's silk." Basia fingered the fabric, assessing. "I've seen it before. That detective—Jesca Ashton, isn't it?—was wearing it, last night at my opening. And apparently here as well."

"Lots of scarves like that."

"I notice clothes, Liam. This is a very distinctive color. The woven bird patterning is unique." Basia scrutinized the hem, a label maybe. "Made in Thailand." She looked up. "The detective was wearing this scarf." His wife's clear hazel eyes held his. "And then not wearing it. Here." Her voice was soft.

"Okay, yes, she was here." Liam looked down at his hand, which still moved the mouse. Uselessly. He stopped. "We were talking...about the girl, she wanted more information." He'd hit rock bottom.

"Honey, the scarf was tangled in the *sheets*. Just tell me what happened."

"I... okay. I messed up. Bad." Liam fingered the tape on his hand while his stomach plummeted down a cliff. "This whole thing with the girl, with Amber, it's hit me really hard. I wasn't...thinking straight." The room was too hot. He stopped, drew a breath. "It's never happened before." What was one more lie, in the scheme of things? "And it won't happen again, I swear. It didn't mean anything."

Basia still held the scarf. After what felt like days, she spoke. Still that soft, loving voice. "Well. These things happen. I guess I'd always thought not to us, but why not? Us too." She shrugged, then inclined her head, as though accepting a weight onto her shoulders. "It's...been a tough couple of days. We've been married for a long time. We'll get through it."

Liam nodded, slowly, relief flooding through him.

"I was thinking..." Basia's fingers still plucked at the purple fringe. "What if we went back to Manhattan? A new start. We were so happy there." She looked up, her eyes bright. "You don't have your job anymore, Cassie's there, we could see her more. And I think I could make the gallery work, probably better than here. Should we do it?"

This was the reduced sentence, the plea deal. He'd copped to the crime and she was making him pay, but not with his life. Or only with part of it. Liam felt as though something was being tugged from deep inside his chest, the roots resisting. Hurting.

She must have taken his silence for agreement.

"The house is worth a ton, we'll make a bundle, plenty to buy a nice place there." She was talking rapidly now, her features animated. Basia loved planning—weddings, graduations. Openings. Moves.

"What about the vineyard?" His throat felt dry.

"Well, I guess you'd have to take care of the problem first—fungus, is it, or mold?—and then you could sell it. You'd likely make a bundle there, too. You've worked so hard on it."

Liam swallowed. "Actually, maybe we could live here...at Vestri. That would be a new start."

Did he want that?

What he *wanted* was not to sell Vestri. Not to leave it. If you had a flawed client—he was representing himself here, and he was deeply flawed—you got what you could while the deal was on the table. Any lawyer knew that. "It's not that far in to the gallery, and we could fix up the house, add on, whatever you want."

"Uptown, definitely," Basia was saying, "East Side or West?" He'd never known whether talking past what she didn't want to hear was a deliberate tactic of Basia's. If it was, it had often served her well.

"I'm not sure what I'd do there. I'd need some time to think about it, okay?" And maybe with a little time, he could get her to change her mind.

"Well, you wouldn't *have* to do anything." Translation: she wanted to move ASAP. And she wasn't going to change her mind.

"I don't like doing nothing." Which wasn't what he'd been planning to say. It was like listening to someone else talk, wondering what would drop next from the guy's mouth.

"Your old firm would take you back, they said the door was always open. And now Cassie's there...that would be nice, wouldn't it?"

"I don't want to sell Vestri, Basia." A step away from the generous deal on the table. The guilty ones always tried to negotiate, even when they didn't have a leg to stand on.

Basia was folding the scarf into triangles now: lining the tips up perfectly, folding, then lining them up again. Smaller triangles, and smaller still, as though to tidy it up and make it disappear. "I've actually thought about that, too. I know you like having the kids work here, like helping them. If you sold the vineyard, you could use the money to found something in Manhattan, or the Bronx or Brooklyn. Lots of kids need help there."

"I've already founded something." His voice came out tight, almost choked. "And lots of kids need help *here*."

"Or you could have Frank run it for you, couldn't you? And you could come up, or we could...weekends, that sort of thing." We. She was trying, but the 'you' had slipped out and he'd heard it.

"I like being here, not just on the weekends. I like working here... *making* something, creating something." A little frown corrugated Basia's forehead. A look of pained concentration on her face. Liam steeled himself. "I don't want to sell Vestri. And I don't want to be a weekend vintner." Suddenly, unbidden, the image of Detective Jesca Ashton, barefoot in the grass, a little drunk. Before he'd followed her into the vines. "It smells good here. Haven't you ever noticed how great it smells out here?"

He knew for a fact she hadn't. She'd never stayed for more than an hour. Of course she didn't want to live here. No A.C. Jumble of random furniture. Dust in her hair, dirt under her fingernails: not her thing. Never had been. He'd changed, not her. And now she wanted him to change back. A perfectly human, perfectly reasonable desire.

But one that he, unreasonable, unworthy human that he was, could not grant.

This was the hushed, tense moment just before the plea deal was whisked off the table. The last nanosecond when he could still turn it around, say the right thing, nod and do what she wanted.

He didn't.

The shine in his wife's eyes came from tears now. He had to look away. "Liam, do you want to know what I think?" He made a noncommittal gesture with his head—yes, no, both, neither. She pressed on, her voice thin and brave. "I think you'd had sex with her before last night."

Like a punch to the gut. The floor beneath his feet slid away, suspending him. But no more lies, what would be the point? "Once."

"Then this isn't what I thought it was, and I don't know how to fix it."

"But it didn't—" He stopped himself. It *had* meant something.

Basia drew a shaky breath, she was trying hard not to cry. "I know you love me, Liam, and I don't think you've changed in how you feel about me, but something has changed here. Something must be profoundly missing from what we have in order for this to happen. You may not want to look that in the face right now, but you have to, because this is what you did: you had sex with another woman, and then you did it again, and when I asked you about it, you lied. Happily married people don't do that."

A bird was singing somewhere. Not a grackle. His sigh was long, from somewhere deep, all the air he'd been holding prisoner in his lungs.

"I'm so, so sorry." And he was.

The computer hummed, the men's voices floated in through the open window, Frank's laugh on top.

"I think maybe we should separate for bit." Basia was suddenly crisp, businesslike. Not unkind. "You can stay out here for a while. Sounds as though you need to anyway." 'For a bit' was Basia-speak for 'indefinitcly.' You didn't live with someone for a quarter of a century without cracking the code. He should stand, shout, wave his arms. Do something. But he didn't.

Basia stepped into the hallway. "I have dinner plans tonight. You could go by the house and pick up some things. Perhaps you'd like some clean sheets."

Liam rose, letting the little dig about the sheets slide. She had every right.

"Please don't. Don't follow me." Her voice was oddly pleasant — still that crispness, but beneath it, something achingly kind. "I think I'd rather not see you right now."

She turned, disappearing from the door frame. The girl of his dreams, a perfect match to each characteristic on the lengthy list he'd compiled during his first year in law school. The ideal woman for the ideal life. She even liked Bartok. Though he'd discovered, with the passing years, that he himself didn't care for Bartok as much as he felt he should. Lately he found himself preferring Bach's sweetest moments.

And the Dixie Chicks. He hid the CDs he didn't want Basia to see in the console beneath the armrest in his car.

Her heels clicked down the back stairs — measured steps, not running. Basia had always known how to stage an exit. And when. Parties, restaurants. Dinners with his law partners and their wives, Christmas and Easter at her sister's. Wakes. Wedding receptions. The girl of his dreams was leaving, and he sat still, letting her go.

He heard the screen door opening. Clicking gently shut. The faint scent of lemon verbena lingered.

Liam approached the window. Some of the men pruned. The others, along with Frank, were maneuvering the second fan between rows of Riesling vines. The third was at the edge of the field, blades a blur, stirring up a twister of dead leaves. Basia walked hurriedly, hair whipping her cheeks, one arm shielding her eyes from the dust. Beside her car she stopped short, looking down at the neatly folded scarf in her hand.

With a precise, contained motion of wrist and fingers—the gesture nonetheless sharp with frustration, he'd learned to read those too—she dropped it to the ground. She got into her car, closing the door firmly. Not slamming, Basia would never slam. But the Peugeot backed out fast, narrowly missing the base of the whirring fan. Tires grinding gravel, flash of bright fabric beneath the wheels.

The car sent the grackles shrieking up from their perches, past the window where he stood, wings snapping like flags in a harsh wind.

And then there was quiet. In the center of the driveway, the scarf was a flattened purple puddle. The men's voices still reached him, the whisper of the frost fans, high and hissing, but what he noticed was an absence of sound.

Waldo straightened, head cocked. Then he ran.

Liam didn't see the birds until Waldo began to pick them up, dull brown instead of iridescent black, maybe grackle young, not strong enough to resist the powerful pull of the fan.

Lips moving, Waldo harvested, big hands gently scooping the small bodies from the grass, examining them. In his big palm one still twitched. With a sure, fluid motion, Waldo broke its neck. Then stroked its breast, lips still moving as if in prayer.

Waldo arranged the dead birds in a circle on the grass. He retrieved the scarf from the gravel and draped them with the mangled purple fabric. Whatever he'd done to the girl, he surely hadn't meant to kill her. But he needed to be in custody, and Jesca Ashton still wasn't calling. Liam didn't feel capable of dialing her number again, not now. He'd watch Waldo, be ready for when she did.

Liam rubbed a hand across his tired face. Some men kept long-term mistresses. Raised parallel families, lived parallel lives; decades of adultery, their wives never the wiser. He'd never wanted to have an affair. He hadn't even wanted to cheat.

But he had, and then he'd done it again. With Detective Jesca Ashton. Yes. And he wanted to do it again.

He sighed.

He was an asshole. An asshole who screwed around. Who took his wife to hear string quartets and then listened to country and bluegrass and vintage rock on the sly. Who ditched important dinners one day and hit the Burger King drive-thru the next—French fries, extra-large, the greasier the better. On the way out to the vineyard that he, in his heart of hearts, didn't want to share with his wife.

He didn't want to live in Manhattan.

It seemed unfair—even absurd—that, until a particular series of papers were drawn up and filed, Basia would still, as far as the law was concerned, have to remain married to him.

The law, at times, could be an idiot.

Among the Riesling vines beneath the window the men were working hard, against the clock and the odds.

Basia had every legal right to take whatever was left of Vestri after the grey rot and the grackles were done with it—adultery gave her all the rope she needed to hang him out to dry.

But she wouldn't. He knew his wife.

His soon-to-be ex-wife.

Basia did everything with taste and class.

Even divorce.

Connor

Connor dropped quarters into the change slot, six for him, six for Megan. Cash for everything—their bus passes might be traceable. Connor kept his face averted, hiding behind his hair.

The driver's seat had a star-shaped hole, stained yellow stuffing. He'd been on this exact same bus yesterday. The driver slouched, snake tattooes coiling his biceps, DroneZone undulating from the radio.

Today it was an Indian dude. This guy sat up straight, didn't smoke, didn't listen to music. Said hi to people when they got on. Saw everything. Saw Megan, all spacey and weird. Connor wished for Snake Man—he was totally checked out.

He took a window seat, letting the pack slide from his shoulders. His back was drenched. His legs ached, lungs still raw from the run. Fingers into his pocket, to check for the lady cop's card. He'd made sure it landed in his hand instead of his sister's.

The bus wasn't going anywhere til everyone sat down. Megan moved slowly down the aisle, touching each seat as she passed it, like she was blind.

Megan was fast when she wanted to be. At school, she won all the races, even beat guys. In the woods she'd left him far behind, fighting through grass high as his knees, her white T-Shirt blinking back at him through the trees. He'd called her and she stopped for a second, not letting him catch up. That was after the cop had showed up again, asked more questions. Said he'd be back. Time to get the hell out of Dodge.

Megan passed his seat, fingers groping. "Where're you going?" Connor whispered.

"I thought we weren't supposed to sit together." Megan answered in her new adult voice, like she didn't care who heard.

"That's *after* Syracuse! There's no one on here, and anyway the driver already saw us. It'd look weird if we didn't sit together."

Megan sat down, not looking at him.

In the woods it was like she was running away from him. If he'd missed the bus, would she even have waited? She had the California Fund. He'd be fucked.

Connor placed his backpack on the dirty floor beside Megan's. Hardly any room for his feet. The bus smelled like cigarettes and old newspaper. He was hungry. For the last three days, they'd had nothing to eat but mushy casseroles made by Jesus freaks. Served on paper plates—no more dishes would fit in the sink.

Definitely time to go.

Connor had never been anywhere. He wanted to see the Grand Canyon, the Pacific Ocean "Hey, Meg, they have a campground in Grand Canyon National Park. We can get a tent. Take pictures of people and sell them. There's a gazillion tourists there."

"This isn't a family vacation." Megan spoke in the new voice, nudging his backpack to make more room for her feet. She looked out the opposite window, faking interest, Connor thought, in the car dealerships and ugly houses she'd seen a hundred times. "You sure Reef's home?"

"He knows we're coming." A spasm of coughs grabbed his throat. Bong hits and running like hell through the woods, bad combination. When he could talk again, he added, "Reef's apartment's huge. And I told you, he has *air-conditioning*."

Megan's voice was flat. "He better be there."

His sister didn't know Reef like he did. She only saw him at raves, when he was high. But Reef knew everything. "He's cool, Meg. Bet he knows all kinds of people in L.A."

"You brought too much shit. Your bag's too heavy, that's why you can't run."

"It's my photography stuff, dip shit." She knew what was in his bag, she'd watched him pack it. "Gonna make us rich!"

Megan ran her fingers over her tattoo. "If we get caught, it'll be your fault."

These days everything was his fault. He hadn't meant for anything bad to happen, he'd just been trying to make them some money. For California. For getting them away from another awful place.

At the bus stop, Reef was sitting in his truck, music thumping. "I need food, man."

"Sure, dude." Keep it casual. Megan hadn't even said hi, not helping with the casual.

"Mickey Dee's," Reef said, gunning the motor. "The cashier's smoking."

At the drive-through, Connor paid: hamburgers, french-fries, and a vanilla milkshake for Megan—he didn't want Reef thinking they owed him anything.

Back at Reef's they ate in the living room. Megan sipped her shake, looking at no one and nothing. The smell of soil and pot, somehow clean and nice, mixed with the greasy tang of fried food. Connor put the phone on the coffee table, where he could see it.

Megan barely touched her food. When they finished, Reef took out a bag of weed. "Are you gonna tell me what you *did*? It's gotta be pretty bad." He licked the rolling paper.

"We stole a bunch of stuff. And then we sold it." Connor grinned, "How else could I afford to take you to McDonald's?"

"Bad-ass, dude." Reef put a fist up and Connor bumped it.

Megan let her head sag back against the futon, eyes closed.

Reef fired up the joint and worked on it. Those were the rules at Reef's: he smoked first, as much as he wanted. "What're you gonna do with all that cash?"

"Move to L.A." Connor tried to sound casual. Now was when Reef could help them with his connections. Megan would see.

"Suh-*weeeeeeet*." Reef took a deep toke. He could hold more smoke than anyone Connor had ever seen. "Once you get set up, you can hook me up—California'd be *amazing*."

Connor held in his disgust. Why was everybody so useless?

"Great, Conn." Megan spoke to the ceiling. "Now what do we do?"

"It's all good." Connor shot a look of warning at Megan, who wasn't looking.

"Hey, where's the hot chick?" Reef passed the joint to Megan, smoke rolling out in blue plumes between his gray teeth. "I was gonna let her sleep with me." When Reef smiled he looked like a dog.

"At some stupid theater camp," Connor said. "She'll come out and meet us later." The lie sounded lame. Megan took a second hit, deep like she was going for wasted.

"She's welcome here!" Reef's tongue slid over his mean dog teeth. "*Any* time."

Megan got to her feet. "I'm tired. Could I lie down somewhere?"

"No problem." Reef stood, all gallant and sexy, "You can crash in my bed. It's dark back there."

Connor waited, tense and stoned, till Reef returned, jingling his motel keys on a big ring. "I gotta work all the way through till morning. Manager's down at the Jersey shore. You get the place to yourselves."

Reef laid a key from the ring on the table. "There's a pizza place over in the mall, or Denny's. Don't let the party get too wild." His eyes were high, happy slits. "Lock up if you go out. Hundreds of dollars under those grow lights. See you tomorrow."

Connor flipped through the channels on Reef's TV—pay-per-view porn came up in the favorites. Wrong kind for him; Connor passed. The air conditioner hummed. He could smell his own sweat, even through the weed. He needed a shower.

Reef's shampoo was in little bottles, and the soap smelled like all the motels they'd stayed in when their mother was hiding from their father. Connor stood beneath the pulsing shower head until the entire bathroom was filled with steam. At the foster home, any shower longer than three minutes was forbidden—Tom had rigged up some stupid contraption that shut the water off, just in case. If you had soap on you, or shampoo in your hair, tough shit, next time you'd be faster. But here there were gallons and gallons of hot water. He thought about the wide boulevards of L.A., lined with palm trees and famous people. In L.A. he'd find them a place with a good shower.

The towels were stiff and rough, but clean-smelling—Darla's smelled like mold—with a Super-8 logo on the edge.

Connor used Reef's deodorant and hair gel. He felt like someone else. In L.A. he'd *be* someone else.

In the living room, the hypnotic rhythm of Sak Noel—Reef's iPod—guided his movements as he pulled on his sweat-smelling clothes. In L.A. he'd buy new ones. Zipping his jeans, he remembered the lady cop's card in his pocket. He'd burn it. Connor reached for the lighter.

But the card wasn't in his pocket. Or on the floor, or under the sofa, or between the cushions.

And the phone was gone.

The door to Reef's room was shut. But she could've opened it, walked across the living room. Taken the card from his pocket, the phone from the table. Called from inside the bedroom.

He'd fucked up.

Megan liked things to be right and fair and even. She got upset about animals in shelters and global warming, about people cheating other people out of things and not playing by the rules. She'd hated making the pictures.

If she hadn't called yet, she would. They wouldn't send Megan to jail. They'd send him.

And he wasn't going.

Megan's backpack was leaned against the wall next to his. Connor ran his hand along the side until he felt the bulging pocket. The zipper opened easily.

No one could stop him. He'd change his route, go through Chicago.

He'd make it to L.A. And when he did, he'd trust no one.

Not even his own sister. Trust was over.

Waldo

Even before taking the bird in his hand, he knew. Suffering. Her suffering hurt his heart. A twist of her neck and her heart stopped. She'd come and gone again. Amber ring round her soft brown eye, open, but not looking. On her way. The changing over continued.

Prayer spoken. Brown-gold feather safe in his pocket.

Vigil begun again, for when he'd see her next.

❧

II

Beatrice

Closing the oven door with her knee, Beatrice clattered the broiling pan onto the cooling rack. The Cornish hens had browned beautifully! On the stove top, greenbeans, blanched to perfection and glistening under a tarragon glaze. Charles's favorite way. And Jes's; she'd loved whatever her father loved. She *must* come. Of course she would, and it would be perfect.

Beatrice popped open a bottle of Pinot Noir and poured herself a glass—a toast, to new beginnings! She took a long swallow. Full-bodied with some fruity notes, yet light enough to be palatable in the heat. Lovely! She examined the bottle: Vestri Vineyards, wasn't that the place Liam Walsh had bought?

Beatrice sipped, happily anticipating. Outside the window was the new gazebo, such a whimsical touch to the back yard—a true inspiration, so picturesque! They'd have drinks out there before dinner, *al fresco*, Jes would be surprised.

Her first conversation with her husband-to-be had taken place in a gazebo. An *English* gazebo, in Kew gardens, just south of London. At first she'd thought the tall, gangly young man a purse-snatcher, she'd been frightened nearly to death. But he'd just been trying to photograph a sparrow. A rare species, as he'd explained later over tea and sandwiches, with a stutter he'd worked charmingly to control. She'd tell Jes the story tonight, they could have a laugh together!

This wine was good; she regarded the empty glass. Onward, silverware, two dinner plates—her wedding china, tonight was a special occasion!—and a festive green bowl for fruit. Nothing too overripe, Jes detested mushiness. A perfect summer dinner, light, casual, effortless. Beatrice arranged peaches and plums into an off-center pyramid, sprinkling cherries over the top. The look pleased her—colorful, insouciant. By dessert time, she and Jes would be companionably discussing the essay.

She wiped her hands on her apron. It must be getting on for seven and she'd run out of tasks. Beatrice allowed herself a glance at the clock. 7:23. Jes was nothing if not punctual. She'd forgotten. Sighing, Beatrice reached for her phone.

"Mom?" Jes sounded disoriented.

"Honey, I thought we'd agreed on dinner tonight, at seven. Did y ou forget?"

Beatrice could hear crackling. It sounded like cellophane paper.

Beatrice elected not to comment on the occasional cigarette in which she knew her daughter indulged. Jes usually made efforts to dissimulate. But not tonight: she heard the tell-tale click of the lighter.

"Dinner?"

"We made a plan, yesterday. You said today." Beatrice left out the "maybe."

"Oh, right." Jes expelled a long breath, and likely a lungful of smoke. "It's been a…complicated day."

"You can tell me all about it when you get here!"

"Tonight's bad. I need to sleep."

"Well, you have to eat," Beatrice aimed for cheerful, bustling efficiency. "I've got everything ready. Even chanterelles, your favorite!"

Charles had introduced Jes to chanterelles before she could even read. Jes would eat anything her father offered her: foie gras, brussels sprouts, escargot even.

Jes certainly didn't have any food in the fridge. Now she only ate take-out.

"Okay, whatever." Another exhalation, she was definitely smoking. "But I need to take a shower first."

They'd eat late. Fashionably late.

Beatrice tried to feel appeased, expectant even. But Jes forgot their plans as often as she remembered them. And she'd sounded so drained. Maybe it wasn't the investigation. Maybe she was having problems with one of her *hook-ups*. Well, that's what you got if you couldn't control your libido.

Passion was strange, to Beatrice, foreign. She was nearly certain she'd never experienced it. Passion must be what drove her daughter to bars, so she could *hook up*. Passion for *sex*. Beatrice felt her lips curl into a grimace of distaste.

For several years into their marriage Charles had continued to offer sex, as one would tea or coffee and a plate of biscuits. Beatrice, not wishing to appear rude, occasionally accepted. There were bursts of experimentation: postures and, once or twice, props, all initiated by Charles. Beatrice had finally protested—it was all so unseemly, she'd felt, for a woman of her age and proportions—and he had politely desisted.

Greater efforts to preserve marital intimacy might have been made, of course, but, in their defense, she and Charles had never quarreled.

And they'd had Jes.

Beatrice poured herself a second glass of wine. A fly buzzed above the cooling chanterelles. She shooed it. It was almost dark. Better to scrap cocktails in the gazebo, too many bugs. And the mint was too wilted for juleps. Another day, after the heat broke. She placed the wine—the bottle was half-empty, how had that happened?—and a basket of bread on a tray and carried it, Geneva following, into the study.

A sudden commotion beyond the window—Beatrice startled. A pinwheel of birds, scattering from the feeders closest to the house. Beatrice still filled them, even in bountiful summer, a small thing she could do for Charles. Jes had tended them while he was alive, but when he died, she'd simply stopped .

Charles's death had changed Jes completely. She'd decided to pursue a Master's in criminology, of all things, after completing an honors thesis on women dramaturges of the seventeenth century—Beatrice had been at a loss for words. Her daughter had become silent, withdrawn. At times, surly.

Even the weekend of the memorial, amid the accolades for her father's work, the encomiums from eminent ornithologists, flying in from the far corners of the earth to pay their respects. The tearful embraces from his students and colleagues, and Jes silent as a stone.

And she wouldn't even hear of a trip to Thailand with her mother to scatter her father's ashes at the bird sanctuary he'd founded. Beatrice had had to cancel the tickets she'd bought. Charles would have been so pleased, but each time she'd brought up the idea, Jes had shut her down with that hard, cold stare of hers.

In the end, Beatrice had scattered the ashes herself a few weeks after the memorial, late one night at the ornithology lab, a quiet garden beneath Charles's old office window. Which had likely been illegal, but she had to do something with them, they shouldn't just sit around the study in a box.

Well, all that was in the past. Tonight's dinner was the turning over of a new leaf! On a sudden inspiration, Beatrice opened the box she'd packed earlier, containing the Thailand paintings. The university certainly didn't need all of these. She'd display them all along the couch here, and how delightful, when Jes arrived, she'd feel as though she'd stepped into a tropical rainforest.

Beatrice hummed as she worked—something Elizabethan to which she almost remembered the words.

"Mom, what are you doing?"

Jes stood in the doorway, holding a round of goat cheese, her offering for the dinner. She was in cutoffs and her hair was wet, her feet bare—there was a nasty bruise on the right one, what had she gotten herself into now? She looked just as she had at fifteen.

Her daughter was finally here! Beatrice contained an urge to hug her; Jes didn't like displays of affection. But maybe later, after a glass or two of wine, and the surprise: the paper—the *essay*—and her father's lovely hoopoe watercolors! Maybe then she'd permit her mother an embrace.

~

Edward

A broad-framed man with a shaved head and a goatee entered the room. His badge identified him as the Chief of Police. "Mr. Friis. Very sorry for the long afternoon. You're free to go." The man held the door open.

Edward uncoiled himself onto unsteady legs. Surprised to observe his feet obeying the impulses sent forth by his brain, moving one in front of the other along the dimly lit hallway, he followed the solidness of the Chief of Police.

He felt exposed, stripped of his skin. Detective Jesca Ashton was nowhere to be seen, but her questions rubbed knowingly against the nameless chambers in his soul, seeping into compartments kept locked tight, even when looking at the magazines or painting the perfect girls.

All because he'd lost control. All because he'd driven to the lake, taken his cock out and jerked off. All because of the perfect girl. Amber. He hated her now. Or he wanted to.

The lobby was empty.

"I can have one of my detectives escort you home," the Chief of Police was saying, "or you can phone a family member." He cracked his knuckles. The sound was disturbing. "I can drive you myself."

He could call Sara on her cell, easiest on his raw nerves. But if Cate were close by, as was likely, she'd know it was him. Phoning the landline would mean talking to Cate herself, since no one ever answered it but her; uncomfortable, but the choice suggested righteous innocence. The third option—appearing unannounced in a police car, just as he'd left, a lifetime ago and under a cloud of suspicion—would seal his criminality into the record of family history.

Edward decided on the landline. "I'll phone my sister." The knot was receding, his voice sounded almost normal. But when he reached for his phone, his pocket was empty—he'd forgotten it.

The Chief of Police seemed to sense his hesitation. "There's a phone here if you need it."

A rotary relic from the 1970s, spiraling cord twisted into knots. Edward hunched over the desk, unable to recall the last time he'd dialed a telephone with his finger.

Two rings before Cate answered. Ice tinkling in a glass. A good sign: a couple of drinks could definitely help his cause. "Cate, it's me. I need someone to pick me up."

"They didn't arrest you?"

"Why would they do that?"

"The same reason they usually arrest people. To keep criminals off the street."

"That's not funny." Detective Jesca Ashton had kept him in that room for almost *three* hours, her questions pelting him like sharp-edged rocks. And now Cate was going to be a bitch?

"I didn't mean it to be."

"Come get me?" Was he going to have to ride in the police car after all? The knot was back, growing.

The Chief of Police was either not listening, or pretending not to.

"I'm busy right now," Cate's voice was tight and clipped. There was rustling, more tinkling, "I'll see if Sara can go."

Arm in a sling and three tequila sunrises to the wind? If Cate was drinking, so was Sara. Edward bit his tongue.

The best possible outcome would have been for Cate herself to insist on picking him up in her white Beemer, a gift from Bill for her forty-fifth birthday. But he would prefer to see Sara right now, sling or no sling. The unsteady feeling returned to his legs. He lowered himself into the receptionist's chair.

Cate was talking to Sara, words muffled by her hand over the receiver. "Take the Volvo," he heard that. For him her tone was harsh, "She'll be there."

Was Cate going to be horrible? They were letting him *go*, for Christ's sake. He hadn't *done* anything. His bright "thanks" was cut short by a click.

"My sister is coming." He didn't add that she was likely drunk.

A tall, thin man with floppy hair emerged from the hallway, nodded tersely at Edward and handed him plastic bags: his clothing, the magazines, and Sara's computer. The magazines were on top. He could see the Chief being careful not to look.

Sara arrived in shorts and running shoes without socks. No makeup, hair in a messy ponytail. Not drunk.

She might look like shit, but she was *sober*. He could tell from the way she held herself, like she'd suddenly found a purpose in life. Drunk wasn't good, at least not for driving with one hand, but he wasn't sure how he'd manage her stone cold sober.

Edward remembered the look on Sara's face when the detective had pulled the mags from under his mattress. Best to toss the evidence bags into the back seat.

He fumbled with the back door. It was locked.

"Hurry it up, I'm in a no-parking zone." In front of a goddamned police station, the world was a pigeon taking shit after shit on his head. Sara turned in her seat, "The fuck you doing back there? Just get in."

He sat with the bags in his lap—there was no other option—covering the computer and the mags with the clothes. Sara didn't look over, but she'd seen. "Thanks for coming." Easy, upbeat, as though he'd had a flat tire, or locked himself out.

No answer. Sara adjusted the radio controls, switching the dial from NPR newstalk to an Oldies station they'd made fun of as teenagers. Now the Oldies were their songs. Fleetwood Mac. *Rhiannon*. Funny that song would be on. He found Sara's eyes. They crinkled upward—a brief glimmer of complicity—then quickly back to the road. Okay, she wasn't trying to avoid looking at *him*, she just wasn't used to driving. The tightness in his chest eased a little.

He needed to get a drink into her. "Want to drive out to the Green Frogge? Happy hour, martinis two for one. I'm buying."

Sara's shoulders slumped forward and she swallowed, probably tasting the clean, cold edge of the vodka, the briny olive. Then she straightened. "I can't keep doing this shit, Edward." She raised her left elbow, the hand attached to the broken wrist dangling from the sling. "I can't even work like this."

Did she not remember he'd had a part in the injury? Maybe she'd blacked out. Good, better for him. "Well, *I* need alcohol. After that, I *deserve* alcohol." He let a trace of irritation grate across his voice—sound put-out at the absurdity of the whole thing. He found Sara's eyes again. He almost had her. "I won't let you have more than one. Promise." Lie. He'd make sure she had five. Which wouldn't be hard, not after the first one. He knew Sara—all or nothing.

"No, Edward. I'm quitting. I'm fucking doing it this time. Otherwise I might as well hang it up."

"Hang what up?"

"Everything." Sara raised the bad arm again, as though the sling were the problem. "Art, my gallery. Men, relationships. Life, Edward. Life." She didn't make the left turn at the light—she was heading for Cate's.

And possibly for a twelve-step program. "I go inside a bar, it's all over." The most self-aware statement Sara had made in a decade. Edward was souring fast on Sober Sara. "There's plenty of booze for you back at the house. And a ton of cranberry juice for me—cranberry spritzer, my new thing. *Cranberry* fucking *spritzer*." There was incredulity in Sara's voice, and pride.

Stopped at the next light, Sara unwound her good hand from the steering wheel, flicked at a film of dust on the dashboard. Sober Sara had a disturbing number of traits in common with Cate. "I see you got my computer back." She raised an eyebrow in his direction—light, sardonic. This was improving.

"Of course. It was a mix-up, Sara. She wasn't murdered. She OD'd."

"Oh. That's good. I mean, not good for her, but better. I guess. For you anyway." Sara pushed a strand of hair back into her ponytail. "But how do you know?"

"I heard the Chief of Police tell that cunt of a cop. I hope they can her."

"I hate that word, Edward."

This was news. "That cunt Cate" was the opening phrase of Sara's go-to drunken rant about privilege and power and the 1%.

Maybe not anymore.

Fuck cranberry spritzer, once they got home he'd have a martini in her hand in nothing flat.

They passed the high school football field, where a group of boys played soccer. On the sidelines, seven girls with tanned legs and long, straight ponytails were building a pyramid.

Cheerleaders. Edward looked away, but not quickly enough. Sara had seen the cheerleaders too. And she'd seen him looking.

"How old are they?"

"The cheerleaders? Seniors, maybe juniors. How should I know?"

"I'm talking about the girls, Edward. In the magazines." Sara's brows were stitched together in a frown.

"Old enough. Legal. Otherwise they wouldn't be in there."

"How can you know that? Who checks their ages?" Sara braked too hard at a four-way stop, sending Edward hurtling toward the windshield.

"Watch it! You wreck Cate's car and we'll be her indentured servants for life. She'll collect the interest in blood and teeth."

Sara was silent. Apparently it wasn't cool to talk about Cate anymore.

They waited while three other vehicles took their turns, advancing at an unhurried pace across the intersection.

He had expected sympathy, despite the sling, despite the new Cate-Sara detente. He *needed* sympathy, for the hours he'd spent seated at a cheap metal table in a piece-of-shit chair, damp khakis chapping his crotch while Detective Jesca Ashton invaded the most intimate recesses of his privacy, determined to make him for a perv, blinded to his cause. He kept his tone easy, nonconfrontational—most of all he needed her back. "I don't know how old the girls are, but I'm sure they have a system. Anyway, they make them up to look younger than they are. Some of them are probably close to thirty."

"It kind of doesn't matter how old they are, does it?" There was a hard, angry edge to Sara's voice. "I mean, from an ethical point of view. Because the desire is for underage girls. And the industry both satisfies that desire and foments it."

One day on the wagon and now she was into ethics? "News flash, Sara: men like porn. It's a huge industry. The young-girl thing is only a very small part of it. There's urination, defecation, S & M, bondage, pregnant women, fat women, women with abnormally large clitorises—pretty much anything you can think of is a fetish for somebody. And plain old, straight-out heterosexual banging. That's probably the biggest seller, actually. Even home videos of ugly people fucking. People will watch anything." Edward would never watch ugly people fucking—they were beyond hope. But it sounded more egalitarian, less fetishistic, to include them.

It was too warm inside the car. Sara wasn't sweating, but then Sara never sweated. He rolled down the window. The air was heavy, moist. Oppressive.

"It's the little girl thing, Edward." The speed with which houses, trees, and fences melted past the window increased. "Little girls are what you like, and little girls bother me."

"Teenaged girls are not little girls." Bad thing to have said. Edward felt his throat tightening.

"Fine. Underage, then." Sara took a curve hard. "As in, illegal."

Edward grabbed the door handle. "If it were illegal, I wouldn't be sitting here right now. And for your information, Miss Moral Majority, age of consent in New York State is seventeen."

"You *would* know that." They were on a tree-lined street now, bordered by houses of two and three stories, all in classic and recognizable styles, a part of town where no one they knew had lived, until Cate and Bill moved here.

"I don't cross any lines." The perfect girl's face materialized in his mind, this time with the makeup, the shot taken from above. The green bra. Amber. Well, how could he have known?

"What about the ones on my computer?" Like she'd read his mind. Sara's voice was rising. "How the hell could anyone know how old *they* are?"

"I'll clean up the computer."

"Edward." Sara turned to look squarely at him for the first time since he'd entered the car. "Have you been jerking off near my computer?" Her eyes were wide, all iris, the pupils pinpoints.

"I meant I'll get the pics off there. I never–"

"I'm supposed to just...*believe* you? They didn't even give you my tools back, did they? Are you sure you're off the hook?"

"I'll get the tools for you, I'll call them tomorrow. They must have forgotten. And yes, I'm off the hook."

"I don't know that I believe that, Edward. You have a totally creepy sketchbook full of me, asleep, done without my knowledge or permission, so God only knows what *else* you've been up to!"

"Not asleep," Edward corrected her, anger creeping into his voice. "Passed out. I draw you when you're soused and passed out, and most importantly, *on your back*. That's the only time your face isn't a wreck. How does that hurt anyone?"

Sara took the sharp right turn onto Cate's street without braking, sending him jolting against the door again. She pulled the Volvo to a rough stop behind Bill's black Jaguar. From here, the view of the lake was unobstructed, the sun, now below the tips of the tallest trees, shooting flecks of gold across the water.

The keys rattled as Sara removed them from the ignition. The house was dark. Cate's Beemer was gone.

"Are they out? I thought we were grilling salmon."

"They're having dinner with some associate of Bill's. The kids are at sleepovers." Sara was silent for a second, seemed to gather herself. "Edward, Cate says you have to go. I'm supposed to make sure you're out by tomorrow, before they're up."

"*What?*" Edward's hand paused on the door handle.

Sara wasn't looking at him, just shifting the keys carefully from one side of the keyring to the other. "She doesn't want you around the kids. Especially Erica."

"Erica? She looks like a little badger. She'd be safe in a basement full of child molesters." Sara's gasp sliced like a shot through the humid air. A week ago she would have laughed. Wouldn't she?

"That, Edward, was a line. A big, fat, bright red line. And you just blew right across it."

"Come on, Sara, you know I'm kidding." Reasonable, sound reasonable. They couldn't just throw him out. "Cate'll forget she even said that by tomorrow. You know how she is."

The keys made soft, precise clinks in Sara's hands. "I don't think so. Not this time. This is bad."

"You can talk to her. She's your buddy now." Edward despised the pleading tone in his voice. He pulled at the wiry blond hairs along his shin until it hurt. "You haven't even tried." He hadn't *done* anything. Except paint perfection. Rid the world of just a tiny bit of its dreary, ironic, nothing-shocks-us filth.

"I don't want to try. You disgust me."

Edward's eyes stung and itched. Only when his vision blurred did he recognize tears. He blinked furiously.

The Volvo bounced a little as Sara stepped out.

Edward's stomach growled. "We already have the salmon — we have to eat, right? I'll start the grill." He could still save this, make it normal again. Maybe even get her to have that first drink.

Sara bent down and looked, for a long moment, into the interior of the car. Her hand near the door, but not touching, as though to avoid contagion. "I'm not hungry." The screen door clattered as she vanished into the house.

Edward sat alone in the car, the humid black night thick around him, suffocating as a wet blanket.

"It's for *Art*," he whispered, to no one. "It's Art."

Jes

The birds were everywhere. Propped against chairs, lining the baseboard. Perched on windowsills and along the mantel, a cacophony of oranges and yellows, greens and magentas.

She'd seen these birds before. She knew these paintings. They were her father's, from Thailand. The air in the study was cloying, damp. For a moment, Jes was back in the rainforest, her father still alive. "Mom, what are you doing?"

"I'm giving your father's library to the university." Her mother gestured toward a stack of boxes, "for the Charles Ashton Reading Room. They're going to frame and hang all his work. Before I pack, I wanted to give you the chance to pick out a couple. I know how you loved it there."

"No thanks, my apartment's way too cluttered as it is."

"Well, at least take a look—there are some lovely paintings here. Once I send the boxes off, I'll give this place a good clean!"

Jes glanced around the room. Her mother's chaos was everywhere. Overstuffed folders strewn across her father's desk, haphazardly sprinkled with wads of plastic that looked like donut wrappers. On chairs, stacks of miscellaneous papers held in place by abandoned mugs, some with a hard-looking sludge at the bottom. Piles of books on the floor. "Better bring in a bulldozer."

"Don't be silly, I can do it in an afternoon. It'll be a nice place for us to sit." Her mother beamed. Jes knew that look: she had something up her sleeve.

On the endtable, a glass of dark liquid—no coaster, no napkin—on top of an original edition of Erwin Stresemann's *Aves*. Stresemann had been her father's hero. "You're giving them the Stresemann?" Jes picked up the book. "Worth a ton, long as you haven't spilled wine all over it. It's a collector's item."

"Then they should have it, shouldn't they? For their collection!" Her mother smiled brightly. "Come back and help me serve—if you can walk on that leg. What on earth did you do to yourself?"

"Nothing, just tripped."

"Well, it looks awful. Maybe you should have it seen to, did you go to the doctor?"

"It's fine, Mom. Really."

"I could fix you an ice-pack?" Her mother looked delighted at the prospect. "Stay here and put your foot up, I'll bring it to you!"

"I *said* it's fine. Just leave it, okay?"

"If you've broken a bone and don't have it set, you could be limping around for the rest of your life. Some day you might decide you want to wear heels! But suit yourself." Her mother started down the hall. "Come along, we'll bring our plates in here."

The kitchen was thick with smells of the elaborate dishes: Cornish game hens in a nest of carrots and quartered onions, cornbread stuffing peeking out between stiff legs. On the stove a pot of gravy, beginning to congeal.

"Let's heat this up." Her mother turned on the burner under the gravy and added a generous splash of sherry while Geneva danced around her feet, attentive to the smells. Simmering in a skillet was her mother's signature chanterelles and shallots, Thanksgiving dinner in August.

"Mom, it's a million degrees outside."

"You've been working so hard, I wanted to do something nice for you. All your favorites." Her mother placed the hens onto plates, arranging carrots and onions like she was preparing for a *Better Homes and Gardens* shoot.

"You shouldn't have gone to all this bother. A salad would be fine." An anxious shadow flickered across her mother's face. "It all looks delicious." Anything but hungry, Jes picked up her loaded plate and followed her mother down the hall.

In the study the coffee table gleamed, a pristine island of order. Her mother had brought out silver flatware, damask napkins, crystal wine glasses. The dining room would probably have made more sense, but they hadn't eaten there since her father's death.

Her mother took up her knife and fork, took a bite of chanterelles. Paused, shook her head. "These could have used a little less stove time."

"They're fine." Jes ignored the dig about her lateness.

A tailor's mannequin caught her eye—draped in black satin, with a small book, a rosary, and what looked like an ostrich-feather fan at its base. "What's up with the creepy still life?"

"I've boxed up the Duchess's costume for Tom and Darla Wilbur." Her mother was pouring wine. Vestri Pinot. "I thought maybe they'd like to bury Amber in it. I needed to cover the mannequin with something—I think it's quite appropriate."

"Mom, that's morbid."

"The black satin? It's a gesture of respect!"

"The costume thing. It's totally creepy."

"She was very proud of her role. I'd have thought she'd be pleased."

"She'd be pleased not to be *dead*." Jes picked up her napkin and studied the intricate Jacquard pattern. "I can't believe you took these out—don't you have to dryclean them?"

"So? I'll dryclean them."

Sometime this century, Jes thought.

"I felt like a celebration. What good are nice things if you don't use them?" Her mother began the delicate task of carving her game hen. "Perhaps `commemoration' would be a better word..." The motions of the knife became aggressive. "Norton called this morning. They're forcing me to teach AmLit this semester. That means no *Duchess*." Displeasure made her mother's usually placid features angular. "It was very clear that he felt poor Amber's death gave him the perfect excuse to cancel my production. He was positively gloating."

"That sucks." Jes inserted her fork gingerly into the plump breast of the hen. Dry. "But it's not exactly a shock—he's never liked you." She took a swig of wine instead. "Here's something that'll make your night. We can toast the fact that I'm officially suspended. If Werner has his way, I'll be out of a job. You never wanted me to be a cop anyway." She raised her glass. "Cheers."

"I thought they'd made you P.I.? You were chasing down Edward Friis, weren't you? And that's absolutely not true—I am fully supportive of any career choice you make." Her mother's lips, shiny with grease, gleamed in the candlelight.

Jes took a bite of stuffing. She hadn't planned to bring up the matter of her job. The words had slipped out, as things did when she talked to her mother. "Edward Friis didn't do it, Mom. He has an alibi." Werner's words sounded equally lame when pronounced in her own voice. Alibi or no, Edward Friis deserved to be locked up. "They finished the preliminary autopsy this morning—girl took a bunch of bad Ecstasy and it reacted with her antidepressants. Cardiac arrest." Jes moved the onions and carrots from one side of her plate to the other, the hen untouched.

"She didn't suffer. Thank goodness." Her mother was talking with her mouth full. "I ran into Friis last night at the vigil. Just after we'd been talking about him. I always thought he was a bit strange, but I must admit I had difficulty imagining him doing...well... *that*."

"He may not have killed her, but he's a pervert. Total porn addict. He had pictures of her, downloaded from some skeevy website called 'Underage Underground.' He's a disgusting fifty-year-old sleaze with a thing for teen-aged girls. Tons of underage porn on his computer, but New York State's stinking legal system makes it impossible for me to lock him up." Forget lock-up. Edward Friis deserved chemical castration.

"How in the world did her pictures get on his computer?"

My mother, Queen of Clueless. "A number of ways spring to mind, most of which would involve her participation." Jes couldn't eat any more of the heavy food. She pushed her plate aside. "Don't you guys have problems with sexting at school? That stuff gets into the wrong hands, you never get it back."

"I can't imagine Amber wanting to do something like that. And I had no idea she was on medications—her file didn't mention anything about that."

"Child Services loves to stick foster kids on anti-depressants. It's practically the default option. And then they don't monitor them properly."

Her mother tsked, spearing bits of meat with the tip of her fork, reaching occasionally for a carrot, an onion, a bit of stuffing, an expression of pure, carnivorous pleasure animating her features. Jes looked away.

The darkness beyond the bay window was complete. Her mother's lamps glowed, lighting up orange bills and yellow breasts, the brilliant greens and blues of crowns and tail feathers, colors so saturated they looked synthetic.

Popsicle colors.

Like the clothes the girls in Bangkok wore, dancing on the stage at the karaoke, pretending to have fun. Her father's grad students had taken her there the week she'd arrived in Bangkok, before the long drive north to the lab. Crazy-short skirts, unbelievably high heels. European and American styles made cheap, ever so slightly off. No bras—the girls didn't need them yet.

"The bars are full of them," one of the guys had shrugged, swallowing half of his Thai beer. Jes had liked the beer, light and lemony, easy to drink. "They have to eat. A lot of their parents force them into it. Unbelievable poverty in this place."

The girls sat with men old enough to be their grandfathers. They giggled and sipped blue drinks through straws, making sure the men drank more.

Instead of slinking into dark corners with their prizes, the men chose central tables, gallantly seating their adolescent companions. They seemed at ease, not bothered about sitting next to German, Dutch and American couples of more appropriately matched ages.

In Thailand, it didn't matter.

Here it mattered—Edward Friis's face conjured itself in Jes's mind. But only to a point—goddamn First Amendment. Disgusted, she swigged from her wine glass.

"I can't believe Edward Friis turned out like that." Her mother's voice pulled her back to the study.

"The world's full of creeps like him." Jes raised and lowered the tip of her fork with one finger, stopping the heavy silver handle just before it clattered against her plate. "Now anyone can go online and download enough crap to keep themselves jerking off for the next twenty years."

Her mother's face blanched, but her features quickly resumed their habitual serenity. "I don't understand why they're trying to fire you. Fine, you were wrong about Friis. But it's better to check these things out, isn't it?"

"It's not that. Drew saw me getting into Liam Walsh's car last night. Took a goddamn *picture*." Jes was feeling slightly lit.

Her mother placed her fork and knife primly together, as though expecting a tuxedoed waiter to appear. "Why on earth were you getting into Liam Walsh's car?"

"I was fact-finding."

"Then no harm done. If that's all it was, you can just explain yourself."

"It's not."

"Not what?"

"All it was."

"Oh, Jes. I *knew* it."

"Whatever, it only happened a couple of times."

"Not everyone has as casual a view of adultery as you do."

Jes felt annoyance creeping up the back of her neck. "Mom, they're not firing me because I screwed Liam Walsh. They're firing me because I fraternized with a person of interest in the middle of an open investigation.

And because I crossed a couple lines with Edward Friis, pervert of the century. Because of course *his* rights are sacred. Werner asked for my badge; this suspension thing's for real."

Pinkie upraised, her mother popped a sliver of shallot into her mouth. "Well. That's a bit of bad luck. But you might be surprised—you're a huge asset to them." She licked her fingers.

"Oh, they'll go after me, all right, this is their big chance. And what internal affairs asshole is going to side with *me* against *Werner*? Those motherfuckers all go fishing together. And hunting, and drinking. Probably whoring too."

"Honey, I wish you'd clean up your language."

"I'm just stating facts."

Her mother sighed.

She could fight this thing all she wanted, the truth was she was going to lose. That was another fact. A month from now she could be living in her car (moving in with her mother was not an option). "But what pisses me off is that Edward Friis goes home scot free and gets right back online."

"Well, at least he's not acting on his baser impulses."

"Mom. Get a fucking clue. Over 70% of sex offenders get their start online." Contrary to *Law and Order SVU*—rerun binges, when she couldn't sleep; at least she didn't download them to her phone—the vast majority of pedophiles offended on familiar territory. In their neighborhoods, within their own families. Their confiscated computers told the whole sordid story of how they got there. Usually after the fact.

"I had no idea…"

"Of course you didn't." Jes emptied her glass, reached for the bottle. "This guy's just getting going. They're not even going to *monitor* him, if you can believe that!"

"He was a good Bosola. And yet shy." Her mother shook her head. "He doesn't seem the type."

"Just because he acted in your play thirty years ago doesn't mean you have the faintest clue what he's like now! And they never *seem* like the type."

There was no type. The male clients in Chiang Mai didn't look as wealthy as the ones in the capital; they looked normal, like nextdoor neighbors or someone's uncle. Like husbands. Or fathers.

The karaokes were smaller, dingier. The girls were different too. Not as pretty or stylish as the girls in Bangkok. And they were even younger.

The men sat beside hotel pools—there were no beaches nearby; they came for the girls—and closed their eyes while small hands rubbed their backs with suntan lotion. They paraded up and down in front of the ancient temples and sat at outdoor cafés, sometimes with the girls on their knees, tickling them, talking to them as though they were small children.

The week she'd arrived in Chiang Mai, Jes had gone to a tattoo place in Old Town. The money had been a birthday present from her father. He'd helped her research the shop, told her to be careful, as he always did, with his one and only daughter. She'd wanted a nightingale, like the ones on her father's carpet. Jes looked down at the floor, prodded a singing bird with her toe, trying unsuccessfully to think about something else.

The tattoo artist had been finishing a bare-breasted mermaid on a tiny black-haired girl, miniskirt pushed down around hips slim as a boy's. One bare foot waving in the air, she giggled as the ink gun crept toward her waist. A tall, sixty-ish man—stork legs, tropical print shirt—stood close, giving instructions to the artist. Jes had left, without her tattoo.

She'd wandered through the market in a daze, buying anything she found—sandals, wooden trinkets, bracelets, a purple scarf. She'd told her father the tattoo place looked dirty, she'd changed her mind. *Good girl*, his hand mussing her hair.

"Oh, my goodness." Her mother blotted at her lips with her napkin. "I almost forgot the surprise." She held out a thin sheaf of papers. "I was cleaning out the filing cabinets yesterday and look what I found!"

Jes took the papers. `Avian Symbolism in the Legend of *Filomela*.' "What's...?"

"It's yours, don't you remember? I'd forgotten how beautifully you write. And the interpretation of the birds is so original. Especially the hoopoe. Just wonderful." Beatrice fluttered, settled herself again, reminding Jes of a clucking hen.

"I don't want it, you can have it." Jes tossed the paper onto the table.

Still beaming, her mother picked it up, smoothing the top sheet. "Now. I have the most wonderful idea. One of your father's old colleagues is putting together a special issue of *Acta Ornithologica*, to celebrate the reading room's opening. They asked me to contribute a little remembrance.

I said we'd do it together, and we can use this little gem as a perfect starting place!"

"*What*? I haven't written anything longer than a parking ticket in ten years."

"Don't be such a stick-in-the-mud. It'll be a lovely tribute. You spent so much time with your father, you'll have some wonderful insights. I've even got the perfect illustration!" With a flourish, her mother produced three stiff pieces of paper. Long, curved beaks, zebra-striped wings, bright orange crests. Hoopoes. Her father's hoopoes. "They're all wonderful! You choose."

"Mom, no." Her mother's face fell. "It's not...I just—"

"It would be such a lovely gesture. He did some important work with hoopoes, didn't he?"

Jes drained her glass. "I fucking hate hoopoes."

"Well, we could illustrate it with another of the birds, maybe the swallow, or the nightingale. I'll get it started, I know you're busy. You jump in when you can." Smile back in place, Jes's mother picked up their plates. "I'll get dessert."

"I'm not writing any goddamn remembrance!" Jes called to her mother's back, as she disappeared down the hallway.

Her mother pretended not to have heard.

The last day of a long weekend in Chiang Mai. August—humid, stifling, like now. Her father had sent his students out to the rice fields to photograph a flock of hoopoes at their nesting ground, told Jes to go along, to help with note-taking. He'd stayed behind to arrange transport of their supplies back to the lab.

The drive was shorter than they'd calculated, they were back before lunch.

As Jes crossed the empty lobby, the hotel owner's wife smiled and waved. The Thai people were always smiling, it could have meant anything from genuine friendliness to utter loathing.

Their rooms were in a row, on the same clean, white hall, with a window at the end overlooking bushes heavy with pastel flowers, like bowls of sherbet.

As Jes fitted her key into the lock, a door clicked softly closed. She turned to see a girl in turquoise camisole and shorts slip her feet into Lahu sandals, like the ones she'd bought at the market. The girl glanced up at Jes as she passed, her face mostly hidden by a curtain of straight black hair.

Two doors away from hers, not three, Jes had counted carefully.

The third door was her father's.

Her mind produced the image: her father in a karaoke, choosing.

How much did it cost, to buy a girl?

Jes opened another bottle of Vestri Pinot—Jesus, was her mother buying this stuff by the case? She filled her glass and swallowed a gulp so big it almost made her choke.

Her mother returned from the kitchen with a bowl of fruit, Jes's round of goat cheese on a plate. Geneva stirred from the oval into which she'd curled herself, sniffing hopefully in the direction of the cheese.

"The peaches are delicious now." Her mother's hand hovered, hesitating between a handful of cherries and a peach. "Fruit, honey?"

"No thanks. I'm stuffed. I'll help you get these back into the boxes." Light-headed from the wine, Jes steadied herself with a hand on the sofa.

Chewing cherries, her mother picked up a stack of onionskin paper. "He had this between each one."

Jes retrieved a painting leaning against the desk. A female peacock—a pea*hen*, her father had always specified—with three brown, fuzzy peachicks, rendered in his precise and perfect way. The mother's tailfeathers were folded, the characteristic bluegreen shimmer limited to her neck and upper breast.

In the lower right-hand corner, where her father usually penciled the date, a series of words. Jes raised the painting to the desk lamp: "*For Mayuree, on her 15th birthday.*"

Mayuree, her father had said in one of his letters—one for every week he was away, with quick, wispy sketches of birds, just for her—was a Thai name for girls. It meant 'female peacock.' And 'beautiful.' "You can't send this one. It has a dedication on it." She held out the peahen and her chicks.

Her mother put her glasses on. "One of his students?"

A cricket sang. Fireflies flickered. A moth beat its wings against the screen.

The joining of pubescent and middle-aged bodies, grossly incongruous, unspeakable. She'd worked for years, drinking those images into the darkest, least visited crevices of her imagination. Forgotten, buried, but back now, as though it were yesterday.

She could feel her father here, in the study. His quiet, contained, exacting presence concentrated and heavy in the air around her, released from between the pages of his books. And the black-haired girl had a name.

Would she have liked the gift? Perhaps he'd thought better of it, given her something else instead. A trinket or a cheap necklace, a bottle of perfume.

Or had he left it unfinished because he'd drowned? In which case, he'd have been fucking a fourteen-year-old. Maybe even thirteen.

"He taught graduate students, not junior high." Jes picked up her wineglass and drained it. "I found out his nasty little secret the last time I was there. He never knew I knew."

Her mother turned the paper toward the lamp. "The chicks are so lifelike, aren't they?"

"He liked pubescent girls, Mom." Jes felt her stomach drop, as though she were sliding down a ravine, her words tumbling in front of her. "The scientific term for such a preference is 'hebephile'. Fifteen's borderline, but they look really young over there."

"What on earth are you talking about?"

"Underage prostitutes. I saw one of them coming out of his room one day, in Chiang Mai, when he thought I was gone."

"What a thing to say! I'm sure you're wrong." Her mother's gaze remained fixed on the watercolor. She moved the sheet slightly, appearing to appreciate the iridescent bluegreen. "Remember how he took those children from downstate birding every summer?" Her mother ran her fingers over the tight pencil script. "It's nice he found a way to continue his volunteer work there."

"Volunteer work?" Jes slammed the wineglass down on the table— her mother started—knocking a crystal chip out of the foot. "That's what you think he was doing with that girl in his room? *Volunteering*? Thailand's the number one destination for sexual tourism, specializing in children and adolescents. Brazil—where his other lab was—is number two. I doubt *that*'s a coincidence." Jes snatched up a watercolor, a hoopoe, and ripped it. "He was a fucking *pedophile*." Her mother put out a hand but Jes grabbed another painting and tore, throwing the pieces to the floor.

"Honey, please…" Beatrice tried to remove a third painting from her hands. Jes brushed her off roughly, ripped again.

216

"You never suspected? You never thought there was anything off about him? Where the fuck were you, *asleep*?"

"We need to get these back into the box, the humidity must be terrible for them." Beatrice was hurriedly gathering paintings, but Jes was faster.

"*This*"—ugly rasp of tearing paper—"is *exactly* why I never told you!" Ripping, tearing, ripping again. Fingers dusty with dry paint, orange from the hoopoes' crests, bright scraps littering her feet. Jes slammed a framed watercolor to the hearth, shattering glass across the carpet, her father's filthy, disgusting carpet. "You never see *anything*, even if it's right under your *nose*!"

She had told the police. Or she'd tried.

She'd invented a paper she had to finish before the start of classes, changed her ticket. Her father drove her to the airport: she could think of no plausible reason to ask him not to. Scrambling to strap her backpack on before he got out of the car—hug-proof. She said good-bye from the curb.

1-(800)-BE ALERT.

She'd found the number online, using a public computer in the terminal, waited until the area around the payphones was empty.

A kind voice, female, thanked her for the call and regretted that the information she had provided was insufficient for any action to be taken. Prostitution, said the kind voice, was legal in Thailand for women over the age of fifteen.

Jes never spoke to her father again.

Five months later he was dead—heart attack while swimming in the choppy waters off Phuket.

She'd celebrated with a six-pack of Thai beer. One less pedophile walking the earth.

Then the paying had started—her father wasn't going to, so it fell to her. Bars, by herself, first near the university, then branching out to the business district. Then downtown San Francisco, the convention hotels. Picking up men she didn't particularly like. No way the girl in the blue camisole had *liked* it.

Each one a punishment for not having seen—her mother might be blind but she wasn't—a payment made on a sleazy, high-interest debt that just kept growing, as predatory loans did. You paid to stay afloat, to keep from drowning.

Sometimes the men offered money; she never took it.

"Honey, please stop." Her mother's voice was pleasant, as though they'd been discussing books or movies. "I won't have anything left to send to the university." She gathered the torn pieces, glancing vaguely around, as if for tape. "You must get this idea about your father out of your head. Perhaps you should see a therapist."

"It's *not* an *idea*!" Jes heard herself shouting. "It's a fact. An ugly, disgusting *fact*." She kicked at the mess on the floor. "How could you *marry* him?"

And make him her father.

May, the spring after he'd died. Her mother had wanted her to go to Thailand, so they could scatter his ashes at the bird sanctuary he'd founded. Jes had refused.

Her mother had given her the money instead. *A summer backpacking in Europe, just the thing!*

Europe was where her mother had met her father.

Her mother knelt and began stacking the remaining paintings in a box, cushioning each one carefully with the onionskin paper. Jes snatched the peahen and chicks from her mother's hand. "I'll take that one after all."

"*Jes!*" Her mother grasped at her arm.

She jerked away, ripping once, then again and again, Beatrice chasing bluegreen scraps across the floor. "That's right, clean up his filth! You've been doing it for thirty years, why stop now?" Furious strides across the room, heels grinding shards of glass into her father's carpet. Brutal slam to the front door, echo ricocheting through the quiet street.

Outside, gulping hot air thick as stew. She felt filthy, worse than filthy, she felt contaminated.

Hitch-hiking was risky. Which was why she'd done it. Up and down the

Italian peninsula, her Italian as broken as she was. Recklessly careless with the one thing her father had claimed to love most in the world: herself.

The truck driver, his truck tricked out with medallions of the Virgin and pictures of his three children.

Around 2 a.m. he'd pulled into an autogrill, its parking lot filled with trucks. His clock had run out, he couldn't drive for more than eight hours or he'd get a fine. No room for Jes to sleep in the back, only him.

The ride he'd found her. Not a truck but a car—where did you even get a Pontiac in Italy?

The steering wheel was loose in her hands. She shouldn't be driving. Her head reeled. She shouldn't have drunk so much.

Lots of shouldn'ts in this shitty world.

She rolled a stop sign, two. Threw off her seatbelt—like a seatbelt ever solved anything. Gunned the gas and ran a light. A pick-up braked, horn blaring, glare of headlights as she barreled through the intersection. She took the curves hard, tires screeching through the dead streets, endless ranks of stupid bourgeois houses hiding god knows what behind their discreetly glowing windows.

Pedal floored, heading anywhere-but-here. When she hit the highway the spedometer read eighty—any cops out tonight, definite DUI. *Bring it, you bunch of pricks, who gives a fuck.* All four windows down, hair blowing into her mouth. Heavy, humid air whipping through the car, she could still smell the reek of her mother's house, her father's study, she could *taste* it.

Being a cop, then a detective, hadn't made it better. Druggies with no options, who shoplifted and stole identities to support their habits—putting them in jail felt like kicking stray, hungry dogs. The druggies' dealers, bad seeds but with their own sad backstories, she could almost always see why they'd skidded off the tracks. If they'd ever been on any track at all.

And the real heartbreakers. The almost-cases, Amber Inglin's being merely the latest one, riddled with loopholes for justice (and porn-addict scum) to slip through. She didn't feel clean after a case like this one. More like dirty. And it didn't feel like paying.

Close-up of twisted old trunks, her palms and knees stinging. She'd landed on all fours in the dirt. They'd pushed her out into an olive grove, in the middle of nowhere. Taken the last of her mother's money. Thrown her pack out as they drove away, an afterthought.

Pre-dawn, mountains looming, black and impenetrable against the dark sky. Tender cool before the relentless heat.

They weren't Italian. They'd spoken in something else to each other, to her in English.

Tough little one, like to fight.

The ripped back seat, her face crammed against foam stuffing that smelled like stale smoke. Caked mud on the license plate, a number with three eights preceded by a Z. Some other digits too, she'd thought she'd remember them for the rest of her life. Already forgotten, like her phone number. Cheap flip-thing, she'd bought it for the trip.

Had they taken her phone?

What would the police say when she told them she'd been hitch hiking, that she'd gotten into the car of her own accord? Some part of her had known what they might do, and she'd climbed in anyway.

Fuck the police.

Walking on shaky legs to the edge of the autostrada, to stand, the toes of her boots touching the asphalt. So the drivers would see her in the glare of their headlights. How else was she going to get anywhere?

Breathing in dust and exhaust, she could feel her face swelling— jawline, cheekbone. A hot throbbing in one shoulder. The faint tang of blood in her mouth, a salty stickiness she couldn't seem to spit out.

She'd lost her water bottle.

Not clear what two men in a car had been doing at the Italian version of a truck stop.

She felt empty, cleaned out. So exhausted she could barely stand. She couldn't remember when she'd last eaten.

From behind the mountains, with the first tangerine flush of day, had come an out-of-body, floating feeling. A flash of understanding with an aura of the oracular about it.

The men had been waiting. For her. She wasn't done paying, maybe never would be.

Sometimes she imagined going back. To that highway, to the dusty olive grove at the foot of the dark mountains. So she could take her poor, brave, furious, nineteen-year-old self in her arms and tell her.

Not your fault. What he did to that girl, what those men did to you. Not one bit of it was your fault.

If there was a hell, her father was in it. Jes was an atheist, but she was willing to make an exception for him.

God*damn* her mother, for having found the goddamned paper and excavated the goddamned hoopoes. For having set off the chain reaction of low blows that had decimated her compartments, rendering her head an official cluster-fuck. And now, somehow, she had to shove everything back into the dank, dark corners and slam the doors shut again. She needed a drink.

Her phone rang. Not her mother—even she knew better. Jes groped across the dashboard, the car swerving jerkily. A number she didn't recognize. "Is this...Detective Ashton?" A young girl's voice.

"Yes." Suspended or not, for the next couple weeks, or until she got stopped for reckless driving, she was still Detective Ashton. "Who is this?"

The girl sounded as though she'd been crying. "Megan Sorensen. I need to talk to you. I'm at Denny's, on Route 96. It's in the strip mall across—"

"I know where it is," Jes interrupted, "be right there."

Concentrate. Eyes on the road. Don't total the car. Megan Sorensen was alive, and she was in trouble. The wine fog lifted a little. Her mother could spend the rest of her life in a cocoon of denial, but Jes was going to *do something*. This was one young girl she could help.

The restaurant was almost deserted. The girl sat at a booth in the back, arrow-straight black hair falling forward, hiding her features. This wasn't Thailand, ten years had passed, but there she was. Then the girl looked up, the mirage faded, and Jes saw the thin, serious-faced seventeen-year-old she'd interviewed at the Wilburs', the one from the pictures on Edward Friis's computer. *Filthy pig*. With its white Formica table the booth looked like a strange boat, the girl floating adrift and alone. Jes felt a surge of protectiveness, laced with fury at a world that took such shoddy care of girls. "Megan?"

The girl nodded, flourescent glare making blue lights in her black hair.

"You okay?" The girl nodded again, wiped at her eyes.

221

"You hungry?"

"I don't have any money."

"Don't worry about that. Order whatever you want."

Megan Sorensen sat absolutely straight, eating her French fries one by one, dipping them first into a fluffy hill of mayonnaise and then into a neat round pool of Ketchup. The peacock on her wrist was a perfect copy of Amber Inglin's. It masked a tangle of scars, ridges thrown into relief by the harsh light: cutters hurt no one but themselves. Jes felt something kick in—she understood this girl.

Her quiet narration of the facts surrounding her friend's death—too much Ecstasy and then an accident? Was it teenage upspeak or did she want help figuring it out, Jes couldn't tell. Her reddened eyelids lowered, she finished the French fries and wiped her fingers on a paper napkin.

"Megan, I'm going to ask you something. And I need you to tell me the truth."

The girl looked up, eyes wary.

"Do you have any idea how pictures of you and Amber might have gotten onto a website called 'Underage Underground'?"

Megan was quiet for a moment, thin fingers worrying the edge of the plastic placemat. "My brother took them, then he sold them to some guy for a lot of money. They're gross." She was shredding her napkin now, making a tidy pile of the feathery scraps. "And they're illegal. I told him that. We could all go to jail, I told him that too. So I guess you can arrest me now."

"Actually"—Jes traced a crack across the greasy table top with one finger—"I have another idea." Fuck Werner. Fuck Internal Affairs. Porn lords thought outside the box, they couldn't ply their trade if they didn't. Tiptoeing around their First-Amendment rights got you exactly nowhere. "How did your brother make contact with this guy?"

"Phone."

"Same number every time?"

"Different."

"He was using burners. And Connor kept these numbers where? In his head? Written down?"

"Typed into our phone."

"The one you called me from?"

"No way." Megan slid away from the table, leaned stiff against the back of the booth. "I'm not going anywhere near him. No way."

"I'll be right there, I won't let anything happen to you."

Megan shook her head.

"It was a super-brave thing you did, calling me. I know you can do this too. I can't get him unless you help me."

"I *can't*."

"I know how you feel. Really-truly." Jes leaned forward. Tried to find the girl's eyes with hers, but Megan was staring down at the shredded napkin, poking the edges of the pile with her finger. "You think I don't, but I do. Lot of scumbag creeps out in the world, and that makes it a scary place. But I know how to take scumbag creeps down. It's why I do this. I can make it happen. Just trust me."

Megan crossed her arms and frowned at the napkin shreds.

Jes could imagine the sorts of calculations she must be making. Risk assessment, Ward-of-the-State style. "I have a gun and I will use it if I have to. I will not turn you in. And no way in hell will I let them take you back into the system."

Megan looked up, was quiet for a few seconds, studying Jes. "You promise."

Could she promise that?

She could. If she quit, first thing in the morning, while Werner was still home mainlining bad coffee. Suspension meant no pay anyway; not working for the shitty system anymore was an appealing thought. Right here, right now, she could *do* something. And then she could hide the girl until they stopped looking for her, which wouldn't be long. Figure out what to do about her, which couldn't be that hard.

"I not only promise, I swear. I will not let them near you, ever again. You have my word."

Megan drew a breath, expelled it slowly, her eyes still on Jes. "Okay."

Liam

Liam's ears still rang with the men's shouts, the birds' screeches. Pots and pans banging, music blasting—relentless pandemonium, the best they could do until the propane cannons showed up. But for tonight, the grackles had retreated.

The smell of grilling meat drifted over the vines, the men's voices tired as they handed cold beers around. Waldo stood immobile at the edge of the field, staring into the trees.

Detective Jesca Ashton hadn't returned his call. Which was just as well. Waldo was weird. More than weird, he was diagnosable. But watching him work—calm, steady, his whole being given over to saving the grapes, he hadn't stopped for more than ten minutes all day—Liam had realized he'd been wrong. For sure he'd been wrong. Waldo wouldn't hurt a fly.

Exhausted beyond his wildest dreams, he still felt buzzily alert. But it was substance-induced: if he weren't so caffeinated he'd collapse into a heap on the ground. The crew was on duty 24/7 now, and in a state of acute sleep deprivation. During the afternoon lull—too hot to prune, though Waldo had put on his hat and kept going—he'd sent Frank out to buy tents, sleeping bags, camping stoves—more damage to the credit card, he'd stopped keeping track. Tonight there'd be hourly rounds to check for signs of spreading rot, all hands on deck at dawn for the next grackle onslaught—hours and hours of overtime, no idea where he'd get the money.

Bankruptcy was a definite possibility. But that would would come later. As a crotchety old aunt used to say, `Sufficient unto the day is the evil thereof.'

Liam washed down the last of his hamburger with a final pull of beer. Frank fished in the cooler for a replacement. "No more for me. I'm going into town to get some clothes." *Home*, he'd almost said, *going home*. "Keep an eye on Waldo, okay? No nighttime wanderings. We can't afford any MIAs right now."

"You got it." Frank lit a cigarette. "Long as he stays down wind."
Basia had left the porch light on. Like she did every night, but the house was different now. Sober, enclosed. Not his. In the entry hall, a lamp glowed. Mail on the marble-topped table, in two perfectly aligned stacks, his and hers.

In the spotless kitchen, he flipped only the switch above the sleek, futuristic hood of the stove; he was an intruder now, stepping quietly, keeping the lights low. He found the big flashlight easily, in the emergency cabinet—candles, matches, a medical kit, an old landline phone. A transistor radio, packs of batteries, ready for a hurricane.

He left a note. *Need the big light at Vestri; batteries good in small one. L.* Tried to think of something else to say. Couldn't.

He found his suitcase beside hers, in the hall closet.

The bedroom looked like Basia: elegant, understated, tasteful. Not his.

He piled clothes on the bed—shirts, socks, jeans, two sweatshirts, a sweater. Wasn't there something else?

He zipped the suitcase, smoothing the bed clothes. Basia hated wrinkled sheets.

Sheets, that was the something else; Basia was right, he needed sheets. Basia was usually right, especially where material comforts were concerned. He pulled sheets from the well-stocked linen closet, starched and ironed, too many, more than he needed. She wouldn't miss them, and he'd have more than he needed of *something*.

Outside a stripe of orange sky hugged the tree line. A pale smear moving along the field's far edge became a dog. Liam shook his head, squinted. Right where they'd found her, found Amber, a tall figure rose from the ground and straightened: Waldo and Galizur, melting into the trees.

How the hell—?

Then his throat went dry. He'd been right, this morning. He should have kept dialing Detective Jesca Ashton's number, over and over, a hundred times if necessary, until she picked up.

This was his fault. It had happened on *his* watch, *he'd* let Waldo near the girl. *He'd* decided, in his single-minded pursuit of organic nirvana, that nature and work would substitute Waldo's meds just fine, no worries. So maybe some criminal charges—at the thought of Detective Jesca Ashton cuffing him, he felt it, that insane little jab of desire—to go along with the bankruptcy.

By the time he reached the fence, heart pounding, they were gone. Pieces of yellow crime-scene tape wound through the brush surrounding a flattened, trampled rectangle of grass. His flashlight beam caught a slash of red. Cardinal feathers, three of them, fanned beneath a cross formed by two brown feathers identical to the ones Detective Jesca Ashton had shown the group. Whatever they meant, the feathers were Waldo's doing, his pockets were constantly full of them. He might not have meant to hurt Amber, but that didn't change the outcome, or his own responsibility for it.

He'd never noticed the path before, next to the bushes, packed earth sprouting twisting roots. Liam ran, the beam from the heavy flashlight bouncing crazily off trunks and branches. Waldo had a head start. Plus he was fast, long, loping strides, like a buck, or an antelope. Breath coming harsh and jagged, Liam gulped the clean tang of pine, the thick loam of vegetal decay.

After half a mile or so the trees thinned suddenly to his right, the path snaking behind a cluster of mobile homes. Naked bulbs alight in makeshift carports, toys scattered over patchy grass. Muffled sounds of traffic: he'd arrived at the back of the trailer park on Route 13, so close to the well-heeled neighborhood where he'd spent most of his married life.

Ahead, footfalls, a different rhythm from his own. Liam slowed, placing his feet carefully heel to toe. Around a curve, the pale glow of the dog's fur between the trees, Waldo walking behind in a loose, easy gait—the broad shoulders and erect posture were unmistakable.

While Liam wondered whether to make his presence known, Waldo stopped and turned, his face serene, "You also like to walk at night."

"Very much." Liam linked his strides to Waldo's. Get him to turn around, lead him back toward the car, contain him somehow. Call Detective Jesca Ashton—the jab again. Tell her where she could pick up the mentally disturbed man who had killed Amber Inglin. Though he certainly hadn't meant to.

Waldo in a cell, an uncomfortable thought. But they wouldn't send him to prison, more likely back to the institution in Utica. There were psychiatrists, medications. Maybe, eventually, a work-release program. If anyone went to prison, it would be him: criminal negligence.

Liam kept his tone conversational, nonchalant—one thing at a time. "Where're you headed?"

"We are following," Waldo answered, pointing upward.

Liam aimed the flashlight and started backward. Perched low in a tall, thin poplar, an enormous owl, eyes glowing yellow. It took flight as they approached, disappearing into the trees.

"My mother is hunting."

OK, now they were in crazy town. "I need you to keep watch on the grapes tonight, Waldo. My car's back that way."

"We must finish following." Waldo adjusted a ragged, overstuffed backpack across his shoulders, arms flexing as he tightened the straps. Items inside rattled and clinked as he walked. Was Waldo running away? If so, then he knew he'd done something wrong. Which opened the door for premeditation. Far worse for Waldo, and way, way worse for Liam.

He had to get him back to the car.

But there was no way Liam could take him, the man was built like a tree. No choice but to walk on. The path widened, gravel mixing with the dirt, trees parting for a ragged parking lot. The hiss of traffic grew louder. Ahead, a neon Denny's sign, red, white and yellow. The dog's ears perked, nose twitching at the smell of hot grease floating through the open door of an industrial kitchen, where two men bent over a steel sink.

Waldo stopped suddenly, tense and still, watching the owl soar over the parking lot. It landed, talons curved, on the lip of a dumpster, silhouetted by the glare of a streetlight.

In a car parked beside the dumpster, a man's angular face reflected bluish light from a laptop screen, then disappeared into darkness as the lid snapped shut. The man exited his car. He wore a suit jacket, too heavy for the hot night, oddly urban against the backdrop of bargain motels, car dealerships and fast-food chains.

As he set off across the lot, carrying a briefcase, the owl took flight.

Waldo lunged forward and began to run—was he reaching for the owl?—face upturned, shouting words Liam couldn't understand. Panting, Liam caught up, yanking Waldo back from the curb and the hurtling traffic—"You'll get yourself killed!"

They stood watching as the man with the briefcase bolted between vehicles onto the median. The owl dove after a small animal, maybe a racoon, which narrowly escaped, scuttling beneath a speeding pick-up. The flapping wings startled the man, who lost his balance.

What happened next was a blur—a dull thud, a loud grunt. Brakes screeching, an SUV spinning, and then the bird was up again, a squall of feathers and talons against a smear of headlight glare.

A chorus of shattering glass, the crunch of metal giving way, and the Denny's sign toppled as the SUV plowed into it, its back fender sideswiping a Frito-Lay truck, which teetered and crashed, contents spilling through flapping doors.

Liam watched openmouthed as the driver climbed through the cab window, hands holding his head. A man scrambled from the SUV, speaking frantically into his cellphone, and began motioning cars around the pile-up. In the far lane, the man with the briefcase was struggling to his feet, miraculously unharmed.

Suddenly, running across parking lot of the Super 8 opposite them, a woman in cut-offs and flip-flops, long hair flying. Gun drawn. What was Detective Jesca Ashton doing here? And why was she stopping at the edge of the parking lot?

In the second or so it had taken for Liam to recognize Detective Jesca Ashton—and feel the jab, dependable as ever, even here, even now—the man with the briefcase had vanished. Wierdly, impossibly.

But the man was his own problem, Liam had others. He tightened his grip on Waldo's arm, pulling him toward the road. "There's someone over there I need you to meet."

Waldo bucked hard, trying to jerk away, but Liam managed to keep his hold. "It's okay." Muscles bunching beneath his hand, hard and ropey, strong enough to bring down a hatchet and sever a girl's hand with one clean stroke. "The policewoman has a gun, she won't let anything hurt you." *But she will lock you up. I'm so very sorry, but that's where you need to be.*

An ambulance arrived, siren shrieking. In the blaze of blue and red lights, Waldo fought like a panicked animal, the dank odor of him sharpened by fear. Freed from Liam's grasp he jumped away, nimbly weaving through the stopped traffic to disappear behind the dumpster, swallowed by the woods, the dog's tail a white comet behind him.

Liam vaguely registered three medics with a gurney, looking around, confused. He'd never catch up to Waldo again. Detective Jesca Ashton had a car, that was her beat-up blue Jetta parked over there. He signaled wildly through the flashing lights but she gave no sign of seeing him. Instead of taking charge of the scene, she retreated into the shadows. What was she doing?

He sprinted across the street, skirting the melee—the medics with their useless gurney, the overturned vehicles; the shattered glass, too many phones. He reached Detective Jesca Ashton as she was opening her car door. He grabbed her arm, harder than he'd meant to—her skin was cool, firm, he felt the jab again, sharper this time, he was actually touching her. She yanked herself free with surprising force and spun around, gun aimed.

"What the *fuck*—" She lowered the gun, but not as quickly as he'd have liked.

"Didn't you get my message? I know who killed the girl. He was just here, the ambulance spooked him."

"She died of an overdose."

"But I saw him, right where he dumped her, not half an hour ago." He fought to catch his breath. "I followed him here, through the woods. He works for me... he's not... he's schizophrenic. I should've made sure he was medicating. We can catch him—I know where he's headed."

"Autopsy says she OD'd."

Relief, a wave so big it almost drowned him: Waldo was innocent. He took a long, deep breath and realized he was staring at Detective Jesca Ashton's bare legs.

A rough-looking bruise spread from her toes across the top of her right foot and up her shin. He hadn't stepped on her last night, had he?

"Did she suffer?"

"Massive cardiac arrest." She looked down at her phone instead of at him. "Happened fast. The hand was severed post mortem."

"How?"

"Lawnmower."

"Jesus Christ..."

"Already dead, it didn't hurt her. But she shouldn't have died."

"I should've watched her better."

"You can't be everywhere. No one can. You did a lot more than most." Which was a kind thing to say, but it sounded like a dismissal. And he hadn't done nearly enough.

He thought back to early May, one of the first warm afternoons, the vines just beginning to bud. Amber had taken a break, climbed the back stairs to the office, to tell him. Him, especially—she must have seen his car drive up, after lunch. She'd been watching for him.

She knew—breathless from the run up the stairs—what she wanted to do. Not accounting and not community college. Drama, at Yale, the best, or the Royal Academy in London. Mrs. Ousterhout had said she could get a scholarship. "I'm going be an actress, a real one."

He'd reminded her she'd need to work on her grades.

"I can make the Principal's List," she'd shrugged, "if I have a reason to."

The whole thing had sounded like a stretch, he remembered thinking. Even preposterous. Which made him ashamed, now. Why not her? Why just a *better* life? Why not a spectacular, fabulous, everything-she-dreamed-of one?

The peacock tattoo on her hand, fishing a pill from the bottle in her pocket. She'd taken a drink from his water glass, washing one down. He didn't ask. He should have.

Why hadn't he?

Because he'd been afraid of her. Afraid of the desire, afraid of being like all the other scumbags who wanted to stick their hand inside her jeans. Which he'd also wanted to do, though he'd never allowed himself to even imagine such a thing. And which maybe she'd been inviting him to do, because maybe, according to the way she understood the world, she'd thought she owed him something like that, or maybe her wiring had gotten so screwed up along the way that she confused the unfamiliar feeling of relative security inspired by having someone actually give a shit with desire.

And he hadn't trusted himself enough to be the adult, so he'd kept a certain distance. That part was his fault, most definitely.

He didn't deserve Detective Jesca Ashton's kind words. Or anyone else's, for that matter.

Detective Jesca Ashton climbed into the car and pulled out a pack of cigarettes. "Want one?"

"No thanks, I quit." Though he almost took one, because she'd have had to light it for him. Now she would offer him a ride. You didn't leave someone stranded in a parking lot outside a Super 8 when they told you they'd just run two miles through the woods. Of course she was going to offer him a ride home. Which, under the circumstances, shouldn't have thrilled him nearly as much as it did. "Did you see that owl?"

"Totally bizarre." She blew smoke with force, in his direction. "They never come around humans except in midwinter, when the rodents are hibernating. And they never, ever miss their mark. She was huge."

"She?"

"Only females have that kind of wingspan."

He was suddenly aware of a presence, in the back seat. A dark-haired girl hunched against the door. She wore earbuds that let through a steady thump of music. She glanced up, saw him see her, then looked away. The pale face tugged at his memory, sharp chin and black pools of eyes.

"Do you need help?" He gestured discreetly with his head toward the back seat. The music still thumped. "Or...anything?"

"Nope, I'm good." A police siren sounded, grew louder. More flashing lights as a squad car pulled to a rough stop, followed by a wrecker. "I have to go. You never saw me here, okay?"

"Ah…sure. Okay."

She backed the car out of the space and headed too fast toward a dirt road behind the motel that he'd never known existed until her headlights raked across it. He felt the jab again, desire with nowhere to go, along with a gutting sense of total devastation, completely inappropriate and adolescent in its proportions: she hadn't offered him a ride.

Exhaustion pulled like lead weights at his legs, his arms, his shoulders. He felt a hundred years old. And no doubt looked it too.

A text from Frank, *where's Waldo? lol*.

He checked his phone. 11:32—he should stop for coffee, there was a long night ahead, keeping vigil over gray fuzz and greeting the goddamned grackles at dawn.

But first he had to get back to his car.

The silent, dark house sat in judgment. His car alone in the driveway, the suitcase he'd left on the ground, the absurd pile of sheets.

The trampled grass at the edge of the field, the scraps of yellow tape, invisible but accusing all the same. The woods loomed behind him, where Waldo might be hiding—he'd looked, to no avail—terrified, maybe even hallucinating, alone except for the dog.

He'd thought he could help them—Frank, Waldo, the girl, the rest of the interns. Make things better for them, give them a chance. Keep his job under control, not let the horrors and incompetence of CS get to him. Run the vineyard too, all while shielding everyone and everything from hurt, from sickness, from pain, from themselves.

Who was he kidding? He couldn't even keep a decent marriage together.

And now here he was, alone, on the brink of bankruptcy. Standing in front of what used to be his house, with his crap in a pile in the driveway.

Connor

The bus entered a tunnel—sudden quiet; dirty cream tiles melting past—and then they were in the city. Canyon of tall buildings, horns echoing off the walls. Out the window, a jumble of shop fronts, the yawning maw of a parking garage. New York. Important people lived here, important things happened. Connor's pulse thrummed.

The driver brought the vehicle to a stop in a bay marked "14" at 7:50 p.m., exactly the arrival time stamped on his ticket. Connor pulled his backpack from the rack overhead—it was heavy, hard to manoeuver, but he didn't trust the baggage area beneath the bus. The part of the California Fund that wouldn't fit into his pockets was wrapped in a sock and stuffed between pairs of jeans. The rest crackled when he moved.

At the Port Authority ticket window the man who took his money barely looked at him, calling out "Next!" before Connor could put away his change and the long ticket that would take him as far as Chicago.

The bus station was cleaner, the ceilings higher, than he'd expected. There was a drugstore, a McDonald's, a tacky discount fashion store. Connor would never do shoots for a place like that, he'd rather be a paparazzi.

A bar. Would they serve him a beer? Better not try, they might card him. And maybe call the police. An electronics store—maybe buy a phone? No, safer to wait until L.A.

Almost four hours before the bus left. He could see some of the city.

Connor crossed the cavernous waiting area, past fifty, sixty, a hundred people. None of them even glanced at him. Walking out the glass doors, the tight, nervous feeling in his chest began to ease. No one here cared what he did.

7th Avenue and 42nd Street, a sign on the corner said. Restaurants, theaters, clubs, delis, all around him a riot of flashing neon—purple, red, blue, pink—cheesy but in a good way. Loud music pumping out of cars, snatches of laughter. A giant billboard advertising men's briefs—cleft chin and five-o'clock shadow, torso and groin in high relief: the ad was cliché, Connor could do better. And in L.A., he would.

Human beings swarmed past, a rushing river of bodies eddying around those who didn't move fast enough. People of every age and skin color. Beautiful and ugly, nice clothes, bad clothes. Fat, skinny, sick, healthy. Everyone hurried toward somewhere else, and no one looked at him. Connor felt safe.

A few blocks from the station he found a tattoo shop, like he'd been looking for it. Maybe he had. His turn now. Connor opened the door. A waiting area with benches upholstered in zebra stripes, a table made out of what looked like car parts under glass, home to stacks of magazines, *Inked* and *SkinDeep*. "*The American In Me*," by The Avengers, was playing, loud, but the place looked empty. Disappointed, he turned to leave.

Beaded curtains rattled. A guy in jeans, biker boots and a muscle shirt stepped through, arms and shoulders covered with tattoos. "Here for some ink?"

"I thought maybe you were closed."

"We're here till midnight, like the sign says. Let's get you tattooed." The guy had an accent. Connor liked that. In cities, you could meet people from other countries. At home, he didn't know anyone who wasn't American. He'd meet lots of foreigners in L.A.

"Yeah, something—" What kind of tattoo did he want? "—cool." Which sounded completely lame, but the guy helped him save it.

"Cool is specialty of the house. You can leave your pack in the corner. Come with me." *Ze house, wiss me.* A hand settled on Connor's shoulder, guiding him toward a zebra bench, then reaching into the pile of mags, a strong hand that knew which one it wanted. Silver rings on every finger, even his thumbs: winged cats, ankhs, scarabs. Ancient Egyptian symbols—Connor paid attention during art history class, the only one he liked besides photography. "A sleeve, I think." The hand briefly touched Connor's forearm. He felt as though he'd stuck his finger into an electrical socket. He'd never sat this close to another guy before, and he liked it.

"Yeah, that sounds awesome." Connor tried to keep his voice cool, laid back. Which was not how he felt. Not at all. "Something people will notice."

"I am sure you are noticed." The guy's eyes found Connor's. Then they noticed him, from his head to his feet. "I'm Alexi, by the way." Alexi's eyes met his. They were the color of steel.

"Connor."

"That is a good name. Connor."

Connor felt his heart seize, like a muscle cramp. He should be telling people his name was Jack. He'd remember next time. But Alexi didn't seem like the kind of guy the police would ask about a runaway kid. Or the

234

kind of guy who would rat him out if they did.

"I like this one." Alexi's hand, with its rings, was holding the magazine open. An arm, difficult to tell if it belonged to a man or a woman because of all the color, wrapped from shoulder to wrist in giant peacock feathers. Like something had brought him here, to do just this. "What do you think?"

"Let's do it." It might be expensive, but he had the California fund. And it didn't seem cool to ask how much right now. If you wanted it you paid for it. That was how the world worked.

"You will look like you have wings." Alexi winked at him. "Right arm or left?"

"Left."

Alexi's hand again, warm on his shoulder, guiding him through the beaded curtain. Something smelled like patchouli, maybe Alexi, maybe the shop, maybe both. Connor breathed in deep, feeling a little light-headed.

Moreso when Alexi told him it would be easier to work if he'd take off his T-shirt.

Face-down on a sort of bed, covered with clean white paper that crackled if he shifted his weight, only the first few minutes were painful. Then he was in a sort of trance, the steady vibration of the ink gun counteracting the pricking sensation until all he felt was a tingle along his arm. The tingling echoed inside him too.

While Alexi worked, they talked. "So you are traveling?" Connor could feel Alexi's interest in him. Something warm and jittery turned over in his stomach.

"I'm going to Florida, to see my cousin. He's in a punk band." The lies were easy. Connor could imagine his cousin, what kind of jeans he wore, his sunglasses. He would smoke. Marlboro Reds, hard pack.

"Excellent," said Alexi. "I like punk."

They talked about The Clash and the Misfits, the Ramones and the Dead Kennedys. Alexi was impressed with what he knew about music, Connor could tell. They didn't talk about families, or school—Alexi seemed like the kind of guy who would quit to do something better.

When the tattoo was done, Alexi helped him to sit up—slowly, explaining that sometimes people felt faint; Connor did, a little—and returned his T-shirt to him, neatly folded and smelling of patchouli. Connor put it on again because he couldn't think of a reason not to, and Alexi led him to a full-length mirror.

Connor caught his breath. Alexi's eyes—they were grey, the color of steel—found his in the mirror. "Your are like a bird boy."

All Connor could think of to say was, "Shit, man."

"So very cool. You look amazing." Their eyes met, and Connor didn't look away. And then Alexi became serious, businesslike, explaining that while some inferior tattoo artists advocated enveloping their recent creations in saran wrap because of its non-stick qualities, he was old-school, only bandages, which should remain in place no less than two hours, no more than four. Connor was lucky because it was summer and his arms would be uncovered anyway, new tattoos liked to breathe. And to be washed, frequently and gently, with a special soap that Alexi was putting into his hand, and extra gauze because when he first took the bandage off—it would be in the bus, maybe in a dirty bathroom, Connor should be extra careful—there would be tiny drops of blood that would need wiping off, and then covering with a special ointment—another tube, cool against his palm, the brush of Alexi's fingers—all of which advice Connor was registering, his brain trapping the instructions for later, because all he could do for the moment was stare at his transformed arm.

The girls wouldn't believe it.

Which he caught himself thinking all the time. It was so hard to wrap his brain around the truth, that Amber was gone. It was so much easier to imagine her back home, with Megan, waiting for pics of his new tattoo to show up on Instagram.

And then Alexi was bandaging his arm, explaining that starting in a few days, scabs would form, he might feel some itching, which would be helped by the ointment, that above all he shouldn't scratch, that the scabs and some dry skin would flake and fall off and then there his tattoo would be, in all its glory, he just had to be patient.

Connor wasn't very good at patience, that was more Megan's thing, but this time he would be. He had to be. There was no one to be patient for him.

"Want something to eat before your trip?" Alexi was sterilizing his tools at the little table beside the bed where Connor had lain. There were tiny flecks of blood on the white paper now. Connor looked quickly away, realizing even as he registered a little wave of nausea that, beneath it, he was starving. Which Alexi had known. It was as though Alexi and he were alone, together, on some kind of wavelength all their own. "I have food in the back."

Alexi's walk was loose and easy, his belt—studded with little silver pyramids—riding low on his narrow hips. Connor imitated him, swinging his own hips a little. Through the beaded curtains was the back room with a table and a couch. There was a refrigerator, too, and a two-burner hotplate. Alexi made him a sandwich. Bread with a thick crust to cut with a knife, a fancy kind of mustard. Big chunks of tuna from a glass jar. On top, Alexi sprinkled things he called capers, sour but good. A New York tuna sandwich. Connor liked it.

When he'd finished eating, Connor stood. "I can wash the dishes for you."

Alexi rose too, taking the plate from his hand. It thunked back onto the table. "Who needs clean dishes?" Warm fingers brushed his forehead, running through his bangs. "You're hot."

Alexi's steel-colored eyes came closer, too close to see. Connor breathed in his smell, expensive, New York. Then Connor only felt. Lips both soft and firm, gentle at first, then moving with more force. Alexi's tongue entering his mouth, playing with his. Connor's tongue played back.

Alexi's hand began to unzip his jeans, and Connor helped. Alexi's head moved lower, until Connor could see that his hair grew in a spiral, swirling from a point at the top of his head. He followed the swirls with his fingers—soft but sturdy, like the bristles on a paint brush. Warmth spread upward, outward, from where Alexi's mouth held him. Like an emergency, but a good kind.

Back in the shop, Alexi was grinning. Connor grinned too. He didn't feel weird, just good. "How much do I owe you?" Was that terrible? Should he have paid first for the tattoo, so it didn't seem like he was paying for sex? But he hadn't known then. He hadn't known *anything* then.

"Three hundred fifty." *Sree*. Maybe Alexi was Russian, or French—Connor hadn't asked where he was from, and Alexi hadn't asked him. He liked that. "Normally it would be five but I have made a special price for you."

Connor knew people gave tips in New York, but did you give a tip to someone who'd just done *that*? Maybe you should give more. He handed Alexi four hundred-dollar bills. Alexi reached behind the reception desk for two twenties and a ten. Connor took one twenty.

"Thanks." *Sanks*. Alexi folded the bills into his hip pocket. "Have a great time with your cousin. You *look* great, anyway. Amazing. And everyone will notice you, trust me." Alexi winked again. "When you're back in New York, come by."

"I will," Connor said, knowing that he wouldn't, and knowing that Alexi knew that too.

Outside, a clock said 9:41. He still had half an hour. He'd see what his camera could do at night. Street lights out of focus, cars blurring past. Off-center closeups of people who didn't know they were being photographed.

At home everyone would have been staring at him but in New York no one even glanced at his bandaged arm. His business and his alone. Connor liked that.

A door opened behind him, strains of techno music drifting out. He turned to see cool-looking people drinking at a shiny steel bar. Connor caught a glimpse of his new self, reflected in the window. He looked older. And cool. He might not get carded. Something in his face had changed. If he went in, would the bartender know he was gay?

There wasn't time. He'd try in L.A.

A vendor on the corner sold hotdogs smothered in onions, must be a New York thing to eat. They smelled good. Connor bought one and hustled toward the station.

Back on the bus—watching the time, he'd decided to leave the bandage on for exactly three hours—Connor flipped through the pictures he'd taken. Some were good. Tomorrow he'd shoot Chicago, and visit the photography galleries at the Art Institute—the bus for Denver didn't leave till midnight. Automatically, without thinking, he put the best pics into a file for Megan. His sister would love New York.

He wondered if she was angry at him.

A shot from the previous Christmas had attached itself to the slide show. Megan, branches tied to her head to look like antlers, nose painted red; Amber in a Santa hat and beard. Their fingers made the peace sign to him, behind the lens.

Connor moved the picture into a file marked "Ithaca." He didn't want to delete it, but he didn't want it to surprise him again.

He put the camera away and stared out the window at restaurants and bars, their lights bright against the dark sky. Sidewalk cafes brimming over with people, some in the kind of clothes he'd like to photograph. Turning

238

onto the West Side Highway, the bus sped up, the river shimmering past. He was surprised how much he liked cities, liked how the experiences came at you so thick and fast you didn't have time to think.

Not thinking felt good.

Waldo

Waldo's feet pounding the earth, chest stretching to pull in air.

Woods in front and all around, no lights. He could stop running now.

Tree bark rough under his palms, pressing to quiet the ringing in his head.

Waldo breathing, the dog breathing. The woods was hiding, but it was open, free. Owl Mother ruled the woods, protecting. Trees and dark sky, spirits and bodies, animals and birds. Birds especially, great and small.

There she was, on the branch above his head. She'd found him. As she always did, as he'd known she would.

He was safe now.

Monday

Beatrice

Beatrice loaded a tray: pot of coffee, pitcher of cream, basket of pastries. Three bran mini-muffins and a single croissant.

And plum jam, from the farmer's market. She'd planned to make her own, but the plums in the fruit bowl had turned to liquid inside their wrinkly skins and she'd had to dispose of them. Never mind, she'd buy some more this week.

As she pushed open the screen door with her elbow, Geneva shot between her feet—causing an ominous rattle of mug, spoon, jam jar—and bounded onto the grass. Beatrice righted the tippy tray and manoeuvered herself down the steps.

Breakfast *al fresco*, such a lovely Italian invention. Or at least the wording was, and words were everything—"outside" didn't nearly do the trick. The gazebo was delightfully cool at this early hour, almost entirely in shade. Golden coins of sunlight filtered through the blooms and leaves twirling up the wrought-iron curlicues, making pleasing patterns on the wooden floor.

Beatrice sipped her coffee, turning her gaze to admire the hollyhocks and dahlias—frothy little summer dresses in pink, peach and lemon. The gazebo would be an ideal spot for a summer wedding.

For Jes's wedding. One day she'd have one, she *must*.

Beatrice envisioned her daughter in a wedding gown with layers and layers of lace and a trailing veil. Jes would never consider such a traditional thing, but it was a nice thought.

And then the Jes of her thoughts was plucking at the petals of a clematis flower, attached to one of the vines climbing up the gazebo. When she was small she'd plucked flowers apart that way—heartlessly, it had seemed to Beatrice—because she wanted to see what was in the middle, and with the petals in the way—the clear bell-tones of a seven-year-old—you *couldn't*.

Jes destroyed everything in her path, looking for truth.

Where on earth had such dark thoughts come from? Beatrice shook her head to clear it; she'd slept badly. Too much wine, and the hot, sticky night. She peered into the pastry basket. So many things not to think about. People thought too much about things.

And most would go to their graves without discovering the secret of life: everything looked better after a mini-muffin! Now where was the butter knife? The coffee spoon would serve. Beatrice slathered jam over the top of her muffin.

Perhaps Jes's paper wouldn't be quite the thing for the memorial volume. Better to just give them the paintings and be done with it.

But first the girl. Beatrice felt a lump rise in her throat, lovely Duchess Amber. Perhaps she wasn't so hungry after all. She flung the last of the last croissant into the yard and Geneva leaped to catch it. Tom and Darla Wilbur had been honored to accept the costume, they'd even invited her to deliver the elegy. She would rehearse thoroughly, so as not to tear up. The service would be appropriate, tasteful. She'd wear something with three-quarter sleeves—it would be hot, but no one wants to look at an old woman's flabby arms. And covering oneself was a gesture of respect. Her Thespian Society pin would shine nicely against the black, and she'd wear a hat, also black. With her hair tamed into a sedate bun.

She was a dedicated teacher, a worthy thing to be, and she must look the part: last bastion against mind-numbing 'popular culture' gaining such a foothold in the souls of young people that true art and literature hadn't a chance.

Beatrice alone had seen Amber Inglin's potential. Who at the memorial service would be truly capable of appreciating what she'd found was another matter—while the Anchor New Life Church clearly went in for drama, most in her audience would be sadly lacking in background for the references she'd be supplying. Pearls before swine, but perhaps some among the swine might be convinced of the value of the pearls. Had that ever occurred to anyone?

Converts to culture, it had a nice ring. Energized, Beatrice picked up the notepad and pen she'd brought along. Writing in her new gazebo! Working *al fresco*! This was no day to mope about inside. Positively idyllic—why had she not tried it before?

"As when the bird of wonder dies…;" a Shakespearean reference to the phoenix, rising from the ashes. A shiver fluttered over Beatrice's bare arms. Perhaps not. Opening lines were always the hardest. "Where late the sweet birds sang…" No. "That birds would sing and think it were not night." That one was nice. Beatrice jotted it down.

But those were all Shakespeare. She needed something from Webster—quite likely no one in her audience would know the difference, but she would. "Blackbirds fatten best…," which referred to bucking up in the face of adverse circumstances, which heaven knew the poor girl had

had to do, but no, the tone was off, and the foster parents might wonder if they themselves were being alluded to. "We think caged birds sing when indeed they cry." Lovely, but so terribly sad. "Cover her face; mine eyes dazzle. She died young." No, no, no.

And then inspiration visited her, in the words of loyal Antonio, noble Antonio, pure of heart and impeccable of character—the Duchess's steward, to whom she was secretly married. "Let all sweet ladies break their flattering glasses and dress themselves in her." The Duchess was peerless, and so too might lovely Amber have been, had she been given her just measure of years upon this tired old earth. She'd reword that sentence, make it a little brighter. Perfect. An eulogy to end all eulogies. Amber Inglin deserved nothing less.

Then—gift from the gods, following a hefty swig of coffee—another flash: Community Arts. They had a decent-sized stage and good lighting, though the ancient red velvet curtains needed a mend and a visit to the dry-cleaner's. The play would be staged after all, and dedicated to Amber. The lead actress—Beatrice scribbled a note, *start search*—couldn't hope to hold a candle, but that couldn't be helped. The entirety of the Anchor New Life Church would attend the opening night—they'd pack the place to the rafters! The Community Arts president, to whom Beatrice privately referred as Lorna the Tattooed Lesbian (she made a mental note never to do so out loud), was a fierce critic of the stifling of adolescent creativity, which was exactly what Norton and his school-board henchmen had done. True, there were no gay or transsexual themes in Webster, which would have made the matter a shoe-in with Lorna, but the sheer pleasure of performing an end-run around stodgy Norton would likely be calling card enough.

And then Norton could read all about it in the local paper—the arts section!

She would need to set about sewing another Duchess costume, immediately. So much to do. Beatrice began to make lists.

And. She could invite Lorna to dinner, to discuss the production. Lesbians appreciated fine cooking, did they not? Or perhaps that was more gay men? But surely she'd be up for a good meal, and mint juleps in the gazebo.

A bird sang, loudly and insistently. *Tweep-tweep-trrit*, finishing on an upswing, as though it were asking a question. Not one of the little gray birds assembled around the bird feeder, Beatrice could never remember what they were called. The bird must be up in the trees somewhere. *Tweep-tweep-trrit*.

Jes would know. And Charles would have. Or they'd have figured it out, together, in the study. Charles knowing exactly which of the volumes to pull down from the shelves, but handing it to Jes, letting her make the discovery. Then they'd return to the window, with their binoculars, the two of them—birds of a feather, cut from the same cloth.

Something pulled her gaze to the study window but it was blank, empty. Of course it was, what else would it be?

She'd call Jes, in a day or two. For now, though, she was so busy. So many things to attend to.

Her sets, for example. For the production. Would Norton let her have them? Beatrice frowned. Not likely. He'd say they were school property.

Well, then she'd take them. In the dead of night if necessary, and with the help of Lorna, who would most certainly be up for such a caper.

So many wonderful ideas, clearly the gazebo was a much better place to work than the dark, musty study. Light and fresh air! Such a tonic. And when the cold came, she'd move her operations to the dining room table, in front of the big picture window—light, light, light! What on earth had ever possessed her, to think she could work in the study?

Beatrice returned to her lists. Dinner, for Lorna. Who looked to be about Jes's age, perhaps a year or two older. Italian, but of course, and *al fresco*! She'd buy bug candles. And maybe one of those outdoor fans, for a breeze.

Edward

Edward reached for his wallet. A bialy, fresh-squeezed orange juice and two cappucinos had set him back $17.73 plus tip. SoHo prices. But eating at home wasn't an option—he could barely stand his kitchen.

He'd slept badly last night. Alone in the boathouse, jerked awake by disturbing sounds he couldn't be sure he'd heard. Ugly scraps of dreams— abandoned houses, vast rooms filled with gray shadows, devoid of a single living creature.

He'd packed and left while it was still dark.

Edward placed bills on the metal tip plate, signalled to the waitress. A tall blond with green eyes. Smooth tanned arms, fresh mouth.

While she made change he fixed his eyes on the storefront across the street— knockoff designer furniture.

Before, he'd have looked at the waitress. Watched from behind his book, waiting for her T-shirt to gape open when she bent forward to serve the table next to his. She'd been one of his favorites.

Today her presence made his stomach clench. Made him remember Detective Jesca Ashton's crossed arms, a look of barely contained disgust on her face—she hadn't even tried to understand.

His bedroom was worse. Arriving home, he'd immediately quarantined the magazines into trash bags, hidden them beneath his bed. He felt their presence even here, violently alive, suffocating in plastic.

Worst of all was the studio. He'd turned the perfect girls' faces to the wall. The smell of turpentine made his head throb.

Three calls to Sara: two from the road, the last one from home. Finally she'd picked up, spoken before he'd had a chance. "Don't call me anymore, Edward." A second or two of Cate and the Perfect Offspring arguing in the background, coffee grinder whirring. Click. Silence. Would he even need his phone now?

Edward gathered his newspaper and Sara's laptop—she wouldn't take it back—and left the restaurant. At his apartment building, he'd left a load of whites in the dryer. Some impatient tenant would have removed them to the folding table by now. A week ago, the idea of anonymous hands touching his T-shirts and briefs would not have disturbed him.

Before facing the laundry room, he'd need some liquid solace.

He stopped at the Korean deli on Hester for tonic and limes. On his way into the liquor store on White Street he smelled smoke. Buying a gallon bottle of Gray Goose—could the doe-eyed girl at the cash register tell he'd be drinking alone?—he heard the sirens.

His entire block was cordoned off, he could get no closer than the corner. From behind the barricade he watched leaden clouds of smoke defile the sky. A burning in his nostrils, acrid incense of loss. Please, *please*, let it be the building *behind* his.

A crowd was gathering. Chic twenty-somethings, SoHo shopping bags over arms. Phones primed, as though to ambush a celebrislut crawling out of a limo. The owner of the bar from the next street over, a messenger boy straddling his brakeless bike; they exchanged looks, shook their heads, *thank god it's not us*. Edward spotted his neighbor, a middle-aged woman who threw pottery. Loose sleeveless dress, bright splashy pattern vulgar against her sallow skin. She'd started up an artist's collective—*Who Needs a Gallery?*

He'd thrown the postcard away.

The woman lived in the apartment below his. She'd invited him over twice for drinks. On both occasions, Edward had declined, pleading a previous engagement. She must have known he was lying, she'd have heard his steps creaking above her head.

Catching sight of him, she hurried to his side, weeping. "Edward! I'm so glad you're okay!"

Deep lines etched her upper lip, forehead all oily pleats and furrows. Inch of gray at her hairline—bad henna job. His age, even a year or two younger. Fellow creative type, comrade in artistic failure. The sort of woman the world would consider appropriate for him.

He'd never bothered to learn her name. "It's our building?" Dread gripped his chest.

"The whole eastern half—my place, yours, a few others. The firemen said it started in the laundry room—some pigeons nesting in the air vents behind the dryers. They contained the fire pretty quickly, but the smoke's bad." A gulping sob displayed too-small teeth. The woman put her hand on his arm. "Your poor paintings!"

Edward flinched, mind reeling. His perfect girls, reduced to ashes. A sick sweat gathered, beneath his shirt. And the magazines, imprisoned in plastic beneath his bed, skin-soft paper fodder for the flames. Or maybe his bed had inhibited the fire and the magazines would be tossed to the sidewalk, drenched with chemicals and water, for passers-by to snicker at, until they were collected and taken to a landfill.

Vertigo tugged at his knees. He had nothing left, nothing at all.

Except a gallon bottle of vodka. And he'd rather die than share it with this woman.

With the pretense of readjusting the packages in his arms Edward drew away from her grasp. Behind the packages, Sarah's laptop thumped flat and hard against his chest. He'd forgotten he was holding it.

There were some pictures left on the hard drive.

Two brunettes, a few blondes—three, maybe four. He could use them, he could paint again. Make more girls perfect. Amber Inglin was there too, many times over.

But something in him had shifted, turned: those were not the images he wanted.

Edward closed his eyes and took himself away from the terrible present. Back to the porch. To the clean, fresh scent of her, something fruity in her hair, warm with young life. Seated beside him on the steps, not because someone had made her, but because it was the natural thing to do. The moment before.

Before he'd ruined everything.

He willed the moment into an image—her mouth, open and smiling; the heavy-headed roses in the beds beside the steps, petals glowing like skin in the dim light. Perfection, no clean-up needed. He didn't want to clean girls up anymore. The colors were like living things. They sang to him, like voices in his head, conjuring her voice, the smells, the humid darkness warm on his exposed arms and legs, like the touch of fingers.

Could he paint her from memory? He'd never done that before. The hair alone, its warm, subtle complexities—he'd never in a million years have been able to concoct such a miracle. Could he reproduce it?

He thought of ascetic medieval monks, painting in their lonely cells. Rendering her perfection from memory, in a product that could not but be imperfect. This would be part of his punishment. Which he did deserve, he saw that now. He'd never masturbate again—which all but guaranteed he'd never experience another orgasm. Instead he'd channel his being, all of it, into preserving that perfect image, that perfect moment. A sort of penitential memorial. And maybe it would make him famous.

But when he finally picked up the brush again, the palette, months into the future and in a dingy apartment in the outer reaches of Queens (the SoHo loft had been a sweet deal, an outlier, and the rebuilding of the burned-out block hadn't been undertaken with people like him in mind; now his commute to teach the largely talentless college students—he had to eat, pay the rent—was even more onerous), he'd find his fingers frozen, his mind blank.

He'd stare, instead, at a scruffy pair of sparrows pecking at something on his windowsill, beyond the grimy panes. The next day and the next he'd try, and the sparrows would be there—together, always, the two of them, while he was so absolutely alone. Every time he looked up, they'd be watching him. Waiting for him to fail.

Which he did, over and over again. Until, one day, he finally stopped trying. He threw the final, offending canvas into a trashbag, along with his paints and his brushes and his palette knives. Dragging the bag down to the curb, Edward wondered whether Sara would care that she alone was the artist now.

On the way back up the stairs, he admitted to himself that she would not.

She wouldn't give a royal shit.

Edward never painted again.

Jes

From the bedroom a board creaked—the sound startled her at first, then she remembered. She'd let the girl have the bed and slept on the couch. Jes put down the bags of croissants and heavy muffins, grease spots already darkening the paper. She'd hit Starbucks on the way back from the precinct: resignation letter on Werner's desk to greet him when he got in. Purposefully early: no face-to-face. Which likely meant no severance pay, but it also meant no awkward questions or suspicions about the girl.

She set the food out. She'd reminded herself to get two of everything, but did the girl even drink coffee? As she laid out the paper napkins, Jes noticed that her fingertips were orange. From ripping up the hoopoes.

"Megan?" Her own voice, too loud, sounded like a stranger's, speaking to the first person besides herself who'd ever spent the night in her bare-bones apartment. "I've got us breakfast, you hungry?"

A second of silence, some thumping—was she making the bed?—then the girl's voice, thin but clear. "Be right there."

Megan brought with her the scent of Jes's eucalyptus shampoo. And she'd found scissors, somewhere, and trimmed her own hair—they'd made a mess of it last night in the Denny's restroom, with the bad light and the tools at hand. Swiss Army knives were never intended to cut hair.

When they'd exited the restroom, the cashier, glued to her phone screen, hadn't seemed to notice them walking past—Jes and a thin, dark-haired boy with a terrible haircut.

"Sorry we didn't get that guy." Megan had rectified things with bangs cut short across her forehead, and a cropped cap of choppy, pixie-ish layers. She was independent. And possibly motivated by a desire to avoid Jes having to do it for her—the girl had flinched, last night, each time Jes's fingers had inadvertently grazed her shoulder or neck.

Jes remembered not wanting to be touched. It had lasted a long time. "Damned raccoon. Could've killed somebody." Jes preferred to blame the raccoon rather than the owl. "Total long shot, but at least w tried."

"That owl was kind of awesome, though." Megan gave her the hesitant beginnings of a smile.

"Owls *are* awesome. Especially the females. Help yourself." Jes indicated the food. "Your hair looks good, by the way. Better than I could've done for sure."

"I found your broom in the kitchen." Megan picked up her coffee—

253

of course she drank coffee. "I swept up the hair, don't worry."

"I wasn't." Jes spoke around a mouthful of muffin. "I'm not exactly a neat freak."

Jes followed Megan's glance around the room—the television set, the beat-up couch, the table at which they sat, their two mismatched chairs. "I could clean while you're at work if you want. Not hard—you don't have any furniture."

"I'm not going to work today. I quit."

"Because of me."

"Let's call it thanks to you. I hated that job." As she said the words, Jes realized she was speaking the truth. Sclerotic bureaucracy and terminal nepotism made it way too hard to do the right thing. "And the uniform's really ugly."

"Yup. Super ugly. Thought so the first time I saw you." Megan let out a little laugh, a coltish whinny. It hit Jes square in the chest and burrowed in. This girl was her responsibility now. It was a new feeling, a strange and unfamiliar feeling, but—shockingly—not a bad one. "So what will you do?"

"Something'll come along." Jes did the math—her wallet, her depleted checking account. Plus maybe one more paycheck. Unless Werner cut off the direct deposit, baiting her to go in and complain. She probably had enough for the two of them for three weeks. Then the rent would be due. She could sling drinks, somewhere—be on the other side of the bar for a change. Not a great role model for the girl, but her skill set was limited and someone had to buy groceries. "For right now let's clean."

Have the apartment in decent shape—if worse came to worst, she'd need her deposit.

Megan had obviously done a lot of cleaning—foster houses, Jes supposed. Dreary, dusty places that any teenager would hate. So she'd at least make sure they were clean. And seem helpful into the bargain. A sly way of taking at least some control.

They scrubbed the kitchen from top to bottom (Megan had already cleaned the bathroom—*before* her shower, she admitted when Jes asked). They dusted everything, even the baseboards. Vacuumed. Stripped the bed and gathered the towels, Jes running to and from the Laundromat downstairs, her pockets jingling with quarters. They mopped the floor with soap and water, over and over until the mop water was clear.

Jes found Megan filling the bucket at the sink for the umpteenth time, tap running hard to hide the fact that she was crying.

"You okay?" Which sounded stupid. Jes reached out a hand, then drew it back.

"I can't believe I did that to her. She was my best friend." A sob, quickly contained.

Shutting off the water, Jes pulled the girl toward her. The embrace was awkward—Megan was a head taller, Jes out of practice—but Megan didn't resist. After a few seconds Jes felt Megan's slight weight collapse against her, rest there, exhausted.

It wasn't good, what they'd done. "It wasn't...ideal." But Megan hadn't done it alone. And turning her over to the system wouldn't fix anything. It would ruin her life. "If I took you to down to the station, they'd book you. You know that, right?"

Megan's shaky "I *knowww*..." was choked off by a sob.

Jes could feel sweat, or tears, soaking through her shirt to her shoulder. "But her death wasn't your fault. You have to remember that, okay? The Ecstasy reacted with her anti-depressants, which are a Child Services specialty—badly dosed, never monitored. You guys should've steered clear of the pills, but you've probably learned that lesson for yourself."

"But I *left* her there, *alone*..." Megan choked on the final word.

"There was nothing you could have done; all the options were bad. If you'd called it in, you'd be in juvie right now. Amber was your friend, she wouldn't have wanted that for you. And she didn't suffer."

"How do you know?"

Whether to say the word 'autopsy' to a grieving, traumatized seventeen-year-old? "Her heart just stopped. She didn't feel a thing. They did tests."

"An autopsy, you mean." This was a girl who liked facts, was comforted by them. Like Jes.

"Those things don't lie." Jes smoothed Megan's hair. "And if you have to die, partying with your best friend by your side is a pretty decent way to go." Something, anything, a narrative to live with. The kitchen was hot, the air stuffy and close. Jes felt Megan's sweat mix with hers. "It'll get better. Doesn't seem like it now, but it will. Swear to God."

Halfway through rubbing the old floorboards with Murphy's oil and rags—Megan: "But I *want* to; you can make more shine if you do it by hand"—they broke for lunch. Jes brought burritos from the Mexican place two blocks over, and more coffee, this time iced. The apartment had soaked up the heat of the morning. Jes brought her fans from the bedroom, to dry their sweat into little trails of salt before it could hit the floor, clean for the first time since she'd moved in.

They played Jes's music, then Megan's, then Jes's again—Rolling Stones, followed by something techno and trancy, then Lucinda Williams. Now there was steady rhythm and no awkwardness, working alongside the girl, who was by turns quiet and softly talkative. She played Nintendo with her brother, or she used to, and she always won. She liked math and science.

Jes had to ask. "You'd tell me if you knew where Connor was, right?" Their hands occupied at a common task, it was easier.

"Only if you promised not to send the cops after him. He didn't mean for any of this to happen. My brother wouldn't survive jail." Megan stopped scrubbing to apply a precise amount of oil to her rag. "But I don't know where he is."

"I could promise—I'm no fan of the system. He doesn't call you or text you?"

"We only had one phone." Megan indicated the device currently supplying their soundtrack. "He'll get in touch with me. Maybe not for awhile. But he will."

"It's crappy that he took all your money."

Megan's lips contracted into a stubborn set Jes recognized—she'd seen it in mirrors all her life. "He *had* to get to California. He'll be a really good photographer some day."

"And what about you? What do you want to do?"

"I was going to help him, in California. With his pictures and stuff. Makeup, maybe. But now…" Megan shrugged and resumed scrubbing.

Jes watched her for a few seconds, all focus and concentration, methodically treating the floorboards a careful patch at a time. She'd made a promise, she couldn't break it. But she couldn't keep it either, not in the way she should. Megan was clearly smart, she could go to college, maybe even a good one on scholarship, but first she had to finish high school.

Her mother would jump at the chance to tutor this girl, any excuse to pretend what was broken between the two of them might be mended.

But that chance had come last night, and it had gone. The thought of her father's study—where the tutoring would undoubtedly take place—made her stomach roil.

And the girl couldn't have friends, she'd only be able leave the apartment under the cover of darkness. Assuming Jes could continue to afford the apartment. Which was anything but clear at present.

And then it hit her. Or maybe she'd known it all along.

Walsh. The vineyard. He was a decent guy. At any rate not a rapist or a pedophile or a porn addict or a sexual tourist. And considering what was out there, that was actually saying quite a bit.

A different school district, out toward Homer, a different police jurisdiction. No one would think to look there; Megan could lay low for the first month or so and then start school as his neice.

He'd offered help. So she'd take him up on it.

Jes scrubbed on, the idea settling. Of course, perfect.

The floor was done, the afternoon headed toward evening. They were drinking giant-sized Cokes—from the Mexican place again; her empty fridge, this was no place for a kid—which Megan had confessed to loving even though soda was bad for you. "Not Pepsi, Coke. I hate it when they try to give you Pepsi and tell you it's Coke."

Jes agreed, she loved Coke too. She finished hers in a final gulp and took a breath. "Megan, I really like having you here." Which was true. Strange but true. "But I have to take you somewhere else. It's not feasible for you to stay here, we'll get found out. And then they'll take you and I won't be able to stop them."

Megan's shoulders tensed, as though for a blow. Quietly: "Where?"

Jes wondered how many foster homes the girl had seen. How many times she'd stuffed all her belongings into a backpack. Been thrown into a new situation that stood a very good chance of being worse than the last one.

"It's a nice place, a good place. A friend of mine." Well, you could call him that. "Out in the country. Actually, it's the vineyard where Amber worked, she must have talked to you about it. There'll be other kids, but it's *not* a foster house. You'll like it, I promise." She could talk things through with Walsh, make clear the sort of arrangement it was and wasn't. Reassure him she wasn't out to bust up his precious marriage. And maybe he knew of someplace that would hire her—vintners must sell to restaurants, and restaurants had bars. "You can call me, anytime. And I'll come to see you, all the time. That's a promise, too."

No calling ahead, that way he couldn't say no.

Liam

A pair of grackles landed on the fence. The first of the evening, they preened and cawed. From the trees, a grating chorus answered.

Liam slumped at the picnic table, watching Frank line up the cannons. The first blast had jolted him out of the dead-to-the-world sleep into which he'd crumpled at his desk. Wiping drool from his cheek, he'd stumbled to the window in time to see the birds scatter, Frank dancing beside the cannon, whooping like a ten-year-old boy.

Dusk was beginning to gather at the sky's edge—soon they'd start firing for real, blasting every three minutes until dark. Pots and pans were piled at the edge of the field. The blue van had its doors open, *Los Tigres del Norte* cued on the sound system.

His head jerked forward, he couldn't keep his eyes open. He shook himself, took the last gulp of coffee. Once the birds were beaten back for the night he'd sleep.

Maybe even four or five hours straight.

Buzz of cicadas, cricket song. His own breathing. The quiet before the storm.

He should get up and do something. Like unpack the trunk of his car. Where his clothes were probably already moldering. Not to mention the sheets.

Halfway to the car he felt an emptiness in his back pocket. He walked back to the table. There sat his phone.

Not that she was going to call. But in case she did.

Right.

He started toward the car again.

All at once, the hellish, pulsating din. Deafening shrieks in surround-sound, solid sheets of bird bodies swooping in from the cirrus-streaked blue, unfurling like black sails over his grapes.

Ear-splitting cannon blast, he felt the ground vibrate beneath his feet. Then another, even louder, followed by a manic mash of accordions and drums, high-pitched staccato of yips and *ayy's*, the frenetic beat driving his pulse. *Por tu maldito amor, por tu maldito amor*, one of the men's favorites, something about bad love. Perfect. He began to run. A raw, ragged roar—he only recognized it as his when his throat began to ache.

He should be manning a cannon or banging a pan. Instead, he was throwing open the trunk of his car, grabbing piles of sheets. Sand, olive, cinnamon, slate—"earth colors," Basia had said they were calming.

An image of Basia in her airconditioned gallery, *not* watching her livelihood get eaten by grackles. Not her fault, any of this.

But why *earth-toned* sheets? Who needed to sleep between sheets that were any color other than white? Another round of cannon blasts covered the jagged sound of rending fabric as he ripped. Tough going, the thread-count was high, but he managed, the birds filling the air with their shrieks.

How had his perfect life turned to shit in three days? He'd tried so hard to be a good person. Okay, he'd done a bad thing. Twice.

This morning brushing his teeth he'd looked in the mirror and seen *that* guy—over fifty, lots of grey, a few bags and sags. A slight paunch (okay, more than slight). Mooning around over a woman twenty years his junior. Like he had some kind of right. All he needed was the midlife-crisis Porsche.

Why was he ripping sheets?

He had no idea, but it felt *good*.

The cacophony covered the sound of the Jetta pulling to a stop behind the van and he glanced up to see a thin, dark-haired girl alighting from the passenger door.

Jesca Ashton got out: the jab of desire, dependable as ever. He felt his face go hot. She stared at the birds, a furious black cyclone wheeling above the Riesling. "Holy fucking shit." And then she was pushing the girl toward the heap of torn sheets at Liam's feet. "Good idea, they hate these. Megan, fly it over your head like this, like a flag. And yell, really loud."

They seemed to float down the slope toward where the men banged pots and shouted in Spanish, their cries sucked up into the bedlam of bird shrieks, banners of olive and slate flapping into the vines. Liam grabbed a sheet and ran after them, cinnamon pennant flying above his head, shouting himself hoarse.

When the sun began to drop, the birds retreated to the trees. The men gathered beside the tents, around the cooler filled with beer.

Liam offered water to Jesca Ashton and the girl. "What are you doing here?" His voice was almost gone.

"This is Megan. I thought maybe she could stay here for a while. Win-win—you've already seen how she can work. But first she has something to tell you."

The pale, angular face slipped into place in his memory, the boy's too, identical to his sister's. Fanning around her left wrist, across the back of her hand, a peacock, tail feathers displayed. The girl's eyes followed his. She spoke softly. "Amber and I got them together. She was my best friend."

Jesca Ashton gave the girl a nudge. "Go on, tell him."

"I'm sorry I stole money from you. I can pay you back, work it off." The girl's eyes stayed on her tattoo. "I don't want to go to jail."

Liam thought of the cot in the kitchen, the green sleeping bag, Amber Inglin's hair spilling. He could have done so much more. "No one's going to jail. Don't worry about the money, we'll work something out."

Megan looked toward the vines. "Amber loved it out here."

"The other interns will be back in a week or two, you'll have company." He'd watch over this girl, give her any help he could. Forget dropping the ball, this time he'd never take his eye off it.

A smile flitted across the girl's serious face. "Cool."

"She could help you build some nesting boxes for owls," Jesca Ashton pointed to the border of trees. "That's the only way to deal with grackles long-term. They'll get used to everything else, even the cannons."

"What's he doing?" Megan gestured to where Waldo stood, apart from the men, scattering grain from a burlap bag.

"Feeding them. Waldo loves all birds. Even grackles."

"What are they eating?"

"Some concoction he makes for them, different mixes for different ones. He knows what they like. You want to know anything about birds, Waldo's your man."

Megan eyes rested for a second on Waldo, then she looked around. "Do I get to sleep in a tent?"

"You'd be better off inside, I think. You're the only girl."

"What if Jes stays with me?" A thin arm twined through Jesca Ashton's.

"Uh... sure, why not? Slumber party."

Jesca Ashton's eyes met his briefly. "Just for one night, to get her settled." She turned to the girl. "Get your stuff. You'll be OK here. This is a safe, beautiful place." Megan ran toward the car. Jesca Ashton took a deep breath. "It smells so good out here."

A woman who decided, just like that, to spend a night in a tent with a teenager.

He liked that.

No overnight bag, no *nécessaire*. She hadn't even asked if he had bug spray. Or sheets.

Pretending not to, Liam studied her. She was angry at the world, or a good part of it. She drank a lot, maybe too much, not that he could throw stones. She smoked. Probably more than she'd let on, people always did. Except for the uniform, he'd never seen her in anything but jeans (or, now, cut-offs, but still technically jeans). She drove a piece-of-crap car. But now he knew. Beyond the sex and the wanting more sex, of course. Which he did. Of course. She pulled at him, stayed with him, because she cared. About Amber Inglin, and about the dark-haired girl standing beside her; about the others, too many others, like them. She cared in a rough, urgent, fix-it-*now* kind of way. And she was doing something about it. Maybe something illegal, but something good.

The law didn't have the last word on good. Not by a long shot.

The sun dipped toward the now quiet trees, splashing fire over the lake at the foot of the hill. He and Jesca Ashton stood side by side on a hill—his hill—watching a sunset. She reminded him of a wild bird, one of those miniature hawks, fierce and fragile. Kestrels, were they called? He opened his mouth—*you remind me of a kestrel; I'm living out here now*—then shut it. Sleep deprivation made you stupid.

"You planning to feed us at some point?"

"Yep, next on the agenda." For tonight, anyway, they had the same one.

"And maybe break out a few beers, or are we only allowed to drink wine out here?"

"Cooler's right over there." Liam started down the hill. He could feel Jesca Ashton falling into step beside him.

Connor

While they all waited for the bus driver to finish his cigarette, Connor stared at the sign over the bus station. His whole arm itched but he resisted scratching. If he focused, hard—word by word, syllable by syllable—he could make the letters stop dancing. *You. Are. No. Where.* He pronounced the words to himself. A weird form of advertising, maybe, to make North Platte, Nebraska, seem a tiny bit cool. Not working. In five hours he'd be in Denver. Maybe that would be somewhere.

When he was very small his mother had taught him the one-syllable-at-a-time trick. Every night after supper she'd sit with Connor on one side, Megan on the other. Reading aloud, her finger following the words, shushing Megan when she blurted them out too soon. Later on they'd all sat on the couch, each one with a separate book, Megan going faster than Connor and their mother put together. His mother winking at him, *we go slow so we can enjoy ourselves, don't we?* Like that every night until sixth grade, and then it had stopped.

When their mother went off the rails, Megan had stepped in.

Megan read the novel or the story or the history book aloud, for both of them. Then she got Connor to tell her his ideas and she wrote the paper as though it were Connor talking. She got A's and he got B's, mostly, occasionally a C, because Megan was strict about only putting in his ideas, otherwise it would be cheating. Megan brought the book smarts, Connor the street smarts. Something for everyone, and Connor didn't get put in the class with the dumb kids.

Connor stared down at the fast food trash on the ground, frowning. The idea had been that he would make tons of cash as a photographer, and Megan would take care of anything that needed reading. And now she wouldn't. He'd managed okay with his tickets and getting on the right buses and buying food, but what about L.A.? Who would read for him there?

As the bus pulled out of the parking lot, the tall man in the ratty jean jacket swayed down the aisle, balancing himself against the seats. Long, greasy hair fell over his eyes, hanging lank to his shoulders. His shirt looked dirty. Connor stretched his legs into the empty seat beside him, shoving the bundle of sweatshirts that wrapped his camera behind his back.

The man grinned at Connor like he knew him. He'd been doing that since Chicago. When he'd gotten back on the bus in New York with his arm in a bandage, the man had pointed and laughed, wagging his head as though they were in on some mischief together. Now he smelled, the sweet-sharp tang of something alcoholic, a lot stronger than beer, mixed with the dusty, intimate sourness of clothes that needed a wash, a body that needed a bath. The man settled himself in a seat across theaisle, still grinning. Maybe at Connor, or maybe at nothing.

Leaving behind the sleepy, nothing-happening town, they were crossing the river again, a flat plate of deep blue between stripes of sand and short, scrubby trees, all beneath a big open sky. At least the land looked clean, swept by the river and the air, not like bus stations.

Bus stations were the same no matter where they were, even if they were new. In Ohio, or maybe Indiana, he'd seen an old scale in a dark corner of the station, with a slot for coins. A quarter, the dingy sign said, for "your weight and your fate." He'd lost his quarter in the broken machine, but he didn't care about his weight and he already knew his fate: Better than this.

Connor thought about moving to another seat—the guy was rocking back and forth now. But that would mean moving the camera, and the bulky backpack with the California Fund inside, all of which would draw attention. Better just stay put—the guy would probably follow him anyway. He was a pain in the ass but he was harmless, Connor was pretty sure.

He had a good eye, like with his camera. Connor could look around a bus station waiting room and see immediately what kind of deals were going down. Who was dealing, who was scoring. The ones selling themselves, the ones looking for someone to buy. He steered clear of all of them.

As the bus rounded the entrance ramp onto the Interstate, the sun raked across the man's face, showing up a scar. It cut from the corner of his mouth to his ear, jagged like a flash of lightning, angry and reddish pink. It wasn't an old scar.

He thought of his sister's wrist, the ridges you could still feel beneath the peacock tattoo. Maybe it was better he'd come alone. Meg wasn't made for the kind of life they'd have to live at first. Amber probably would've done okay, but not his sister. Amber rolled with whatever you threw at her. Like the money shots. His body clenched.

"Your girls get tons of hits," the guy had said, five weeks ago at the bus stop. "But these are fluff." He'd handed Connor back his flashdrive. "I'm getting requests for money shots. Solo, getting off. Or girl on girl. Not with a dude—in their heads the dude is them. The individual relationship thing and all."

Connor hadn't wanted to imagine his sister doing those things. Or Amber. But money was money. And they'd needed more. Especially if all three of them were going to California. "How much?" Connor folded the twenties the guy had just given him.

"Depends. A good shot'll get you a thousand bucks. A video, five grand, maybe more. Make sure the blond gets a lot of action."

Five K. They could have their own place in L.A., no more foster squats or Jesus freaks. "I don't know if they'd go for that."

"Your call." The guy headed off across the parking lot. Connor didn't watch him—he knew the rules.

"That's gross." Megan had squirmed in her chair, wrapping one leg around the other. "Seriously, Conn, that's nasty. And illegal." Megan always thought about the consequences.

"It's all illegal, Meg. But it's not like anybody knows who you are. He doesn't even know our names. If anybody goes to prison, it'll be him. We could make thousands and thousands of dollars."

"Hell, *yeah*!" Amber gave Megan's shoulder a little push. "We can get really, really high, we won't even know what we're doing. And when we come down we'll be rich!"

"No fucking way." Megan never said the f-word. She turned back to his math homework—stupid summer school make-up course, but Megan could print just like him, so he was aceing it. That was another Megan thing, math. Math, reading, running, and consequences.

Connor had dropped the subject, but he hadn't forgotten. Neither had Amber. The two of them, lined up against Meg for a change.

"Get some X," Amber had told him, right before she left for camp. "Couple pills, couple drinks, she'll be fine."

Connor had been doubtful from the start. "What if she won't take the X?"

"She will if I do."

"Got it extra strong, just like you told me," Reef had counted out six chalky tablets into Connor's hand. Suns stamped on one side, hearts on the other.

"Two each. Take one, wait an hour, take the second." Reef rubbed his hands on his motel-issue pants. "You'll be tripping all night."

The party would be for Amber, to welcome her home. Megan had gone for the idea, just like Amber said she would, buying Cool Ranch Doritos and chocolate-covered Oreos, Amber's go-to stoner food, downloading Amber's favorite music to her iPod. Connor had used some of the California fund to buy Reef's old speakers. An investment.

At the cabin, they'd waited. Lit candles. Drunk a warm beer left over from last time. When Amber called after her babysitting gig, Megan had answered. Connor had heard her voice, excited. "That's so awesome, you guys—no one ever had a party for me before!" Amber's fake surprise had sounded so real.

But she'd gotten there late, after 9:30. They'd planned on more time. Connor shot her a wtf look, but Amber had just shrugged. So he'd pulled the X out of his pocket—a special welcome-home present, he told them, and Amber acted all surprised again.

Amber had swallowed hers first, then Megan. While Megan helped Amber open the beers she'd brought—still cold, she'd been to the convenience store—Connor had spat his pill back into his hand. He needed to be sober. He'd lit a joint, passed it to his sister; pot would make the X kick in faster.

Twenty minutes later nothing was happening, the girls were just laughing a lot. Reef had said to wait an hour but they were short on time. At ten, Connor had handed out the second tablets. Again he'd spat his out.

When Kito and Reija Lee's *Sweet Talk* began to spool out of the speakers, Amber had jumped onto the table. "I couldn't even get a beer at that camp. Not *one*! For two whole *weeks*!" She threw her head back, arms swaying in the air. "Woo*hooooooooooooooo*!"

Then Megan was on the table too, copying Amber's moves. They were getting somewhere. Connor had slipped the camera around his neck. A good one of Amber gyrating and swinging her T-shirt over her head, but it was already 10:10. They had to be home and in the TV room by 11:30—Darla and Tom were coming back from a church retreat.

Connor dug the two remaining tablets from his pocket. "Come on, guys, one more so we can see the stars!"

Burned into his brain, he couldn't forget if he tried: Amber's hand reaching out for the pill, bright peacock feathers fluttering. Her body crumpling, a puppet with its strings cut. Megan catching her before she hit

266

the table, doubled over laughing. Amber's shoulders and legs jerking, in a way that wasn't dancing. Head drooping forward, but her eyes were open.

"Meg!" Connor ran to the table. "Something's wrong with her."

Megan still danced, eyes closed, swaying Amber's convulsing body in time to Bare's "*Bring It Back*."

"She's sick!" Connor shouted over the music. "Lay her down!" This was not-not-*not* going the way it was supposed to.

Megan stopped dancing, looking confused.

"Over here. This way."

Megan took tiny steps, hauling Amber like an oversized rag doll. When she reached the edge, the table wobbled, tipped. Slow-motion replay, Megan and Amber tumbling. Amber's head hitting the floor, a flat, hollow thud. The table had just missed Megan, landing on Amber's chest. Megan looked dazed for a second, then stumbled to her feet, but Amber didn't move. The convulsions had stopped.

Connor moved the heavy table off of Amber.

At least Amber wasn't bleeding. But she wasn't moving.

Megan had put her ear against Amber's chest. Held Amber's hand, fingers wrapping the peacock tattoo. "I think she's dead, Conn." Squeezing Amber's wrist, repeating in a whisper, "she's dead."

"People don't die that way. She just passed out. She'll be fine." Connor grimaced as he remembered shaking Amber's shoulder, lightly at first, then harder. "Come on, dude, we have to get home before Darla and Tom, or they'll fry our butts." Amber's head had rolled loosely, lips slack. Her wide-open eyes staring up at at him, not seeing.

Then he'd slapped Amber's face, like he'd seen on TV, it was what they did to wake people up. "Come on!" Again, hard. Once more. She wasn't dead. She couldn't be.

"Stop it, Conn! *Stop hitting her!*" Shoulders shaking, Megan hade clutched her friend's hand, gasping like she couldn't breathe. Sobbing and gasping.

Connor felt Amber's other wrist. No pulse, nothing. He'd put his hand over Amber's mouth and nose, close but not touching. Counted to ten. No breath. "Shit."

He'd felt inside his T-shirt until he found his own heartbeat. Racing, jumping, a panicky, syncopated rhythm.

Then found the same spot on Amber's chest, an inch or two above her bra. Nothing.

She *was* dead.

This was death. Death was stillness. Open eyes that didn't blink, curled limp fingers. He'd felt the music pounding through the floor beneath his feet, but—for a moment—he couldn't hear it. Death was silence.

He'd seen, then, that everything was his fault.

"Meg." He'd shouted at her, at his own sister.

Nothing. His sister wasn't going to be any help. Plan. He had to have a plan. If Amber had still beenl alive, he'd have called 9-1-1. But she wasn't.

So he'd thought of something. On TV, psycho guys were always killing girls. Then doing weird things with the bodies.

It could look like someone else had done it. On purpose. Guys who killed girls stripped them first. When they were finished doing whatever they did with them, they left them in fields. "We have to take her clothes off."

"*Whyyyyyyyyyyyyy?*" The word trailed off into a wail. Megan still rocked.

"So it looks like somebody killed her. Help me get her shorts off."

Megan shook her head, moaning.

"They'll separate us, Meg. If they don't put us in jail."

"No." Megan's head rolled from side to side. He'd been afraid she might faint. "No, no, no, no, no."

He'd grabbed her shoulders, meaner and harsher than he'd ever been with anyone. "You have to do what I tell you. Okay?" He hadn't known his voice could sound like that.

Megan stopped rocking and sat absolutely motionless.

He'd tugged the bra and panties down, unaided. Nude and dead, Amber had seemed no longer their friend--her body a problem, a horrifying liability, a trap.

Connor had tried to be careful, tried to remember everything. Amber's phone in his pocket, her clothes in his backpack. He'd collected the beer bottles, the candles, the sheets. Megan's iPod. He'd had to leave the speakers. His sister just stood there, frozen.

He'd opened one of the sheets, laid it on the ground. "Take the front corners. Face forward." In the dark, without the candles, Amber's pale body was almost as white as the sheet. "Just walk. I'll make sure she doesn't fall off."

After several feet, they'd had to stop to fix the head and shoulders.

They'd started again, made it a little further, but the right arm wouldn't stay inside the sheet. Megan had turned, reached out a hand.

"Leave it, Meg. It's okay. She can't feel anything."

Amber's fingers dragged and scraped along the ground, all the way through the woods to the open field.

They'd stopped. No clouds, bright moon. His sister was silent but her face glistened, tears running down her cheeks. The road was closer than Connor remembered; they'd have to be fast. He'd pulled the sheet from under Amber's body and used it to cover his hands. They could find fingerprints even on skin, he'd seen it on TV. He'd positioned her against a tree trunk, sitting up. A freak-o serial killer had done that once on a cop show. He'd wiped Amber's phone on the sheet and left it beside her hand. She looked ready to make a call. Totally sick. He'd had to look away.

"What are you *doing*?"

"It has to look creepy, like she was murdered." Connor stuffed the sheet into in his backpack—evidence all over it.

"We can't leave her here like this!" Megan sank down beside her friend's body.

"Don't touch her! Someone will find her tomorrow, Meg. Come on."

Megan wouldn't move. From behind his sister, he'd forced his hands under her arms, tugged her upright. She'd fought him but he'd finally gotten her to her feet–they were the same height, nearly the same weight, but she was slighter.

He'd looked back and Amber had slumped to the side, doing a slow-motion fall to the ground. He blocked Megan's sight with his body and shook her lightly, "Pull it together, okay?" She was sobbing again. "We'll get sent away for the rest of our lives. We have to be in the house before Tom and Darla get back. Come on."

Megan had begun to walk, wobbling a little on her feet. Connor put an arm around her waist to steady her, pulling their phone from her hip pocket. He'd be in charge of the phone now. He'd glanced at the screen. No calls since Amber's. Impossibly, it was only 11:13.

They'd made it home and into the TV room before the freaks got back from communing with Jesus. They'd said good-night to Darla like nothing had happened. Once they heard Tom's snores, they'd gone upstairs to bed.

Megan had said only one sentence to him before he fell asleep, "Everything's different now." Her voice had sounded weird, deeper, not like her at all.

Farms slid past the bus window, a red barn, cows. Neat white fences and grass so green it almost hurt his eyes. It all looked so bland, dull even.

This time tomorrow he'd be in L.A. He'd find somewhere to stay, and it wouldn't be a big house with palm trees and a swimming pool. It might not even be a motel. Some place like the Y, if there were even YMCAs in L.A. Or a park bench or the floor of a bus station, until the cops chased him out and then he'd find somewhere else.

There'd be creeps he'd have to deal with, like scarface over there, or worse.

But Connor could take care of himself. Megan couldn't, and he wouldn't have been able to take care of them both. He knew that now. He felt a stinging in his eyes. He blinked several times, hard.

But the tears won. He swiped at his cheeks with his palms, keeping his face toward the window so weird dude wouldn't see. More tears came, and he wiped those too. He hadn't hated Amber, he'd liked her. Why hadn't he been nicer? What was wrong with him? It wasn't her fault Megan wasn't with him, it was his, and no one else's.

If Amber had come it would have been the three of them, and it would have been okay, it would have been fine. No, it would have been *better*—someone else with street smarts, of which Amber had plenty. And the other kind too, her brain was like Megan's and Connor's all rolled into one. The three of them together, unstoppable.

He should have been her friend.

Instead he'd used her, used them both. She'd teased him about it, in her theater voice and using old words, while they took the pictures; she was just kidding, but she'd been right. Sex was supposed to be nice, like what had happened to him last night. With Alexi. Two people enjoying themselves, each other. Agreeing. Not a bunch of nasty pictures for guys who found girls on the internet and told them to do things. No matter how much they were willing to pay.

Amber had tried, she'd wanted to be his friend, but he'd kept her away, to punish her for taking Megan from him. And so she wouldn't figure out his secret: he could barely read.

The tears were coming too fast to swipe now, so he covered his face with his jacket and pretended to be asleep, concentrating on keeping his shoulders from shaking. And his left arm free and clear of fabric, not touching anything that could make lint. It itched like fuck but he wouldn't scratch. He would not.

He couldn't make it up to Amber. That chance was gone.

But he could make it up to Megan. Give her everything she'd ever wanted, and then some. Even things she hadn't dreamed up yet to want.

He'd save every single cent he made, except for buying camera stuff and food and enough clothes not to look like a street bum so people would give him work. When he got real money, he'd buy his sister a plane ticket out, first class. He'd give money to poor people and street people and animal shelters and homeless shelters and anything else she asked him to. Lots of money, tons. Until he'd paid for the horrible thing he'd done. On the way out of the bus he'd stuff a hundred-dollar bill into crazy dude's pocket—Megan would totally have done that, and probably without asking him.

When he got the house with the pool and the palm trees, his sister could live there and never have to work. He'd get her a peacock-feather sleeve just like his so they could be twins again. Bird-twins. Megan could do exactly as she liked, all day long. Every single day of every single year, for the rest of her life. And he'd hire someone to clean the house. She'd never have to scrub a bathroom again.

A Friday in November

Jes

Jes was in the bar, polishing glasses, post-Thanksgiving dinner. Theirs had been pizza, delivery. Her idea, sans relatives, including her mother, who'd likely have had other plans anyway—she'd somehow become the darling of the Community Arts theater crowd, her weekends now filled with readings and screenings and benefits. Jes had left the others cleaning up in the kitchen and come in to get the tasting room ready for the Black Friday onslaught. She smiled, hearing Megan boss Liam about the proper way to load a dishwasher.

Megan was doing better, only cleaning the bathrooms once a week. She'd struck up a friendship with Waldo, and now the two were practically inseparable. They'd made a sort of shrine—which Jes probably shouldn't have discovered, it had been an accident, she'd been looking for somewhere private to smoke—behind the barn, up a sharp rise that led into the woods. A small clearing, dry brown grass and pines, Waldo's handmade birdfeeders hanging from the branches. At the edge of the clearing, a big rock; at its foot, waving from a dust-covered blue glass vase, a bouquet of peacock feathers, oddly beautiful in their effect. The rock was hollowed out, cracked and worn smooth by centuries of frozen winters, hot summers. Inside the hollow were more feathers—cardinal, blue jay, nuthatch, sparrow.

A small, honey-colored stone, amber. Jes had picked it up, warmed it in her palm. Put it back, gently.

That was where they went, Megan and Waldo and the dog, when they disappeared. A place surrounded by trees, open to the sky. Smelling of outdoor smells. An alive place, a vibrant place. Not like the cemetery, where Megan hadn't wanted to go.

Megan was eager to start school again in January—Liam had said she should sit the fall semester out while CS went through the motions of looking for her; with Amber's case officially deemed an overdose, they'd stop soon enough. For now she was reading books Jes or Liam picked up for her, and becoming close with one of the new interns. The sister, Yanna. Helping her work on the apartment above the garage, the deal she and her brother had struck with Liam, in exchange for free room and board. Every few days Megan would grab Jes by the arm, wanting to show her the wall they'd painted purple, a chair they'd found somewhere to stain.

Megan so desperately wanted a home, and now she'd found one. Jes had helped her do that, at least one truly good thing she'd done in her life.

And the tasting room bar, which had been her idea. It was now her territory, bartending officially her thing. A sort of business within a business, Wednesdays through Saturdays—a simple menu of snacks, nothing anyone had to cook. Which meant the clients stayed for a glass, two. Paid drink prices at the bar instead of just tasting, tried more wine, took more bottles home.

They liked Jes and they tipped. They came back, bringing friends. She'd been lucky thus far: no former drive-bys.

The new accounting system, fully computerized, was also hers— Liam's mess of a payroll book had set the bar particularly low, it hadn't been hard to be a hero.

She was living at Vestri now, accidentally. In something that looked and sounded like a relationship, also accidentally. She'd slept here through the harvest season because it had made sense, all of them working around the clock. Soon enough she'd been slinking in and out of Liam's bedroom like a guilty college freshman.

Predictably, she'd stumbled over Megan one night, coming out of the bathroom.

"Why are you sneaking around?" Megan—strangely grown up— had squinted at her through sleepy eyes. "It's totally fine. And it's not like no one knows."

At the end of September Jes's lease had run out. So it had made practical sense to bring the rest of her stuff up—storing it at her mother's was not an option. Liam paid her, like he paid everyone else. The weekly paychecks a layer of safety, of separation. The difference between close and too close.

Hearing the shuffle of jackets and boots being donned, Jes called out that she was driving into town for bar supplies, did anyone need anything. Liam answered—no, but thanks, see you in a bit. She heard the squeak of the back screen door, heard everyone troop outside together.

The bar was actually fully stocked, she needn't go anywhere. But her car had become her haven, a place to smoke and listen to music and be completely alone. Holidays, even anti-holidays, made her inexplicably sad. And the bar could always use more olives and crackers.

Jes grabbed her jacket, alone on its hook, and hurried down the back steps. She started the Jetta down the long, steep driveway. The leaves were brown now, mostly on the ground, the lake at the bottom of the hill shining silvery through the naked trees. Beneath a leaden jumble of clouds that threatened snow, the old farmhouse promised a warm kitchen, a fireplace, a safe harbor to wait out the cold months until spring woke everything up again.

From the car she saw them all. Megan and Waldo, tending their owl houses at the edge of the woods, the dog close by. The new interns, raking leaves. Brother and sister, two years apart, more casualties of the system. The sister graceful and tall, blond with a swan-like neck, the younger brother still new to adolescence—floppy bangs and gangly limbs, a light sprinkling of acne.

And Liam and Frank, stringing pine boughs and lights around the porch railings. Liam smiled and waved. Jes waved back.

At the end of the driveway Jes braked, waiting for a string of trucks to lumber past. Once she'd rounded the curve, Vestri slipping out of view, she rolled the window down a few inches and lit up, blowing smoke toward snug houses and barns. Not minding the cold—the heater was on, she liked the clash of the two.

As she passed the exit that led to the Velvet Dog, Jes's stomach took an awful dive. She'd almost wound up there two nights ago, with Liam in the city working on placing Vestri wines in bars and restaurants. Jes had been headed out to her car, not quite admitting to herself what she was doing, when she'd stumbled over Frank, sitting on the porch, smoking.

Something inside her had declared, even better, and she'd gone back inside for a bottle of whiskey and a shot glass. Gotten steadily, deliberately drunk, smoking and shooting the shit with Frank. Late, everyone else asleep. The air weirdly warm—a last flashback of Indian summer. Along the way from good buzz to tipsy she'd inched closer and closer, and then she was doing it, like she'd had a plan all along. She'd landed her hand on Frank's thigh, taking a perverse pleasure in finding the exact same spot where she'd first touched Liam.

Frank had given her her hand back. "Not that I wouldn't, under normal circumstances. But I couldn't do that to Liam. He's into you. And you're bombed." He'd clinked his Coke bottle against her shot glass. "To things that never happened."

Heart in her throat, she'd waited two days for the boom to lower. Of course Frank would tell Liam, any friend would. She hadn't counted on his loyalty extending to herself as well, or maybe more to what was between her and Liam. She'd kind of been hoping Liam would cop to having hooked up with Basia in the city. It would have hurt, badly, but it would have justified what she'd almost done. What she'd tried to do. But of course Liam would never do that. And even if he'd tried, Basia was the kind of woman who turned pages and left them turned.

No, the one who'd almost messed up had been her.

She was the one who always had to fuck the best friend.

Sooner or later she'd be back at the Velvet Dog, she wouldn't be able to stop herself. She turned the radio on.

The Rolling Stones. Wild Horses. She turned it up. Loud, louder, as she thought back to the quietly happy scene she'd left at Vestri. Everyone outside, working together, after a communal meal. Picture-perfect, perfect without her.

She drove past her exit, leaving the supermarket and its overflowing parking lot behind. No need for wild horses.

There was a bag in the trunk, a few basic clothing items and a toothbrush. She'd never taken it out. She'd see it there while she was doing something else, driving Megan somewhere, opening the trunk for some reason, and it would make her feel safe. Still her own, armor fully intact. And prepared, for whatever.

For now.

The loneliness was familiar, like slipping into an old pair of shoes, broken but still serviceable. Even a little comfortable. She could bartend somewhere, now that she knew she was good at it. It would be easy to disappear. Look how effortlessly she'd separated her world from her mother's.

Chicago if the grey Lexus in front of her took the next exit, Boston if it didn't.

Boston. Boston was full of bars, at least one of which would need an extra pair of hands for the holidays. Someone who didn't mind working straight through them.

She would miss Liam. She already did. But he deserved good things, better things. Better than her.

Jes's chest ached. But this was necessary.

She turned the radio off. To hear the silence of being alone.

They wouldn't know yet, wouldn't suspect. Black Friday Eve, the pre-sale sales, she could be standing in line or stuck in traffic. By the time they realized something was up, she'd be halfway to Boston, her phone buried in a rest-stop trash bin.

Ten more miles and she'd have reached the point of no return, beyond which turning around and high-tailing it back to Vestri would require more of an explanation than crazy crowds and long lines. After that, at the next rest-stop, she'd pull over and smoke.

And send a text to Megan before she tossed her phone. Tell her she'd be in touch. Not to worry. They'd see one another again, soon. Promise.

Megan would be fine. Liam would be fine.

And maybe, some day, she would too.

❧

Waldo

In the last bright scraps of day, the blackbirds pecked cracked corn close around his feet. Up on the hill, Frank and Liam were hammering and laughing. Somewhere nearby was a fire. Leaves burning. The smell filled his nose. Everything peaceful today, all in its place.

The new girl came running down the hill, zipping her fluffy jacket. Drawing close to Waldo. She touched the dog, who did not spook.

The girl dropped cracked corn for the birds at their feet, pecking. Around her wrist folded a peacock feather. Like the Amber girl's.

When the new girl had first appeared, he'd received a message. That she would help him, that they would work together: they would choose trees at the edge of the woods, bordering the vines. They would draw plans. They would saw and cut and hammer and nail.

And so it had been.

Waldo and the peacock wing girl had built houses for owls—mothers, and then their babies.

The houses were now full, the owls had found their homes. The peacock wing girl was his friend.

And the Amber girl had come back. She was here, among all the silent beauty, sky and cold lake and woods. For some time he'd felt her nearby, in the bare trees that waited for snow.

Today was the day, the day of thanks, with the world in joy and order. Today was the day he would explain his secret to the peacock wing girl.

The Amber girl was a small bird. The smallest of all.

Tiny enough to fit in his pocket, hide safely in his hand.

Too small to see, even. Small enough to live forever.

Acknowledgements

Alphabetical order; here goes. To Ana Cortils, dear friend, for picking fights with me until I wrote again, *sans* footnotes. *Gracias, hermosa.*

To Andrea Ingham, reader, writer, and friend. Especially during the dark times; she reads a mean deck of Tarot.

To Bob Colley, my editor at Standing Stone Books, for patiently making this book infinitely better. And for some great dinners at Mercato – whose turn is it?

To coffee, and whoever discovered it.

To David DeVries, María Fernández, Simone Pinet, Rachel Prentice, and Shirley Samuels. For reading; for having high standards. For standing up for what's real, and for encouraging my little rebellions.

To Gil Dennis, who knew how to find the story.

To J., for dreaming this book up with me: in spite of everything, I get to thank you for that.

To Leslie Daniels, writer, reader, *editrix extraordinaire*; teacher, mentor, unflagging supporter. And, above all, friend.

To Leyla Rouhi, for always telling me to do this.

A Lola López Mondéjar, por los ánimos, y por sus novelas y relatos, que no tienen precio.

To Mercedes García-Arenal, for reading, and for being brilliant.

To Michael Carlisle, prince among agents. I'm a lucky writer.

To Palmer—in peace may you rest, little one—Petal, and Sarge. For being rabbits, and for sharing their lagomorphic lives with me.

To R., for not minding that I hide away to write even while on vacation, long as I'm back by five.

To Viola Monaghan, for introducing me to Leslie Daniels, and for existing in the world.

And to everyone at the Squaw Valley Community of Writers, for everything you do.

Thank you all.